The Wolf And The Siren Song

S. L. Phanes

2

Cover Design: S. L. Phanes

Editor: J. S. Elliot

ISBN: 979-8-9898008-1-0

Here starts a journey that I have long ached to share with you.
Welcome aboard.

This book is dedicated to my mother and sister; to endless innocence and boundless joy.

Part I

1

James

Fine, I'll get us a crew

He coughed and hacked into his sleeve. With a strangled gasp, he pulled his arm away and looked at it. The dark splatter of the Shadow Bite, gray and viscous, soiled the cloth. He looked away, the Bite piercing his chest and fingertips with ravenous hunger.

The Silver Rose, his ship, his only home, his only friend since that terrible night at the cliff ten years ago, growled as he stepped off of her floorboards and onto the pier of the Pirates Isle. Caressing her wood, he swallowed. "Fine. I'll get us a crew."

The Bite recoiled at the mention of a crew, and James drew in a soft breath, hanging on to this brief respite. The creaking of the Rose's deck slowed into a whisper, as though wishing him luck and safety.

He knew he needed luck to find the proper crew mates. The Devil's Trap was the only place he could find a crew who would join his ship with the reputation he had.

Though he denied it, Captain James Wolf was, in every way, a pirate.

He hated pirates. Especially the ones on the Islands of the Devil's Trap—but he had a crew to find. He adjusted his gait, hiding his weakened step. He was walking into the Captain's Relief, one of Pirates Isle's biggest and busiest taverns. He did not want to risk anyone sniffing his weakness.

The gathered pirates momentarily paused in their music, gambling, and drinking. He glared at them, corner to corner, wall to wall, before he stepped to the bar. The music and pleasantries continued.

The barkeep placed a cup before him and poured a drink, the sting of liquor radiating from it. James eyed it, then eyed the barkeep.

"What's the matter, captain? Afraid of a little rum?" The barkeep rested his palm on the wood bar-top, a grin framing uneven teeth splitting his face.

Another pirate approached the barkeep, Ainsley, and put a hand on his shoulder.
"Hey, Ainsley, take it down a notch. You know how Captain Wolf is…"

Ainsley's grin turned downright contemptuous. "Well maybe if the Captain still had his soul, he'd get a lick of sensation out of wha' I served him."

With a flick of his hand, James pinned Ainsley's sleeve to the wood with a knife. Their audience murmured in the background, the tune that floated through the room wavering again. James took the glass of rum and swirled it, before pouring it on Ainsley's head.

Ainsley blinked the rum off his face, otherwise outwardly unfazed. "That all you've got?"

James turned to leave.

"Come back here, you bloody pirate."

The music stopped dead.

James turned. Rage seethed in his chest like a spitting cobra, and the Bite responded greedily. He knew he shouldn't react. He knew this would only feed into the Bite.

He approached the barkeep and plucked the knife out of his sleeve. Without a second thought, James lashed out. Ainsley staggered back with a wet wheeze, holding his bleeding throat.

James faced the tavern, the bloodied knife in his hand. The music resumed. He dropped the knife before he could be tempted to put it to use again, the Bite skittering in every corner of his chest, nibbling on his fingertips like a thousand blades. The cutting sensation swelled, threatening to spread to his throat. He had to get out of here. Fast.

James had been living with this *thing* for ten years, and any scant relief was worth gold.

But he had no chance of finding a crew in this tavern after Ainsley's comments and James' outburst.

He hastened out of the tavern and walked down the paths of the island, away from pirates and rum and frenzy. The Shadow Bite—the affliction of the soulless—wrestled in his chest, and he doubled over, a hand flying to his heart. He coughed again, hoping to release the tension that undulated in his torso.

James wiped the swath of ashy fluid and walked down a desolate path, one of the few calm ones on this island. He shuffled his boots through the sand, his clenched hands in his father's old jacket pockets. Leaning against an abandoned hut's wall, he stared out at the ruthless and beautiful waters. Flipping his jacket's collar up, he put his hand to his chest, feeling for the necklace's outline under the fabric. He looked to the horizon where the inky black sea met the freckled night sky.

This night reminded him of the same night he left his home and arrived on this island. In fact, he had been standing in this exact same spot after he first docked his ship on Pirates Isle. Diamond stars had been decorating the sky, and a cool breeze relieved the night's heat. It had every traditional element of an enjoyable night.

But James remembered it differently. To him, that was the night he swore to take his revenge against Commodore Henry Gregory Mitchell. Even if it killed him.

His vision blurred from the eternal movement of the sea to his hometown, Il Porto Dell' Armonia. His bedroom had overlooked an often-visited cliff; it was also the last place where he saw his town, his home, and his mother.

The Bite rebounded against his ribs, a cough escaping him. He shook his head, attempting to dissuade the Bite from rushing the memories back to the forefront of his mind.

It was a fight he always lost.

He knows, Giacobbo. I can't hide your symptoms any longer. His mother's words resounded in his head as if it were yesterday. *You have to run.*

And young James ran. A boy of fifteen, he had run to danger first before he heeded his mother's warning. The Commodore was the High Ambassador of the Shadow Ordinance in James' hometown, and he enforced the laws against selling souls to the Shadows fiercely. The Commodore's quarters were the last place James should have been. It was only a matter of time until the Commodore caught him and his mother and charged them with Shadow Treason. But it was the only place James thought that would give him something to incriminate the Commodore, and dissolve the Shadow Ordinance in Dell' Armonia, permanently.

It was a dark, moonless night. The only light that illuminated the door to the Commodore's quarters was the hazy flickers of lamps. He crept to the windows facing the sea and picked the lock. *Thank you, Anamaria,* he had whispered his thanks to his friend who taught him how to pick locks, whom he knew he might never see again should he fail.

He entered. The chambers were empty, quiet, save for the whistle of wind that entered the window. Eerie. No Commodore. He swallowed and ventured through the chambers, like a mouse moving through a den of sleeping cats.

The sounds of skittering whispers drew near. He recognized those whispers. *Shadows.* He followed the sound to what appeared to be the Commodore's study, stealing glances behind his shoulder for any sign of officers.

The Bite threaded through his arms, crawled up his neck, and James could have sworn he could feel it slithering through his head. He could not stop the memories from swarming again, a swell of pain gathering under his skin.

When he had entered the study, James beheld a sight that struck fear and relief in his chest. The Commodore's study was littered with strange glyphs, and a presence that James was intimately familiar with.

Shadows.

He crept inside, the whispers moving with him as though they recognized him.

The doors creaked.

"Search and find him. I will not have a little lad toying with Shadows running free while this embassy remains!" The Commodore's voice had bellowed throughout his empty quarters.

In a moment of panic, James had shoved whatever journals with strange glyphs into the bag his mother had packed for him and rushed to the nearest door. He hadn't run for long before his foot caught something firm, and he tripped. He fell upon something cold and clammy. When he put his hands to it, his blood froze under his skin.

Flesh. His hand was upon flesh. He drew back, his mind attempting to deny what his eyes saw.

Admiral Fleming. A colleague of the Commodore, an Ordinance ambassador of Dell' Armonia. His face was shrouded in ash. Strings of shadows swirled from his right eye. His once clean collar was charred. He had been killed, no doubt, by the Shadows.

The metal clang of muskets and officers drew near.

Move.

His gaze immediately went to the cliff that his house overlooked. He scampered out a door to the cliff, submerged in darkness, to the only place he thought he could hide while things died down. His every muscle ached for him to stop, his breath scratching his throat, until he reached the cliff's leveled peak.

Mother. I need to find mother. He clutched his bag close to his chest. *I need to find mama and take us to The Rose. We have to get out of here!*

He had heard the footsteps before he saw the figure step out from the gloom cast by the rocks. Tears stung his eyes and blurred his vision at the sound of his mother's smothered pleading.

"Now, now, young Wolf. You wouldn't want anything terrible happening to your mother, now would you?"

The scene froze James' limbs. His mother, shackled in the custody of the Commodore.

"No," he said, struggling to keep his voice level. "Don't hurt her."

"I wouldn't hurt a resident of Dell' Armonia while my embassy resides here. But you…" He had stepped to James, pushing him closer and closer to the edge of the cliff. "You killed the Admiral. You threatened the safety of this town with your reckless actions. And with it, your very own mother's. I did not want to do this to you, young Wolf—especially after your father's death. Alas, you leave me no choice but to apprehend you. Both of you."

"Giacobbo!" His mother's distressed voice echoed across the cliff. He looked to her, his face strangled with tears, his voice knotted in his throat. "Take care of the Rose, *mio caro*."

James clawed at his chest, but the Bite clawed back ferociously. He clutched the necklace to bring himself back to the present moment, away from the harrowing memory.

But he failed, again.

The feel of the necklace brought the memory back with accuracy. The Bite twisted in his abdomen, as if taking pleasure in reminding him of the moment his mother tore herself from the Commodore's grip and shoved James off the cliff.

The ground had disappeared beneath his feet. Gravity took over, his satchel with the journals floating around him. He clawed at the air that lashed against his back, reached for the sky that kept distancing itself from him, until he felt sails cradle his fall, envelope himself and his belongings.

He rolled onto the Silver Rose's deck, her wood groaning against his thud, his belongings falling like hail around him, the papers and journals of The Commodore gliding like snowflakes toward him.

His first reaction was to run to the Rose's helm. He pulled, but the helm wouldn't budge, his muscles hauling against the Silver Rose's strength with all his might as she sailed away. The cliff behind him began to shrink, and its level peak revealed a scene that was forever burned into James' memory.

Just as a pirate killed his father, the Commodore killed his mother. He pounded his fists against the Rose's helm and begged her to turn around. His fists ached. Red, swollen, pulsing. But she kept sailing. Away from Mitchell, from danger, and from his mother.

That night, James had sat on the bow, staring out to the sea, numb and overwhelmed. Starlight was sharper in the open ocean than on land. The air was thicker, the water vaster. The Rose sailed to the one place she knew better than her trading routes. The Devil's Trap.

Revenge had been on his mind since that night.

He gave a blood-churning head shake, purging those memories from his mind. He looked at his shaking hands. The ink gray of the Bite spindled through his fingertips, and he clenched his fists, waiting for it to dissipate.

James tried to occupy himself with other things to move his attention from the unforgiving, acrid emptiness. This night offered a gentle breeze. And the moon hung over the sky like a lone candle in a lone room.

He turned his attention to the pirate ships that suspended over Pirate Isle's drunken, dirty dock. James always made sure he docked the Rose as far away from crowded ships as possible. He didn't want anyone boarding her, or have their nasty shoes, or no-shoes, tarnish her deck. Filthy pirates. Not that she would let them. Most pirates in the Devil's Trap knew the stories about the Wolf and the Rose, and often avoided getting near them, especially if the Wolf was in a foul mood.

It was just him and her, and it had been for ten years. But being soulless wasn't as easy as he thought it would be, and the Bite was getting progressively worse. The Commodore had a loyal fleet and unwavering influence. James and the Silver Rose were just one man and one ship.

The crisp slice of an unsheathed sword drew his attention. James rolled his eyes. Whoever dared fight him this far away from his ship was a coward.

He turned, unsheathing his own blade, to find a man peering at him under the veil of shadows. Their swords met with a clang as the stranger stepped out into the moonlight. The faint silver light and dim lanterns that lit this path were enough to sharpen this man's features.

"To whom do I owe the pleasure?" James said. His opponent's deep arctic blue eyes fixed on James' keen brown eyes, scrutinizing him.

"Couldn't help but notice you in the tavern back there," his opponent said. "The name's Charles Bruno." His fine nose and well-defined jaw shone like his sword's metal under the light, and his hair rippled in the night wind like a wheat field.

"Let Ainsley be a lesson then."

Their swords clashed and a fight commenced. Charles' swordsmanship matched—if not out-skilled—James'.

He eyed Charles' nimble steps. "Nice footwork," James remarked. He was taught how to handle a sword and sail a ship when he was old enough to join his mother and father on the Silver Rose. But Charles' movements were exceptionally fluid, and his sword looked almost weightless. Quick feet like these could be useful aboard the Rose. "Where did you learn all this?"

"My sister and I grew up with swashbuckling stories," Charles answered, "and naturally, we nagged our uncle to teach us so we could become as close to the characters we read as possible." Their conversation didn't interrupt his dueling. "And so here I am. I could teach you a thing or two."

James evaded a blow from Charles, and parried Charles' sword, exposing his abdomen.

"Besides," Charles recentered his sword to protect himself, "there's only one person in the Trap who doesn't like rum."

The Bite wrung in his chest, wiring around his heart. His peculiar dislike for rum often made him the target of mockery. "And who might that be?" James asked.

"James Wolf, of course," Charles replied.

"You've got gall. Not afraid of the Wolf and the Rose?" James said. The two halted, coming nose to nose with each other, their swords crossed between them.

"Only a little," Charles grinned, revealing his charming teeth.

Spools of the Bite spread through James' hand, and his fingertips began to shiver and tremble. With a growl, he pushed Charles back, breaking their interlocked swords. Their boots sprayed sand into the air, and the lanterns cast a precious light over these sandy clouds. The moonlight was gracious enough to illuminate the dangerous dance the two performed, and the sea added to their symphony an adventurous hum.

James advanced toward Charles, forcing him to guard against a deadly blow.

Charles seemed to notice James' advancement. Their swords crossed again when Charles blocked James' attack. He replied, his tone confident and teasing. "Don't get all defensive. I was only looking for a little adventure and thought one Captain James Wolf might need a hand on deck."

The Bite withdrew wildly, skittering away somewhere in the recesses of his soulless body. The sudden throb in his heart nearly caused him to stumble. He swallowed hard and spoke before the Bite could fight back and weaken his grip on his sword. "Joining the Silver Rose and the Wolf is no adventure—what did you say your name was again?"

"Charles," he grinned, his grip still intact.

"Charles," James repeated the name, savoring it. "You are aware of what you are getting yourself into, eh?"

"Very aware."

The two eyed each other for a second longer before Charles disengaged. "Nice to finally meet you." He resheathed his sword and extended a greeting hand. "And thanks. Your footwork isn't too bad, either."

James took Charles' hand and gave it a firm shake. Eagerness, however naive, was new to him. And somewhat… refreshing.

Charles smirked. "Oh, don't act all humble."

"Humble?"

"Almost everyone knows that infamous name. Stories spread like wildfire," Charles said, throwing an illustrative hand in the air and moving toward the shore.

The Bite writhed and shrank, the tight grasp around his heart loosening. The relief was transient, but he welcomed it. He spoke, grateful that the Bite was no longer clawing at his throat. "What stories have you heard, I wonder?"

Charles drew in a deep breath. "Lots of stories, different versions, all the same conclusion. That you're a soulless monster." He glanced over his shoulder, the sweet glint that passed through his pale eyes contrasting his cruel words. Charles turned his gaze back to the swaying waters. "But it's best that I listen to stories from their very source."

James opened his mouth to respond when muffled but very loud thuds came from a shack behind them. James and

Charles turned and neared the commotion, when a man with frazzled, untied hair, a frantic yet amusing look on his face, came barging out of the shack. He ran toward the two, his head preceding his speedy heels.

He clutched their collars and yelled, his voice cracking, "We gotta go!"

Before James could push the man aside, a dagger whizzed past the three and struck a tree behind them, missing the crazed man's head by mere inches. Being rather short had its advantages sometimes.

"Mendez!" A gruff voice came out of the shack. Three figures broke out of it, shattering its door in half. The one who appeared to be the leader of that band of misfits—the Devil's Trap was full of those—clutched her sword in hand, her face red with fury. Her two other followers were behind her, their swords in their hands, ready to fight when she gave the command. The leader was of average height and big build. She was clad in an off-white shirt, an untied waistcoat, and a belt that held her surprisingly neat trousers up. That dagger must have belonged to her, as she had three to spare sheathed on her belt.

The man who stood next to her had his hair tied back in a low ponytail, a messy stubble and a jacket that had all but one of its buttons missing.

The third man, well, he was a mere lad. A boy of fifteen, perhaps. He half-heartedly held his sword, but seemed ready to fight if the need arose. The embroidered shirt he wore was tucked neatly into his trousers. He wore a concerned yet steady expression that told he had been through his many times before.

"I didn't think you were the double-crossing type, Mendez," the leader yelled.

"Can't we just forget about this, Max, and just be friends?" Mendez said, slowly backing behind James and Charles. "Do something!" He pushed them toward her.

The leader—Max, apparently—dashed toward the three and raised her sword. It met James' blade with a sharp clang.

"You want to fight?" Max growled.

"No, not really. I don't want to fight. It's getting quite late for a third brawl in one night," James said, blocking Max's blow with ease.

Max's accomplices joined the fray. The boy headed for Mendez and the other ran toward Charles, who unsheathed his sword again. The symphony that Charles and James started on this side of the island wasn't over yet.

"Anmar, why?" Mendez muttered as he and the boy exchanged blows.

"I'm so sorry, Santiago," Anmar said. He thrust his sword at Mendez, who clumsily avoided it and blocked the blow with his own cutlass.

"All I wanted to do was have a nice walk in a nice quiet alley after Ainsley's idiocy," James shouted as his sword and Max wrestled, the gleam of the taverns and lanterns twinkling against the blades.

"Well, Pirates Isle isn't exactly the best place for a nice, quiet walk," Charles said in James' direction, balancing his words and duel effortlessly. "Lagoon of Cabins is a quieter island. But if I were you, I'd go somewhere like the south of France. Lovely place, lovely weather." He breezed through his attacker's parries. "My sister and uncle and I always go there each year. Well, we used to—"

"Oh, shut up!" Max shouted, struggling to keep James' sword at a safe distance. "After I get it back, Mendez, I'm going to kill you!"

Anmar grumbled and swung Mendez's sword out of hand before he elbowed him in the chin, sending him to the sands of the beach.

"I'll be back," he whispered and rushed to Max and lunged at James, who barely blocked it in time.

"I don't want to fight you, boy," James said.

"Don't call me 'boy,'" Anmar said dryly and sent a blow.

Max left Anmar to deal with James and tread to Mendez. He was groaning and holding his hand to his chin, sand peppering his clothes and hair.

"Mendez, watch out!" Charles yelled out to him. He surveyed his surroundings for anything of use, and his gaze landed on the outline of barrels tied to a hut's wall. He grinned and moved backward, defending against his attacker's blows, until he had him right where he wanted him. Charles kicked sand into his attacker's eyes and hacked at the pile of barrels held together by the flimsy rope. The rope snapped, sending barrels rolling into Charles' opponent.

Charles gave a cheeky smile, proud of himself. He ran toward Mendez and Max, jumped and swung on a tree and his boot hit Max dead on in the face. She hit the ground with a groan of pain, and he landed neatly as if he'd meant to do that.

"I have no idea how I did that," he said, and smiled unashamedly.

When Anmar saw Max and her accomplice on the ground, he took two steps back and surrendered with the nonchalance of a young lord.

James and Charles put their swords away and Anmar did the same. The symphony finally finished, and the sea's ambiance remained.

Charles joined James and Anmar. "Can we all calm down now?" he asked.

Anmar glowered at them. His expression was cold, but his eyes shot a glare like fire.

"Owed you money?" James asked. Most brawls in the Devil's Trap started because someone cheated in a game or with goods.

"Not money. And not me," Anmar pointed to the two on the ground. "Them."

James glanced at Mendez, who staggered off the ground, leaving an outline on the sand where he lay. "Then why stand with those two?" James asked.

"Don't test me—" Before Anmar could finish, Mendez landed a fist to his nose and knocked him out. James shook his head and Charles frowned at Mendez.

"He elbowed me," Mendez grumbled, pointing at Anmar. "And *he* double-crossed me."

Charles raised an eyebrow and James sighed. Silence settled between them.

"Thanks for that," Mendez finally said.

"Don't mention it," Charles laughed.

"You're welcome," James mumbled.

"What was that all about?" Charles continued.

"It wasn't money that I owed," Mendez said, and James didn't miss the bitterness that made its way into his voice.

James turned to talk away, but stopped, his hand flying to his heart. The ache in James' chest seemed to tighten. When he faced Charles and Mendez again, the Bite shriveled.

James didn't want to admit it to himself, but he found Charles rather delightful, and something about Mendez made James smile. He was fun to be around, even in these circumstances. James could use more laughter on the Rose.

But he didn't know what Mendez's intentions were just yet, or what stories he knew about the Wolf and the Rose, and it was still too early to judge.

"I suppose we should properly introduce ourselves," James faced the two squarely, injecting some vitality into his demeanor. He let them start.

"Charles Bruno." He put out a hand.

Mendez shook Charles' hand. "Santiago Mendez."

They both turned to James, expecting an introduction.

"Right," he said. "I'm James Wolf." He rubbed his fingers together, hoping the Bite wasn't visible on his fingertips before he extended a hesitant hand.

"*The* James Wolf," Charles told Mendez, a smirk on his lips.

"Never heard of you," Mendez replied, entirely nonchalant as he shook James' hand.

James' mouth quirked with a little smile. A little bit of ignorance of the Wolf and the Rose might serve him well.

One of the gang members let out a throaty groan. James' lip twitched, annoyance visible on his brow. He turned to Mendez and Charles. "How's about a drink?" He asked. *A drink perhaps in the Captain's Relief might help me discern who's a good candidate and who's not.*

James turned in the direction of the loud taverns, and Charles and Mendez followed him without a word.

2

James

There's always a test

The Devil's Trap was ancient. Comprised of thirteen islands in a minefield of shipwrecks, it stood in a vulnerable spot; in the Atlantic, deeper into the ocean by the West African coast, southwest of Spain and England. Any Royal Guard could bring it to rubble. Yet, the Devil's Trap has been a place for pirates to drink, party and smuggle for many years. No Royal ship survived the wrathful shipwreck that surrounded the islands.

James used to think that only pirates and outlaws were protected by some sort of magic innate to the Devil's Trap.

But the real why these islands were safe was because the shipwreck was sentient.

The Silver Rose was released from her world and landed near Pirates Isle by a sunken ship. The rift from the Rose's arrival caused the aura from her world to spread into the surrounding islands, and the graveyard reef had grown ever since the Trap gained awareness of who was friend and who was foe. Unfortunately for the Royal Guard, the Trap did not discriminate between Royal Guards and pirates, and when pirates began to make homes and outposts out of the wreckage, the Trap learned to protect its benefactors from the Guard. One attempt at a time, the islands' defense multiplied through the massacred, drowned, and destroyed Royal Navy ships. The scar from the rift still seeped energy, like blood in water, giving the islands an unnatural sentient presence.

James turned to face the dock where he had left the Rose. Her crow's nest hovered in the air behind the congregation of shacks and ships, the moonlight breaking between the masts and structures. He remembered her words. ***You need a crew, Giacobbo***.

Charles was grinning, looking around him like a little boy who had first come to realize that such a place existed. He followed James and Mendez, who knew this place better than he did, down the cobblestone paths. The lights from the countless taverns, shops and markets foamed like snow around them. The windows of shacks framed bottles of rum, carpets, cushions, drunken sea folk and an assortment of equally fine and ultimately useless trinkets.

They reached the tavern. A sunken galleon's captain's quarters served as its main structure, the large windows of the ship angled to face the sky. Barrels upon barrels of rum crowded it. Part of the sunken ship's crow's nest was planted firmly in the middle of the structure. Atop it fluttered a flag that read *The Captain's Relief.*

Mendez sauntered to the doors as if he owned the place, and opened them wide, arms at full extension. Though no one's eyes in the tavern turned to the trio, James sensed that the patrons tried their best to pretend that they weren't disturbed by his re-entry. James paid them no heed. Charles appeared a little apprehensive. His eyes shifted around, probably looking for Ainsley.

"They must have dragged him somewhere. Probably to some infirmary island," James said to Charles, answering his unease. James walked to the bartender Ellis—thank goodness—poured rum for Charles and Mendez, but for James, she poured something else. James picked up the flagon and gave it a little sniff.

"Anisette." He wished he had a soul for a moment to savor every sensation of this drink.

"Only the best for you, captain," Ellis said. "Apologies about Ainsley's vulgarity."

"No harm done," James said. He dropped a few coins on the table, one of which was a gold coin. "For your troubles with Ainsley."

Grinning, Ellis pocketed the coins and spoke in a breathy voice. "No trouble at all, captain."

James turned to the seats by the windows, Charles and Mendez following behind him. They each grabbed a drink and took a seat. James sat by the window. The tavern was spacious, with the bar at the end of it sitting under an arch, terribly stained, but beautifully decorated. To the left of the bar, surprisingly talented pirate musicians played the accordion, piano, and violin. When James last docked here, the tavern had a Ladies' Night, where only women played a mix of uplifting and tragic music. Tonight, there were two women and one man. Their lively music matched their boisterous mood but contrasted their disheveled state. Appearances didn't stop pirates and outlaws from living full lives.

The tables and walls were laced with bullet and sword slashes. Even more barrels of rum and ale were stacked against the wall. Candles were stuck on whatever shelves or unused tables by wax, and lanterns made halos over the bar and the musicians' heads. Although the tavern was an unsightly place, it had a certain welcoming and happy presence to it.

"So," James said, "what brought you to a place like this, Santiago?"

Mendez huffed. "That boy and I robbed Max and were planning on running away from her and that annoying Edward." Mendez made a face impersonating Max and gave a throaty voice at Edward's name. "It sounded like a good plan so I thought I'd celebrate and have a drink. I passed out. Next thing I knew was Max and Ed and that little traitor after me." He threw his hands to the table.

James adjusted himself in his seat and looked out the smudged window that obscured the shimmering moon. His chest throbbed, and he felt as though the Bite was baring its teeth, hungrily gnawing on his heart. Clenching his fist under the table, he turned to Charles. "And what's your story, Charles?"

"My story?" Charles repeated. "I'm the brother of a wonderful sister. Son of a kind librarian." He blinked slowly. That must have meant he knew his fair share of pain. Yet his expression did not betray him. If anything, his voice was a little eager. Eagerness masking pain often meant secrets. "I set out for a little adventure before I take care of the bookshop. Maybe pick up a few stories and write them with my sister." His expression sank as he wrapped up his little story, his tease of an abbreviation. "You?"

"I thought you knew my story," James said. He took a gulp of the drink. There was no sting, no burn as it went down his throat. Yet, the Bite seemed to release its grip on him when he met Charles' eyes. How curious.

Charles leaned forward and rested his elbows on the table. "Tell us more."

James tapped the scarred tabletop with his fingers, staving off the numbness that dug under his skin. "Why don't you tell me what you already know of the Wolf?"

"Oh, I never knew there'd be a test," Charles teased.

"There's always a test," James retorted. He could keep a six-volume log of stories that roamed about the Wolf and the Rose. But at this moment, he was particularly interested in Charles' version of the stories.

"You lost your ship, the Silver Rose," Charles began. James nodded and winked.

"I heard the one James Wolf sold his soul. The highest word says he sold it to the Shadows. Most people just like to say the devil," Charles continued. "Of course, any interactions with Shadows are outlawed by the Ordinance. And so, Wolf planned to murder one of Dell' Armonia's Ordinance ambassadors. A bloody murder it was too. The poor Admiral was unrecognizable."

James put his cup of anisette down and gave Charles a quiet clap. He had to give Charles credit for trying. His story wasn't half wrong after all.

Charles didn't look amused. He held his cup and leaned forward like it was a challenge. "Other stories say he used the Shadows' Influence to raise his ship from the depths."

James' face was plastered with a mirthless smile. He sat back in his seat. Shadow Influence to raise the Rose? That wasn't how it worked. James couldn't control the Shadows. If he could, he would've brought his father back after he lost him in the pirate attack.

Charles fixed him in a stare, his gaze entangled with scrutiny and intrigue, bordering on caution.

"You missed a few details here and there, but—" James shrugged and raised his cup, "nice try." He turned to the other. "Tell us more about your story, Mendez," James said, bringing the anisette back to his lips.

"Nothing too special about yesterday," Mendez said.

"Well, you weren't born yesterday," Charles pointed out.

"I'm not as interesting as you two," Mendez said.

James laughed. "Oh, try us."

Mendez sighed. "I was in an orphanage ever since I can remember. I never had a name for a while. They called me Monté," he said and took a hot gulp from his drink. "Once I learned how to read, one story stuck out to me. The hero's name was Santiago. I loved that story. So, I took the hero's name. I became Santiago Mendez and I escaped the orphanage." He paused and took a small breath. "Unfortunately for me, I was very young. I got into some trouble, and joined this band of idiots you met earlier for seven years." His usual confused and lively air dissipated with a forceful exhale. "I wanted to leave them and find my own meaning and path. But seeing as Anmar is a no-good traitor, guess I'm better off as a one-man band." He chugged whatever was left of his drink.

James was fascinated by how Mendez seemed entirely unbothered by the rum.

"If you ask me, that's very interesting," Charles said.

"To a bunch of idiots who don't know what they're doing," James said and raised his cup. Charles and Mendez did the same. They all drank out of their wooden tankards. Mendez knocked his chest twice, letting out a hiccup.

James set his flagon on the table and looked into it. He caught himself smiling, the tension that he was so used to in his abdomen loosening. He had been alone for an uncomfortably long while. Ever since he sailed with his Rose from that cliff. Maybe it was time to stop being the lone wolf. A few crew members wouldn't hurt, right?

Both knew pain. Charles masked it with joy. Mendez seemed to forget about it with good company and good adventure. Charles knew some stories about the Wolf and the Rose. Which was perfect. Whatever Charles knew about the Wolf and the Rose would be enough to keep him mindful of what they're capable of. As for Mendez, the less he knew, the better, and the more loyal he would be.

"Well Mr. Bruno, Santiago Mendez..." He raised his flagon and took another sip. "You've passed the test... Would you like to come aboard the Silver Rose?"

"Would I?!" Charles exclaimed.

"Anything to keep me away from those bunch," Mendez said, putting his hands into his pockets. He frowned and pulled something papery out of them.

"What's that?" Charles asked.

"My treasure map!" Mendez said and leaped in his chair.

"Oh no, not a treasure map, please." Charles grimaced. "Characters always die because of treasure."

"It's a. *Treasure.* Map," Mendez said his words clearly.

"Shh!" Charles said, "You don't want a bunch of pirates knowing we have a treasure map, do you?"

Mendez leaned closer to James and Charles and lowered his voice. None of the people around them seemed to hear the word 'treasure.' Probably because they were intoxicated. Pirates and buccaneers were drinking and laughing. Others, drinking their misery away.

"Where did you get that?" James asked.

Mendez slid it across the table to him. "I stole it from Max and Anmar when I planned to escape. It's mine now."

The map had no headings, no marks of land, no north, south, east, west. It had strange lexigrams. *The* strange lexigrams that James has seen in the Commodore's journals for ten years.

He ran his fingers over a familiar mark on the map. "That's not a treasure map, Santiago."

Max must be looking for it. She might be running through Pirates' Isle, searching for Mendez and whoever stole the map with him. James needed the map, and Max could not take it away from him.

"Mendez!"

The tavern door burst open with a crash and the crowd snapped to attention, finding Max unsheathing her sword in a frenzy. "Get back here, you bastard."

The music, babbling and fighting halted and everyone turned in the direction of Max and her accomplices.

"Time to go." Charles shuffled out of his seat. James pocketed the map and headed to the back of the tavern, Mendez following him.

Anmar pointed with his sword to them. "Over there!"

Now the tavern turned in unison to James, Charles and Mendez, who made for the nearest exit. Max and her misfits darted in their direction and the trio scurried out the back door nearest to the musicians.

James bolted to the dock, holding the map dear in his hand. He didn't look behind him, but he heard the other two on his heels. Has he already found a crew?

Their boots slammed down the cobblestone path, the pirates around them did not bat an eye. It was a normal night in Pirates' Isle.

James gestured with his hand for the two to follow. "Follow me!"

"Where?" Charles panted.

"To the Silver Rose."

They arrived at the dock, the wood echoing with the thumping of their boots. It was a brittle dock, built on an incline of land, weathered from enduring years upon years of storms, with mossy and rusty piers supporting its minimal form beneath the low, murky waters.

"Going somewhere, captain?" a gravelly voice resounded from the shadows.

James halted and turned to the voice. "Thaddeus."

"In flesh and blood." Thaddeus stepped out of the shadows and into the moonlight. He wore an eyepatch that hid a scar that traced down his left cheek. His mouth split in a grin. He unsheathed his sword and directed the end of his blade at James.

"I wouldn't fight here," James said.

Thaddeus stroked his eyepatch. "I may have lost an eye to you, Wolf. But I won't be fighting alone this time." Footsteps emerged from behind him. Boots and bare feet jumped off a ship's gangplank. "I've got a whole crew."

"They're surrounded," came the far cry voice of Anmar.

Max and her accomplices arrived at the scene. She gritted her teeth, a muscle working in her jaw as she did. "Hand it over, Mendez."

"Ha! I don't have it anymore." Mendez splayed his empty hands, almost mockingly. "It's with him!" He pointed to James.

"Then I'll rip it out of you." Max advanced to James, and he blocked her blow.

Thaddeus came in for an opportunity attack, and Charles parried his strike. "What are you doing? Fighting the Wolf?"

"Get out of my way," Thaddeus spat back. Thaddeus' crew advanced toward Mendez and Charles, taking advantage of the distracted Wolf.

But James grinned. "This close to my ship. Really?" he called out to Thaddeus.

The dock shook as a cannonball collided, momentarily staggering the fight. James kicked Max in the abdomen, and she stumbled back. He saluted with the map, and hopped off the dock.

There was no splash.

Charles ran to the edge of the dock, peering down at the water. Mendez blocked an incoming blow from Thaddeus and jumped, screaming.

Charles followed.

He landed on wood, and then noticed where he was: on a rowboat, with James standing at the head of it, one knee bent on the bow of the boat, his arm over it.

The boat moved on its own, the oars rowing themselves. Mendez didn't seem to notice. He turned to the stern of the boat. "She doesn't have a ship. I'm free!" He turned to the stern of the rowboat and screamed to the dock. "So long, *amiga*!"

Another cannonball crashed into the sea, dousing the boat in the bay's salty waters.

"Missed!" Mendez called out over the boat.

"Stay down!" Charles pulled at Mendez's collar, jerking him out of the path of a whistling bullet. Charles whirred on James, "Captain."

James still had his foot on the boat's bow, his eyes frowning not at the chaos behind him, but at the calm waters before him, his eyes searching for something, or someone. He flicked the map out of his pocket, and Charles saw a hint of a grin across the Wolf's face. "Captain!" he repeated, yelling.

"Hang on tight." James pocketed the map. He held out his hand, the motion so natural as though he had done this before.

His hand met a rope as one would meet a handshake. After only the barest of pauses, he turned to his little crew and winked. "Come aboard."

The rope went taut and pulled him, his features blurring behind the frame of a dark, looming ship. Charles and Mendez exchanged glances before looking to the dock of Pirates' Isle. A ship was hurtling out of the docks into the bay.

"That's Thaddeus. Let's go." Charles gestured for Mendez and stood at the edge of the boat. He held out his hand, skeptical.

A rope dangled in front of him. Unsure of what he was doing, Charles reached for it.

And it reached for him. It wrapped twice around his wrist and forearm like a snake and pulled. The rowboat disappeared beneath his feet before the yelp even fully left his throat. Bodily scooped over the railing by an unassuming coil of hemp, and he landed on the deck of a ship, only just managing to keep to his feet with how it deposited him. Regaining his bearings, he looked around for the Spanish man. "Mend—"

Mendez's scream swelled, and his frame thudded into Charles, throwing both of them onto the deck. Mendez was cackling.

"You two just going to stand there?" James' voice resounded from the quarterdeck. "Get on the cannons!"

Charles and Mendez shuffled to their feet. "Cannons?" Charles called out.

His captain pointed. "There."

A low whistle rushed in their direction, and a cannonball splashed into the sea, water splashing onboard. Charles ran to the barrel of cannonballs by the quarterdeck stairs and loaded the starboard cannon. He aimed at Thaddeus' ship.

"No!" James called out to him. "Let her aim. Mendez, where's Max?"

"No need to worry about her, captain," Mendez answered. He trimmed the main sail and the ship picked up speed. "She doesn't have a ship."

The words settled into Charles' mind a little too late. *Let her aim...*

But he did not need to comprehend the words. A grinding sound rumbled as the cannon moved on its own, turning its muzzle away from Thaddeus' ship and onto the wreckage. Charles' eyes widened in disbelief as fire flicked on the cannon's line on its own. He took cover and shielded his ears.

The deck vibrated beneath his feet when the cannon fired. He watched the ball hurtle in the air.

And miss—or so Charles thought.

The cannonball landed near a broken bowsprit in the wreckage, water sloshing over the clinging drapery of seaweed and wood. The sea beneath the remains of the ship rumbled and boiled, against all logic.

The bowsprit quivered. It turned in its waters, other wreckage and shipwrecks following suit. Another cannon fired, landing yet another ball in the waters by a submerged hull. Thaddeus' ship tore through the bay, its course now direct with the quaking remains of the beached ship.

Charles braced for impact, as if he were on Thaddeus' ship himself.

The submerged crack of wood resounded in the dark waters as the ship collided with the wreckage. The ship slowed, the water roiled as if it hosted a furnace. The wreckage eroded and rumbled, masts careening toward Thaddeus' ship, wood and debris gathering at its bow.

James let go of the helm and headed to the quarterdeck stairs. "He was a pain in my neck."

Something cracked in the devastation, and shouts erupted across Thaddeus' sinking ship.

James descended the stairs, his hand on the railing. He flicked a matchstick and headed to the lamps, as the helm steadied itself, adjusting his ship's course away from the carnage in Pirates Isle's bay.

He lit the quarterdeck lamps of the Silver Rose. The ship chirped a creak from his cabin, and two more lamps shone on their own, opposite to James, the warm light traveling in succession toward him. The Rose sent another squeal under Mendez's boots as he gawked at the ascending shimmer of lights.

Charles didn't miss the smirk on James' face, and he faced his captain. "What's so funny?"

James lit a starboard lamp as the Rose lit the adjacent port lamp. "The Rose says she likes your boots, Santiago."

Mendez turned on his heels, his eyes taking in every detail of the Rose's woodwork. He glanced at the helm and cannons that returned to their place. "What is this place?"

"The Silver Rose," Charles answered. He locked his gaze onto James'. "So, the stories are true." The Rose sent a low rumble that began at her bow, traveled up her mast and dissipated near the quarterdeck. "She can speak with you, then. I can't hear her."

James blew the matchstick and ascended the stairs back to the helm. "Correct. I alone can hear her." He glanced back to his crew, his voice curt. "She, however, can hear all of you."

Silence stretched, thick and languid. Charles shifted his weight, his steps charged with tension. The air around the Rose's masts seemed to sigh as her sails rippled.

"You've been sailing this ship on your own?" Mendez spoke next.

"No, I'm not entirely alone." A glint passed over James' eyes. "The Rose is here with me, after all." His voice was pensive as he stroked her railing, his palm leading up to her helm tenderly, as if waking a loved one from a nap. A flicker of her lamp near the helm appeared as though she smiled at him.

"I've always wondered how the Silver Rose slipped through Navy ships, so much like smoke," Charles said, as if that was something you could casually say to any seafaring fugitive.

"The Ordinance's ships, you mean," James said, not even attempting to check the rising rage in his voice.

The Rose groaned a gravelly sound from her mighty belly at that word, silencing the night ambiance around her, the wind between her sails fizzling out.

James knew the Rose was eyeing Charles closely, whose hand hovered over his sword, tension galvanizing between the soles of his boots and the floorboards. He walked over the deck as though he were walking on coals. A rope slithered from the Rose's mizzen mast down to Charles, snaking a path to his boots. He froze and swallowed.

"I thought you knew my story," James said and held the helm.

Whatever stories that roamed out there didn't concern the Rose and her captain. Any story that struck fear and awe, or tenderness and kindness, was a story they could use to gain the loyalty of their new crew. James was willing to use any story, good or bad, to do just that. He was desperate for one, he needed the manpower.

Mendez approached the slithering line. The woven hemp swung to face him, like a snake ready to strike. But he extended his hand to it. The frazzled rope approached him. She wrapped the line around his palm, but not tightly. It was almost friendly. He smiled and she shook his hand. Mendez looked up at the sails. The Rose's sails and sheets breathed the air around her high mast. She rippled them a little, enticing him.

James gazed upon his new crew. Their contrasting images, one fearful, the other welcoming, made the Bite quiver in James' chest. He cleared his throat, swallowing down the unfamiliar sensation.

"What do you want from us?" Charles' voice brought James' attention back to focus.

"All I need is a crew." *I am desperate for one.*

Charles drew in a deep breath. "I've always wanted to sail under the Rose's flag, and I've heard lots of stories about it," he said. His stride grew more comfortable walking over the Rose's floorboards, and his hand finally left his sword. The Rose shone her lamps brighter where he strode, his shadow sharper and clearer across her deck. "Well." He shrugged and turned on his heel. "This is it."

"Captain James Wolf," Mendez declared, "you want to get out of here or what?"

"Glad you asked," his captain replied.

The Silver Rose squealed from her bow to her stern and her until-then unlit lamps shone awake. The light cast her wood with a warm hue. She untied her lines, let her sails unfurl and aimed for the wind. James turned the helm, and her sails cupped and caught the gust with a snap of fabric. Her bow turned away from the dock, toward the open ocean. She felt the water beneath her hull lash as she cut through it, the fresh air of the sea getting heavier as she sailed further into it. The shipwreck slowly materialized over the horizon. But this time it was different. This time, the Rose had a crew.

Charles and Mendez turned to their captain.

James held the helm, the moon silhouetting him. "Welcome aboard."

3

Charles

He had a promise to keep

Charles put his journal in his bag. He stuffed the bag into his pillow and placed the pillow between his hammock's creases, making sure the bag was as deep in the crease as possible. Running his hand over it, he couldn't feel the journal. Good.

He walked to the water bucket. His reflection stared at him in the liquid. It didn't smile, nor frown. The image was clear, his features moving with the water's ripples. He cupped his palms and dipped them in, eager to distort the image of the man he saw.

He climbed up deck. He was usually the first one up in his family. Not on this ship. On this ship, the Silver Rose was the first one up, metaphorically speaking. She was anchored somewhere deep in the sea, but the water was still, and quiet. Unlike his mind. Charles breathed in a quivering breath and sauntered over to the railing. He ran a finger along the well-worn wood, then carefully set his elbows on it. The Rose's hull made a small squeal where Charles stood, almost as if greeting him. He breathed deeply, the sting of the sea and the aged scent of the Rose's wood unknotted his resulting frown.

Wood and salt. That was all he'd smelled in the past two years as he searched for the Wolf and the Rose on the high seas. The scent of wood and salt now seemed different, tasted different. Sweet and final.

That finality settled into his chest. He would never again have to smell wood and salt and rotten barnacles again after he finished this job. After far too long, he'd be back with his family, to his bookshop. It would be the smell of aged paper and leather, Uncle Wilson's tea, and Gabrielle's stories.

A shadow passed behind him, only just catching his peripheral vision. Charles twisted around and found the Rose dangling a line, frayed fibers spiraling from its edges. It hovered near his face. The rope slithered closer and he leaned back. Stories always said her lines were like snakes. Visceral images flooded his mind: Strangled. Hanged. Drowned.

Sweat coalesced on his neck. The line curved down. He followed its movements with his eyes but didn't move his head. Not his head. With a quivering breath, Charles closed his eyes when he couldn't see the line anymore.

Something tugged on his collar. He opened his eyes and found the rope straightening his vest and promptly pulled him forward, away from the railing.

An uneasy smile slipped through his lips. "Thank you," he said. His mind went back to his journals, retracing his movements hiding them.

"You're an early bird."

Charles flinched at the voice. He turned and faced Mendez.

"*Dios mio, amigo,*" Mendez said. "You look like you've been hit by an anchor. Did you sleep?" He joined Charles by the railing.

"I slept better than I have in two years, thank you," Charles said. His hands went to his hair, matting his temples and ruffling the back.

The door to their captain's cabin creaked open. Their little crew turned in time to find him stepping out of it, adjusting his blue embroidered jacket and peculiar necklace. The Rose's sails moved as if she breathed a sigh of relief, and the rustling of her ropes and ratlines became softer. The tone of her creaks shifted, and Charles followed the sounds of her creaking wood from the bow to James' cabin. The sound stopped exactly where James stood.

Their captain managed a smile, and Charles noticed a twinge of pain behind those lips. The Rose's shrouds rattled, and her masts creaked. James appeared as though he was listening to something she was saying. When he spoke, his voice was as coarse as sand. "On deck, sailors. The Rose needs a heading."

"Aye, captain!" Mendez sprang into action. He aided the Rose with unfurling her sails this time, rather than let her do it all by her lonesome, while James headed to the helm. A deep croaking sound came from her capstan, and Charles moved to help her raise the anchor.

He couldn't help but be proud of himself. Raising an anchor on your own was no laughing matter. Though it was mostly the Rose who did the heavy lifting.

Gradually, the anchor towed upwards before locking into place, and the sails were trimmed. When they caught a solid wind current, they were soon in pursuit of the horizon. The Rose moved fast and nimble, not unlike the clouds that floated above her. Charles stepped on the railing nearest to the bowsprit. Looking below him, he noticed the wooden rose vines and leaves that decorated the figurehead. The stories he had heard of the Rose had failed to capture her structure's beauty.

The Rose let down a rope for him. It went to his hand and made its way into his palm. He held it tight, and it wrapped twice around his wrist as he hopped onto the bowsprit, maneuvering his steps around the wooden rose vines. Leaning forward until the line was taut, he let his free arm over the edge. The wind brushed his cheeks, and the occasional spray of the sea sprinkled his face. He closed his eyes and let the sensations refresh him.

It was easy to forget why he was here.

He wanted to believe his journey was coming to a close; that he would face no more problems, no more barnacles, no more traveling alone, no more sleepless nights. But he was nowhere near finished. Though he wanted to deny it, the most arduous part of his job had just begun.

"Well, I'm hungry." Mendez brushed his hands together.

The Rose's line tugged Charles' wrist twice. He walked and hopped back onto the Rose's deck. His eyes followed the line's path back to the jib mast.

"So am I, Santiago," James said. "We deserve a treat after that. Phew! What a load of work."

The Rose gave a long cackling rumble from his cabin. James headed to the hatch and Mendez followed. Charles surveyed the Rose's main deck, a certain heaviness draping over his shoulders. He shook his head and followed his captain and shipmate's steps.

"So, what would you like to eat?" James asked, his voice muffled as he entered his galley. "Hardtack. More hardtack. Err… dried apricots. And… I don't know what this is." He rummaged a little more and finally settled on an apple. He threw a piece to Mendez who held it without hesitation.

"Gracias."

Charles smiled and took the tack from James. Charles looked over James' supplies. Walnuts and almonds. Dried fruits, dates. Jars upon jars of spices. Barrels of stuff the colors of dried and aromatic nuts and fruits. He turned his attention again to James as his captain handed him and Mendez a handful of walnuts and pistachios and another hardtack biscuit.

"There's quite a lot of food here for one captain," Charles said.

"A captain's gotta stock for his crew," James replied.

"How long have you been planning for one?" Charles asked.

James shrugged. "For a good long while." He threw his apple in the air and caught it. "You lot wouldn't be here if the Rose hadn't pressed me to find a crew." He took a bite. The Rose's brig rumbled. "Also, with all of these extra rations, I *had* to find a crew, otherwise it would be a waste. And I hate to waste."

"These rations must have cost you a fortune, captain," Mendez said.

"I have my ways," James winked.

Charles looked to James' eyes. Meagerly noticeable dark circles rimmed his eye sockets. Charles' mind remembered his employer's words. *He's dangerous, Mr. Bruno. Are you sure you're for this assignment?*

Charles shook his head lightly and hoped neither his captain or crewmate noticed. He found no one around him, and he turned to find James turning to go up the hatch to deck, Mendez trailing behind him. Charles' steps followed.

"I appreciate that and all," Mendez said. He found a barrel and sat on it, gnawing on his tack. "But if you want me on board, you'll have to get more rum than that."

"Whatever you need," James said.

The Rose's lines squealed and rattled and the wind brushed a whisper in her sheets as she sailed through the waters. Sunshine blanketed Charles' eyes and he felt it become part of his being. A smile materialized on his lips. Then he remembered why he was here. His short-lived smile dropped like a stone.

"Feeling a little seasick, are we, Charles?" James asked.

"Not at all." Charles expanded his chest and gave a brave smile. "I've sailed many times before. I'm a man of the sea."

"He just wants to take a look at the map, right, *amigo*?" Mendez hopped off his barrel.

"So do I." James turned to the captain's cabin. The doors framed James as he sauntered through them, creaks and rumbles emerged from his cabin as the doors slowly groaned open.

That had been his job for two years. Find the Wolf and the Rose. Bring them back. Alive. Here he was. On the deck of the Silver Rose. He has heard all too many chilling stories about the Wolf's cabin. He had a promise to keep. *Come back alive, Charles.* All he needed to do was get the Wolf and the Rose to—

"Charles, are you coming, *amigo*?"

James

Whatever is important to The Commodore is prey to us on this ship

"Welcome to my humble abode," James said, and sank into his aged mahogany chair. The intricate carvings along the frame gave James' silhouette a royal presence. The creaking wood in his cabin paced the breath of the Silver Rose. The space had a warm tint in the morning sun. Light blurred through the curtains covering the stern window and made a startlingly orange pillow appear luminescent. He gestured with his hand for Charles and Mendez to sit, and laid the map across the table.

"Let's take a look at this treasure map," Mendez said.

"Are you *sure* it's a treasure map?" Charles asked.

"Yes. Max got it off some relic-collecting contractor. That's why she's mad at me for stealing it." Mendez pointed to a spot on the map etched with a peculiar symbol. "He said he'd pay us a big sum if we find where this map leads to."

"It could just be a map out of an atlas that you tore out of her pocket." Charles slid the map closer to him.

"Oh, please," Mendez said, snatching the map. "Max can't read." He put the paper closer to his side of the table. "And for your information, I didn't tear it. We split the map between us and the other two contractors involved."

"What the blazes are we going to do with half a map?" Charles grumbled, leaning in to take a look at the paper in Mendez' hand, who turned in his seat away from Charles' view.

"They said this map is special. And I couldn't leave the group empty-handed so—" Mendez backed away from Charles, who was reaching for it, "—I took the spoils of Max's first ever, possibly conned, contract."

"That doesn't make it a treasure map." Charles leaned beyond his chair, reaching for the coveted parchment again.

"The contract did promise a generous sum. If so, then who knows where this map leads." Mendez swung it behind his back and leapt away from Charles.

"Give it." Charles reached behind Mendez. Charles was taller, and he would have snatched it out of his hands had it not been for the Spanish man's quick movements. "You know, you belong in a circus with those moves," Charles grunted, jumping out of his seat to Mendez, who twisted away from him in response.

"Will you stand still so we can all read it?" Charles grunted, grabbing at the air.

A quiver reverberated in James' chest. He frowned and his hand flew to his heart. He had lived with the Bite for ten years, and almost became accustomed to its sensations. He leaned in his seat and steadied his breathing. His cabin hadn't listened to human voices aside from his own in a long while. And his chest hadn't felt this quivering sensation since he last attempted to visit Damascus.

He turned his gaze from his new crew to the shuddering map. Though the figures and symbols on the map were blurry in Mendez' grip, James saw something that caught his attention, like a hunter spotting his prey.

"Settle down." James stood from his chair and snatched the map from Mendez' hands. The two stopped arguing and Charles straightened his red vest.

"I'm more flexible than you," Mendez said to Charles.

"Yes, but I'm the tallest," Charles retorted, completely ignoring the fact that James was almost a head taller than he was.

James set the map against his dagger-hole riddled table. Strange. The lexigrams looked a little different now than they did in the tavern. He inspected the symbol that caught his attention, his immediate impulse was to reach for his drawer, where he locked away the cipher of lexicons. The symbol on the map looked identical to the glyphs on the walls in Mitchell's study five years ago.

James reached for some parchment and scribbled the symbol he saw. He opened the drawer and sifted through the journals and his ciphers.

"What have you got there, captain?" Charles leaned over the table, his eyes searching the papers.

The Rose creaked again. Charles and Mendez exchanged frowns.

"Are we missing something?" Charles said and crossed his arms. "You look more interested in the mark than the alleged treasure map itself, captain."

"There it is," James said when he matched the glyph of the map to the lexicons on his journals. A triangle with an eye in the middle.

"What is?" Charles asked.

James held the lexicon scribble to his crew. "Whatever this symbol marks is important to the Commodore," he continued, his eyes locked onto Charles. "Whatever is important to the Commodore is prey to us on this ship." James set the parchment down.

Charles set his eyes on the scrawl. "I see."

"Well then we found a heading!" Mendez said.

"We're not exactly sure where this place is, though," James said.

"Let's figure it out together," Mendez replied. "Like a crew." He wrapped his arms around his captain and shipmate.

All three hovered over the map. James put his hands to the table, squinting between his stack of codes and ciphers. Charles crossed his arms, more so eyeing his captain and his enigma of papers and glyphs than the preternatural chart, while Mendez put his hand to his chin, seriously giving it his best to try and uncover the shifting surface of this map.

The map had the strange glyph in question, some stranger looking sigils that resembled a cluster of islands. But that was it. No landmarks—no North, South, East, West—nothing. James sifted through the key for the Commodore's journals, but nothing provided any clarity on the symbol in question nor the lexigrams in the journals.

The Rose was thinking right along with her crew as well, leaving intermittent ticks of thought that only James could understand. But the map remained a puzzle, even to the otherworldly Silver Rose.

You want to get to the talismans first, don't ya?

They had spent three days trying to decode the map with no luck, the Silver Rose getting restless and her captain agitated with no headway to be had.

The captain lay down on his bed, arms crossed over his eyes. Sitting on a chair, fiddling with some paper, Charles glared at the ciphers and papers on James' table.

Mendez lay flat upon a plush blue carpet, arms outstretched, map covering his face. He abruptly bolted upright, the map sliding off his features. "Did you hear that?"

"Hear what?" Charles frowned, turning to face him.

Mendez flinched and stood, listening intently. "That."

James' eyebrows knotted and he tuned in. "I hear it too." It was whistle that morphed into an eerie hum. The captain stood from his bed, attuned to the voice that swirled in his cabin, faint yet clear. It came from the sky, and sea. Everywhere and nowhere at once.

"Like a siren?" Mendez pushed the map away from his path.

"Surreal," Charles said, his voice slurred.

"Magical," James cooed. His vision hazed, but his eyes traced the sound as it seemingly whirled around his head.

Their gazes slowly went blank while they listened to the head-whorling, ethereal voice that echoed in the cabin and ricocheted across the sea.

"So beautiful," Charles slurred, his speech slow and drowsy as he wandered to the cabin door. The Silver Rose made a heavy creak under his feet.

"It's all right, *mia Rosa*," James murmured, trailing after Charles. "It's all right. It sounds lovely."

The Rose creaked again, louder this time, trying to muffle the voice that held her crew captive.

Charles blinked. "Heavenly."

The voice was ear-piercing, clear as a crystal bell. The three streamed out the cabin door.

Night had fallen. The Rose luffed her sails loudly and groaned a guttural sound from her brig, but she couldn't mask the eerie humming that came from the moon, then hung over the sky, horizon, and sea.

"Hello, boys." The voice funneled from the crow's nest to the Rose's stern. "Did it really take a siren's song for you to notice me?"

The three winced, turning to face the source of the voice. James blinked owlishly and held his pulsing head. "Did you have to make it hurt?"

When James' eyes finally adjusted, he discerned a husky figure resting on the Silver Rose's great stern lamp.

"So sorry, dearie," the voice hummed, "I can't control the side effects."

The Rose's sails snapped peevishly in response and ropes slunk to the merman, aiming to bind him. But the mysterious creature's reflexes were unearthly, catching her snaking lines with grace, a certain familial kindness in his touch. "Hang on, darling," he said, "we're from the same world, you and I. You wouldn't want to hurt a fellow Nahidan, would you?"

Not a single creak came from the Rose, silence piercing the air as she pondered the idea. She withdrew her lines back to her masts, and when the lines finally nestled into posts, she gave a soft, whispering creak under James' boots. ***Hear him out.***

"Who are you?" Mendez asked, breaking the uncanny silence.

"Aereon," the figure said. "Member of the aquatic community of another world, a mystery to yours. Or as your people like to call us—" he lifted a shoulder and batted his gold-yellow eyes, "Mermaids."

The crew blinked stupidly at his scaled tail that glimmered a calm blue and a warm orange under the lamp lights and moon. Aereon must have noticed. He smirked. "This your first time seeing a merman?"

"We'll be quite honest with you." Charles flicked his index fingers at the merman. "Yes."

"You're sailors," Aereon remarked. "You're bound to see merfolk at some point."

"Merpeople don't glow," Mendez countered, staring at Aereon's impressive tail.

"Of course we do, honey." Aereon winked. "We're a much more diverse beings than the stories you've heard." His eyes locked onto Charles' for a moment before surveying his friends. Then Aereon wore a dreamy smile as he traced a glistening finger on the Silver Rose's form. "Mystery ship," he said. "I see you got what you wished for, Wolf." His gaze now pierced into James'. The Rose creaked in the sea in response to the merman.

"Hardly," James scoffed, his voice coarse, almost inaudible. He never wished for his mother to be killed by the Commodore. All he wished was to bring his father and the Rose back after the pirate attack. The consequences of his actions had seemed marginal when he had listened to the whispers of the Shadows that dreadful night in his room.

"This is a much bigger world than you can imagine, Wolf. Not just Ordinance ambassadors and mermaids and Shadows." Aereon rested his elbow on the lamp's ridge, his chin in his palm.

"What do you know?" James chided.

"Only that we want you to get to our doorway first. Before the Shadows and the Xanahan Guardians do."

His words were a riddle, but James only heard one thing. *The Shadows.* "What do you know about the Shadows?" James called, his voice rising.

Aereon giggled. "What indeed." He adjusted himself on the Rose, his tail curving with the ship's arches, as he readied himself to tell the crew a story. He raised a scaled palm and flicked it to the crew. A splash of faint yellow, rubescent pink and blue light flung from his fingers and hovered over the crew's eyes.

"There were three worlds in alliance," the merman said. He beckoned the lights to him and they swirled into a blurry image. "Simraash, Xanahae, and Nahida." The lights bubbled before they focused into three spheres, with faint movement within them that made it as though they were their own microcosms.

"Simraash, or as you call them, the Shadows, relied on the light source of their world. But it was dying. And in turn, The Shadows were dying." The miniature world on the left turned an acrid gray and began to melt, strings of light falling like viscous paint and disappearing before they hit the Rose's deck. "Afterall, there can be no shadow without light." Aereon's voice swelled and echoed everywhere, a mournful melody in his voice that made James' head spin.

"The Shadows asked their allies for help," Aereon continued, and the two worlds next to Simraash's rippled. "But they were too busy preparing to introduce themselves to your world, and they ignored their nearest allies. And so Simraash waged a war on Nahida, their closest access to light and hope."

Simraash crept through Nahida, like ink in water. The gray spindles of Simraash drained light of Nahida, dousing it in darkness. Little beings flitted about the graying world, falling from Nahida onto the Rose's floorboards. Some bounced like little fireflies on the Rose's wood before winking out, other's light diffusing before they reached the Rose's deck.

James didn't miss the small wince that passed over Aereon's face, brief and nigh imperceptible. *There's something in it for him.*

Test him.

But the mask of charm and allure returned to Aereon's face as he continued his story. "Xanahae did not take that kindly."

At his words, the world called Xanahae flashed and rumbled, arbors twisting out of it and dug into Simraash like knives. The arbors and spindles wrestled against each other within the bubble of Nahida, the world too small to contain the battle between the two angered allies.

Flecks of gray fell out of Simraash, too, some scrambling to Nahida, others falling onto the Rose's deck, and diffusing in a plume of smoke. Simraash's world dripped before the arbors wrapped around it like snakes, squeezing the air out of it. The dark world cracked, and shattered, shards of it frittering away in an explosion of smoke, while Nahida lay sloshing with gloom and destruction.

The smoke and ash and shadows, although were merely an illusion, sent a chill skittering through James' blood. The Bite responded hungrily, amplifying the awful memory in James' mind. He balled his fists, a meager attempt to hide his growing tumult.

Aereon's melodious voice brought him back to the narrative. "Long story short, the alliance broke. Simraash was banished out of it." The worlds cracked and shattered into pieces. The lights collapsed and the three worlds merged together and retreated into Aereon's closed fist. "But there still remains a threat to our world, Nahida," Aereon concluded. "There are weak points in this world. Points that act as doorways between your world and ours. The map will lead you to that vulnerability."

The familiar image of gray and smoke and snaking Shadows raised bile in James' stomach, the Bite in his chest threatening to dig an icy path through his throat. He swallowed thickly, hiding the swaying in his posture.

The three stood in silence, unsure of what to make of this narrative. Tragic as the story was, it meant nothing to James. Not unless it brought him closer to his sole purpose. *Revenge.*

Test him.

James stepped forward, the merman eyeing him with those cool, golden eyes. "How do you know all this?"

"Let's just say I have a responsibility. I must be privy to such things."

"What's in it for you?" James pressed.

Aereon seemed to take in a breath, and in the soft glow of moonlight and the Rose's lamp, James could see geometric shapes on the merman's face, shoulder and chest glint and twinkle with Aereon's inhale.

He clasps his hands together, his gaze softening. "Oh, Wolf, always the one to calculate." The merman flashed James a delightful grin and leaned against the Rose's lamp. "Nahida is my home. I want your help to protect it from the Shadows. Is that so wrong?"

"We tried using your treasure map," Mendez said, pulling James out of his unease. "It doesn't work."

"Treasure map?" Aereon laughed, his voice surging over the Rose in waves not unlike a breaking tide. "That's no treasure map, darling. Though if you consider the doorway to my world a treasure, then I'm deeply flattered." Aereon turned his attention back to James, addressing him directly. "You know more than anyone the ways of the Shadows."

The Bite now reacted to that, all but crushing James' heart with a wild frenzy. He gritted his teeth, and his first reaction was to clutch at his chest. He was glad his crew was behind him. *Don't let them see weakness!*

Hissing, he glared at Aereon. "What's in it for me?"

"Still looking for the talismans, Wolf?"

The merman knew exactly what commanded James' attention, whose lips twitched as words knotted in his mouth.

"Ahh, yes, dear Wolf," Aereon mused. "The Shadows want them, the Guardians want them … and now a few humans want them, too."

Aereon could be lying, but if he could get James any closer to the talismans than the Commodore, he was going to take any chances. "How can I trust you?"

"You want to get to the talismans first, don't ya?"

"Yes. Yes, I do."

"Then follow us," Aereon said. He leapt with unerring grace back into the sea. The crew ran toward the railing, scanning the deep, black waters for any sign of his shimmering tail.

"Aereon!" James yelled and leaned at the railing, completely forgetting that the sea was a mere shove forward.

Aereon's voice echoed inside their heads again: "Over here, boys."

Mendez pointed toward an obscured light under the waters. It shone brighter as Aereon's voice jumped at them from the sea. "Follow us."

The Rose's sails luffed and cracked when the sea around her burst a cocktail of pastel colors. The lights grew bright and lit the Silver Rose's hull in hues of orange, yellow, blue.

"Are those…?" Charles began.

"More merfolk," James told him. His eyes followed the stream of light that emanated from the Rose onto the sea. Merpeople flicked from the iridescent waters, their tails camouflaging in the night's stars.

The collective song of the merfolk frothed over the waters and swept around the Rose.

"Yes!" James cheered. He jumped and kicked the air on his way to the stairs. "Thank you, Aereon," he called to the air around him.

The Rose stretched a rumble through her wood and braced more lines and sails.

"Let's catch the wind, *amigos*!" Mendez dashed to the jib lines.

"And hoist the colors." James clapped Charles' back and ran to the helm.

4

Charles

Why is anything dear to the commodore prey to us?

His captain had been in good humor as the Rose made her way through the waters, sailing through the night and into dawn. After their brief morning meal of hard tack, pistachios, and wine—rum for Mendez—they had gathered in their captain's cabin. Charles and Mendez had been charting the Rose's course, while James attended to his peculiar ciphers and map.

He had been intently focused on his work, as though he was the only one in his cabin, sifting through the papers with strange glyphs and scribbling stranger notes. He only looked up from his papers when he appeared to be listening to the Rose's creaks.

Day stretched into dusk and into night as they worked. Experience and habit had made charting a course come naturally to Charles. His hands worked deftly with navigation instruments, but his mind was elsewhere.

The Shadows. What are they? What is this merman on about?

If they remained on the same course, their destination would take them to New Orleans.

And what are these glyphs?

New Orleans was nice. He could send a letter to home there.

Whatever is important to the Commodore is prey to us on this ship.

I have to finish this job. I have to save the bookshop.

New Orleans.

Does James mean the Commodore harm?

Stop thinking about it!

"You just going to stand there, mate?"

Charles flinched at his captain's voice, who was standing at his cabin door, eyeing him.

"I'm coming," Charles said.

James fixed him in a scowl as he joined his crewmate and captain. The Rose creaked under James' feet, and he squinted before he broke his gaze.

Charles' steps slowed as he stood on the main deck. The moon cast long, blurry shadows on the Silver Rose. She was confident, and her sails gave a strong crack in the wind. He looked out to the sea over the railing. The waters around the Rose moved almost as if they cleared the path for her. One wave after another, organized and coordinated as much as they were chaotic and dangerous.

If this were truly a treasure map, he could have forgotten about this job. The treasure could have been worth a lot more than what his employer promised. He would grab whatever fortune his pockets could fit, and forget about the Wolf and the Rose—charlatans who would do anything for treasure. And, truthfully, Charles believed he was no exception.

But this wasn't a treasure map.

He drew in a breath and gazed at the sky, and on his exhale, he spotted the flag that the Silver Rose flew. He studied it. The flag looked like it had been sewn together from mismatched fabric that was of no use anymore. Hues of blue flecked with gold and a patchwork of orange and red. It had no crest or heraldry, but was instead rimmed with embroidery. It appeared that whoever made this took great effort to maintain the impeccable detail, even despite the ragtag nature of the cloth itself.

Charles' eyes darted to the Rose's quarterdeck. There was no one at the helm as she sailed steadily. And there was no sign of the captain on deck.

Whatever is important to the Commodore is prey to us on this ship.

Lost thought, and Charles dueled against his impulse to sneak into his captain's cabin. He had made a promise to Gabrielle: Come back alive. But he would not return empty-handed.

So, he turned to face his captain's cabin.

The doors weren't too extravagant, or overly large. But at that moment, he felt dwarfed. The stairs that framed the cabin curved as they lead to the helm, like a crown above a pedestal.

Charles knocked on the doors, thinking that perhaps it would be best to give the Rose a little notice in advance. Wouldn't want to catch her off-guard, if such a thing was possible. He did not want to enter his captain's cabin without his ship's invitation.

He reached for the handles. But the doors creaked open before his hand touched the wood.

"Hello? Silver Rose?" he said, a stutter in his voice. "May I re-enter? I think I forgot something inside," he lied.

The cabin rumbled and creaked, and Charles assumed he had gotten the Rose's approval.

As he searched for his phantom-something, and he spotted the pieces of tapestry that hung on the hull walls. To Charles' left, there was a book cabinet. He turned his attention to it and prepared himself to see something he didn't want to.

But the cabinet only held charts and books with Italian, Turkish, Arabic and even Latin titles. He'd never known James was a linguist, even with all the stories about him. One book read *Poems of Rumi*. Another title said, with ornate gold letters, *The Ultimate Guide to Forgotten Languages*. Charles even spotted titles in languages he didn't recognize. He was the son of a librarian; he should know what those titles meant.

The Rose tilted, the cabin creaking in response. Her movements made his vision swirl. He moved with her tilt and found himself in the heart of the cabin, by the grand table. It was large enough to fit nine crew members, a swath of quills and ink scattered over it. To the right of the table, there was the captain's bed. It looked like it could fit two people. Charles assumed James liked a big bed. By the bed, James kept a container full of swords and empty scabbards, placed strategically within arm's reach.

The Rose's aft growled and Charles turned his attention to it. Forward of the bed, there was the captain's wardrobe. He had only seen James in the same slightly oversized jacket and the same waist belt, and he wondered what his captain kept in that closet. Over the closet, there were more tapestries and some unfinished pieces of clothing, orange thread dangling from one end of it.

"Not in the chart cabinet nor the table," Charles murmured and rubbed his hands together. His head moved as though he was casually searching, but his eyes darted fast, troubled, searching for something more, though he did not know what.

The wide aft window, half covered with curtains, led Charles' view from the right to the left of the cabin. The curtains held soft tears, but they still retained their embroidery. There was a small table with candles, one more quill and music sheets, but no instruments. A small sitting cushion by the table with sheets, blankets and a few pillows thrown over it.

Most of the cabin looked the same. Tapestries and thread, quills and ink and charts.

The cabin shifted again in the rough waters, and Charles had to steady himself on the captain's table, his hand falling on the locked drawers.

He frowned when a realization occurred to him.

The Rose was guiding his search, tilting the cabin this way and that, groaning creaks here and there to guide his attention. She led him right where she wanted.

She creaked and clicked in his direction, as though addressing him.

He suddenly didn't feel the need to keep up the act. Inclining his head above, he addressed her. "Silver Rose. Why is anything dear to the Commodore prey to us on this ship?"

The Rose responded to him with a groan. He wrung his hands together and turned to face the source of the sound.

The captain's desk. A drawer creaked, and he reached his hand to it. But before his fingers twined around the metal, the Rose slid it open.

Charles' hand shrank away, as if avoiding a poisonous flower. The floorboards creaked beneath his feet, and the Rose lit a candle on the table. The light illuminated a small painting resting in the drawer. He held it, delicately. The edges were faded, but the art retained its color, no mote of dust so much as freckled the paper. In the image, there was a man, a woman and a young boy. Charles leaned into the candlelight and studied the drawing.

The boy was rosy-cheeked, smile so pearly and genuine. The woman was adorned in a gown that looked like a medley of Venetian and Levantine designs. She had her hand on her young boy's shoulder. The man was tranquil, eyes relaxed, lips parted slightly in a reverent smile. Charles flipped the paper over. He mouthed the words, written in Italian:

To the Wolf family,
Thank you for making Il Porto Dell' Armonia a place of peace.
Happy anniversary.
~ Messer Emiliano

Charles flinched when the candle snuffed out with a hiss.

No sooner did he put the painting back than the doors to his captain's cabin creaked, an accusatory sound grating within the wood.

And through the doors, stepped Captain James Wolf.

The Mark of The Wolf

Captain Wolf strolled to his shipmate, apprehension spreading across Charles' features.

James regarded him with a nod. "Having fun?"

Charles swallowed and opened his mouth to speak, but James interrupted. "No no, please," he waved a hand, and Charles thought he saw threads of gray along his captain's fingers. "Let me save you the trouble. Come." He walked outside his cabin.

The Rose rumbled as she tilted in the waters, the portrait sliding back into the drawer before it closed. Charles followed his captain, trepidation rising in his every step.

"Over here," his captain beckoned for him to join at the helm. His gaze followed Charles' steps as he mounted the stairs. Those steps carried weight, tension. He sensed his captain's calculating gaze, and Charles swallowed.

"Would you like to steer the Rose?" James asked.

Charles blinked.

"I thought you were a man of the sea." James laughed, his tone unexpectedly jovial. "You look like you've never seen a helm before."

"I have," Charles said. His shoulders sank and he rubbed his hands together. "Would she allow me?" he mumbled, glancing around as if scanning for danger.

James stepped away from the helm, his hand lingering at the handles, and whispered over Charles' shoulder. "She allowed you into my cabin, she'll allow you on her helm."

Charles averted his eyes from his captain and looked to the Rose's helm. James opened his palm to it.

Now Charles saw it. The tips of his captain's fingers were dusted in the gray of the Bite. His eyes darted from James' palm to the handles of the helm, his jawline tense and his hands clenched.

Charles approached. His palms quivered over the wood, finally closing his fingers around the handles. He scanned the deck of the Silver Rose.

"Looking for someone?" James asked, and a mirthless laugh weaved in his voice. "Mendez is below deck. It's just you. Me…" The mizzen mast ropes and lines snaked down and curled around Charles' wrists. The Rose rattled under Charles' feet with something akin to a giggling sound. "And the Rose," James finished. He regarded his hands, rubbing them together as though to warm them. "The Rose tells me that you snuck into my cabin."

Charles swallowed, his hands working under the ropes. "I—I thought I misplaced something in there." He continued steering the Rose, his eyes flicking between the horizon, James and the Rose's lines.

"Save me the lies, Charles," James interrupted, not attempting to check the vexation in his voice. But when the Rose creaked toward him, his expression shifted from sour to confused.

"He saw it?" James frowned, his hands clenching for a moment.

Unable to understand what dialogue his captain and ship shared, alarm bubbled in Charles' chest.

"Why, *mia Rosa*?"

Charles saw no point in diversion, and when he spoke, his words came with confidence, as though he was not bound to the Rose's helm. "The portrait that the Rose showed me. That's you, isn't it?"

James glared at Charles but ultimately averted his gaze, a pained expression stiffening his features. He turned his attention to the horizon instead and swallowed thickly. "Yes."

"What happened to them?"

"Gone. Pirates took him and the Commodore, her," his captain croaked, his voice weak, burdened.

Charles frowned and faced his captain, lost for words. The Commodore was not capable of something like that, was he?

The Rose's hull rumbled, and her mizzen mast creaked to James, a consoling sound.

"The sea is full of violence," was all that Charles could mutter.

The Rose rumbled under James' feet, and his expression slowly relaxed. He lifted his palm, examining the gray rivulets under his skin like diseased veins. "I thought I could get used to this. So cold and numb," he rasped, resting his hand on the railing. "The Rose believes differently."

The Rose withdrew her ropes, and Charles let go of the helm to face his captain, relief spreading across his face. "What does the Rose believe, then?"

"She believes that having a crew will slow this down," he wriggled his fingers, his gaze almost vacant. "I, on the other hand, believe in nothing but revenge."

Revenge against the Commodore, Charles finished in his head.

"Relax, Charles. I'm not going to hurt you," James added when he saw the tension in Charles' posture. James winced, and Charles did not miss the way his captain's hands quivered with concealed pain.

"I need you to slow this down," James said, waving his gray fingertips before he held the helm, his hands meeting the handles as though cupping a lady's for a dance. Winds picked up and the Rose's sails luffed. Along the thundering of her sails, the crack of a flag above the mainmast followed.

James pointed and Charles followed James' gaze to the flag. "See that flag up there?" The moonlight seemed to spotlight it. The stitches gave it a ghostly silver shimmer. "It's called the Mark of the Wolf. You be sure to call it by that name."

"Aye, captain." The words escaped Charles' lips and tasted like a lie.

5

Charles

Your future? It's full of poison

It would take an ordinary three-masted brigantine six months to arrive—but the Silver Rose was no ordinary three-masted brigantine.

"Charles, we're nearing port. Get up here!"

Charles blinked from his journals, startled by Mendez's yelling. He marked the date, hid his journals, and made for the deck. He looked out from the bow of the Silver Rose and found a city beginning to materialize on the horizon.

"Is that New Orleans?" Charles said, peeking from the railing. Mendez did the same. He was in high spirits, as usual.

"If that's where the merfolk led us, then yes," James said.

"I've only seen it in books," Charles remarked, the thrill of new places bringing a gusto to his words.

"Good." James steered the helm. "At least one of us has some idea what we're getting into."

None of them had any idea what they were getting into, and especially not Charles.

James helped steer the Rose around the busy harbor. She rumbled through the waters past an array of ships, from sloops to frigates to fishing boats.

"They might ask for papers and what have you," Charles called out to his captain.

"What papers?" Mendez asked.

"I mean the Silver Rose isn't entirely a regular ship." Charles turned to James. He rubbed her railing just in case. "Sorry, Rosy," he added.

She creaked a *none taken.*

"What if we get caught?" Mendez said, threads of anxiety woven into his voice. Guardsmen made their way onto the docks. Mendez swallowed hard. Charles' jaw tensed.

James let out a prickly laugh and slid down the stairs' railing, and the Rose handled the helm on her own.

"We can get by, don't worry," he said, heading into his cabin.

Charles frowned as shapes became clearer near the harbor. Sailors, traders, visitors. Guardsmen. He wasn't ready yet. He told himself he needed more information first.

The longer he stayed, the harder it became for him. And the longer he stayed, the harder it would become.

"I hope I don't bump into any guards I know." Mendez raised his shoulders. "I'm awkward at introductions, right, *capitán*?" he called out to his captain's cabin.

Some guards knew Mendez by name, appearance, and crime. It would be an uncomfortable encounter indeed.

Their captain walked out of his cabin with a thin stack of papers in hand. "Just relax," he said. "Everything's going to be fine."

"What are we doing exactly?" Charles crossed his arms.

"Nothing too questionable," James said. "Remember when I said I used to go on trading trips with my father on the Rose?"

His crew nodded.

"Well, I still have some papers from those trips. All right, look lively men. We're on a trading trip," he beamed and waved the yellowed parchment in his hands.

"How are we going to convince them? Don't the papers have dates? And destinations? And look at us." Mendez waved a hand at himself and pointed to Charles. "We don't really look merchant material."

Indeed, they weren't. James' boots were worn, and the jacket he wore hung down to his thighs. Not to mention his wind-ruffled hair. His embroidered waist belt could have passed as merchant material, but it had lost some of its color and had some tears and holes in it. And he was the captain of the ship. His crew wasn't any better. Mendez's beard was unkempt, and he still, somehow, smelled of rum. Charles might have passed as a well-dressed, highly esteemed trade shipmate, but he could use some grooming. He had a growing stubble, his hair hung in strands by his temples and his red vest really needed a wash.

"We'll figure it out," James said, fixing his hair to one side and adjusting his jacket. "Now, Mendez, your name is going to be Quartermaster Twidle. Charles you are Boson Shh—" James stretched his word trying to think of a name, "—middlestein. That's it. Boson Schmiddlestein."

Mendez clapped his hands, erupting in a spasmodic laughter while Charles rolled his eyes. The Rose squealed a laugh, too.

"Ugh, you too?" Charles looked to the Rose's masts. Her mainsail gave him a little wink. He turned to James. "I hate you."

"I know." James smiled, amusement twinkling in his eyes. "And I will be Captain Goldheart."

Easy stuff, easy stuff. All they needed to do was play their Twidle and Schmiddlestein roles, get past the dock, and follow the map.

The Silver Rose rolled through the waters and neared dock while Mendez wiped tears of laughter with his torn sleeves. They reached the dock, their "papers" ready, their names butchered, and disembarked the Rose.

The dock thumped with boots and strides. Sailors dismounting, goods and cargo sliding down, guards patrolling. A man in a uniform approached them. He had a very fine nose—even finer than Charles'—and skeptical, squinting eyes. "Welcome to New Orleans, gentlemen," he said. "I need your names and your purpose here."

Charles and Mendez let James do the talking; they were too embarrassed of their names to approach anyone.

"Trading trip," James announced in a cheerful and confident tone. "I am Captain Goldheart and these are some of my fine and seaworthy crew, Quartermaster Twidle and Boson Schmiddlestein." He waved at them.

Mendez's smile was broad, while Charles' was politely fake.

"Ship name?" the man asked.

"The Silent Raven," James replied.

"I wasn't expecting a Silent Raven any time today—" the man began, pulling a book out of his jacket pocket.

"Ah, yes, but we have our papers right here." James pointedly waved them in front of the dock officer.

Charles gritted his teeth and resisted the temptation not to slap the back of James' head.

The officer opened a hand for James pass him the papers. Charles and Mendez exchanged anxious glances. James bit his lip, but retained his smile.

Charles' gaze flitted around the busy harbor. The place was riddled with guardsmen. Any officer could have a connection to an Ordinance embassy. He could end it right here, right now.

The portrait. Could I really do this to him and the Rose?

Stop being soft-hearted! This is all for Gabrielle and uncle. I'm so close.

A cold sweat formed on his neck. *It's just the humidity. I don't have enough information,* he told himself.

"Where is the rest of your crew?" the officer asked, examining the papers. He looked like he had a hard time reading it, which was a good sign.

"Why, they're aboard the ship, getting the goods ready, my good man." James slapped the man's back and slipped him a few coins in his book. Three full livres.

The officer looked at the coins then stared into James' eyes. The captain just smiled back a wide, toothy smile. He gave James his papers back and snapped his book shut, the coins safe inside. "Welcome to New Orleans, Captain Goldheart," he told James and made way.

Charles let go of a breath he didn't know he was holding. Mendez's shoulders relaxed. "We were so obvious," Charles muttered as James and his crew strolled past the harbor.

Mendez lifted his chin. "I think I played a good Quartermaster."

"Yeah," James hummed.

"How did you convince him?" Charles remarked.

"I slipped him a few coins," James said nonchalantly as they walked, off to his side.

Charles turned to him. "We can't afford that right now."

"Yes, we can. We're on a treasure hunt. We can afford anything," Mendez responded.

"There isn't any treasure, Mendez," Charles grumbled like an old man draining hope out of a youth.

"You never know. Not all treasure is silver and gold," Mendez replied.

Charles shook his head and huffed. He didn't argue any further. He just continued walking along the city's streets. Small buildings flanked a church, which stood uphill at the head of the city. The trio walked around the square blocks, small vendors left and right were calling for customers to buy their jewelry, love potions, charms, clothes.

"Come get your protection charms! Charms for sale!"

"Clothes, anyone. All the way from France, *non*?"

Mendez's pace slowed down by a small market stand, musical instruments outstretched on the market table. He ran his fingers over a guitar.

"Twenty livres, *chére*," a woman said behind the table. Mendez instantly wriggled his fingers away, picking up the pace and rejoined his captain and shipmate.

They were deeper into the city. Charles glanced again over his shoulder. The dock looked a distance away, sailors and guards became indistinguishable figures ghosting across the harbor. If sailors and guards looked fuzzy and distant to Charles, then so would the Rose's crew look to them. He needed to act, now.

James was admiring the city around him. His gaze landed on a charm stand, the blue shimmering hues catching his attention. But something snapped him out of his path.

A figure caught James by the arm. "Want to hear your fortune, young man?" Charles and Mendez suddenly stopped by their captain before a tattered tent, incense and smoke slithering out of the holes in the fabric.

"Oh," James said, pulling away slowly. "No, thank you."

"It's about your future," the stranger prompted. The figure was veiled with a mahogany and gray shawl. The rest of their body was covered in a dark blue gown. They wore a pale porcelain mask that covered their entire face, lips painted on in a vibrant red and eyes outlined with a kohl black. Not an inch of their skin was exposed to the air of the market, nor the audience inherent in the public space. They pulled James in again.

"I said no thank you." James frowned, attempting to pull away. But the stranger gripped James' wrist tighter. Charles approached, his hand over the pommel of his sword.

"Even if it's about *the Commodore*?" the figure whispered.

James stopped pulling. Though he could not see the stranger's face, he sensed a smile behind that red-lipped mask. Spindles of charred, smokey gray weaved their way through James' wrist, spreading like catching fire where the masked figure clutched him.

"What about the Commodore?" James asked.

"Captain, I think we should just—" Mendez began.

"Hang on a minute," James raised his free arm, holding Mendez back, not taking his gaze away from the masked stranger. "What about my future? Tell me."

The figure cocked their head to the side. "Your future? It's full of poison."

"Poison? What poison?" James' eyes flicked around the teller's mask. The spindles of gray dug through his veins, as if his very blood was a frozen lake. Their captain flinched, the Bite snaking under his skin clearly causing him pain. It looked as though it was about the burst through his flesh.

"You need not worry about that danger just yet, *captain*," the figure drawled, a certain mockery woven into their tone. "For now, there is a much bigger danger nearby." The teller's head slowly turned to Charles.

His heart dropped, and sweat spread on his neck. As Charles eyed the figure, he felt their hidden eyes bore into his very soul, a certain knowing in their shrouded gaze.

Please don't tell him, please don't tell him, please don't tell—

They must be lying, casting arbitrary words to gather a few coins.

Charles tugged at his captain's sleeve. "They're bluffing. Let's get out of here James."

"I said hang on." James shook Charles off. "Do you know anything of the talismans?" The question about his soul came so close to leaving his lips.

"Mhmm," the soothsayer hummed, their tone playful, their voice ever slow and sly.

"What about the talismans? Will I get to them before he does?"

The soothsayer laughed, somehow simultaneously frail yet confident. "Who?"

"You know who!" James hollered.

"We need to get out of here already. Come on!" Charles grumbled and wrung James' arm loose from the figure's grip, the dark spindles of the Bite receding slowly across his skin.

James

James massaged his wrist, his gaze focused on his skin, but his mind was elsewhere.

That fortuneteller spoke of a danger. It could be anything, anyone, anywhere. Mitchell, The Shadows, a traitor, an ambush.

What was the poison about? Could it be the Bite? Could it consume him before he reaches all six talismans? And what was the closer danger? The poison could very well be the Bite consuming him, rapidly, right here, right now.

He blinked himself back to the present moment. Dusk had settled over the city like a mantle, creeping in from the horizon.

"So, what was that all about?" Mendez asked.

Charles clasped his hands together and stopped walking, his captain and shipmate stopping with him. He faced his captain. "Don't listen to them, James, all right? They're just trying to attract attention."

"What do you know?" James grated.

"I don't know. But I'm wary when a fortuneteller speaks of doom and lies just get a few coins," Charles said. "Believe me, I've had an experience or two in my travels."

"Aye," James muttered noncommittally, his tone betraying his scant words. An acrid constriction rose in his torso and he clawed at his chest as an unavailing frost tightened around his heart. His knees felt weak. "Let's just sit down somewhere for a moment."

They sank onto a bench on an elevated spot of ground. The sun came after a brief blanket of clouds, nearing the horizon. James drew in a depth breath, and remembered there were two people next to him. Charles and Mendez.

One thought ambushed his mind. The night the Shadows slithered on his bedroom floor, forced themselves down his throat and came out with a smokey orb that glimmered the color of the moon and fazed like a dipping sunset, leaving him feeling emptied, drained. And a few days after that, the Silver Rose's sails appeared on the horizon. But his father had not returned with her. He was still dead.

With a shake of his head, James pushed the thought from his mind. Anyone would sell their soul for someone they loved and lost.

He pulled the map out of his pocket and beckoned his crew to inspect it. Anything to turn his attention away from the skittering in his chest, the chatter in his mind, and the cold digging itself through his fingertips.

As if in response to the crew, the map's surface rippled like water, the figures and lexigrams hazing before they settled into another enigma. Three lines streamed from a single source. James surveyed the area around him. He would never have visited this continent if he didn't need to. His eyes wandered from the streets to the map when he spotted something a little too coincidental.

"Hey, look at this." He pointed to the map where three lines diverged from one. It matched the streets to the right of James and his crew.

The three stood and let the map guide them, following the main path briefly until it forked into three.

Charles ran a finger over the parchment. "But which to follow?"

"Now what?" Mendez said.

He stopped dead and sniffed the air. "Wait a minute," Charles whispered.

"What?" James asked.

Charles' eyes widened as if the fragrance spoke only to him. He sniffed again. "Is that—" he said and sniffed each path's direction, each time his nose twitched and his eyes adjusted.

"What? What is it?" Mendez asked impatiently.

"Croissants," Charles cooed, passion glazing his voice. He faced the middle path.

"We need to follow the map, Charles. Not now," James said.

"Then follow my nose," Charles replied, his eyes in a daze.

James held Charles by the shoulder. "You better not be leading the Wolf astray, Charles."

Charles sniffed the air again. "I would never."

James and Mendez followed the path that only seemed visible to Charles' nose down the middle street. His impeccable sense of smell led them to a small inn and bar with tattered walls, and aroma cascading out its windows.

Charles immediately went to the shopkeep and got himself a croissant, Mendez following to get his own. James grabbed them a seat and laid the map over the table.

"I thought we couldn't afford this right now," James teased when Charles returned and sat in the seat in front of him.

"I have enough to eat not to bribe, James," Charles said, biting into his pastry.

James smirked. "I'm only teasing."

"Why would the merfolk bring us here?" Mendez asked, peeling a piece from his own croissant.

James couldn't answer. He trusted no one. But if the merman had stakes in the talismans, then this is exactly where James wanted to be. He looked around him, scanning the area for anything that resembled a symbol he could recognize.

"Don't doorways usually have need keys or something?" Mendez said, and rotated the map toward him.

"Keys for what?" Charles asked.

Mendez polished off his last bite. "You know. A key to a door."

"Mmhm," James hummed. He looked behind over his chair, inspecting every wooden block, every table, every cloth.

Charles finished his croissant quietly and pushed his plate away. He and Mendez looked out the window. James' gaze finally reached the window and he looked out with them.

Sunshine slanted from the sky. It turned a bronze-orange as the sun neared the edge of the city. James slipped the map to his side of the table and examined it again. He turned a brief glance to his crew, and his eyes found Charles. He looked pensive, still gazing out the window as if it reminded him of something.

James let go of the map. He was a captain of a breathing crew now. He released a slow breath he didn't know he was holding. The longer he looked at Charles, the more a frigid feeling rose in his chest and settled into his abdomen. He nudged Mendez to Charles' direction, urging him to speak first.

"Are you all right, *amigo*?" Mendez asked Charles, his voice soft.

"Yes, I'm fine," Charles nodded. "Just tired."

"Would another croissant cheer you up?" James asked.

Charles gave a weak smile. "Why not?"

There wasn't much to be cheerful about. The place they sat, although it had a good view and tasty pastries, was a rundown old establishment. Not worse than the tavern on Pirates' Isle, granted, but it still needed renovations.

"Maybe I'll get myself one as well," James stood. "I'll go ask."

He approached the shopkeep opposite to their table when a man had entered and stood before him. James waited politely and looked out to the sea from the window. It reminded him of something, too.

It was a dusk just like this one nearly a year ago when he and the Silver Rose were floating off the shore of Pirates' Isle. Taverns muffled the sound of glass bottles breaking, music and laughter. The sea was still, the Wolf and the Rose suspended by shipwrecks. The sun was just setting, and the sea gave its last breath of color for the day. He had been sitting at the Rose's bowsprit, fixing the sea in a blank stare, his eyes empty, his breathing mechanic. The Rose's figurehead shifted and curled an elegantly carved petal around his arm.

The memory commanded his mind with such tyranny, no other memory nor the senses of the present moment obscured its clear image. On the Rose's bowsprit that night, he'd begun to cough his first wisps of black smoke. The dark rings had sharpened. The ache and unyielding grip in his chest had begun to tighten, with no respite.

You need a crew, Giacobbo.

The Rose knew soullessness was without a cure. But she also knew that it did have some remedies that cushioned the progression of the Bite. He lifted his head and looked to Pirates' Isle amidst a shipwreck shrouded in mist and fog. Its lanterns just had begun to flicker as the sun's highest point dipped below the waters. If the Wolf had a chance at a crew, it was at these lawless islands.

He had been nine years without a soul, alone at sea. Empty, lonely. Immeasurably lonely. That yawning, abyssal loneliness could have been remedied, although not without difficulty. But it still wasn't without a cure.

But it wasn't just loneliness, which could be remedied. It was the Bite, a disease without a cure. That's what James knew. He was used to the sour compulsion to meet his festering desire for revenge. Anything beyond revenge was foreign to him, and to the Bite. Any emotion, any desire that the soul would have carried was left without vessel, and the Bite feasted upon it greedily.

But now there was another desire budding within the hollowness left behind by the absence of his soul. And the denizen of that cavity did not take kindly to this nascent wish.

James blinked and his mind returned to the present moment, his gazing wandered to Charles and Mendez. Although he only met them recently, it felt as though he had known them forever. He was treading a very fine line. This respite and relief came with the possibility of danger and betrayal.

He glanced across to the innkeeper, who was not too happy looking of a fellow. James surveyed the pastries before him when a shimmer obscured his vision. He followed that shimmer. It came from the man standing before him, somewhere on his arm. James squinted and the shimmer revealed itself on the man's wrist: a bracelet with one angle of a triangle as its centerpiece, a symbol that James had seen on the journals and map.

The triangle with the eye.

He needed that jewelry. James turned his crew and waved his hands. He caught Mendez's attention first, who then told Charles to turn around.

Wrist, James mouthed and gestured with his hands.

"What?" Charles whispered.

Wrist. Jewelry. Need it. He turned a finger around his own wrist and brought a fist close to his chest.

Charles turned to the man James was motioning toward when he saw it. He nudged Mendez and pointed at the bracelet.

Charles studied the man a moment and nodded before approaching their target. He stood beside him and pretended to examine the drinks at the bar. The man glanced and smiled at him, and Charles smiled back. Mendez crept up behind the two.

James bit the inside of his lip. Mendez didn't look like he knew what to do, but he was about to do it anyway. He began to reach for the man's wrist when James held Mendez's hand. He held out a hand, subtly signaling for him to wait.

"*Bonsoir, monsieur*," Charles said.

"*Bonsoir*," the man replied.

"What brings a man like you here?" Charles asked, leaning toward him as he spoke.

"A drink," he said dryly.

Charles nodded. He glanced behind him and spied Mendez edging closer.

"Long day today," Charles claimed, drawing the man's attention away from Mendez. "What a storm out there. And what a terrifying monster that was."

"You saw it too?" the man said. "Long and big and covered with seaweed?"

Mendez pulled his hand back when their target replied.

"Yes," Charles said quickly. "Yes. Of course I saw it. You wouldn't be able to miss it."

"I knew it. They call me a liar. I'll tell everyone that *monsieur*... what's your name?"

"Clement Chevalier," Charles offered smoothly.

"Antoine," the man said. "What say you join us tonight at the bayou and share what you saw?"

"Err, yes," Charles said. "Yes of course. But not before a drink, what do you say?"

"*Accord*," the man smiled and pulled out a hand. Charles smiled back and shook the man's hand, giving his captain a good angle of the bracelet. James fixed a look at the jewelry. One angle of a triangle, bronze, its sides the size of a pinky finger. James nodded to Mendez.

"So, what are you getting? Not sure what to grab for myself. I'll have what you have," Charles said.

"As usual. Some good ale," Antoine said.

"Excellent choice." Charles smiled and clapped Antoine's back just in time as Mendez unpicked the bracelet and slid it off his wrist.

"*Une tasse de—*" Antoine pointed, then stopped, staring at his wrist. Before Charles could warn his crewmates, Antoine turned to see James and Mendez gazing at the precious jewelry. Charles slapped his palm to his forehead.

"*Voleur*!" Antoine drew his sword. "Give it back!"

Mendez wrenched the piece into his pocket as James tucked his necklace inside his shirt, unsheathing his own sword.

Antoine started in their direction before Charles shattered a glass onto his head. He swayed and then held steady. But he kept to his feet and charged at Mendez, who leapt to the side with a shriek. Antoine crashed against the tables that Mendez cleared a way to and they broke under his weight.

"Damn it, not again," the innkeeper grumbled and ran to the kitchen.

"Couldn't you have done this any swifter?" Charles shouted at Mendez.

"I was swift as a feather!" Mendez retorted, awkwardly drawing his sword.

"Give it here! It's mine," Antoine bellowed. He regained his position and delivered a blow only to meet James'.

Charles' sword struck at Antoine's side, but Antoine parried just in time. It was the two against one, but the man was fierce. He grabbed a bar of the broken table and struck it to Charles' side. Charles staggered back at the sudden pain. Antoine charged at James, who parried his blow.

"You did *not* just do that!" Mendez screamed and lunged.

Antoine kicked a boot into Mendez's knee, sending him stumbling with an inarticulate grunt of pain.

Now it was James and Antoine. And it just got personal.

"Bastard!" James hollered. The slashing of swords and clanging sounds of pots filled the small inn, but James' voice was clear and resonant. "I will cut you." He lunged with a fiery thrust at his crew's assailant.

"I'll hurt whoever steals from me" Antoine parried James' blow. "Now give it back!"

"No," James said plainly. The anger and irritation that bubbled in his chest treated the Bite, and his next blow came calculated and guided. He slashed at Antoine's shoulder, and scored first blood, causing the man to drop his sword with a clatter as he grasped at burning flesh.

James approached, the coarse emotion fueling his intent. He raised his sword.

But Antoine elbowed James in the jaw, and reached a quivering hand to his blade. He grabbed it and threw it in Charles and Mendez's direction.

It missed both. But hit the intended mark. The sword's blade dug deep into the door hatch, locking it.

Charles and Mendez turned around, the man stomping in their direction, grasping his sword in one hand, and his bleeding shoulder in the other. The two were ready to defend themselves when Antoine took a pan to the face. It echoed throughout the room with a resounding *thunk.*

Charles and Mendez looked from the unfortunate Antoine up to the pan where his face had been. There, the innkeeper stood, arm outstretched with the decisive kitchen utensil.

James stood from the floor and headed to his crew. The Bite swarmed his abdomen, goading him to gut the unconscious Antoine like a fish.

But he had a crew now, who was watching.

"Thanks," he said hoarsely, rubbing his aching jaw, breath leaving his chest sharp and uneasy.

"Don't mention it. He deserved it, anyway," the innkeeper said. "He never pays his tab and he always walks in with a bad attitude."

"Thomas, *que-ce ... que c'est?*" a man said and approached from a back door.

"*Monsieur* Croix." The innkeeper turned to him, troubled. "I can explain."

The man looked around him, his disapproving gaze jumping from broken boards and glass scattered around the inn. Finally, he said, "Look at this mess."

"*Non monsieur*, I didn't—"

"Is that Antoine?"

James saw irritation on Croix's face, and read tension and anxiety on Thomas'. "Pardon us," he intervened. "It was our fault. We started the fight."

"And just who are you supposed to be?" Croix asked, turning to the crew rudely. He lifted a cold eyebrow upon a colder gaze.

"I am Santiago Mendez," Mendez said and thumbed his chest. "And we just saved Thomas' life, right, *amigos*?"

Charles opened his mouth to say something, but Croix interrupted.

"Hmm. A Spaniard and two fugitive-looking beggars in my shop. Get out of here before I call the guards." Croix turned to Thomas and flicked a hand to the unconscious customer. "You, pick him up and put him outside," he said. He fixed a stare to Thomas, whose head hung, actively avoiding looking Croix in the eye.

"I knew I shouldn't have taken you in after your father's death," he said.

James grit his teeth. He glared at Croix as he walked to the back door, like a hunter would glare at prey. Every muscle in him compelled him to charge at Croix, to sate the Bite's hunger for raw emotion. He balled his fists until James felt the sting of his nails against the meat of his palms, resisting the urge to satisfy the Bite with more violence.

"I don't like him," was what James said instead.

"*Désolé, messieurs*," Thomas mumbled and bent to pick up Antoine.

James and his crew approached to help. Mendez carried Antoine by the legs like one would carry a wagon, and James and Thomas held him by the arms, while Charles pried the sword from the door hatch.

"You have to leave soon before *Monsieur* Croix comes back. I need to clean and lock up." Thomas stumbled but led James and Mendez to the door.

"Sorry about the mess," Charles said. He sheathed his sword and opened the door.

They set Antoine on the side of the road. Mendez made sure he let go of Antoine's legs with as little care as he possibly could.

"No, it's all right," Thomas said. "*Bonsoir.*"

"No, Thomas, let us help," James said. "It's the least we can do."

"Just leave." Thomas walked back into the shop without a backward glance.

James glanced at Charles and Mendez, and the three of them seemed to share a simultaneous thought judging from how they shared a wordless nod. They all trailed after Thomas.

"I can still see you," Thomas told them, sounding exasperated. The crew simply kept walking until they reached the door. Thomas crooked it open a little and looked behind them back to the three of them. "Fine," Thomas grumbled, and opened the door.

6

James

One more crew member won't hurt, right?

The air was thick and heavy with moisture. The early night blanketed the sky in a deep indigo, and the three helped Thomas clean the fairly destroyed inn.

"Thomas, is it?" James asked as he collected broken wooden boards and piled them on the once intact table.

"*Oui*, Thomas Lamont." The innkeeper swept dust and splinters to the side. "*Iel en Français.*"

"Pardon?" Charles asked.

"My pronouns. *Iel en Français*, they *en Anglais*. Croix never listens," Thomas said. "And you are?"

"Charles Bruno," Charles replied as he collected fallen cups and plates on the table. "*Il en Français*, he in English," he added.

"I'm Santiago Mendez. And yes, I'm a Spaniard. I'm a *neat* Spaniard, too." Mendez put chairs back by their tables, making sure the corners of the tables paralleled the corners of the walls. "And he *en Inglés*."

"*Enchanté*," Thomas said, a light laugh escaping their chest.

"And I'm James Wolf, he *in Inglese*," James muttered. He'd almost forgotten he was a wanted man.

"Really?" Thomas said, amusement in their voice, resting their palms over the broom's tip. "I think I've heard of that name before."

"Finally!" Charles exclaimed and threw his hands in the air. "Someone who actually knows him."

"Aren't you the man who sold his soul to the devil or something and killed some important Ordinance General?" Thomas said, casually returning to sweeping.

"I didn't sell my soul to the devil. And I wasn't the one who killed the Admiral."

"*Pardon, monsieur*," Thomas said. "I didn't mean to offend."

"You've got the wrong story." He studied the talisman that shimmered under the lamplight. "And don't call me *monsieur*. My name's James."

Thomas nodded and laughed. "So, what's your story, James?"

"He was the son of a sailor and a tailor," Charles said.

"Good, you know my story now," James said.

"I'm all about stories," Charles smiled. He turned to Thomas, shining a glass with his sleeve. "He was the son of Angela and Badr Wolf, their home was Il Porto Dell' Armonia."

"His father's ship got raided by pirates," Mendez added.

Thomas rested the broom on one palm, their gaze engaged.

Sensation brewed in James' chest and diffused through his limbs. His fingertips tingled, his legs shaky. Turning a chair around, he sat with one arm to the seat's back. He had to stop himself from swaying with this surge of emotion. He was about to share his story. It was dangerous to share, but the urge twisted in his chest, tightened around his limbs, and wouldn't leave until he spoke. He was exhilarated, but also frightened.

But the blooming sensation suddenly shriveled up, the Bite winding and coiling around this estranged emotion like a snake choking its prey. The abrupt shift of feeling left him breathless. His hand flew to his mouth, attempting to hide his gnashing teeth.

"What happened next?" Thomas asked, their voice soft and intrigued.

He spoke, hoping that the words leaving his mouth would relieve the war between The Bite and its new victim. "The captain of the pirate ship, the Calypso's Wrath, killed my father. I had woken up in a fever back home with a grieving mother." The distant ebb and flow of the shore drifted through the open window, and gave his story a somber melody. "I had lost father and the *Rose*, and our means of sustenance. So, I did what need be done." He swallowed down the building Bite in his throat. It competed with a lump in his throat.

It was an unusual feeling. He hasn't had to cry about his mother, his father, his soul, in ten years. He continued speaking, forcing steadiness into his voice. "I sold my soul to the Shadows. Dark, manipulative things. Of course, the Shadows weren't specific about who they would be bringing back from the dead. A few days later the Rose came back to 'Rmonia, back to me and my mother."

His gaze met Charles' again. The Bite skittered around his heart and a dull whistle buzzed in his ears. It took everything in him to focus when Charles spoke.

"Perhaps the Ordinance had a reason to be there, then," Charles suggested.

"I wasn't the only who sold his soul in 'Rmonia," James countered, the words leaving his mouth in a rush.

Confusion, intrigue, caution swam in chaos on Charles' face. "Are you suggesting the Commodore sold his soul to the

Shadows too?" Charles sat back in his chair and folded his arms. He glared at James, a challenge in his eyes.

"I know he did," James said, confidence and pain weaved in his voice.

"*Mon dieu*," Thomas said. They leaned back in their chair and put their hands to their knees. A smile spread across their face.

"You like that?" James murmured to Thomas, shooting a glare to Charles.

"I haven't heard something like this in—" Thomas said, "ever! But why are you here?"

"A merman told us to find something and protect it," Mendez answered.

"Ah," Thomas said. "I see you found it."

Changing the subject brought him nothing short of relief, and he took a deep breath. "What, this?" James pointed at the bracelet, and then picked it up once again. "It's just a piece, a fragment, that'll get us there." James rolled it in his palm.

"What's so important about them?" Mendez asked. "They look rather useless to me."

"Not to Mitchell they're not, and certainly not to Aereon," James said. "There are six total talismans. This is one of them. That bastard Commodore and I have been chasing after them for years. They can be anywhere, disguised as anything."

"You think the Commodore is consorting with the Shadows?" It was Charles who spoke, his voice wry and distant.

"Mother and I tried to hide my soulless symptoms. I know them when I see them. But of course, nothing flies over the Commodore's head." His fist tightened around the chair's wood. "He wouldn't leave us alone. He took her." James fixed Charles in a cutting glare, his shipmate's gaze failing for a moment. "She

90

told me to run—so I ran. But not without a fight first. His headquarters were *riddled* with these Shadow glyphs and I—I stumbled on Admiral Fleming's body." Hot tears threatened his eyes. He blinked them back, his words charged with raw emotion. "Whatever Fleming found out, the Commodore wanted buried. He's a liar and a murderer."

Tension rose in James' chest, as though his heart anchored one end of a taut rope, and Charles held the other.

Silence settled and James swallowed and broke his gaze from Charles, hoping that no one noticed his tears. The long fingers of the Bite scathed his chest, taunting a sob in his throat. He secretly fought for breath.

"So, both you and the Commodore, allegedly, sold your souls to the Shadows. Both of you are after these pieces," Thomas' voice broke the tension between the two. "And the Commodore's going to do what, exactly, with them?"

"Something personal, some lost lover; I don't know," James murmured. He shuddered. "One of the talismans is in the Silver Rose, my ship. And I will not have him hurt her while I draw breath." *Which might not be long if you remain without a soul.* He stifled a cough.

Mitchell has everything. A fleet, unwavering influence, the trust of the Crown, the entire Ordinance. James only has his Rose and a few of the Commodore's cryptic journals to decipher.

And, perhaps, a crew now…

"You've got to be the best crowd I'll ever have," Thomas gleefully said. "Everyone else never talks to me. And they're boring and drunk."

James turned to Thomas, eager to change the subject again. "So, you're the cook here?"

"I'm the cook," Thomas said. "The cook, the cleaner, the brawl settler, the bartender. Everything but my own person." They looked to the ground and played with their nails. "*Monsieur* Croix owns all this." They gestured with their hands. "He does nothing. I can barely keep a roof over my head, and I'm just one person. It didn't get any easier after my *papa* died."

"I'm sorry, Thomas," James said.

Thomas fell silent.

"You get too little credit for how good those croissants were," Mendez said.

"*Merci, chére*," Thomas said with a genuine smile that brightened their entire face. "Good to hear someone likes what I love doing."

They resumed tidying the inn silently, and after they finished, they stood and admired their work. Although there was a pile of broken wood and glass in one corner, the inn seemed more polished than it had been when they first entered.

Thomas returned the broom to a tiny closet near the bar. "How about a small treat as a thank you?"

The crew turned to their captain for a response. The throbbing he had tuned out while they cleaned and shared stories eased in his chest, as if his crew's attention diffused it. "Sure."

An innocent smile spread across Thomas' face as they headed for the pastries. "Drinks?" they asked, skillfully retrieving four cups out of a cupboard.

Charles took a seat at one of the four remaining intact chairs. "I don't mind at all."

"You don't have to ask. I never mind." Mendez seated himself.

"You don't happen to have anisette, hmm?" James asked, strolling to his crew's table. He sank deeply into the chair, exhaustion weighing on his limbs so much like an anchor in the deep. He knew very well this depletion did not come from tidying the inn, nor the fight with Antoine.

The sounds of bottles full of drink clanging against each other came from the cellar as Thomas spoke. "No anisette." They popped their head from the cellar. "I've got rum."

"I'll take that!" Mendez said.

Charles drew his fingers across his neck and shook his head to Thomas, flicking his eyes to his captain.

Thomas shrugged and dipped back into the cellar. "No rum for the captain. Ale, ginger. I've got red wine."

"That'll do," James said.

Thomas re-emerged from the cellar, two bottles in one hand, four cups in the other. They laid out the cups on the table, their movements light and fluid. Setting the pastries down, they poured James and his crew the drinks before taking a seat.

"These are good!" Mendez exclaimed, sinking his teeth into his pastry.

"*Merci*. I baked them this morning," Thomas responded, their cheeks red with a smile.

James took a bite of the pastries and a sip of wine. Charles was saying something, but James couldn't process whatever it was. Thomas' voice slipped through as James' mind drew inward again.

The pastry and wine touched something within him. That touch rippled and expanded, draining sensation out of him, only to return, soothing yet raging.

Dell' Armonia. Home. Mrs. Graham and her biscuits during English lessons. Soft and rich. Messer Emiliano, the town baker. James was his favorite child in the town.

The taste in his mouth intensified. He gulped down some wine to drown it, but it only brought back more memories, drenched with emotion.

Wine. I wasn't allowed to drink it, but I snuck some from the winery. Niccolo warned me and Anamaria against. But we snuck onto the Rose and tried a sip. We had Niccolo to thank for alerting our parents. The Rose had tried to hide the wine, but helped Niccolo find us.

She is dear.

He was fun and cautious.

She was fun and spontaneous.

It was all fun and happy.

Then it was all gone.

The sensation swelled, and something in his chest writhed as his mind churned. He tightened his fist, nails digging into his palm, and James snuck a look at his hands. A small speck of smoky gray effused across his skin, like ink in water. The spindles of gray carried a bite of cold as it dug its way through his fingers. But it was fighting against something, digging through his skin against a new intruder. The Bite was not used to connection, and it recoiled at the new taste. It was accustomed to callous emotion. Anger, and vengeance. This feeling was new. The change in the Bite's attention sent a fleeting relief in James' heart. Warily, he welcomed it.

Thomas' voice brought him back to the present moment. They were laughing. Charles was taking another sip, Mendez speaking.

James set his cup down vacantly. He stood.

"Something the matter, James?" Thomas said.

"No, no, I'm fine," James said. "Just getting some air."

"I hear you. It gets stuffy in the inn sometimes. I once had to…"

Their voice fizzled out, overwhelmed by the buzzing.

He stood at the window and opened it, fighting despair. It won't leave him alone. And it would never leave him alone so long as he was without a soul.

James breathed in, the air viscous and humid, but any bit of air would help ease the confinement in his abdomen and chest.

The vista blurred. He blinked. Something wet escaped his eye. He touched it as if it caused him pain, numb confusion on his face. He hasn't had tears in five long years.

He wiped the tear as if wiping away shame and turned to face his crew and Thomas.

One more crew member won't hurt, right?

Thomas

Sad bunch, on a quest

The night's darkness dripped through the inn's windows and the four walked out, Thomas locking the creaking door behind them. They meandered around New Orleans, from Thomas' inn, past the church, prison, and toward the marsh. The mix of sweet and sour smells still floated through the streets with them, beckoning the group along. Thomas led the way. They knew the streets like the back of his hand, unlike Silver Rose's crew.

Thomas didn't care where they were going. They wanted to stretch as much time as they could before they headed back to Croix's quarters.

"So how long have you been here, Thomas?" Charles asked.

"A long time, *chére*," Thomas said and kicked rocks and pebbles with their feet. Two pebbles collided, one cracked, and Thomas remembered their father's fever. "Anything new, James?" they asked, hoping company would offer a welcome distraction.

For a moment, the innkeeper felt part of this little assemblage. Thomas did not know where the crew came from or where they were heading, but they craved leaping into this uncertainty. They blinked and breathed in, and remembered where they were. Back in the streets. Stretching time again.

They and the crew stopped at a spot of elevated land that overlooked the church and harbor. All four of them sat at a long bench, staring out, alternating between the sea, the map, and the key.

"Why did you steal the map in the first place? Why come with us?" Charles asked, turned to Mendez.

"Max has been blabbering about this map for a while." Mendez clasped his hands. "We've been thieving for..." He squinted an eye, thinking, and settled on, "... A long time. When Max finally found this job, she took it."

"Job?" James asked.

"Max made a deal with a contractor," Mendez said. "He said he'll make us rich if we find where this map leads to. Naturally, Max took the deal."

Thomas eyed James and the strange jewelry, wondering why such a strange piece seemed important to him. They found themself wanting to ask question after question. Who were they? What was this piece? Why do they want it? What is the portal? And could Thomas meet a merman, too?

"I've been in an orphanage ever since I can remember," Mendez continued. "I followed Max and Anmar, then Edward joined. Anmar and I thought maybe we could do this one last job and then we could leave." He shrugged and blinked at the ground. "But Max found out. She always does. And now I'm here."

"Well, I'm glad you're here," James said, looking out to the quivering sea. "What about you, Thomas?"

"*Moi?*" Thomas asked, surprised. They haven't had anyone ask them about themself with this much interest before. If people asked them, it was mainly to know if their father was married or not, if their mother was Christian or not. Thomas breathed and studied the trio. They all had intent eyes, light smiles. Thomas exhaled, back arched against the seat.

"I don't know. I never knew my mother, except through the stories my papa told me," Thomas said. "She died when I was only a year old. My papa told me she was a great woman. He said she saved his life when he first arrived here."

Thomas lapsed into a smile, blinking slowly. They had learned everything from their father, and their father had learned everything from their mother. Thomas' father learned how to navigate the lands, how to cook, and how to be open and full of life. They kept all that they learned from their parents in them, locked in a little box deep in their chest, waiting for the right moment to share it with the world. Or perhaps even just the right person.

"My father always told me to look for something new and good in life," Thomas said. "Whatever that meant to you. To me, it meant cooking. That kept me alive and motivated, until my father got the fever. I was only ten. I took care of him, and worked at this place in the meantime." They pointed in the direction of the shop. "He died when I was twelve. And I've been under Croix's supervision since."

The crew and innkeeper fell silent again, the sleepless city's ambience and the chirping crickets frothing them.

Thomas found themselves filling the silence that yawned between them. "We're a sad bunch, aren't we?"

"Sad bunch, on a quest," Mendez said.

James turned to them. "Why don't you join us, Thomas?"

Thomas glanced towards the sea. It was beautiful. No walls, no cleaning, no settling the brawl of the evening. And most certainly no Croix giving commands, no snide remarks on Thomas' mother, no lectures on why Thomas should be more grateful.

This wasn't the life they worked for. Maybe now, it was giving them another chance. Maybe this was a moment to unbox what they learned.

"I—" Thomas began, "I don't know."

"Oh, come on." Charles nudged Thomas, playful and encouraging.

"You'd make great dinners on the Silver Rose," Mendez said.

Charles turned to Mendez and fixed him with a scathing stare, not unlike a parent might to their child. "We, of course, don't want Thomas just for their good cooking, Mendez."

The sea tantalized Thomas and a heavy warm wind began to blow, as if trying to convince them. The innkeeper clenched their jaw and breathed deep. They opened their mouth, about to say something, but stopped.

Were those soldiers holding muskets, with Croix at the head of them?

"We have to go!" Thomas jumped to their feet as a flock of guards stampeded toward them and the crew, arms at the ready.

"*Arretez*," a voice commanded behind the crew, the head of the troop putting a musket to James' back.

7

James

The Ordinance will get nothing

"James Wolf," the commander said, poking James a little harder with his musket's blade. James was ready to pounce on the commander, and he drew his sword. He begrudgingly held still when the commander shook his head; his men cocking their muskets.

"I wouldn't challenge us this far away from your ship," the commander said, his voice icy before he turned to Thomas. "Thomas Lamont," he said again. "*Monsieur* Croix tells me plenty about you. Steals more often than he pays the rent."

Affronted, Thomas declared, "I stole nothing." They gave Croix a sidelong look but brought their gaze down when Croix's eyes settled on them.

"And *Monsieur* Croix tells me otherwise," the commander replied blandly. "Do I trust the child of an ex-guard, or do I trust my local official?"

Thomas was about ready to say something before the commander raised a hand, turning to Charles.

"Don't I know you from somewhere?" he asked, tilting his head a bit as he leaned in to examine Charles. "You're a recent hire, *non*?"

Tension tightened Charles' frame. "You've mistaken me for someone else."

The commander gave a terse smile and turned to James. "A certain Ambassador will be incredibly pleased to see you."

"I don't think so," Mendez said and kicked the guard holding him. He swung away the musket resting against Charles' back in a flash just as a rifle fired, the bullet missing Charles' head by a hair. James drove his sword into the nearest guard, throwing his aim off course.

Another guard fired a musket into the air, signaling for more soldiers from the garrison.

Terror gripped Thomas' throat. It was fast. Too fast for Thomas to think. The commander launched for James, who slashed a guard to the ground.

Charles elbowed one in the jaw, sending the guard's teeth flying through the air. Officers swarmed James like ants. He snarled and thrashed as they grabbed hold of his arms.

Thomas didn't have a sword, nor did they know how to handle one. It wasn't fair. Thomas turned around, looking for something to use. They spotted a knot of birds on a roof. They knew these birds, and they knew how much trouble they gave them in the shop, especially pecking red pastries. Thomas turned to the officers, clad in their white and red raiments when an idea sparked in their head.

"*Allez. Allez!*" Thomas flailed their arms and ran towards them. The birds swarmed and attacked the men red clothed men. "It worked!" Thomas yelled.

James wrenched his sword-arm free and slashed at one of the officers. The guard cried out and dropped his musket, loosening his grip on James. He seized his opportunity and impaled the officer restraining Mendez, who kicked the shin of the guard holding Charles.

Thomas watched the scene unfold before them; their mind registered their limbs' movements far too late. They began to run and swung their hand for the mysterious crew to follow.

James ran down the street alongside Thomas. "Clever. Thanks for that!"

Thomas was out of breath, not because of their sudden sprint, but because of the irrevocable choice they had just made. "Croix's going to kill me," they groaned.

A musket ball whizzed and exploded onto a brick wall as the crew ran past it. "Don't let them slip away!" the commander hollered as the four of them ran down past the church. With a mix of rage and frustration, the commander disentangled himself from the dark cloud of birds and ran forward.

"This way!" Thomas gestured for the trio to follow a path deeper into the city. "Follow me."

Charles pointed towards the docks. "But the ship's that way."

Thomas turned to their right, running by the armory and to the living quarters. "I know, just trust me," Thomas called out to the crew. Just as they spoke, a bullet whistled past their heads and splintered a wooden column, and the trio burst into a sprint, hot on Thomas' heels.

"Quickly!" James shouted.

Thomas turned and ran down the street, against a crowd of people going the opposite way.

Mendez knocked into someone's freshly made pastries, sending them hurtling to the ground. "Sorry!" he yelled over his shoulder. "Oh, that looked so good." Charles snatched two catapulting pieces of pastries out of the air and bit into one while handing another to Mendez. Charles held out a hand and Mendez gave it a high five.

Another explosion of gunfire interrupted their celebration.

The guards followed hot on their heels but lagged behind in the irritated crowd. The commander whistled, and five soldiers came around the armory. "After them! Get those criminals!" he barked at the officers.

"This way!" Thomas panted. The crew ran with Thomas until they reached the dock—but they couldn't stop there.

"Papers pl—" the man at the dock began before James and his crew bolted past him "*Arretez*! I said papers please!"

"Don't let them escape!" one of the guards yelled. They lined up and reloaded their muskets.

The four reached the dock but to no avail, for they were surrounded, the soldiers' bayonets aimed at them.

Thomas looked around for another way out when the sound of a low whistle whizzed past them, followed by a thundering boom.

The dock rocked violently as a big, black object crashed into it. Sailors and guards were flung into ferociously into the dark waters after the blast, and the harbor erupted in chaos. Thomas almost tipped into the water, but Charles snatched them by the collar and swung them back to the dock. Smoke slithered from the brims of the cannonball-shaped hole in the dock.

"*Mia cara*!" James exclaimed. He turned around to face her as she slid to the dock, a stream of smoke dancing from her hull cannon. As she neared, some of the ardent guards regained their balance and were ready to fire again.

The Rose came nearer to the dock, and James took cover behind barrels and cargo, the other three following his lead. Mendez shrieked as bullets narrowly missed him and hit the Rose's hull.

"My Rose!" James screamed. The ship's creaks came clearer as she neared, her grating sound sending an ache through

James' heart. "I'm coming!" he called out to her from his cover. "You'll pay for this one!"

"Is he *talking* to his ship?" Thomas asked as they took a careful peak around boxes.

"You'll get used to this," Charles said.

The Rose let down her gangplank behind the crew just in time. She fired again from her aft cannons and plunged another half-dozen men into the water.

"Hurry!" Mendez cried out, making way for Charles to board.

Thomas turned to the gangplank when something yanked them by the collar. They were twisted around, and they faced Croix.

"*Tenez,*" Croix said, his voice icy. The few men behind him aimed their arms at Thomas and the ship. Thomas wheezed and grimaced. They tried to form words, but they couldn't catch their breath.

"You have to make me wake up the whole town just for you, *non*?" Croix said in a rancid tone, throttling Thomas by the collar.

Thomas struggled against Croix's grip.

"Your meaningless mewling never fails to surprise me," Croix said. "But this one," he glanced behind Thomas, shooting a wry glace at the Silver Rose's crew, "this one tops it."

The metal of a sword hissed beside Thomas' ear, its point against Croix's neck.

"What do you think you're doing?" Croix snapped, glaring behind Thomas. But even with a sword against his neck, Croix still wore a smile. Thomas knew that smile very well, and feared it. It meant Croix thought it was in a better position.

"James, don—" Thomas choked.

"That's a sword," Croix interrupted. "I have muskets."

"Aye, but," James said, "my ship's got a lovely view of your men and your barracks."

"So, it's really you." Croix's gaze focused on what Thomas could only imagine was James' ship. "Afraid for this little child—" Croix said, giving Thomas' collar a shake, and drawing a wheeze out of them. "He's nothing but a mistake."

"*They* are not a mistake and certainly not a child," James said. "And no. I don't fear anyone. You're rather bothersome and I'd just as soon kill you."

Croix's hand flashed from Thomas' collar to their hair, twisting them around. Thomas gasped for air but Croix's free clamped over their mouth. They thrashed against Croix as he restrained their arms and positioned them as a living shield against James' blade.

Tears threatened to obscure Thomas' vision as Croix tightened his grip on their hair. James' sword didn't waver.

"James, please—" Thomas wheezed. "He'll kill m—"

"You're surrounded," Croix interjected. "And if you kill me, you're going to have to kill the child first."

Thomas tossed against Croix's restraint.

"You're going to let Thomas go," James said. "And if they're not out within ten seconds, good luck getting your men together when the fires spread. Ten."

The Rose's cannons turned in unison in the direction of the government quarters. The men wavered.

"Stand your ground!" Croix barked. "The Wolf is bluffing."

"Nine, eight," James counted in a bored tone.

Croix tightened his grip. Panic bubbled in Thomas' chest and they fought for air. Croix shouted, his voice bellowing in

Thomas' ear. "You all know who this treasonous fugitive is; he's the Wolf!"

"James, please! I don't want to die—" Thomas pleaded, their voice smothered.

"Seven."

"Arrest these men!" Croix shrieked.

James rolled his eyes. "Three-two-one." And the ship's hull erupted in cannon fire. Cannons landed in succession at their target, and the barracks crumbled, an explosion belching within the rubble.

Whatever command Croix had over his men vanished, replaced by panicked urgency. Some dropped their muskets and others ran to their devastated homes and quarters. Shock seized Croix and he staggered, his grip fell from Thomas' neck and Thomas fell to the ground, coughing and gulping air.

When Thomas' breathing stabilized, they looked up to see a scene that stole their breath once more: Many holes ate through the barracks and soldiers' living quarters, the columns that once held the entrance doors now is ruins.

A hand appeared in Thomas' peripheral vision. They turned and saw James. With a shuddering sigh of relief, Thomas grabbed his offered hand as James helped them up to their feet.

They'd seen sail ships before. But nothing quite like this one. Their eyes landed on the rose figurehead and followed the form of the great ship's hull, masts and sails. She was beautiful.

The captain turned to the mighty ship, smoke still slithering out of her cannons.

Croix's voice came from behind. "He'll find you, you know." James stopped dead. Thomas had never seen Croix's smile waver like that. Croix shrieked, "My men are nothing. But *he* is everywhere. The Ordinance will get its hands on you."

Thomas looked to James again. In an instant, the icy glare that James possessed in his eyes was replaced with wrath.

He strode to Croix, his blade still in hand and slashed him across the cheek. Thomas' hand flew to their mouth, muffling a startled gasp. Croix staggered and held his bloodied face. He screamed, "How dare y—"

James plunged his own blade through Croix's abdomen, and Croix dropped his sword, the metal resonating as it fell against the dock. James twisted his blade and pulled Croix close, leaning to his ear. "The Ordinance will get *nothing*." Oh so slowly, James drew his sword from Croix as he spoke.

Croix fell, hissing in pain against his wound.

Thomas lowered their quivering hands and looked to Croix, who was spitting blood on the dock. Thomas' eyes went to the quarter where they had lived most of their life. Then they turned to James, his ship and crew. Charles and Mendez stood at the railing, getting the lines ready. They looked oddly at ease on that ship despite the violence that had just occurred. Thomas traced the Silver Rose's form, and she gave a strange feeling in Thomas' chest.

Thomas glanced back at Croix one more time and made sure they looked him in the eyes. Croix had no retort, for his face had frozen in eternal dismay.

And so, Thomas turned to the Silver Rose and walked toward the ship. There was no one at the helm. James headed up the stairs as Thomas walked up the gangplank and stepped foot on the ship.

The Rose's sails gave a strong crack in the wind, and she raised her gangplank. The ship turned her on own helm without help. Thomas glanced back at the town they could never call home. Men bobbed in the water, others scurried around their crushed homes and stations. Croix lay dead on the dock. The scene blurred in front of Thomas as the ship cut through the open waters.

8

Anmar

But the outside world also had Mendez…

It was midnight on Pirates' Isle, and Max just found out that Mendez had been planning to leave her group.

"Who left him alone with the map?" Max eyed Edward and Anmar.

The boy swallowed and hoped Max didn't see. She had been eyeing Anmar's steps closely ever since they got this new contracting job. It was her first, and the sum their contractor promised was greater than all of Max's thieving history. Even with two other contractors, the amount left Max baffled—and it lifted Anmar's spirits. Up until he and Mendez had the bright idea of taking the whole sum for themselves and leaving Max's petty little group.

But first they needed the map. And who had to pickpocket it from Max? It was Anmar. Mendez didn't exactly have light hands and feet.

Anmar felt a sharp pang of guilt in his abdomen. If he hadn't left Mendez alone with the map, Max wouldn't have found out. They would have still had the map. And Anmar wouldn't have been alone.

Max's stare forced Anmar to keep his eyes to the ground. "Anmar," she said. "Do you know something?"

The boy shook his head mutely. Max crossed her arms, the same way she always did, ever since she found him in the alley six years ago. He owed her the truth for taking him in after all the trouble she gave her. Even when she had nothing to her name, she'd still offered him protection. Anmar scratched his forehead, obscuring his eyes.

Swallowing hard, he mumbled, "I sort of left him alone with it." Instantly, Anmar regretted it.

Max approached him. "Why, Anmar?" she asked softly. She always started softly.

He remembered the night he and Mendez planned their escape. Mendez's hands were flailing around and above his head while he explained the plan Anmar had just described to him five minutes ago. It had filled Anmar with hope and strength.

Anmar felt another jolt of strength in himself, now. He'd wanted to say something to Max for a long time. "I shared it with him because we were planning something different," Anmar said.

She fixed him in a glare. He tried to hang on to his strength, but it melted like wax under a fierce candle.

"Something different?" Max echoed, bowing her head.

The silence felt hollow in Anmar's ears and the air in his chest slowly, meagerly, began to form words. "We couldn't stand another day with you," he said. "And we were planning to escape."

"You *what*?"

Anmar's lip quivered.

"You wanted to leave my group?" Max fumed. "After we finally got a good deal?" The softness in her voice withered away.

The last of Anmar's strength dissolved like seafoam did on beach sands. "It's too late now. Mendez is out," he mumbled again, half-heartedly hiding his words from Max.

She walked closer to him, the wet sands making a slushing sound beneath her furious steps. Anmar could hear his heart in his ears, and his gaze fell to the sand.

"Hmm," she mused. "How long have you been planning this? You two?"

Anmar had been here before many times. His pocketknife was only a flick away, but he had never used it on Max.

Max abruptly seized Anmar by his hair. "How long?" Max demanded.

The boy's limbs shook like a branch in a storm, hot tears filling his eyes.

"How long?" she barked, shaking him by the hair.

"Two months! Two," Anmar blurted and reached for his head. "Since that Ginysis guy sent us the letter."

"Do you know what you just did, Anmar?" Max gripped his hair tighter. "The map was our one chance out of this pathetic life. And you just threw it all out!"

The jolt inside Anmar changed from fear to guilt and self-hatred.

"So, you want to leave? Is that what you want?" Max gave the boy another shake that gave made his head pound. "I try to find what is best for group and all you want to do is leave?"

His head began to pulse against Max's grip. Anmar looked to the one person he had left. But Edward stood still, arms crossed, a statue of contempt and indifference.

"I can easily leave you here, Anmar," Max threatened. "Isn't that what you want? Hmm?" she gave another shake. With each jostle, scalp burning, Anmar grimaced harder. "I can leave you on this island right now. See how you fare. Would you like that? Hmm?"

Anmar imagined scenarios if Max left him. He knew no one, and with what little experience he had, he was sure he'd end up dead and alone. He begged, dread rising in his throat, "No, no! Please, Max. I'm sorry. I'm so sorry," Anmar cried. "I won't do it again." He reached for Max's hand before she abruptly let go of his hair, thrusting him away.

"Don't forget where I found you," Max retorted. She rubbed her forehead, and her fingers left a transient red imprint on her skin.

That again. Anmar had been here before.

And this was the part that he hated the most. Not the gnawing pangs of hunger, the cold, nor the thieving life, but the part where he felt like a wet rat again. Any sliver of strength that ventured to armor Anmar crumbled when Max reminded him.

She'd found him under a bridge, cold, alone and hungry. She'd agreed to take him all the way back to Damascus to return to his family, only to find them long gone. Or, worse still, how she generously took care of him despite her own struggles in life, the surplus that she distinctly lacked. Every time Anmar remembered that, the stench of shame overwhelmed the fragrance of strength. And this time, there was no Mendez to make him feel better.

"I'm trying my hardest," Max said, pulling Anmar out of his thoughts. "The one time I find something good for us all—" she spread her arms, gesturing to her group, "—you decide to throw it all away!" Anmar opened his mouth, but Max cut him off. "You think I trusted that Ginysis and Alexandra? Hmm?" She treaded closer to him and Anmar felt his heart shrivel. "This job was our only way out of this miserable life. Our only way to getting a ship of our own."

A painful frown knotted Anmar's forehead. "Max, I'm so sorry. I didn't mean to harm our group, I swear."

"Just get out of my sight," she yelled, a tuft of her hair bouncing on her forehead.

Edward waited until Anmar went in their opposite direction before he began bickering with Max again. Anmar walked somewhere far away from them. But not too far. He found a chair tucked away behind a log. He could still hear Max and Edward yell over each other's voices.

He sat down, kicking his feet up on the log. A cool coastal wind blew and stung his face. The boy pulled his jacket's collar up and crossed his arms. Anmar blinked slowly and huffed.

He wanted to cry. But he didn't feel anything in him. Usually, he would stir up the memory of an achingly beautiful song he'd heard in one of the taverns on Pirates' Isle. A song that he always tried to hum and recreate. It always gave him a good cry when he needed it, relief when everything else failed to offer escape. But he wasn't sure he had any tears in him tonight. Anmar stared into the blank sea. The shipwreck mouthed the bay, an entrance to this particular island. The debris shielded the shore from the heaviness of the waves, and the water splashed onto the shore in a gentle welcome.

Although being a crewmate of Max's hypothetical ship wasn't his favored option, he found himself longing for it, longing for a more permanent state of being where abandonment no longer haunted his mind.

But the map proved to be a riddle, and their final destination wasn't any clearer. Their employer was also clueless. He even had to hire them, and another group. A man named Ginysis and his wife Alexandra. What a strange but beautiful name. Ginysis. If Mendez was here, he would've started making jokes about that.

Their employer was Lord Edenton, a highly esteem gentlemen and Londoner. Anmar remembered his quarters: Trinkets behind glass, glass behind trinkets, globes, golds. Ginysis and Alexandra were already there when Max and her group were summoned. Max had heard about him on the streets, and thought she'd pay a visit. Of course, Max and her group weren't nearly so infamous as Ginysis and Alexandra. Anmar even found it strange that Edenton would hire their group at all when he had the other duo.

Edenton had cut the map in half. One for Max's group, and one for Ginysis and Alexandra. The pair didn't even flinch when Edenton tore the map, a saccharine smile on his face. The map shifted to regard each of them present, and then he spoke. "Do not lose sight of this map. It will lead you to the keys and the island. Find it for me, and I will make you rich," the Londoner had said.

Exiting Edenton's quarters was like waking from a dream. Between the freshness of reality, and the heavy desire of the un-reality. And that un-reality was Max's only chance.

Anmar's thoughts turned to his own dream. Back with his father from work during a parade. Parades in Damascus were his favorite time. Music, people, dancing, cheering, food. Someone had pulled Anmar to the side and whispered to him stories of a lost treasure. The treasure the man spoke of was an un-reality to Anmar, then. He was ten years old, and he took it upon himself to venture out and find this treasure, and bring it back to his family; triumphant, wise, and rich. He thought he would become back a hero. The savior of his family. The savior of his neighborhood, even.

How naive he had been. His misadventure got him lost, hungry, and cold. Instead of treasure, he found bandits and misfits. And upon his return, empty-handed and empty of the stomach, and found no one left in his neighborhood. Everyone, gone.

Look at where that stupid treasure hunt took him. Stuck with stupid people, repeating the same stupid mistake. He couldn't leave, however much he wanted to. Where would he go? The world he lived in now wasn't any better than the outside world, but at least this world kept him somewhat fed, protected, and clothed.

But the outside world also had Mendez…

He swung his feet side to side, thinking of the Spanish man. Anmar missed him. At times like this, he and Mendez would walk away from the bickering and just talk, taking shelter away in their own little world. Mendez would tell Anmar stories of how he escaped the orphanage. Mendez would tell him stories about the ring that a wonderful woman once gifted him, a ring that he wore at all times, which he claimed would lead him to her when he needed her most.

Anmar always thought Mendez would never run out of stories. He, himself, would talk about anything to keep himself from the shame and guilt. And Mendez would double those efforts. Sometimes the efforts were worthwhile, like drumming and dancing. Sometimes they were ineffective, like sneaking some rum and trying it out together. Anmar tried rum three different times, and each time he would hope the taste would— perhaps—be better. It never was.

This time, however, Anmar sat and let the shame swallow his chest and slither through his mind. No matter. At least Mendez is now safer, happier with that pretty blond boy and the brunette captain with the strange necklace and even stranger demeanor.

The breeze danced across the beach again, and he shoved his hands in his pockets, shielding them from the cold. The wind became more punishing. Sharp, chilly. The cold seeped through Anmar's pockets, and he clenched his fists against it. Perhaps this was a punishment. Punishment for believing in a stupid un-reality. Punishment for destroying Max's only way to her un-reality. Punishment for betraying Mendez.

He looked out to the sea and it rewarded him with another boisterous gust to his face. Anmar leaned forward and closed his eyes. He received the wind's words. The cold drew water from his eyes; a tear traveled his skin and left a chill in its wake across his cheek.

Anmar opened his eyes when the squall died down. He wiped the tear from his cheek and rubbed his hands together when he caught a glimpse of something fluttering on the lingering breeze. It landed on the log at Anmar's feet. The paper lodged itself on the log's bark, fluttering against the wind. Anmar studied it closer. Jagged edges. Torn. Faded orange in color. A color too familiar. He frowned and took his feet off the log. He picked it up.

It was the size of his palm, a strange symbol across it and three dots in the bottom right corner. It was a piece of the map! Anmar grinned.

Maybe the wind wasn't a punishment but a blessing, a message.

He bit the inside of his lip, glancing at Max and Edward. She would be furious if she found Anmar with this alone.

His heart pounded, and he had a sudden urge to fling the map into the sea. Better to leave it unknown to Max. Or perhaps sell it to some vendor on the island, make some spare change.

Anmar was about to fold the paper back when an idea scrambled to the forefront of his mind, his gaze shooting to the sea with widened eyes.

The wind gusted into him again, as if to affirm his idea.

Could he do it? Could he possibly take this piece, whatever chance this scrap of paper may have, and run away and find Mendez?

But the idea deflated as he considered the reality of his situation, and his shoulders slouched with it. He wouldn't be able to escape on his own. This island was surrounded by shipwrecks, and beyond that, an archipelago proper that'd be difficult to navigate without knowing the way. Sand bars. Submerged dangers. The tide itself, without the right equipment. Anmar would ask for a ride with one of the pirates, or perhaps stow away, but it was too dangerous for him alone.

Max was right. Anmar would not fare well on his own. If Max hadn't found him all these years ago, he would have starved or frozen to death.

He wouldn't be able to go anywhere on his own with this map, anyway. The map wasn't useful at all, and without Edenton's aid in the beginning, and Alexandra's direction, they would have never found a way in the first place.

Disappointed at his only option, he sat back in his chair. He lifted the fragment of the map up and tried to make sense of it. It was as every bit as enigmatic as the ring on Mendez's finger.

Once Max and Edward's bickering calmed down, Anmar could hear the jaunty, distant music and shattering glass from the tavern.

He brought his focus back to the map and tried to straighten the edges out on his lap. It was very small, and he feared tearing it again. It looked ancient. Its once white leaf now faded and rippled with folds. Curious, he thumbed it a little.

"What the…?" He turned his head to the side, rubbing his thumb on it again. Something felt solid within the thin, delicate paper.

It moved. Amazed, he followed it with his index finger, careful not to lose its tracks. It turned in a circle and moved up, plummeted down diagonally before coming to a stop at a place no less nebulous than the first. Anmar tapped on it, looking for an answer. It rippled under his touch, like a rock in a still lake, until the map began to show clearer lines and continents. He stared at it, the wind blowing and playing with its corners.

He had another idea. He didn't have to stay with Max and Edward for long. Just long enough.

"Thank you," he whispered to the wind and sea, and smiled. Anmar stood with a jump and walked to Max and Edward's direction.

"What do you propose we do now, huh, Max?" Edward asked.

"Go after them," Anmar said.

Max's attention shifted to the boy.

"Mendez has a strong grip." Anmar pulled out the torn piece of paper. "But a clumsy one."

They all moved closer to the small paper Anmar held between his index and thumb. It luffed like a whisper in the wind.

"Well, what the blazes are we supposed to do with this small bit?" Max asked.

"Edenton said the map was special. Ginysis and Alexandra weren't worried about tearing it." Anmar swallowed thickly, and hoped Max didn't see. He just needed her to agree to move forward with the map and they'd lead Anmar to the un-reality. To Mendez, and the Silver Rose. "I found it in the sands, and thought you'd like to see it," Anmar added. Max held out a hand and Anmar gave it to her.

Edward leaned in and read.

"Veracruz?" he said.

Anmar nodded.

Max looked at the map for what felt like forever to Anmar. He held his breath.

"All right. Good lad," Max said.

Anmar exhaled, relief filling his chest.

9

Charles

It's us against The Commodore

The sea glistened like gold coins under the evening sun. Thomas rested their elbows on the railing, the sun warming their back.

It had been three days. Three days since the Rose sailed away from what Thomas once knew as their home. Three days since Thomas last gazed upon Croix's bleeding body.

"He killed him." The words slipped Thomas' mouth before they even realized.

"You better get used to that, Thomas." They flinched and glanced behind them. Charles joined them at the railing. "How are you feeling?"

Thomas gazed out to the sea as it ebbed and flowed like a thing alive. "I don't know." Their voice was heavy and coarse, but their eyes twinkled with something that Charles recognized as courage. Silence fell between them, interrupted only by the crashing of waves on the Rose's hull.

Thomas rubbed their hands, wanting to say something but unsure of how to phrase it. They put one hand on the Rose's railing and faced Charles. "Are you bound to this ship and crew?" they finally asked.

Charles swallowed but faced Thomas squarely. "I am bound by a certain promise, yes. But I want to be here. You?"

"I don't know what to expect," they admitted. "I knew exactly what to expect back in New Orleans."

Silence filled the air again. The Rose placed low squeals and creaks as she cut through the waters. She had kept her course for three days, not furling her sails for a second, her helm steady without a waver, carving a path in the sea away from New Orleans.

Thomas gazed to the helm. Their gaze then wandered to the Rose's sails, masts and riggings. Their fingers however over the railing, as if they took care not to touch her too heavily. The Rose gave Thomas a reassuring creak under their fingers. "What a ship," they breathed.

The doors to the captain's cabin creaked open, and James marched out. A crack snapped from the Rose's sails as James walked onto the main deck, greeting him.

"Ahh," Charles faced his captain. "Speak of the devil."

"We don't speak of the devil here, Charles," James said, coyness in his eyes.

"I suppose the devil's a bit tired," Charles replied. The two held one another's gaze for a while, tension in their posture.

The bilge hatch squeaked and Mendez emerged from below, breaking the simmering tension between James and Charles. "You two are just going to stand there or are we going to find a heading?" Mendez said.

"Of course," James said in a droll tone, pulling his gaze away from Charles. "Come, come." He turned back to his cabin and the crew followed. Thomas' steps were eager, yet hesitant. The Rose opened the door with a soft squeal.

He seated himself at the head of the table. "Welcome to the captain's cabin."

Thomas held their hands together, looking around, their curious gaze jumping from one object to another. Mendez was already standing before James' chart cabinet, looking through his captain's maps and atlases.

"Did you expect to find Shadow hosting my cabin?" James addressed Thomas, but his words caught Charles' attention.

"What? No," Thomas said. "It's just that… I've never seen something as magnificent as this." They wandered around the cabin, grounding themselves at chair handles and the table.

The floorboards creaked under James' feet.

"Oh, you're making her feel sheepish," James said with a smile.

Thomas laughed and gave the table one last brush, fond.

"You still don't have a sword, do you?" Charles asked Thomas.

"Allow me to fix that." James stood and strode to his well-made, humble bed. He pulled out a sword with a bulbous head. He unsheathed it and gave it a light swing before he handed it to Thomas.

"*Merci!*" Thomas held the sword, examining the workmanship. It was lovely, a work of art. "I don't know how to handle it though."

"Don't worry. You've got an excellent teacher," James nodded to Charles, who nodded to Thomas with a reassuring smile on his face.

"*Dios mio*, captain, do you ever organize your charts?" Mendez said.

James' eyes widened and he leaped out of his chair. "Don't touch anything without putting it back right where it was! I have them in perfect order."

Mendez spread the charts across his captain's table while James carefully inspected each chart and reorganized them in a way that made sense to him.

He joined his crew, rolling the map between himself and them. James rested his palms on the table and looked at Thomas. Mendez and Charles exchanged glances. "You know how important the destination of this map is to me, right, Thomas?"

Thomas gulped. They glanced at Charles and back to their captain then nodded.

"The Commodore is after the destination of this very map. The same Commodore Croix dared to threaten me with. And you know that on this ship, the Commodore is game for the Wolf and the Rose, right?"

"Aye, *capitaine*," Thomas affirmed, a certain gusto in their voice. They stood upright and put their hand to the hilt of their sword. "I'm aboard the Silver Rose now. This is my home, and I will protect it."

A faint smile made its way on James' lips. But alarm rose in his eyes, and he turned away from his crew, stifling a cough, his hand clenched in an abrupt fist on the table. He swayed and turned to his chart cabinet, steadying himself on his chair's handle.

Thomas side-eyed Charles, who merely shook his head.

"I don't suppose you have any experience with Shadow Glyphs before," James rasped over his shoulder, his gaze briefly locking onto Charles' before he turned his attention back to his cabinet. He reached for something on his shelves, hiding the contents with his body.

He returned to his crew, whisking a key and unlocking his drawer. He splayed a stack of journals and free papers on his table, yellow with age, ink charred. "There are the journals of Commodore Henry Gregory Mitchell."

The crew tensed, their eyes darting around the captain's cabin as if expecting the Silver Rose to respond with hostility.

Her creaks and rumbles only continued at an even pace, not wavering for a moment at the forbidden name.

James seated himself and perused through the journals until he found what he appeared to be looking for. He pushed a stack of bound papers over the table, keeping them out of reach from his crew. "The Commodore is consorting with the Shadows; the very crime he has charged me with."

"But it's true, isn't it?" Charles challenged.

"I suppose it's not a secret that I sold my soul to them, yes."

A frown furrowed lines in Charles' forehead. "Then what are you suggesting?"

"You know what I'm suggesting," James said. His gaze left Charles' and he turned to his other crew mates. "The Commodore sold his soul to the Shadows. He's not as unblemished as you seem to think he is," he finished, shooting a sharp gaze to Charles.

"How did you get your hands on these?" Charles leaned close over the journals, his eyes inspecting the parchment.

"I stole them." James swallowed thickly. "When he charged me with Shadow Influence, I stole his journals before… before the Rose and I left."

His captain appeared to be scanning his crew for any signs of rejection. As Charles surveyed his crewmates, he found himself unsurprised. Mendez was intrigued, as always. Thomas wore a quizzical expression.

Charles didn't miss the glance that James threw in his direction. His captain's focus was deadset on the papers, his fingers twitching toward them. He retracted his fingers and crossed his arms, as if to tame his wild interest—or, perhaps, to tame the cryptic *thing* in his chest.

Mendez was next to speak. "You think we can use the journals to decipher the map?"

"I hope. I need to get to it. Fast."

"Before the Commodore gets to it," Thomas said and James nodded.

Charles tried to temper his own expression and failed. Disbelief marred his features. He remembered when he and his sister would often read a forgotten grimoire in their Uncle Wilson's bookshop that told terrible tales up until Uncle Wilson found out and hid that grimoire away with dire warnings to Charles and Gabrielle of those wicked creatures.

The Commodore wasn't capable of consorting with such beings, was he? Charles remembered the night he pursued the offered by the Commodore's embassy. He was genial in his demeanor, confident in his words. Charles truly believed that the Ordinance was doing good work. When Charles took up the bounty hunt for the Wolf and the Rose, he thought he was doing right by everyone. Right by his family, right by his community.

"It's not just us against Max," Mendez said, pulling Charles from his thoughts. "It's us against the Commodore."

"Like you said captain," Thomas said, confidence in their voice. "Whatever is dear to the Commodore prey to us on this ship."

James centered the map between his charts and Shadow Glyph cipher over the table. "Let's get to work, then."

The four of them leaned over the map, trying to match the new markings it gave them against James' Shadow Glyph key. As if in response to their rapt attention, the map's markings shifted and changed, rearranging its surface into unknown borders and letters.

Thomas put a finger to the map, and another to James' index of ciphers. "V," they said. "That's a letter V."

James clapped Thomas on the shoulder. "Thank you. I've stared at these journals for so long."

"Sometimes you might need a new pair of eyes, captain," Mendez said.

"Indeed," James said and glanced to Charles again.

He took a seat, away from his captain and pretended to join his crew's efforts. But his attention was no longer on the map's destination. His attention was not acutely focused on this troubling thread to the story of the Wolf and the Rose.

James

A storm is coming

Evening stretched into dusk. Dusk stretched into night. They deciphered two more letters—V and Z—and a landmass that was not recognizable in any atlas. The map had teased them with an odd illustration of a warrior statue that would shift across the parchment's surface, mocking their attempts to find an answer.

The rest was still an enigma. The Rose's tilting movements slid the key down to James' side of the table. He held and rolled it in between his fingers, perhaps with more force than was necessary.

"Careful not to break it," Charles said.

"I won't break it," James grunted irritably. "I just need to—" he whacked it on the map, "—Why are they never helpful?" he muttered behind his palm.

126

Exhaling sharply, he closed his eyes. When he opened them, he caught a sight of the inky, gray slithers of the Bite creeping on the flesh of his fingertips. Dread bubbled in his chest. He couldn't be caught coughing, heaving for breath—weak and vulnerable—in front of his crew.

My men are nothing. But he is everywhere. The Ordinance will get its hands on you.

Clenching a fist, he stood and without a word, paced out of his cabin.

His crew exchanged frowns and followed.

"What's the plan, captain?" Charles asked, looking about deck for James.

James' voice came from the quarterdeck. "We're lowering anchor for now."

The Rose's sails breathed the air, rippling as the wind rushed through her riggings. James gave her helm a squeeze.

"Anchor? Why?" Charles walked up the stairs.

"The Rose says there's a storm coming ahead of us," James lied. *And we barely have a heading.*

Charles approached his captain. "So we're just going to anchor here, idly?"

James didn't take his eyes off the horizon. The Rose turned her capstan, her lines and sails rattling with the wind and waters as she coming to a halt.

The only sound that permeated in the night were her intermittent squeals and creaks and the bubbling water against her hull. She sent a creak from him to the stair rails, and James descended.

A storm was not coming.

Mendez sat on a barrel and threw a gaze to his captain. "You'll find a heading soon, right?"

James' index finger was fully engulfed with the disease gray of the Bite. He balled his fist, hiding his fingers away from his crew. He nodded over his shoulder to Mendez's direction and disappeared into his cabin without a word.

10

Charles

They both want something from each other. And they both will stop at nothing

Morning came, and Thomas was the first one up. They immediately headed to the galley to see what reservoirs James had. Charles woke next and turned to the direction of Thomas' voice.

"Peas, biscuits, walnuts, almonds, oats. All right, not bat. *Trés bien*, some dried figs." Thomas helped themselves to the dishes. "More almonds. Where's the meat?"

The Rose steadied herself while Thomas worked in the galley.

"*Merci, madame*," Thomas smiled, naturally putting together the crew's breakfast.

The Rose's galley had not seen aroma in a long time. James had a few spices, organized alphabetically in glazed ceramic jars, though James rarely used them. Thomas knew each spice by smell. They artfully organized hard tack next to dried figs, walnuts, oats and cinnamon, prepared wine and the crew's breakfast was ready.

They had their breakfast under the sun on the Rose's deck. The air carried no scent of a storm with it, and the Rose's wood did not look wet with rain. The crew glanced to the extra plate they left for James on a barrel, then looked to each other.

"You think he'll come out of his cabin any time soon for that?" Mendez asked.

The silence was unsettling. Even the Rose was quieter than usual, her subdued creaks and rumbles coming in disorganized directions.

"Doesn't look like it," Charles said. He turned to Thomas. "Would you like to learn how to handle a sword, Thomas?"

Thomas smirked. "Right after you help me clean this up!" They scooped the plates and headed below.

After they were finished—and James' plate was left in the galley—Charles and Thomas took the main deck as Thomas' training grounds.

"Keep your hips facing your opponent, Thomas," Charles said. "Good. Now, left leg forward, and keep your weight evenly distributed."

Thomas adjusted their position and delivered a blow.

"Wonderful. Watch your footwork."

Thomas smiled and parried Charles' next attack. "Doesn't being with a captain and a ship like this terrify you?" Thomas said, and their conversation proved distracting, for they readjusted their footwork again.

"Yes, a little." Charles waited for Thomas as they took the proper position. "But if this is part of my story, then so be it."

The two went quiet again and the Rose gave them their silence. The creaks of her wood and riggings matched the water's tempo. She tightened a knot on her reefed sails and adjusted her helm.

Thomas' eyes flicked to her moving ropes. "You still haven't told me how she can do all this."

Charles parried Thomas' incoming attack. "He claims she's out of this world, that she was found like this," Charles said in a hushed whisper.

Thomas lowered their voice as well. "Found her?"

"His parents found her."

"What happened to them?"

Charles' features darkened, and his brows furrowed. "His father was murdered by a pirate. And his mother…" Charles knew the Rose was listening, and he chose his next words wisely before he continued, "he says the Commodore killed her."

"*The* Commodore?" Thomas exclaimed.

Charles only nodded. "James committed the highest crime against the Shadow Ordinance, you've heard of it, I'm sure."

Although they lowered their voice, a condemning croak traveled across the Rose's floorboards and up her main mast. Charles' gaze flitted around her deck, always scanning for any signs of danger.

"I've heard of it a little," Thomas replied. "Croix spoke of it often."

Charles lowered his sword and leaned in towards Thomas, as if hiding his words from the eavesdropping ship. "The two have been hunting each other for years. They both want something from each other. And they'll stop at nothing."

A shaky rumble traveled through the Rose's deck in Charles' direction, the creak diminishing as it reached her masts.

The sun dipped below the horizon and the deep, dark blue of the sky spread its veil over her wood. The Rose's masts left long, creeping shadows on her deck.

Charles

What was he doing in there?

It had been three days.

Three days since they last saw their captain tread into his cabin. Thomas and Charles, and occasionally Mendez, have been dedicating their evenings to practicing their swordsmanship. It's been one day since their practice sessions have started to feel a little awkward and a little too quiet.

"Does he usually do this?" Thomas asked, parrying Charles' oncoming attack and delivering one in return.

Charles shook his head.

"I won't say I didn't expect this," Mendez said, "but I kind of did." He was sitting on a barrel, drumming while he watched Charles and Thomas practice. "Wish he had some instruments." Mendez returned to drumming, and the Rose added a timed rumble to his tunes.

Even when Charles stayed up writing in his diaries, he never saw a glimpse of the Wolf. Creaks from his cabin were sparse and quick.

He couldn't find an answer to this among the stories that he had heard, and all he could do was resort to the story that was the most credible. It must be the Shadows. James' cabin could be flowing with them. Why else would he isolate himself from his crew?

But those journals with Shadow glyphs? By the Commodore's own hands? Charles found himself wondering which side of the fight he was truly on.

Thomas delivered a lunge at Charles and if Charles hadn't noticed and parried at the right time, he would have had his shoulder seriously cut.

"Good. You're using your opponent's distraction," Charles said as they both halted. "You learn fast."

"I have a great teacher," Thomas smiled. They sheathed the sword they can now call theirs and shook Charles' hand and he pulled them in for a pat on the back. Mendez drummed a swift, improvised fanfare on his barrel—he may not have had a trumpet, but the spirit brought a smile to their faces. The two bowed and then clapped for Mendez.

Then the awkwardness and silence settled again.

Night came. The Rose creaked in the direction of her masks. The crew had learned to listen to her creaks, and Charles was becoming especially attuned to what those sounds might mean.

This time, the Rose seemed to want help with her sails, tightening knots and untangling lines. They had no heading, and they were sure James had no heading either.

So, they went below deck. Absently, they ate hard tack and head to their sleeping quarters.

Charles lounged in his hammock and waiting until he heard Thomas and Mendez's breathing slow with the mantle of sleep as it settled over them. He laid still, wakeful and dry-eyed, staring at the wood of the Silver Rose.

What was he doing? What is he hiding?

Such strange behavior, yet typical of the soulless. The stories say that the soulless will isolate themselves, a symptom of their emptiness. They may become listless yet hot tempered, emotionless yet tumultuous. His captain was often withdrawn and ill-tempered. Charles was now seeing isolation. And if the progression of symptoms continued, he dreaded what their captain was capable of.

The same goes for the Commodore, if James' claims were true.

Charles tried to shake the crude thought out of his head, but the questions persisted, torrential and raging.

How could I have missed it? The Commodore's penmanship is unmistakable. But he's the High Ambassador of the Shadow Ordinance.

And what better position is this for someone who committed the same crime he preaches against?

I'm a pawn in a game of chess, and neither side is my own.

What am I condemning him to? What am I condemning the Rose to? The crew…"

Charles shook the remorseful thoughts out of his mind and reminded himself why he was here. It was either him, or the Wolf and the Rose. Charles had a promise to keep, and he had a family to return to.

James did not.

Did he?

He took his vest off, put his pen and diary in a pocket and wrapped the vest into itself. But he felt that was enough. Undoing the end of his pillowcase, Charles stuffed the diary in and tucked away the bundle in the hole of the mast that his hammock was tied to. He sat upright, his back to the cavity that held his secrets.

Charles blinked and became aware of his furrowed brow, tension gripping the middle of his forehead. He rubbed at his face and listened.

The Silver Rose was resting at sea. It was eerie. Quiet. The Rose and the waters around her hull were the only sound he could hear. He dismounted the hammock and headed up the main deck, careful not to let the hatch door squeak too loudly. He'd have to remember to oil the hinges later, and hope that it didn't offend the Rose in the process.

A moonless night on the main deck. The Rose commanded silence. Alto creaks slithered across her main deck and up her main mast. Her foresail sheets followed the creak with a low rumble. A wind blew the shrouds against her masts. He couldn't tell which was the sea and which was the sky if it wasn't for the rhythmic waves distorting the mirrored image of the stars.

Charles took cautious steps over her wood. He did not know if his breath was his own, or the wind around her wood until he felt the cold breeze on his neck. He felt watched, her planks anticipating ever step he took.

He was standing in the middle of her main deck, facing her bow. She was submerged in darkness. Her main mast towered Charles' head and his eyes traced the floorboards to her foremast, then followed the star-dotted sky to her crow's nest. He spotted the flag. *The Mark of the Wolf.*

Turning on his heels, his eyes followed the mainsail back down all the way back to the floorboards. The Rose received his journey with a long creak, as though she knew he was inspecting her.

Thud.

He faced his captain's cabin.

Thud thud boom.

Tension tightened his shoulders. Shadows could burst out of his cabin any second.

Was I found out already? What is she going to do? What will he do?

"Is he all right?" Thomas' voice came from the hatch as they stepped on deck, Mendez followed behind.

"What is he doing?" Mendez asked, agitated. "He hasn't been out in days. Charles, go knock on his door."

"What? Why me?" Charles protested, his eyes still plastered to the cabin's door.

"He likes you." Mendez shoved Charles' shoulder. "Go ask him."

"I don't know what he's doing in there," Charles shot back in a strained whisper.

Thump.

"Ugh," Thomas groaned. "I'll do it myself."

Knock knock knock.

"Captain?" Thomas asked. "You all right?"

Charles tested the doorknob. "Locked," he mouthed to the crew.

"Yes, yes. I'm fine." James' muffled voice came from behind the wood.

"We heard noises," Charles said.

"I'm fine, Charles, I'm fine. Just—just figuring things out."

"Have you had anything to eat?" Thomas asked and bowed their head to the door, eyes to the crew.

"Yes, I'm good."

"What's that supposed to mean?" Thomas whispered to Charles and Mendez, who shook their heads and shrugged. Silence from the cabin again. The crew went silent, too.

"Rose, you'll tell us if he needs anything, *non*?" Thomas asked the Rose's wood. She creaked under their feet and across her hull.

"He's the captain." Mendez shrugged and headed below. Thomas followed.

Charles lingered. He stared at James' cabin with an unblinking stare, wishing he could see right through. *What is he doing in there...?*

11

James

James had no heading. He hated it. And the Bite knew that. He clawed at his chest and winced, his other hand forming into a fist. He groaned, fighting the urge to claw the Bite out of his chest. It writhed and twisted and wormed in his heart, whispers skittering in the space where his soul should be.

The sound of crumbling paper brought him back to the present. He unclenched his fist, releasing the paper that wrinkled beneath. His fingertips were doused in gray, wisps rising through the length of his fingers like smoke from a candle.

Tears formed in his eyes. It was new, fresh, almost relieving. He hasn't had tears in a long ten years. The Bite slithered in his torso, searching, and slowly, the tears diminished, as though afraid of the peckish Bite. He shook his head and stifled another groan.

"It's getting worse." His voice barely made it out of his throat. He palmed his face and shut his eyes. "What if— what if I don't make it. You'll be—"

Mio caro, do not think of that right now.

He heard her but couldn't respond, his voice frozen in his throat. He tried to swallow down the Bite that weighed so heavily in his chest.

The Rose creaked across his cabin a raspy sound that traveled from his table to the great window at the aft. He drew a quivering breath and turned his thinning attention back to the Commodore's journals. He had forty of them. Each one ranged from three to twenty pages, some in loose papers, other bound into a notebook with cloth covers.

And they were all written in the Shadow Glyphs. The language was strange, and incredibly complex. James had scoured endless dictionaries, numerous languages, and countless civilizations. Nothing matched the journals. It was almost like this language belonged to another world entirely. The lexicon consisted of strings, dots, circles and lines. Every minute arrangement meant a different letter, a different meaning. Even after ten years of studying it, James didn't fully understand the language's rules. But he knew enough to slowly read through Mitchell's pitiful journals, enough to learn his motives, and more importantly, his dreads.

All James needed to do was find out how to toy with the Commodore's dreads. He opened the journal entry that had the most deciphered lexicons and leafed through his key.

Fleming has been overstaying his welcome in my
q¹   ense his suspi
ment to this n

the remaii

The Rose. I will get her. Fi st, I must get through the ¹ oy and his mother. Looks like De¹' ·monia going to see he· t Shadow rance in years.
y of some sort

He turned to the map, a few marks strewn across its surface. Then, James frowned, studying it closer. He could have sworn the marks were on the bottom left yesterday. There was a mass that resembled land on the parchment, but nothing matched the atlases on his table. The glyphs were all connected; the first to the second, the second to the third at the fourth. He browsed through his Shadow Glyph key and the journal entry for any sign of the marks that he saw on the map. There were two letters in his key that looked similar to the map's.

A

U

Hours crept by. He rubbed his palm against his jaw. He was growing a stubble. He hated having a stubble. His hand flew to his head, aggressively turning it in his hair then slammed his fist to the table.

"Damnit," he huffed.

His gaze went to his wardrobe, the Rose's creaks leading him there. He stumbled to it and opened it, wistfulness coating his movement. There sat his mother's sewing supplies. He had used up most of his mother's yarn over the decade he had spent alone at sea. Some was on his cabin walls, a small piece of tapestry of blue, brown and red. He kept one last ball of yarn untouched. It was the last piece of yarn that his mother touched, and he could not get himself to use it. He reached for it. This last ball of yarn was bright orange, fuzzy and bright.

He's getting ahead, James. You won't be able to catch him at this rate. You don't even have half of the journals deciphered.

It will consume you before you can even have another piece. He'll get the Rose. He will destroy her, tear every floorboard until he finds what he wants, and you'll watch—

Smoked erupted from his fingertips and snaked through his skin, cold and numbing, digging beneath his flesh like knives. His fingers spasmed at the sudden pain, loosening his grip on the thread. It fell, part of it unraveling as it rolled on the Rose's floorboards.

James picked it up and put it back in his wardrobe, closing the door on his precious supplies, as though hiding it from his own suffering. Tears burned his eyes once more, and he hammered a frost-bitten fist against the wardrobe.

Knock knock knock.

"Captain?" Charles' voice came from behind the door. "Are you all right?"

The doorknob turned. Clicked. Remained closed, thankfully.

"We heard some noises," Thomas said.

"I'm fine. I'm fine. Just— just figuring things out." James stifled a cough against his hand. His palm came away with darkness, gray in color, smoky in texture. Panic bubbled in his throat as he wiped his lips, a viscous string of the Bite clinging from the side of his mouth. Shakily, he turned back to his table, grimacing with silent horror.

I have to do something. Fast!

"Have you had anything to eat?"

"Yes, I'm good," he rasped. He was not hungry. He felt nothing but a blend of dread, anguish, and urgency, the Bite feasting on it with a fierce gluttony.

Silence. He waited to hear their footsteps move away. He resumed his work.

The night stretched into the early hours of dawn. He grabbed his stash of walnuts, hard tack, and one of his mother's favorite embroidered blankets and headed out to the crow's nest for the third night in a row.

The deck was quiet, and the crew was asleep. A slither of a crescent moon smiled in the slowly waking night sky. James climbed the ratlines into the crow's nest and sat, his left leg folded, his right knee bent. He rested his elbow on it as he nibbled on his walnuts and tack. The stars still took the stage of the sky before the sun. A brush of clouds smeared a stark blueish white against the western sky, and a few tufts of pale orange clouds foretold the sunrise.

He gazed at the scene before him. It reminded him of the Dell' Armonia. The fountain and sunsets, the moonrises and trees. Messer Emiliano's bread.

A shiver traveled down James' spine, prompting him to adjust his mother's blanket around his shoulders. It was the blanket she made him while he was away on the trading trip with his father. The blanket was supposed to be a gift for their return. Little did any of them expect the pirate attack. James had been ill with an oppressive fever for a week after he had lost his father and the Rose to the captain of the Calypso's Wrath. Their home had been silent, empty. He had rarely seen his mother weep, though he knew the only hours she truly felt safe to grieve was when her son was asleep.

It had continued like this until he heard the whispers of the Shadows creep to him through a necklace of his father's, the very necklace James now wore at all times. He had listened to those whispers, promising him a quick and easy escape from his grief.

And so, he had struck the deal. Little did he care about the consequences.

All in one year, he had lost his father, his mother, and his soul. After a decade alone at sea, he had forgotten how to feel such things as grief. For so long, he had only known the emotions that fueled the Bite. Wrath was its favorite. But something else smothered the emptiness where his soul should have been. Something akin to connection. It was new, confusing, and James chose to tuck it away, unsure how he or the Bite would react to it.

He took a sip of anisette and hugged his knees in. "Do you think their souls rest at ease, *mia Rosa*?" he whispered.

The Rose creaked a soft whisper across her crow's nest. *I am sure their souls are at peace, watching over us, Giacobbo*.

"I hope so," James said. His throat tightened, a stabbing pain blossoming in his chest. He would have wept for his soul, for the chance of reuniting with his parents in another life. His soul was no longer his.

He downed more anisette, aching to swallow down the weighty lump in his throat, before he stood. He breathed the crisp air, closing his eyes at the height of his breath.

A head-spinning sound rang in his ears. It swelled in his head, morphing into quiet hushing, then refocused into a hum. The voice left his head and circled toward his cabin. The Rose welcomed the hum with a gentle rumble. A whisper hovered over the crow's nest, beckoning him.

He opened his eyes. "Aereon."

12

James

I swear to you and The Rose

He sprang to his feet and clambered down to the main deck. Moonlight and twilight washed over the Rose's wood, and the sea was quiet and still.

James turned to the Rose's stern, searching for the merman. No Aereon.

"Over here, Wolf." The voice strung him along, leading James off. It came from the Rose's starboard. Aereon was at the railing, resting his chin on his palm, his elbows to the Rose.

"How are you doing that?" James said, approaching the railing, wonder in his eyes.

"I can do lots of things, wolf." Aereon winked and lifted his tail behind his head. A fountain of water gyrated around his tail, carrying him to James' height, his scales winking obscure lights in the water. "For instance," Aereon hummed and leaned closer, resting his palms on the Rose's wood, "I can sense a soul's messages." He eyed James, a small smirk playing about his lips. "And I sense none from you."

James averted his eyes from the merman's amber gaze.

Aereon smiled and touched a wet hand to James' chin, the touch eliciting a quiver in James' muscles. The merman faintly turned the captain's gaze back to him and continued, "That's why I thought I'd pay a visit, impatient one."

"I suppose it's not a secret to you that I told my soul," James finally said, shame touching his voice. A twinge traveled across his chest, the sensation moving to his throat and lingering.

He hadn't felt anything with such acuity since he sold his soul. His gaze met Aereon's.

The merman responded, his words honest, his voice gentle, "Selling one's soul is forbidden where I come from. Part of my duties as a commander is to find those who are close to trading their souls and save them from such a fate."

"You're a commander?"

"One of Anahiya's, yes. That's my community in Nahida," Aereon said gently, tenderness in his voice. His hand moved to James' clenched fist, draping his webbed fingers over James' and unfurling his tightening fingers. James winced as his fingers unfolded, the Bite's gray wisps pinching the nerves under his skin like needles. Aereon continued, "But you won't see any judgment from me."

Something about Aereon's accepting words and soft regard kindled warmth in James' chest, warming away the tyranny of shame, chasing away the Bite's hunger. The sensation seemed like it moved in a circular pattern in his chest, massaging away tension, melting away the Bite's spools within his very muscles. He wasn't sure what this sensation was, if it existed at all. He could be imagining it. He had been without a soul for ten years, and he was no longer sure what it was once like to have one.

James cleared his throat. He needed to ask. But as soon as the question formed in his throat, it broke under the weight of shame and fear. "You mentioned you're from another world," was what he said instead. "Like the Rose?"

"Yes," Aereon said. "It's called Nahida." The Rose creaked under her captain's feet and across her hull where the merman rested. Aereon ran a finned finger over her railing. "She's an exquisite ship." The Rose's mast creaked and her ratlines rattled, Aereon turning his head to the Rose's voice. He smiled to her before he returned his gaze to James. "The Rose, dear Wolf, was released here from Nahida with a purpose."

"Because she has one of the talismans," James said, his voice flat. He gazed out at the sea, somewhere above Aereon's shoulder. "I'm assuming the key to the island is another one of those talismans."

"How do you know that?" Aereon whispered, concern breaching his veneer of calm.

"Because the Commodore of the Shadow Ordinance is after those very same talismans," James shifted where he stood. "I read his journals. He's after them for some reason, I don't know what it is. But I will find it. And I will take it away from him."

"There's an Ordinance now?" Aereon asked, his forehead tightening with a small frown.

James swallowed, biting his lip. He noticed the growing frown on Aereon's face. "What's all this Shadow talk and talismans got to do with the Rose?" James muttered.

Aereon's frown melted as he returned his attention to James, a smile tugging at his lips. He blinked, looking away from James' face. "There are things a commander should not share with a human, Wolf."

"Guess I'm very lucky," James said.

Aereon laughed, the sound pleasantly melodic. "Yes, you are."

The merman had translucent scales on his left cheek and part of his forehead where it covered his brow, casting a shimmer over his skin. A string of intricate geometric shapes lined one side of his head that stretched from his forehead to the nape of his neck. The right side of his hair was short and waxy, flecks of water twinkling on it like glistening adornments, and the left side of his hair was long and wavy, bunching at his shoulder, heavy with water. The fins on his arms were a translucent orange, and even more geometric markings covered his chest, shoulder and forearms.

"These enable me to breathe above and under water." The merman noticed James' attention to his geometric markings. "Especially the air and water of this world. Among many things, of course."

James flinched, suddenly all too aware of the way he was eyeing the merman's body. "Apologies, I didn't mean to—"

Aereon cupped James' cheek, a reassuring glint in his golden eyes. "Not at all, Wolf," he said. "I admire your curiosity."

James looked away. He didn't want to face Aereon's eyes. They had something precious, something James had heedlessly sold years ago.

"Wolf, look at me."

He raised his gaze, just enough to meet Aereon's chin, still avoidant. Silence stretched between them, each waiting for the other to say something.

Finally, the merman said, "I trust her in your hands."

James faced Aereon's gaze. "Why? I don't have a soul. What makes you trust me?"

"You're a careful steward of her." Aereon closed his eyes. "I can tell."

Calm condensed from the air around them. Along this calm came fear. James readied himself to feel it physically manifest in his chest. Long, cold fingers of fear massaged his abdomen, gripped his throat. He steeled himself, ready to ask the question that gnawed in his heart for so long. "I'm afraid,

Aereon." The Bite noticed that, turning in his chest, ready to devour emotion. "This *thing* inside me. It's—" He swallowed down the tears that tightened his throat. "What if it consumes me before I can—who's going to keep her safe? She's the only one I've got and—"

Aereon reached a hand to James' chest, his movement abrupt but soft. James shrank back, but the merman steadied his hand. At Aereon's touch, James' heart felt like a dried lake quenched with gale. It was sudden, almost painful. He staggered back, his voice quivering, "What—what are you doing to me—"

The Rose groaned in their direction, lines slithering toward the merman like a water snake. ***Leave him!*** Her lines wrapped around Aereon's wrists, attempting to pull the merman away from her captain.

But the merman kept his hand firmly on James' heart and faced the Rose's slithering ropes, his eyes not betraying his resolution. "Be calm, Rose. I'm not going to hurt him." He turned his attention back to James. "You've been without a soul for so long. You almost forgot what it's like to have one." His gaze softened, a certain warmth enveloping his eyes. "Almost painful, isn't it?"

The Rose creaked a grating sound, and Aereon let go, slowly, gently putting his hand back on the Rose's railing as though reassuring her even as her ropes still twined around his wrists.

The tight and acrid sensations reformed in James' chest, settling back in his heart with sour speed. He sucked in a dry breath and steadied himself on the Rose's railing, his legs suddenly weak. Her ropes, reluctantly uncurled around Aereon's wrists and went to James' forearms, steadying him.

"The Bite will not loosen its grips on you," Aereon said finally, his voice blunt and honest. "The soul, dear Wolf, is the connection between the mind and body. Yours will ultimately collapse under the weight of the Bite."

James' lips quivered as he stroked his throbbing chest. "How long—"

"Oh, Wolf," Aereon whispered. He started to reach a hand out to James, and then withdrew it. "However long it takes. A month. A year. Ten years. It doesn't matter. The Bite *will* consume you."

A sharp breath left James, and he leaned closer to the railing, still holding onto the Rose's lines as his head stopped spinning. "I need to know how long I have left. I need to protect her—"

"Connect," Aereon finished. "If you so want to slow down the Bite, then connection weakens it. I see you're already doing that with your crew," he said, casting a glance across the Rose's deck. "But it will only temporarily slow the progression of the Bite. Nothing can substitute the soul. I've seen it happen countless times." A pained expression passed over his features, ever so briefly.

A crushing weight of despair pulled on James' shoulders. And Aereon could tell. He leaned over the Rose's wood and put a hand to the captain's cheek, running a finger along his jaw. It caught James off guard; a shiver ran down his spine, and he closed his eyes. Words did not form.

Aereon spoke for him. "You need the talismans to get your soul back. It's not an easy process."

James could hear a thread of doubt in the merman's voice. But his eyes still retained a certain kindness that James was unaccustomed to. Any mention of his soulless condition was forever coupled with disdain. Yet, not so with Aereon.

The merman's webbed fingers found James' wrist, and as they wrapped around the captain's hand, a small shiver traveled up his arm. He savored it. "Tell me more," James said.

Aereon breathed deep before he smiled. He faced James squarely, his eyes compassionate and warm; a stark difference to the words he was about to share. "The only way to get a soul back would be for a Simraashi—a Shadow being—to pluck it out of their light source." He shook his head. "I don't know what Simraashi would be willing to betray their home and life source for a human."

The merman hesitated, and James did not miss that. He gazed into the Aereon's eyes as he challenged him. "There's more beneath those guarded words and soft gaze. Tell me."

That drew a smirk from Aereon, an endearing laugh escaping him. "You always know what to say when you want something, hmm?"

Aereon removed his hand from James' skin. That left James aching for the merman's touch, but he held back, waiting for Aereon's next step. He leaned closer to James, resting one elbow to the railing, and opened his palm in the space between them. Little figures of light began to form on his palm, shaping and reshaping until they settled.

"Is this one of your tricks again?" James teased.

"Give it a chance," Aereon said, mirroring James' playfulness. When he spoke again, the tantalizing siren elements of his voice shone through. "Besides, I've practiced this one especially for you." James smiled, cautiously relishing the closeness between them and the sweet ringing that the merman's voice sent in his head. Aereon continued as the shapes settled into what appeared to be a council seated beneath a vast tree. "Those six talismans were once what kept our Three Worlds in alliance."

The shapes rippled as two renditions of the talismans appeared, a distinct glow obscuring their sharp edges and they appeared as though they were a watercolor painting of light. But the shapes were clear to James; a triangle with a gem at its center, and a rose. The Rose rumbled, recognizing her figurehead.

"When Simraash was cast out, those talismans needed to be broken apart and scattered where Simraash can't find them." The key and rose exploded in a puff of light and Aereon continued. "Of course, the Ministers of my world would not make it easy to find those talismans. I doubt Xanahae made their talismans easy to find, either, and I'm certain they made it true hell for the Simraashis to find their own." He thumbed James' necklace, knuckles brushing James' skin as he held it in his fingers. "I'm surprised those necklaces found their way into your hands, and into the Commodore's." Aereon paused, noticing the confusion that flitted across James' face. "Apologies, I didn't explain very well."

James leaned in, which drew a small smirk from Aereon.

"The talismans were a symbol of alliance between our Three Worlds. But they were more than just a symbol." The light in Aereon's palm began to dim, and the tree itself withered, flecks of light falling from its branches like leaves. "They were a source of strength, allowing the three worlds to share connection and resources between one another. But when Xanahae disregarded Simraash's pleas for help, the Simraashis were left with no choice but to attack my world."

Aereon's words were chosen carefully, but James did not miss the passing shadow of sorrow on the merman's features. He continued, "Combine all six talismans, and the Shadows might have a chance against Xanahae and my world. The things Xanahae has done to Simraash and my world during the Crisis. I can only imagine what they are willing to do to avoid another."

Though Aereon was outwardly focused on the withering tree, his thoughts were elsewhere. James recognized that look. It was charged with lament, a requiem so close to his lips. James reached a hand and placed it to Aereon's, who broke out of his reverie and turned his full attention back to James, a smile melting away his mournful look. "But these troubles are all too foreign to be your own," Aereon said.

James felt no remorse nor concern for the little glowing figures in Aereon's palm, which was not unusual. But what was unusual was the unrelenting tug James felt in his heart toward the merman. He felt an urge to say something, anything, to soothe the grief that lurked behind Aereon's features.

He swallowed, parting his lips to say something, but Aereon spoke before him, the layer of allure and confidence returning to his voice. "You have two out of six talismans. The key would be the third," Aereon divulged. "Find all six. Destroy them and the gates between the worlds will collapse."

There was something left unsaid beneath his words, but James caught it. The merman opened his mouth to say something, but it was James who spoke first. "If the gates collapse, what will happen to my soul?"

Could he really get all six talismans and find a way to his soul? Could he cure the Bite?

Revenge first. I need him to bleed and beg.

Aereon spoke, as if sensing the warring thoughts swirling in James' head. "Those talismans are dangerous. They may appear mundane at a glance, yes, but to utilize them releases great power." Concern settled into his features as he closed his hand, drawing the little figures back into his palm. When he spoke next, it was just shy of a whisper. "Those who get their souls back… not many of them survive that transformation."

"And you're here to warn me of such danger," James said, challenging the merman.

Aereon said cunningly, "I am here out of my own will, dear Wolf." He graced James with a sly smile. "I was tasked with giving you the relevant information you need to get to our doorway. Nothing more," he insisted.

"Seems like you gave me a touch more information than that."

Amused, the merman continued, "You sly wolf." He shifted to face James again. "The talismans were made deadly for a reason. The Ministers didn't want other beings' hands on them so easily. This first talisman, the key, it's—it's perilous." He went quiet, calculating his next words. "Just take care. Please."

"So, you truly were sent to caution the Wolf, then."

"I am *choosing* to caution you. I'm not supposed to." Aereon studied James, contemplating him with a faint smile. "I love your coyness," he said, and his hand went back to James' for a moment. "I'm here to protect our world from the Simraashis. But I don't see why I can't help you out along the way as well." He leaned in, as if sharing a secret. "You very well could find a way to get your soul back *before* destroying the gates." He winked. His face was very close to James', their noses an inch away. The merman tensed and closed his eyes. "But be warned. It is not easy."

James closed his eyes too. Serenity washed over him, casting the Bite in a veil that soothed his body. The Bite had never been so subdued. Only when he was this close to the merman did he feel a sense of tranquility. "How can I find them?"

"Check your map again, Wolf," Aereon said and opened his eyes. "And be patient." His hand lingered at James' lips. James leaned towards Aereon's finger. A flowering feeling swirled in the void of his chest. A blend of pain and sweetness formed its own, unnamed sensation.

The air around them tightened. Before James could respond, Aereon spoke, a promise on his lips. "I will make sure that you reach this third talisman."

James' hand rushed to Aereon's cheek, but the merman caught it before it reached his skin. "Don't thank me," he said, his voice coming in a hot whisper. Aereon brushed his cheek against the captain's fingers, the merman's scaled skin grazing the tips of James' flesh. "Remember, don't let the Shadows get all the talismans. And by Shadows, that includes their proxy, the Commodore. Help me safeguard my home from them, and I will help you get your soul back."

Aereon lowered James' hand, indecisive.

James gave Aereon's hand a light squeeze rather than allow the merman to release him. "I will do everything I can. I swear to you and the Rose."

The two leaned close, their foreheads almost touching. Aereon smiled, and James could see a collection of constellations in the merman's eyes. Aereon brushed his hand along James' cheek one more time. He slowly sank downward as his fountain drained into the ocean, his fingers sliding below James' chin.

"Where are you going?" James leaned toward him.

"Back home." His siren voice hovered over the waters. "I have to attend to my duties."

"When will I see you again?" James called out, leaning out at a dangerous angle over the railing. The waters around Aereon whipped and churned as he descended, the sea behaving as though a storm were brewing.

Aereon hummed, his voice a haunting echo over the water. "Very soon, dear Wolf." His head lingered over the sea for a moment before he winked and disappeared into the black waters.

James stayed at the railing for a while, engulfed in the void of the night and silence of the sea. Eventually, the Rose sent down a rope and slowly brought him back to a safe distance from the edge.

He heard scurrying below deck and the squeak of the hatch door.

Mendez's voice came from behind him. "Captain?"

13

James

Day of the Dead

"Where are your boots?" Charles asked as James turned to face his crew.

The sun began to peak above the horizon, casting strings of golden light on the Rose's wood. "I think we finally have a heading," James said, a smile blooming on his face. He ran to his cabin, and his crew exchanged glances.

"Welp," Thomas said. "I'll go get us something to celebrate with." They head back below deck. Mendez and Charles followed their captain.

"James?" Charles entered his captain's cabin. His captain was scrambling through his papers and charts at the table, deeply focused, almost frenzied. Charles walked closer and crossed his arms. "Care to explain?"

James continued to rummage through his papers, knocking over his chair in his pursuits as he circled the large table.

Mendez frowned. "I thought you didn't like messing with your charts, captain."

His captain finally found the map he'd been looking for, and his smile grew wide when he gazed upon it. A smile that his crew had never seen him sport.

"Mm," Mendez said, as if put off. "That's new."

"It is!" James beamed, lifting the map. A shining scar shone across its surface as shapes began to materialize.

"I meant that smile," Mendez added.

Thomas re-entered the cabin, two cups and a plate in their hands. They paid no heed to the map and charts and directly made for their captain's table, setting down the plates, but not the cups. "Now eat."

James surveyed the fruits and oats. "What about the wine?" he turned to Thomas.

They waved a cup of date wine in front of James, who gave it a quick sniff. James reached for it, but Thomas drew it away. "Water first." They set a cup to the table.

James drew in a breath as he set his chair upright. He took a seat and reached for the water and fruit.

"Never thought I'd see you in a stubble," Charles mused as James drained the cup of water. Charles took a seat beside him, Mendez and Thomas following.

"All in good time, Charles," James said, setting his cup down.

The Rose was still anchored, and James could feel her charged with desire to sail in a new direction. His thirst was quenched, and he hardly noticed how hungry he was until he'd nearly finished the fruit and oats that Thomas had prepared. "Thank you, Thomas," James said.

"*De rien*, captain."

"Wine?" he turned to the ship cook, his eyes almost pleading.

Thomas slid the cup to their captain, a satisfied smirk on their face. James took a swing and pointed to the marks that were now at the top left of the map.

"Those letters kept shifting and made no sense at all," he said, and ran a hand over the paper, smoothing it against the surface of the table. "Finally, they settled. I think we're close." The map's glowing surface reached a peak and finally dimmed.

As the light settled, marks shimmered in its center, as though the light burned those shapes into place.

James leaned close, eager to decipher their new riddle. "What letters are these?" he muttered to himself, sifting through his journals.

Thomas shifted in their seat, leaning in to take a closer look. "I know this sounds silly." They pointed to the shimmering shapes. "But this looks like a skull to me. And that," they pointed to another mark, "that looks like bread."

Silence fell in the cabin as they looked between Thomas and the map. Flustered at the attention, Thomas hunched over.

"They're right," Charles said. "What's the date today?" His crewmates turned and blinked at him.

"October 29th," James responded.

"How far is a course from here to Mexico?" Charles asked.

The Rose creaked, and James listened. "A few days. Three, tops." He frowned as the puzzle pieces fit together. "Bread and skulls," he grinned, turning to Thomas. "Day of the Dead."

At those words, Mendez sifted through the chaos of papers on James' table, searching for the relevant charts of Central America. A string of new symbols appeared in place of the skull and bread. James stroked the new markings. He felt a thrum within them, like the map had something hidden between the fibers of the old paper. "This symbol here and here," he pointed to them, "look like the letter S if you put them together."

"This and this look like an E." Mendez flicked his finger between the two lexigrams. They shivered in their place when Mendez lifted his hand.

"Do that again," James said.

158

Mendez put his fingers over the letters and moved his hand. The letters followed as if Mendez's fingers had commanded it. Thomas took another three symbols and moved them together. They formed a broken, but very distinctive W shape. James did the same to four more shapes and they formed the letter N.

"NEWS?" Mendez said.

Charles crossed his arms. "Or… North, South, East and West."

"Now we're getting somewhere!" James exclaimed. He moved the letters to the top right. The map glowed again, and shapes materialized over the faded paper.

The Rose swayed starboard, and a chart fell from the pile that Mendez had gathered, the left corner of the paper aligning with the center of the map. It responded in kind and shone brighter, the map's light bleeding through the chart, illuminating shapes that overlapped between the two papers. Thomas adjusted the parchments over each other so that a clear shape aligned between the map and the chart. The skull and bread made their next destination crystal clear.

Mendez turned the atlas to his crew. "There," he said.

James leaned over his seat. "Veracruz."

14

Charles

I'll stay however long you need

"So, captain," Thomas said, "where do you usually resupply?"

"There are scattered outposts in the Atlantic. And some in the Mediterranean." James took a sip of wine, stepping out of his cabin. "But the one that has the best supplies is Thieves' Den." Charles raised an eyebrow at that, and James continued. "Best smuggled goods by far. Especially this time of year."

"What do you have for meat?" Thomas asked.

"I don't know. Just salted pork." James shifted as he headed to the helm.

"That'll have to do. But you'll need variety," Thomas pointed out. "Next time we reach the Devil's Trap, we'll need flour, peas, chickpeas and definitely some salted beef."

"Whatever you need." James smiled behind the helm. "You're the master cook on the Silver Rose."

"And rum," Mendez added. "More rum."

Charles' attention slipped away from his crew and captain. His mind trapezed back to the experiences of the two years he had spent at sea before finally arriving in the Devil's Trap. Fishing ships, pirate ships, navy ships, trade ships. Ropes, sloppy dinners, hard tack, harder tack. Uncomfortable sleeping quarters, lashes, cuts, letters to home, a broken heart, and stories abound. Lots and lots of stories.

He finished his ship work absent-mindedly before he went below deck and sat alone in his hammock; the first hammock that his body felt comfortable in. But his mind tossed in this hammock more than any other.

Charles was afraid that these stories were true. Even more afraid that they weren't. Afraid that he would finish his job. More afraid that he wouldn't. Afraid that James would hurt him. More afraid that Charles would hurt his captain and his Rose.

Mendez's hearty laugh pulled Charles from his thoughts. Thomas and Mendez came down the hatch, Thomas' hand around Mendez's shoulder, laughter bouncing between them as they headed to their sleeping quarters.

"Goodnight, Charles," Mendez said, lying down under his covers.

"*Bon nuit*!" Thomas added.

"Hmm," Charles acknowledged.

Within an hour, Thomas and Mendez were deeply asleep.

Charles did not. He had been sitting with his back to the mast, his arms around his knees. James was right. They were getting close. But the closer Charles got, the more weight his job carried.

The Silver Rose's creaks were low in their tune below deck. A creak came, another rumble followed, almost as though she was humming.

He hopped quietly off his hammock, wore his red vest and headed up deck. There was a slight chill. The Rose sailed ever onward, her helm unmanned. They would be in their next destination in no time at all.

Charles shambled to the starboard railing and stood by a lamp, close to the bow. It shone brighter for him, a subtle heat radiating from it and warming Charles' cheeks.

"You look wonderful tonight." The words escaped his mouth before he could think of them, and her lamp turned a red hue. He tried to face the lamp's light, but he couldn't. It wasn't the brightness of the light, but the brightness of the Rose's life that made his very soul feel small. His gaze fanned from the sea, to the speckled night sky, to the Rose's masts and wood. "Aren't you tired? Do you need to sleep, or something? I don't know. *Do you even sleep?*"

Her hull groaned softly beneath his boots.

I do not need sleep.

He nodded.

Then frowned.

He stared at her lamp, as if looking for the Rose's eyes. "I—I can hear you!" Charles said under his breath. "I can hear you?"

You can.

He glanced behind him, expecting his captain.

He's in his cabin. Sleeping. This is no ambush, Charles. I am speaking with you.

Her shrouds clattered and Charles followed the sound of her voice as the creaks reached his hands on the railing. "H— how? Does he know?"

I will tell him. I tell him everything.

He swallowed. "Why are you speaking to me? Why now?" He let go of her railing and stepped back, afraid that she would hurt him. There was a grinding and snapping sound that came from her bowsprit, drawing his attention. The figurehead was moving, rose vines cracking and popping as the wood extended itself, blossoming in his direction.

I am speaking with you because I need to know. Her vines approached Charles as she spoke. It curled, facing him, swelling at the apical bud. A wooden rose bloomed, and thorns popped out of its stem. ***How long do you plan to stay aboard?***

He blinked. What a specific question. Charles drew a slow breath, calculating his words. "As long as you'll allow me."

Her floorboards clicked and creaked, and her main rose twirled slowly, as if contemplating his answer. *Be more specific. How long?*

"Why does it matter to you?"

Because, dear Charles, the rose twisted and extended again, twirling around Charles' shoulder. The thorns were not blunt, and they nipped at his collar. *I need you here.* The rose faced him as it bent around his shoulder, the wooden petals a perfect lie, the thorns hiding a biting truth that he ached to know. *Tell me, what do the stories tell you of the Bite?*

"I know it consumes its host," he said. "Eats them up from the inside out."

And you know that I have a strong interest in preventing that fate from befalling Giacobbo, right?

He nodded, his cheek lightly brushing against her petals.

Do you know what slows it down?

"I'm afraid I do not."

The rose vine unfurled itself from Charles' shoulder and returned to the railing, still facing him. *Companionship. Connection.* Axillary buds bloomed, small and beautiful. *A crew. Like you.*

"I suppose that remedies it, then."

No. Her voice swirled through the wooden rose, ricocheting within the petals and reaching Charles like waves on a shore. He was listening intently.

This crew is only a temporary remedy. It will consume him. I can sense it.

He frowned. "You can?"

Every inch of it that grows, an inch of him shrinks.

One thought ambushed his mind. *What if it consumes him before I finish the job?* The words escaped him without thought. "How long does he have?"

I am unsure. But you, the rose perked up, her petals fanning in a way wood should not, ***this crew, this company. It slows it down. I've been sensing it since you've arrived.***

So, she needs me and the crew.

You see why I asked how long you'll stay? Her voice was pensive, the petals almost wilting and the small buds at her stem shrank back.

"You need us to save him?" Charles asked.

The only way to truly save him is to get his soul back. For that to happen, I need to get to the talismans. Her vines slithered back to the bowsprit, her wood creaking as the flower nestled itself back within her figurehead. ***He's all I've got left.***

Her words hung in the air for a moment. His heart sank, his throat dried.

She creaked once more, and left Charles in silence. Sadness brewed within it, and the waters and wind made it simmer with choices. He rubbed her railing, felt every crack, fracture, dip, etch. Decisions billowed in his mind, but he had already made his choice.

His hand dropped to his thigh, unable to bear the weight of guilt. The lie on his lips felt like daggers. "I'll stay however long you need."

15

Anmar

He had to get out of here

Anmar rubbed the back of his aching neck and his nose wrinkled when the smell of fish irradiated from him. He groaned. Of course it was Max's stupid idea to stow away on a fishing ship from Pirates' Isle all the way to Veracruz. There were dozens of ships on the island that were bound here. But she chose that one. There were smuggling ships filled with spices. Ships carrying textiles, carpets, swords even. Fish-free ships. Anmar didn't even mind stowing away on a pirate ship. Though these vessels weren't any better than smugglers and illicit traders, they at least didn't smell like a thousand barrels of rot and salt.

He dragged along the harbor, trailing behind Max and Edward and pulled out the map. Max had trusted Anmar with the map as they stowed away from the fishing ship and approached Veracruz. He had played his cards well and earned her trust, just for a little longer. Long enough for Anmar for find the Silver Rose and leave. He hoped.

It was dusk and they found themselves walking amidst a celebration. Light quivered behind shops, like ghosts over a graveyard, the smell of bread, sugar and pastries hovering over them. The cemetery next to them was adorned with food, pastries, clothes, toys. It was the Day of the Dead.

"What's this all about?" Max asked. She had very few redeeming qualities, but Anmar was grateful that Max was in possession of the ones she wielded with such gusto. One quality was her undying love for celebration.

"Can we please follow the map, Max?" Anmar said to her.

"All right, all right," she replied.

"Anything new?" Edward asked. He peered over Anmar's shoulder. The map didn't say much. Its surface had shifted again the moment they were on the fishing ship. It now had a light pulsing out of its left corner, and a line that always pointed toward the cemetery, however they turned it.

"Why would it bring us here?" Edward asked, disturbed. They entered the gateway and walked between the headstones and pastries, lights and musicians.

The Rose would be here any moment, or so Anmar hoped. He just needed to get to where the map wanted first. She could be a more permanent home to him, and the crew a kinder, more permanent family. Especially because Mendez was there. At least he hoped. The map blurred in front of his eyes as he played and replayed scenarios in his head of taking the key, boarding the Rose, and leaving Max and Edward behind forever.

"Oh, bread!" Max cheered. Her voice snapped Anmar back to the map. They continued between gravestones, the dirt beneath them lush with a recent rain. Max's swift and quiet hand snatched a loaf. Among the ongoers and festivities, Max only looked like a participant.

"Oh, necklaces too," she mused, reaching a sly hand over a gravestone.

"Don't—" Anmar began, but Max had already pocketed a necklace from an altar. "Have respect, Max," Anmar said quietly, "people are commemorating their dead."

"Ah, you lot don't know how to party," Max waved her hand in the air.

Anmar rolled his eyes. Spirits of the dead, celebration, bread, and sugar mixed into the air around them and wove a dance in the chilly November night. Festivities made Max seemingly an entirely different person. Most of the time she was tense and angry. But celebrations and parties loosened her immediately. That was why Pirates' Isle remained one of the best places to be, if he had to be around her.

"Back to the map," Anmar said to himself.

"You lot need to let go. We're going to be rich," Max said. "Party a little."

"We didn't find what Edenton needs yet." Edward pronounced his words very clearly.

It was hard enough to keep them on the right track, and now Max was inspecting every gravestone and altar on her path. "We're going to be rich," Max repeated. "And we're going to have our own ship and crew."

"Not a chance in hell I'm joining," Edward grumbled.

Max shoved him. "Oh, come on!"

"Will you help me read this thing!" Anmar snapped. He immediately shrank back, and if it wasn't for the festival's lively music and chatter that wafted even into the confines of the graveyard, he would've disturbed the peace of the dead. But truthfully, he was more afraid of disturbing the peace of Max. He gulped, but he was relieved when Max and Edward leaned behind him to examine the map.

"What's this supposed to mean?" Max said over Anmar's shoulder and pointed to the light on the map.

Anmar twitched at his ear. "I don't know. The pulsing light might mean we're close. But I don't know where."

The celebration pulled their attention from the mystery of the map to the mystery of the dead. They followed the music around the cemetery and found somewhere to sit, under a hulking tree and dominoes of tombstones adorned with flowers and belongings. The pulsing of the map's light continued at the same frequency.

"Do you think Edenton's lying to us?" Edward asked.

"No." Max shook her head. She examined a ring she stole along the way. "Did you see his quarters? The man's mad for treasure. He'll do anything for it."

"And what about that Ginysis and Alexandra?" Edward asked again. Neither looked at each other. The festival music shifted into something calm and steady, ominous but cheerful.

Max lifted an eyebrow and slipped the ring into her index finger. The festival lights flickered against the aged ring and reflected in her eyes. "We will be *regrouping* with these two in the Trap before we report to Edenton, eh?" Max said, emphasizing the word. She eyed the ring some more. "We'll make sure those two are dealt with. There are lots of lies we can tell Edenton about what happened to them."

"If Mendez doesn't find it first," Edward grumbled.

Anmar lifted his shoulders, bracing himself against Max's incoming wrath.

"Mendez will be dead long before he reaches it," Max said, her face suddenly stern. "And if he's not, I'll make sure he is."

Traitor. Anmar was a traitor. His gaze jumped from gravestone to gravestone, altar to altar. *Stop thinking about death!* he scolded himself.

"Are you hungry?" Max asked, a shift in her tone. "I'm hungry. There's so much bread and sweets. Let's go."

"What? No. Max," Anmar said, but before he could do anything, Max was off into the cemetery again. Anmar groaned heavily.

"Let's just get something to eat. We'll come back to this rubbish later," Edward said.

Anmar sighed and followed. Of course, they had no money. At least, not enough for all of them—so someone had to steal something. And that someone was Anmar.

He was fifteen, but people always mistook him for ten or twelve. He didn't care. He had a small frame, and could easily slip into any small crack, any door. He often wondered if that was the only reason Max kept him. He was good for thieving, and thieving was all she did.

The cemetery was full of festive foods; bread, sugar, candies, tamales. But Anmar was not going to steal from the dead, but he'd steal from the living any day of the week. Most of the time, they deserved it anyway.

He walked slowly between the altars and gravestones, Edward and Max behind him. Someone played the guitar at the cemetery entrance. Everything was in contrast. Laughter and cheerfulness warmed the chilly November air, and sugar and sweets mixed with skulls and tombstones. But Anmar didn't immerse himself in the contrast. He wondered if he was the only one like this in the celebration, unable to connect with joy and wonder. He tucked his hands into his pockets and tried to muster gratitude over guilt.

Outside the cemetery, the smell of food and fresh bread intensified. Anmar followed his nose to a bakery shop, pastries of every kind visible everywhere across its windows. He gestured for Max and Edward to the front door as he entered the back.

The door was cracked open, and he snuck through. Mendez would have helped him, but tonight Anmar had to do everything himself. Anmar hopped quietly, and peeked over each counter, inspecting the bakeries as though he had all the time in the world. He hoped no one heard a thud when he bumped his head against a cabinet in his search.

Quietly, he slipped as many goods as he could fit into his pockets, and used his shirt as a pouch for more. He popped one into his mouth. Anmar thought he'd give himself a little treat. Once a while couldn't hurt.

He turned back to the door to make his leave, but when he tried the knob he found it was locked.

"Fiddlesticks," he mumbled behind a full mouth. He reached for another pastry and took an angry bite.

Anmar peered into the rest of the shop, and when no one was in sight, he snuck forward. He moved a few steps when he found someone enter a side door, whistling and singing. Anmar could have pretended he was one of the celebrating children, but his pockets were full of sweets, and his shirt-pouch was conspicuous.

"I've told you countless times," Anmar said through clenched fists, "not to leave me while I'm doing my work." If Mendez was here, he could have helped him. But Anmar had to figure it out for himself.

He turned his head around, surveying the room. Around the corner in front of him, there was a bucket with a mop inside. How unsightly for a bakery.

Anmar had nothing on him but his sword and sweets. He attempted to lean forward, but the floorboards creaked in his direction and he pressed his back against the wall again. The person appeared to walk in his direction. He waited a minute then picked his least favorite pastry, aimed it at the mop and threw it. It hit perfectly. The mop fell with a clatter and the bucket spilled.

"*Dio mio.*" He heard the person say. "*Antonio?*"

Anmar held his breath while the person walked over to the mop. He waited for him to kneel down and then made a mad dash for the front door.

When he finally was outside, he ran into Edward who was walking toward the bakery, the sweets and food squished against their clothes and faces.

"Where the hell were you?" Anmar screamed, wiping the sugar and crumbled sweets off his face.

"I came to get the back door for you. And Max found her food," Edward said.

Anmar turned his head to Max and found her standing with what looked like one-third of a triangle in her hand.

"Look what I found," Max said, waving it. Anmar could barely make her words as her mouth was so full.

Anmar stood, brushing the demolished bakeries off his clothes as Max pocketed the odd jewelry.

"Where did you get that?" Anmar asked.

"The bread? You took too long, so I just took from the cemet—"

"I mean the piece," Anmar said. He took a breath and continued. "Don't—don't answer that." His pocket felt a little warm, and he pulled the map out. As Max's hand moved near the map, it glowed warmer.

"Oh my God," Anmar said. "Look." He moved to the wall behind him and tilted the map toward candles. Max slowly pulled the piece away. The map dimmed. Then she put it closed. It grew brighter. She did it two more times and laughed. Max and

Anmar kept pulling the map and piece closer and away from each other, watching the map put on a light show under the candles.

"All right, we get it," Edward said. "We need the trinket."

Anmar examined the map. The left corner that pulsed earlier was now shining.

Now was Anmar's chance. The Silver Rose's crew should be here any time. All he needed to do was get the map out of Max's hands, without her knowing. Sleight of hand was in Anmar's wheelhouse, so it shouldn't be a problem, right?

"*Ladrón*! Come back!" Someone said in the direction of the bakery that Anmar just robbed.

"Someone was sloppy with his work," Max said, pointing a finger. She and Edward turned to run and handed Anmar half a loaf of sugary bread.

Anmar's eye twitched and he followed. He had to get out of here.

16

The Crew

I am not a pirate!

The voyage took the Silver Rose and her crew to Veracruz, and they found themselves in the midst of a celebration.

As they walked past the harbor, Mendez noticed the Spanish flag that luffed on top the buildings. "I don't like this place," he said, shifting his gaze. "Too many Spanish soldiers." He and his group had caused loads of trouble back in Spain, and guards might recognize him, by name and by crime.

"They won't be able to spot you, Mendez," Thomas reassured him. "They're probably here because of the celebration." Thomas turned their attention to the sound of music brewing deeper into the town. The crew stepped toward the distant strum of strings and shake of percussions. The rich aroma of fresh bread and sugar swirled in the air around them.

Mendez picked up the pace, making way toward shops and bakeries adorned with calaveras. "Good on the map to take us here during the Day of the Dead festival." People danced and sang, and laughter buzzed louder as they neared the cemetery.

"Looks like fun," Charles mused.

James grimaced. "Now's not the time for fun, we have to follow the map."

"There's always time to have fun," Mendez said with a wink, and Thomas nodded.

"Aereon did bring us here for a reason," James said, his pace slower than that of his crew.

"Come on, we won't take long." Charles leapt in front of James and walked backwards, meandering at a comfortable pace as he took in the sights. The festival's ebb and flow immersed them with corals of colors, masks, face paint. By the cemetery, the smell of sweets and the sound of melodies intensified.

"Come on, captain." Thomas nudged their captain's elbow. "Have a little fun."

"Are they—" Charles looked to the cemetery ahead of them.

"Decorating bread!" Thomas yelped. They clutched James' collar and shook their captain's shoulder. "*Mon dieu,* look at them!" they shrieked as they dashed towards the stand.

"Fine, just the pastries and then we move forward," James said, faintly exasperated, and followed Thomas.

"Promise?" Charles lightly punched his captain's shoulder, who gave a nonchalant nod. He pulled the map out and gave it a quick scan.

"Can't we just enjoy our time just for a moment?" Charles asked, pulling James' attention away from the map.

Unable to focus his attention on the map among the captivating music and the aroma of bread, James sighed. "I suppose we can," he said and put the map back in his pocket.

Thomas joined in with decorating. The shopkeep under the tent moved aside like he was making way for the sugar and bread's rightful majesty.

People gathered and decorated their own loaves, as children ate tiny bites, their mouths and noses covered with flecks of sugar. Thomas decorated their own and bit into one, sugar puffing over their cheeks.

Mendez reached for a loaf but paused when he spotted a familiar satchel among the crowd by the cemetery. Leathery, with a strip of red on its seam. He looked closer and found a cutlass, the hilt a striking orange. He looked to its owner's shoes. Beige and black. That could only mean one thing. He looked to the woman's right. Sure enough, there he stood. Red hair tied back, mahogany jacket, deep blue gloves. Ginysis.

"Oh no," Mendez gasped. He grabbed James' and Charles' collars and raised his shoulders, eyes widening. They both frowned at him.

"What is it now?" Charles grumbled under his breath.

"Behind us. By the cemetery," Mendez whispered, his voice barely audible through the festivities.

"What's going on?" James asked.

"Contractors. They were working with Max and her employer," Mendez whispered.

"Who?" Charles said.

"I'll explain later! Right now, we need to find the key and get out of—" he glanced behind him and let out a small shriek before he scurried behind James and Charles. The two turned around, confused.

Thomas soon rejoined their crewmates, offering them the bread they'd decorated. "Where's Mendez?"

Charles shook his head and shrugged. "Hiding behind us."

"It's not that scary," Thomas said. "It's just Day of the Dead. We're supposed to be celebrating."

Mendez tugged at James' back. "I have a bad feeling about this. We should probably get going."

"Is he all right?" someone asked beside them. It was not the Spaniard's voice. It was a Scottish accent.

James and Charles turned to the source of the voice, and Mendez pivoted to stay behind his captain and shipmate. They faced the figure. Red hair pulled back, bread in his ungloved hand. His satcheled friend held two pastries, one half-eaten and the other still steaming hot.

"Oh, he's fine. Just a little spooked," Charles said.

"What brings you—" the man turned to see who was behind James then returned to his position, "—four here."

"We thought we'd make port. See what comes of it," James said. "It's been a long journey."

"Well, you made port in just the right time!" the man exclaimed. "Enjoy your—" He stopped and squinted behind the two. James and Charles smiled as naturally as they could. "Don't I know you from somewhere?" the man said, peeking behind Charles a little. Charles stretched his arm and shoulder out a little and shook his head.

The woman raised an eyebrow and took a bite and casually walked behind James and Charles. Mendez shrank away.

"Santiago," the woman said, not too brightly.

"Alexandra!" Mendez peeked his head out. "Fancy finding you here," he said with a smile.

"How's the hunt going?" the man asked.

"You know what Ginysis, I gave that life up," Mendez said, he slowly emerged behind James and Charles' backs.

"Don't play stupid, Mendez," Alexandra retorted.

"Where's Max and Ed?" the man said. "And where's that young man?"

"I wouldn't know. Although it would be nice if you helped me look for—" Mendez started. He scanned the area around him, and in that moment, he spotted familiar and not very welcome faces exiting the cemetery. Another small shriek escaped him and Mendez hid behind James and Charles again.

"What's the matter with him?" Ginysis said. "I know it's the Day of the Dead, but can't you…" He turned around to see. Max's gaze locked onto the six and her tread quickened.

"There you are," Max called out under the cemetery gate.

"Time to go," James said and dashed in the opposite direction. Thomas stuffed the bread in their pocket and ran, Charles and Mendez followed.

"Mendez!" Alexandra shouted, "I saw the key. Come back here!" Drawing her sword, she and Ginysis ran after them.

Thomas presented their crewmates with their own loaves of bread as they ran. Charles and Mendez didn't hesitate to take a handful from Thomas' hold.

"Don't mind if I do." Charles brought it to his mouth. All four of them ran, kicking little clouds of dust behind their boots. The festivalgoers didn't pay their haste any heed as they ran through the still-playing drums and flowing colors.

"Friends of yours?" Thomas panted, looking behind.

Charles shook his head, chewing on bread. "Uh-ah."

"*Oye!*" a performer shouted at Mendez as he tipped over the man's guitar set.

"Hey, I've always wanted one of those!" Mendez snatched a small guitar that miraculously survived the crew's stampede.

"Hurry!" James called out to him. Mendez jumped over the battered wood and flung strings.

"How did they get here?" James said under his breath, vexed. They rounded a corner and onto the paved paths.

"They must have figured it out from the other half of the map," Charles said. "Mendez!" He frowned at him.

"Oh, be quiet and run, Charles," Mendez huffed.

Alexandra and Ginysis cut a corner in front of them, swords unsheathed, and the crew stumbled to a halt.

Charles caught his breath, the air coarse in his dry throat. "Oh, come on, we don't want any trouble."

"Just hand us the key, and we'll be through," Ginysis said.

"No," Mendez said. He spotted Spanish guards marching toward the chaos. He shoved James, Charles, and Thomas aside, barely evading a bullet that whistled by. They ran ahead, away from the guards, Alexandra and Ginysis disappearing in the opposite direction of them. The four didn't get far before Mendez thudded into Max's big frame as they rounded a corner with an audible grunt.

"There you are," Max grumbled and snatched him by his hair.

Thomas elbowed Max in her side. "Get your hands off him!"

Max heaved and Mendez fell from her grip, his bandana crooked sideways. Charles helped Mendez up and they hastened to run.

"I think this belongs to us," James said and took Max's part of the key. He put it in his pocket and made for his crew. "I have the key," James shouted as they all ran, their legs pumping and their hearts pounding.

"Good. Now to get to the Rose," Charles panted.

It was too crowded, and the path to the harbor was now blocked with people dancing and guards surveying the area, arms at the ready.

James unsheathed his sword and turned, barely blocking Alexandra's blow in time. He glanced around for his crew, but they were busy with Max.

"Good reflexes." Alexandra lightly swung her sword away. "Been a long journey, eh?"

"Believe me, it's been one hell of a journey," James said, blocking her brisk attack.

"Embroidery, necklace," Alexandra mused. "You look a little familiar."

James tucked the necklace in his shirt and parried Alexandra's incoming blow.

"Yes, you look a little too familiar," Alexandra continued. She parried James' attack and delivered another. "James Wolf."

He gnashed his teeth and blocked her attacks, unwilling to give her any more information.

"Only silence now, huh?" Her onslaught of blows never flagged. "Stories in the Trap do mention that you're a bit… prickly."

"The stories mention a lot of things," he said.

"The latest stories say you're on the hunt for something," she smirked and smoothly deflected James' next move. "He's getting a little closer, isn't he? The… Commodore," she said slowly, stretching the word.

James' hand wavered and he nearly missed her next attack. He barely blocked it in time and brought the two's arms above their heads, their gazes locked. Music dimmed in his ears. Dusk was nearing and brought darkness with it. The Bite hungered in James' chest.

"Ahh," she said. "So *you're* James Wolf. I never thought I'd meet you."

"What of it?"

"Oh, the stories that wander," she said. Their blades swung and separated momentarily. "I'd love to know more," she said as their swords met again in another strike.

The sun dipped below the city's jagged horizon, and shadows grew longer across the ground, stretching toward James. Her words lingered in his mind, quickening his breath.

"Surely we can reach an accord," Alexandra said, "isn't that what pirates do?"

"I am not a pirate!" James bellowed. His head seethed like the inside of a furnace. If he hated anything more than the Ordinance, it was pirates. There was no difference between them. To one, he lost the Rose and his father, to the other he lost his mother.

The Bite engulfed his mind, and he wanted nothing more than to strike something down and sate his fury.

"You've wandered and plundered the seas. You even dress like one," Alexandra taunted.

James grunted and aimed for her shoulder. "I don't dress like a pirate."

Alexandra parried his blow and their crossed swords traveled about their heads. She smiled, like she knew something James didn't.

Something ripped the key out of James' hand, and James whirled to see Ginysis.

"No!" James slashed with his sword towards him. "I need that!"

"Cheers, love," Ginysis chuckled as he and Alexandra ran off towards a stone bridge behind James.

He ran after them, but he lost them in the crowd. James looked for his crew but they were swarmed with guards.

"*Merde*," he grunted and turned to help them. He slashed a guard across the back and swept the man's legs out from under him.

"Hey," Charles said to his captain, wiping blood off his lip. "I had this under control."

"Clearly," James remarked dryly and headed to the next guard.

Mendez tripped over and fell to the ground, his guitar sliding in front of him. As the guitar came to a stop, Mendez saw Alexandra and Ginysis whiz by him. He reached out just in time to grab one of Ginysis's ankles and trip him to the ground, the key slipping out of his hand.

Mendez scooped up the key as he scampered by. "Ha ha!"

Ginysis regained his footing with an inarticulate sound of rage, sword in his hand, and darted at Mendez, who screamed and bolted away.

"*Lo siento amigo*," he cried and left his guitar behind.

"Gin, behind you!" Alexandra shouted. The remaining group of guards who surrounded the Silver Rose's crew came to fight the contractor duo.

"The Blue Fox and runaway ward. The Crown's been looking for you," a guard said.

Ginysis scoffed. "How many times do we have to do this?"

"This will be the last time, I assure you," the lead officer said as guards drew closer in a ring around them. For once, the duo and the Rose's crew had to cooperate.

Gin landed a dagger into the lead officer's shoulder before turning to another guard. Charles slashed another behind Thomas before the guard reached them.

"*Merci*," Thomas said to Charles, slaying one in the back.

"*De rien,* my friend," Charles replied, parrying a blow. Mendez cut down an oncoming officer before he reached Charles and Thomas.

Another guard swung Alexandra's sword out of hand and was ready to fire his musket. "Gin, my sword," she shouted. Ginysis whipped out a dagger and threw it, landing it in his chest.

Alexandra winked. "Thanks, dear."

Ginysis smiled and moved on to his next target.

"Told you we can reach an accord," Alexandra called out in James' direction. Ginysis chuckled, digging his dagger into a guard's neck as he loaded his musket.

James grunted, taking out his mounting fury on an officer with a wild slash in the back. "Don't get any ideas."

Something tugged on James' collar and thrust him to the bridge's wall.

"You're coming with us, Wolf," a guard said and cocked his bayonet. Thomas smashed a bottle into the officer's head before James forced his sword to his target's abdomen and kicked him to the ground.

"That's the last of them," Mendez yelled as he threw a guard over the bridge. The crew and the duo stopped mid-battle and stared at each other. An uneasy silence hung between them.

Mendez, who had the key in his hand, sprang and made it down the bridge. James, Thomas and Charles ran after him.

Ginysis threw a dagger. It missed their heads as they arched down the bridge. The two resumed their pursuit, but the crew was nowhere to be seen amidst the festival that had resumed.

"Damn it," Alexandra said.

James

The four walked toward the docks, catching their breaths. They moved against the festival's flow and kept their heading toward the harbor.

"Sorry about the guitar," Thomas said.

"It's all right." Mendez put his hands in his pockets and shrugged.

"Once we find the island, we'll get you all the guitars you could want in the world," Thomas offered.

Mendez grinned. "You'd better!"

James stayed quiet as his crew walked and spoke of things they would do after they find the island. Conversation passed over his head like clouds, unnoticed. *Guitars, family, food...*

Finally, the second part of the key was in his hands. Mitchell would soon be the one to beg him. The thought, that feeling, made his heart thump with ruthless fervor. His fingers tingled, and that feeling in his chest radiated into his throat. A hot yet cold sensation, heavy and constricting, surged in his head, casting his vision in a swirling gray smoke.

Gabrielle, music, drums, peppers, hats with feathers...

A plume of thoughts clouded his crew's words even further. The colors and sounds seemingly around him vanished like a cloud of smoke from a candle's flame. Then there was nothing but the thoughts and acrid tightness.

What does she know about the Commodore? Did I miss a lead? Why is she after the key? I certainly don't need any more people after the talismans, and I'm not a bloody pirate.

Is the crew going to leave after we find the island? What will I do to slow down the Bite? Even if I had a crew, it's no substitute. I need my soul back.

What if Mitchell gets to the island first? Is Aereon in danger? Maybe—

"James!"

He startled. "Mmm?" Sensation returned to him with abrupt clarity, and he made out his crew behind bushes and hanging branches of trees. They were gesturing for him to take cover with them. He made for the branches and hid, not knowing why.

"Spread out and find them!" he heard Max's voice shout out.

James drew his sword silently and waited. Behind the leaves and branches, Max, Edward and Anmar each took a direction.

Their skirmish was exhausting, and he didn't think his crew would be able to fight Max and Edward again. But he was ready. He could fight beyond the point of exhaustion when the Bite fed into his rage.

But he was so close to the harbor, so close to the Rose. He just needed to climb aboard, and he'll be a step ahead of the Commodore. Just one more piece of the key and he'll have the upper hand.

Footsteps drew nearer. Cautious, intent.

The crew held their breaths. James was read. Charles wobbled and fell on Mendez, who furiously whirred on him.

"Move over!" Mendez whispered forcefully.

"There's little space, how do you expect me to move?" Charles whispered back.

The two started arguing behind whispers. Thomas slapped their forehead with their palm.

James brought his sword inches from his face. "Shhh!" He shook it in front of his lips, miraculously escaping a cut.

The leaves suddenly cleared and Anmar appeared before the crew. The boy smiled, something relieved and innocent. James regarded him but didn't lower his sword, and Mendez parted his lips to speak.

"Anmar! Find anything?" Max's voice broke through.

Anmar shrank back and his smile dissolved. He turned his head to Max's voice, still keeping his gaze at the Rose's crew. He put his fingers to his lips and called back to her, "There's no one here."

Anmar let go of the leaves with a faint rustle, and the boy's footsteps dimmed with his retreat.

James lowered his sword, his shoulders tense, his heart heavy in his ribs.

17

The Con Artists

Shadows aren't that *bad*

"I searched. Couldn't find anyone," Alexandra said, rubbing her forehead and pulling out their half of the map. "It wouldn't change without the other half now."

She gave a deep exhale, a small puff of vapor dissipating as soon as it left her mouth and nose. The sun had set. It was the second day of the festival.

The two were under the stone bridge. Ginysis eyed the guitar that Mendez dropped, flicking a stick of red and applying it on the lips. The red-haired contractor walked to Alexandra and gave her a long kiss. She felt for Ginysis's hair tie and undid it. "You know you can be Virginia now," she said.

"I know." Virginia grinned. A breeze blew three strands on her face. She tucked the strands behind her ear and wiped the smudged red on the side of Alexandra's mouth.

"That's *the* James Wolf," Alexandra said.

"How can you be sure?" Virginia asked.

"Oh, I'm sure. Hates the Ordinance. Wants the talismans. Afraid of Shadows. Hates pirates. He's the Wolf alright."

Virginia's hands slid from her wife's shoulder to her wrists. Alexandra held her hand and looked to the ground in thought, digging her thumbnail into her forefinger under Virginia's grasp.

"I think," Virginia said, rubbing Alexandra's hand to relax, "we should check the harbor."

Alexandra nodded.

"And join their crew."

"What?" Alexandra twisted away, sliding her hand out of Virginia's. She shook her head stiffly. "No."

"Oh, come on!" Virginia protested. "You heard. He said he wasn't a pirate."

"That's not my point."

"Alex, please." She approached her, palms lifted. "We've come a long way for this. That's really the Wolf and the Silver Rose." She held Alexandra's hands again. "This might be our chance to finally get that bastard Elian."

Distant strings strummed and the smell of pastries thickened as bakers pulled fresh batches from their ovens. People lit their candles and lanterns, little flecks of orange and yellow lights materializing over the bridge's view.

Alexandra breathed in the aroma and frowned. "It's dangerous." She faced Virginia again. "Elian's Ordinance has had a bounty on us for years."

"All the more reason to join the Ordinance's worst enemy." Virginia's lips twitched into a smirk. "Besides. Mendez is there. He can help us. Or something."

"This is risky. I don't want both the Commodore and Elian after us."

"Then we kick their arses with the Wolf and the Rose on our side, Alex come on!" She huddled closer to Alexandra and reached for her cheek. "We can finally have our freedom."

"What about the Shadows?" Alexandra gazed into Virginia's eyes, concern laced with thought in her own.

"Shadows aren't *that* bad," Virginia said.

Alexandra's expression softened. She brushed a lock of red hair behind Virginia's ear. "Shadows aren't to be trifled with, dear. You know that."

Virginia lifted a brow. "But wouldn't it be fun?"

Alexandra gazed into her wife's eyes and saw her own reflection. A lock of red hair curled over Virginia's eyebrow, and Alexandra tucked the strand behind her ear. Her hair never stayed in place. Alexandra loved it. Virginia was always the one for fun, always the one for risks. That was the first quality that pulled Alexandra from her chambers to join Virginia in their nighttime soirees by the fountain.

"Alex, remember when we sat by the fountain?" Virginia cooed.

"Please don't go there." Alexandra's lips formed a reluctant smile. She always thought Virginia had an uncanny ability to sense what was on Alexandra's mind.

"Remember what we vowed?"

Embarrassingly, Alexandra's smile grew. The memory transported her to the fountain of *Chateaux Lucas*. She remembered Virginia's serenades, the time they stole in the gardens at night, away from Alexandra's ward, the courtesans, the servants, the officers. She was Ginysis, the court boy by day, Virginia the dreamer by night. Those nights were Alexandra's tiny breaths between splashes of empty, regal life.

The memories fragmented and reformed into the night she learned that her father had died. That her guardian had hidden this news from her. For weeks—months even—while he planned for her marriage to Elian, son of one of the most influential members of the Viennese Shadow Ordinance.

It was that night when Alexandra was torn apart. She would not have been reborn if not for Virginia's daring—and nearly fatal—plan to escape with her.

"We swore to allow ourselves to live. However ridiculous it got, we still had an oath to life." Virginia's voice brought her back to the moment.

"Oh, Ginny," she cupped her cheek. "You're always so risky."

Virginia gave her hand a kiss. "Risky is what got us together."

Alexandra took a deep breath. "Fine. Let's find them."

"Yes!" Virginia jumped. "Thank you!" She kissed her and picked up the guitar before grabbing her hand and bolting to the harbor.

The Silver Rose's crew walked in silence across the harbor.

Finally, Mendez spoke, concern lacing his words. "What's he planning?"

"I don't know. But what he did just saved us back there," James said.

Mendez glanced behind him, hoping to see a glimpse of the buy, but instead spotted the con artists catching up to him and the crew. "Ugh, let's get out of here quick, *amigos*."

"Wait. You dropped something." Virginia presented the guitar to Mendez.

"My guitar! I thought I lost it." He grabbed the instrument and strummed a swift little tune, the music shifting his spirit.

James frowned, studying the pair. "What's this supposed to be?"

"Let's call it a peace offering," Alexandra replied.

James gave her no heed and walked faster on the harbor, the crew following him. But Virginia intersected and held up her hands before the crew. "Look, we're sorry we were a bit…"

"Rash," Alexandra finished for Virginia and stood beside her.

Charles scoffed. "Rash is an understatement."

"We just want to get to the island," Virginia said. "Mendez, tell them."

James turned to Mendez. "You know them?"

Mendez frowned and aimed his guitar at her. "They were both with us when Max took the contracting job. Said Edenton needed as many contractors on this job as possible." He turned away, gripping his guitar tighter. "But you can count me out of it now." He held the instrument, ready to play another note but he paused. "Hang on, what happened to Genesis?"

"It's Ginysis," Virginia said. "The name's Virginia. But sometimes you can call me Ginysis." She adjusted her gloves and winked.

James fixed Alexandra with a glare. "This is more than just the contract, isn't it?"

Alexandra's gaze shifted, as though surveying the area for any more officers and guards. "Listen, you have a lead, and a ship, and we have some—" she looked for the right word, "—experience. Maybe we can help each other."

He rolled his eyes. "I've heard that one before," he said and took a step toward the Rose.

Alexandra followed him, her steps urgent. She held her hands in front of her, away from her sword. "You're not the only one whom the Ordinance is after. The Viennese Ordinance ambassador Elian has pursued me and Virginia for years."

"They're your problem. Not mine," James retorted, moving past her again.

"Still enmeshed with the Shadows?" Virginia's voice cut through the air.

That made him stop. The crew exchanged glances.

He turned to her, a frown tightening his forehead, his eyes narrowed in interest. Virginia was smirking, ambling to the captain. Alexandra seized the opportunity. "Over the years, I've learned much about the Shadow Glyphs. We can work together."

James' gaze flitted between the two. "And what makes you think I can trust you two?"

"The Bite, I'm sure you're intimately acquainted with it." Virginia had reached him and stopped two steps away from the captain of the Silver Rose, a challenge in her eyes. The captain's hand tightened in a fist, and he hid a wince. Virginia raised an eyebrow at that. She continued, her voice carrying an edge to it. "Perhaps we can help."

"Fine," he said through his teeth. He turned to Alexandra and pointed. "But don't call me a pirate again!"

"Fine," the two said in unison, ever so faintly wry.

The captain turned to his ship. "Welcome aboard."

18

Edward

That's it?

The little stone bridge had its share of stomps and strides that day. It had festivalgoers running across it, feathers dropped on it. Drums thundering over it, food spilled onto it. It had been slid over, run over, tread over. It had a guitar slide against it, daggers thrown across it, swords dancing above it. And now, it had Max and Edward arguing under it.

"Damn it!" Max rubbed her face with fury. When she had enough, she hacked with her sword at a bunch of unfortunate and indifferent bushes.

"I told you." Max rushed to Edward. "I told you to keep an eye on him. How can you let Anmar slip away on his own like that?" She rubbed her face furiously again before she continued in a blast of anger. "And Mendez! You had him. Why didn't you just—do something? Are you even listening to me?"

"I'm listening." Edward headed to a boulder and sat heavily. "All I hear is '*Edward you screwed up like you always do and*—I was too busy fighting and looking for the talisman, you idiot!" he snapped, his voice echoing under the stone bridge.

Max stood silently, anger eating at her words.

"You are an idiot, you know that, Max," Edward said. Max's face flushed red. She thumbed her chest and opened her mouth to speak, but Edward interrupted. "You're an idiot, that's what you are." His lip curled with open contempt and he crossed his arms. "Because of you, now we're really getting nowhere."

Max thumbed her chest. "I kept this group together."

Edward watched Max's face shift from anger to what seemed like sadness.

She rubbed the back of her neck. "I shouldn't have left him to scout alone. Who knows where he is now." Max ran her hand over her nose and mouth and turned her back to Edward. "We were supposed to finish the contract together," she said.

Edward looked to the ground, where Max's shadow met her boots, her undercut neck waxy under the dusk sun.

"We were supposed to finish off Alexandra and Ginysis or whatever and get the whole share for ourselves. We could have at least found the island together first," she finished, her arms slumping. She opened and closed her palms nervously. Edward watched.

Max was right. They were supposed to find the island first, get Edenton's whole share. But that was where Edward wanted to stop. He had no place in the ship and crew that Max envisioned. He was going to leave the group with whatever treasure he could fit into his pockets. He was going to go somewhere far away. Somewhere safe. Somewhere where he could be with Alicia.

Edward found it in him to pity Max. Pity her hope of using the treasure to buy a ship, make a name for her and her crew, this broken and shattering group.

"So what are you going to do now, *ringleader*?" Edward jeered, arms still crossed.

"We're not getting any closer to the island with no map." She whirled and swung her sword into a tree. The blade bit into wood and stuck.

"Gentlemen," a smooth voice said from behind Max.

Edward, still sitting with his arms crossed, leaned to his side to see this new intruder. The sun was setting, and the man stood right in the middle of the sun's disc, as if by design. But even with the bronze light behind him, Edward could still make out the man's tall, firm form, and his fine features.

He was well-dressed. Likely worked under the Royal Navy, or the Ordinance. His outfit spoke of it all. Collars up, cuffs rimmed with beautiful embroidery, a cutlass and a pistol on his clean and polished belt, and a golden pin affixed to his collar. The words *Lex Umbra* shimmered briefly within it. The shadow of his silhouette wore a cold yet magnetic smile, only just visible in the low light.

Edward scoffed. Any man looking like this, carrying himself with this air means trouble. "And who the hell are you supposed to be?" he asked.

"I see you're in a bit of a predicament," the man replied, eyeing Max's effectively discarded sword in the tree trunk.

"Yeah? And what do you care about it?" Max said rudely, turning toward their visitor.

"I am only here to help," the man responded to their cold and disgusted welcome.

"Oh, yeah?" Edward retorted. "We don't take help from people like you. Not anymore," he added, standing up. He was repelled by this man's presence. All of it. The prim posture, the tailored outline. Edward knew Max didn't trust this man either. At least they could agree on one thing, he supposed. The only reason they agreed to take Edenton's contract was because of his promising reward. Alas for the map. Behind the titles and embroidery, the man before them was a shell of a promise.

"I understand your reluctance." He stood firm. "But we can help each other."

"Oh?" Max shuffled loudly to him. "Pray tell. The first one double-crossed us. And what are you going to do? Promise us a one-way trip to the gallows?"

"I can help you find the island," the man said. "I see your first contract didn't end well. I can offer you a better one. Beat your competitors to it. And I assure you," he bowed his head slightly, "No tricks."

Edward couldn't suppress another scoff. No tricks. Always the same. 'No tricks' meant 'turn the other direction and walk away, preferably after slitting this man's throat.'

"Yeah, well, you heard Edward," Max said, her hair bouncing as she jerked her head at him. "We don't work with people like you." Max sauntered to the man's face. They both eyed each other. "Bugger off."

The man did a little hop. "Very well gentlemen. You've spoken." He put his hat back on and turned into the setting sun's direction.

He took two steps. And those two steps were enough for Edward to rethink. This reminded him of many moments that carried a promise with them. A promise that flew past him, like an autumn leaf on a windy day. Like that time he let Alicia fly in the wind. That day, she took two steps toward Hansel. Edward hadn't gone after her, asked her to perhaps not go where the wind took her. He watched her go with the richer, sweeter wind that was Hansel. While Edward, the dry, wretched wind stayed where wind never left.

This man may be a golden shell and hollow like the rest of them. But at least he had power. Perhaps even more power than the Silver Rose and her crew.

"Wait! Wait," Edward held out his hand. The man stopped in his walk.

Edward joined Max. They were truly far behind, nowhere near the island. James and his crew were—well a ship and a crew. Edward raised his eyebrows to Max and nodded in the man's direction. Max thought for a minute.

She rolled her eyes. "What do you want?"

The man turned to face them, a cool smile spreading across his features. It didn't reach his eyes.

"All I ask from you, gentlemen, is the key."

Max and Edward blinked at each other.

"That's it?" Edward asked uneasily. Just a worthless key? Was that the only cost to sweeten his wind?

The man held his smile and nodded a yes. He held out his left gloved hand. "Do we have a deal?"

Edward and Max exchanged glances. This man was Max's only chance to her own ship, and Edward's only chance to see Alicia.

Edward nodded and Max shook the man's hand.

19

Anmar

What are you?

Anmar sprinted and pushed against the festive people, almost hurting himself twice. He resisted every urge to look back. He wasn't leaving anything too precious behind. Max and Edward. Nothing good ever came from them.

He reached the harbor, and suddenly, everyone and everything around him dissolved. Nothing mattered. Not the people marching to and fro, not Max and Edward. The only thing that mattered was finding the Silver Rose.

She shouldn't be too hard to find, right? He searched between the masts and sails, flags and hulls, looking for a special figurehead, or sails with roses, perhaps. He took a few steps forward and looked around nervously when he spotted the captain.

"Fine." He heard James say. Anmar found a hiding place behind a barrel.

"But don't call me pirate again!"

"Fine."

"Welcome aboard."

The crew began to move toward a ship. The Silver Rose, no doubt! Anmar froze, his nails digging into the barrel's wood. He needed to approach them. And fast. But he studied their faces, and his strength dwindled.

He watched their boots board the Rose one by one. The captain stepped aboard first, then Santiago, followed by the blond pretty boy and a new crew member with a hat. Then Alexandra and Ginysis—

Just as the last foot fell upon her wood, Anmar saw the Rose's sails unfurl, and the sound of her cranking capstan and raising anchor seized his attention. The crew just arrived on the ship. Anmar stole a glance to her helm. It was turning away from port. Without a helmsman…

He sprang from behind the barrel and ran. The ship moved fast. Her gangplanks raised and the crew was in the middle of the deck, scattering. He reached the edge of the harbor, seawater before him. He searched for a way in. There was a window within jumping distance.

He took two steps back. The Rose's bow was heading portside, her rose figurehead disappearing behind her hull…

He ran and jumped.

Everything slowed down. His arm reached as far as it could towards the fabled Rose.

And he missed.

The boy fell into the water, the splash muffling sound around him. He moved his arms around, bubbles streamed and tickled his face. He opened his eyes. So much salt. But he made out the Rose's giant hull in the murky waters and swam to her.

Dusk cast Anmar in the ship's long shadow momentarily. But the shadow shifted away as the Rose cut through the water, moving fast.

No. No, no!

He moved his arms twice more before he felt something wrap around his right hand. Tight.

The water's current pushed against his skin as he was pulled forward. He panicked and splashed around, pulling out his knife. Suddenly, his neck jolted as a rope pulled him from the sea. He gasped for breath, water lashing his cheeks.

Some rope was wrapped around his arm. He must have caught something, or something caught him. He didn't know, but he held onto it strong as he swung lightly and—*thud!*

Wood. He hit wood. Anmar pushed himself away with his free arm… It was a ship. His eyes traced the few barnacles lodged on the hull and caught sight of the vine, petal and rose carvings that decorated the wood. The bow was barely visible, but he recognized the floral figurehead. The Rose!

Anmar twisted the rope around his wrist twice, and lodged his legs against the Rose's wood. He climbed until he reached a window, and tried to open it. Locked. Anmar looked behind him. The harbor wasn't within swimming distance anymore. No turning back now.

The might ship rumbled as she cut through the waters. Anmar adjusted his boots against her wood, held the rope tight and pushed himself away from the Rose. He readied himself as he came hurtling toward the window when something stopped him, the sudden change in his inertia drawing a choked breath from his chest.

Another rope had wrapped around his arm and wrenched him away from the window. The rope slithered down his arm and wrapped around his wrist, the sight freezing Anmar's breath in his throat. Fear and shock warred in his limbs, and he eventually drew his sword.

More frazzled lines twined around his sword's hilt, and he fought with the stubborn ropes that tried to twist his sword out of his hand. Bobbing along the ship's path in the waters, tied with snaking ropes, his grip was clumsy. He slashed anyway and cut his sword free of the rope. He aimed for the lines on his waist and cut it. Gravity took ahold of him, and he dangled by the arm and crashed against the ship's hull again, her damp wood scratching his cheek. Anmar adjusted his feet on the window platform and kicked at it. It shattered and he jumped inside, missing a slithering rope that came whipping for his ankles.

The boy rolled on the Silver Rose's floorboards, sucking in a shivering breath. Pulling himself from the ground, he coughed and blinked the salty waters out of his eyes.

Creaks and thuds echoed upstairs. He looked around for a hiding spot, fresh fear still obscuring his judgment. There was a cooking station, a pot, bags with beans, oats, neatly and oddly organized boxes of spices. Anmar was in the galley.

He rested his back against the hull and looked around, orienting himself and catching his breath. But his focus dissipated as he took in the Silver Rose's design. He listened to her. She creaked often, high and low, deep and croaky.

She was distracting, calming. He took a cautious step over her floorboards, and they creaked beneath him. He took another step. Another creak. Something moved in his peripheries, and he turned to it.

No one was there. The galley was still, pots and utensils swaying with the ship's movement. He continued and took another step, his breath shaky and quivering in his chest. Something growled and his hand flew to his mouth, covering his startled gasp, before he realized it was his own stomach grumbling. He rolled his eyes, tension tightening his shoulders as he made his way through the galley.

Something snatched at his foot, and the world tipped upside down as he hurtled onto the floorboards. He turned on one elbow and drew his sword, ready to face whoever had caught him.

But it was still only him and the empty galley. Anmar stood, his sword still in his hand, a shallow breath rattling his body.

"Diego?" The word escaped him in a flimsy whisper before he could even stop it. Wood and metal grated just as Anmar spoke Mendez's name. He whirled to the source of the sound, expecting Mendez behind him, ready to throw himself into the only person who he thought would show him mercy.

But there was no one.

"Hello?" he whispered again, failing to keep the growing fear out of his voice. The ship's wood rumbled again in response, fueling the boy's alarm.

He was deeply attuned to any sign of movement that he didn't notice the sound of a rolling barrel until it was too late.

Anmar stumbled out of the way but it caught up to him, and he ran in whatever open direction he saw.

He made his way out of the galley, hoping that the commotion below deck did not alert the crew. The barrel was catching up to him, and he turned a corner, out of the galley. "Oh no," he panted when he registered where he was.

He came to a jarring halt, and the barrel crashed against him, sending him sprawling inside an open brig. Anmar rolled and adjusted his footing, aiming to jump out of the brig.

Something moved in his peripheries again, but this time he caught it, slashing his sword in its direction. It was a rope, and he had cut short before it reached his arm. But another wrapped itself around his sword and flung it out of hand. It collided with the brig's metal, ringing wildly.

The barrel that had stopped rolled again and tossed him further into the brig. He stumbled and lost his footing, falling face-first onto the harsh wood.

He rolled onto his back, hoisting himself upright on his elbows just in time to see the brig door rattle shut. Baffled and afraid, he stared at the cell's ringing metal. The creaking and groaning of wood intensified, closing in on him from every direction of the prison cell.

"What *are* you?" he choked out, a scream lodged in his throat, crawling deeper into his cell. He pushed himself against the wall and huddled his knees to himself. Tears burned in his eyes.

The rumbling and groaning escalated, but at its peak, the creaking softened.

Then stopped.

It was quiet, the only sound came from the muffled gurgling of the ocean's water against the ship's hull. The creaking shifted direction. It carried itself across the cell, toward the door. The metal squeaked and it opened slowly. Blinking at it, once, twice, he stood warily. She creaked underneath his boots toward the open door.

"You—you're letting me out?"

She creaked again at the door. Shaking steps took Anmar outside the cell. She creaked some more, softly this time, in one direction. He turned to the direction of the creak. A bag of hard tack and another of dried apricots tipped towards him. He approached cautiously. He picked a biscuit and an apricot. She creaked. He ate a bite.

The ship tilted gently left and right. Were they out in the open already? He hopped to a few bags of goods, shifting his gaze to the stairs behind him. The Rose creaked across the galley's floorboards and groaned towards her starboard. A rumble gave a dull hum in the basin of wood and salty air.

He peeked over the bags. Beans, oatmeal, tack. Uncooked rice, a small amount of salted beef. More tack. Walnuts, pistachios, almonds, raisins. Cardamom, nutmeg and tea. Lots and lots of tea. He bit his lip and stole a quick look to the stairs. No one there. No long shadows on the stairs, no footsteps.

The Rose tilted again and another bag tipped over to Anmar's feet. More biscuits. Those looked softer. And tastier. He turned around and checked for anyone. No one was there. The Rose creaked and tilted again. A circular biscuit rolled from the bag and landed near Anmar's hand. He picked it up and took a bite. Not too terribly hard. Flaky. Slight sweet aftertaste.

He scratched a biting itch on his arm and took off his wet shirt. Max had stolen the shirt on his back for him, once upon a time. He took another feeble bite, but he couldn't finish the biscuit. He threw it forcefully to his side and it broke into two uneven pieces. The mighty ship creaked again, softly. He looked around him.

"What have I done?" Anmar whispered through tears. He wrapped his arms around his knees and began to cry.

20

James

That's why I hate pirates

"The infamous Captain Wolf," Alexandra said, "Tell us more."

Thomas, Charles and Mendez exchanged anticipated glances. They leaned toward the table and gave their captain *the gaze*. James knew that gaze. It was an unmistakable you–have–to–talk gaze. He clenched his jaw, the words trapped in his mouth.

"All right, I'll make this easier," Virginia said, sitting back in her chair at the captain's table. "We'll ask you questions, and you elaborate. How are the houses in the Devil's Trap?"

"Ginny!" Alexandra turned to her, appalled.

"What? I'm only asking?"

"We won't be living there."

"You never know!"

"We're not living with pirates, Gin."

"We've sailed with them before, living in the Trap wouldn't be any different."

"Well, the houses aren't too terrible. Some islands have a nice view and good supplies," James replied. "But I'm with Alexandra on this one. I wouldn't live on an island full of pirates."

"All right, I'll play this game." Alexandra leaned over her seat. "Did you start the blockade in the Mediterranean?"

"That was three years ago!" James countered.

Alexandra laughed. "So you did!"

Charles' mouth dropped and he let out a laugh. He looked to Thomas, who put their face to their palm and smirked, while Mendez gave a wide grin.

"No, I didn't," James conceded. "Well, yes. Not entirely my fault!" He shifted in his seat, adjusting his arm on the armrest. "I was on my way out of Spain." His gaze flicked in the direction of the drawer.

That trip had been all for an alleged talisman that wasn't even there. He breathed deeply and continued. "There was a pirate ship to my south and the Spanish Ordinance to my north. So the Rose and I opened fire on the Ordinance ship, alerted the pirate ship to it, and sailed."

James remembered that day, and it sent a small rush of triumph in his heart. Although there was no talisman in Spain, he still got a little joy out of watching the Ordinance and pirates blow holes in each other's ships. "I didn't know it would cause a blockade. What was I to do?"

"All right, how about this," Virginia started, "Why did you sell your soul to the Shadows?"

The Rose rumbled after Virginia finished her words, and Alexandra's eyes followed the Rose's creaks. James' gaze flittered between his crew's faces. Five pairs of eyes gazed at him, expecting, intent. That made him shift in his seat. The Bite in his chest quivered, as if it knew it was the subject of inquiry. An acrid emptiness writhed within him, distancing emotions and words from his tongue. The Rose rumbled under his seat and a squeal tilted across his cabin.

Tell them, Giacobbo.

He swallowed thickly. Charles' gaze locked onto his.

We need their trust if you're to slow down the Bite. Tell them.

He turned to Virginia, whose eyes were darting around his cabin, following the Rose's creaks and sounds.

"Relax, Virginia," he said, his voice no more than a scratchy whisper. "She won't bite." He rested his elbows on the table, leaning forward. His crew exchanged glances, save for Charles, who leaned over his seat in rapt attention, a frown painted across his forehead.

"We were off the coast of Egypt, returning from a trade ship," James began. He interlaced his fingers together and dropped his gaze. He has never told anyone about the pirate attack. The fragmented memories that he had tried so hard to erase came surging back, displacing his mind from his body. It was hard to be here, in his cabin, with his crew, when the images and sounds of cannon fire, chaos and brutality raged in his mind, threatening to shake his very frame. He viciously rubbed his hands together, attempting to bring himself back to the moment, with his ship and his crew. He needed his crew's trust. Even if he didn't trust them back. "The pirate ship ambushed us. It flew an Italian flag. But the closer we got, the more the Rose warned him."

"Who?" It was Charles who asked.

"My father. Captain Badr Wolf," James said. "But it was too late. The ship opened fire. And—"

The Rose squealed under his boots as he spoke. He rubbed his face, trying to dampen the ferocious memories. Fire and smoke and ash. The Rose's pained and panicked cries, the rattling of her floorboards as the cannonballs gorged through her hull and splintered her wood. His mind echoed with his father's commands across the cacophony of the disoriented deck.

"He disappeared, and I took the helm. I found him, amidst the—" he gestured with his hands, the words tied on his tongue, "—amidst the chaos. He was standing in front of the pirate ship's captain. Captain of the Calypso's Wrath."

"I've heard of it before." Alexandra was frowning, her attention focused. "When I was a child living in Egypt. She was a terror on the coasts of port cities."

"Then you know her brutality," James finished for her. He turned to face her but looked away when his eyes brimmed with tears. The Bite clawed back those tears, feasting hungrily on James' reawakened grief. It left him hollow. "She killed him. My father. Right before my eyes. Maybe it was my fault. If I hadn't screamed his name, if she hadn't known he was my father, maybe she wouldn't have shot him. The Rose was taking on water, drowning. Someone pushed me overboard into a longboat before I could reach him. Next thing I remember, I was in the water. Then I woke up in a fever back home in 'Rmonia to a grieving mother."

A deafening silence settled in his cabin when he finished his tale. "That's why I hate pirates," he said to Alexandra. "And as for your question, Virginia." His attention shifted to her. "I was fifteen. My mother and I barely managed without the Rose. And the house was empty without my father. Mother was silent. I was desperate. So, I did what need be done. I gave them my soul." He finished his sentence like someone downing a revolting drink. "Of course, the Shadows promised someone back, but they did not specify who. Five days later, the Rose came back to us. But my father was still dead."

"I see," Virginia said, her voice barely audible.

"I suppose that did not sit well with the Ordinance embassy in Dell' Armonia." Charles was the next to speak.

"It did not." James sat back in his chair, exhausted. "My mother knew what I had done. She couldn't let the Commodore find out. She tried. She really tried to hide the signs. I tried too. But it wasn't enough." His words were thick and heavy in his mouth.

"And he sentenced you," Charles said.

"Sentenced us both. Hiding someone in contact with the Shadows is a crime. My mother risked her life helping me leave 'Rmonia with the Rose. But the Commodore wouldn't let us go. The Rose and I have been on the run since."

Alexandra scratched the back of her neck and grimaced, and Virginia bit her inner lip.

"I knew it," Virginia said.

"Ginny, stop," Alexandra whispered loudly.

"Another question," Virginia asked.

"Last one!" James said, breathless.

"What do you know of the Viennese Ordinance?"

"Nothing. I only know of the Commodore."

"We've had a brush or two with the Ordinance," Alexandra said. "The Viennese Ordinance did not take kindly to my research on Shadow Glyphs."

"Among other things," Virginia said, and Alexandra put a reassuring hand to hers. "We've been hunting our own Ordinance enemy, if you will," Virginia continued. "Ambassador Elian Krenn."

James laid a few pieces of paper on the table, little sketches strewn around them with notes and scribbles along the edges. "The Commodore wants these talismans. The Rose's figurehead is one of them. This necklace is the second," he lifted it briefly, "the key to this doorway is the third, and others." He leaned over and plucked the journals from the drawer and placed them in front of Alexandra and Virginia. "If you help me decipher these journals and find all talismans, I will help you bring down the Ordinance, Mitchell and Elias or what's his face."

Alexandra and Virginia's gazes met, then Virginia turned to James. She took off one glove and pulled it through her fingers, stroking the material. "Well, captain. Looks like our paths merged for a reason. We're not friends of the Ordinance. And the Commodore looked quite interested in these talismans. And by extension, I suppose, so does Elian."

"There are five of them, I think?" Alexandra said.

"Six," James corrected.

"Finding them was the biggest challenge. Hence, Edenton's contract. If we find all six, we will have the Ordinance in our palms," Virginia concluded.

"You think we'll find the Commodore at the doorway, then?" Charles said.

"I'm sure," Alexandra said.

The wind blew stronger, and the Rose's wood clicked aloud. James unrolled the piece of the map that he had, and Virginia pulled out her other half.

"When we first took the contract and Edenton gave us half the map, we split the half in half and hid it away," she said.

Mendez scowled at Virginia. "Why…?"

"You know, for safe keeping," Virginia grinned. "Alex and I never thought we'd be members of the Rose's crew when we took the deal. We had to have a backup, lest you lose your half or something happened to ours."

"Relax, Mendez," Alexandra said. "We hid it in the Devil's Trap. If we join the three, the map will be easier to read."

Thomas lightly tapped the chair's arm. "Let's get to it, then."

The crew began to shuffle out James' cabin. Thomas spoke with Mendez about what dinner to prepare next, while Charles and Alexandra conversed about what it *really* was like sailing with pirates.

Virginia lingered. She replaced her glove on her hand and faced James. "Hey, captain."

"Hmm?" James organized his papers and charts, trying not to show his troubled and pained face to the newest crew member.

"About selling your soul to the Shadows," she began. Virginia approached him, and he was forced to face her. "There's no shame in that. Anyone would sell their soul in a heartbeat for someone they love." Her voice was a little hushed, as though she was sharing a secret. "I know a Bite when I see one. Whatever the Ordinance has taught you about your soul, it's all wrong."

His brows furrowed, and he nodded, swallowing down the knot in his throat. He took an extra breath to force his words out, but they wouldn't form.

"I almost sold mine," Virginia admitted. "But she helped me keep it." Virginia's eyes trailed to Alexandra, standing on deck by the mainmast.

Silence stretched between them, and James' eyes locked onto hers.

"I'll go help the crew," she said and left the captain's cabin.

James lowered his gaze, and his hand flew to his chest. In his periphery, he saw gray strands of the Bite swell in his vision and dig beneath his fingertips. He tightened his fist and collapsed into his chair. He closed his eyes and drew in a shaky breath. James was afraid to open his eyes and still find the wisps of the Bite plaguing his vision. So he kept his eyes closed, back resting against his chair and wishing he could catch a moment of reprieve.

The Rose creaked above his head, and he turned to face the source of her voice, keeping his eyes closed. "*Grazie, mia cara,*" he said to her. She rumbled back, a small breath of serenity making its way through his uneasy mind.

His attention moved to the sound of his crew outside of his cabin. More voices on the air, more hands on deck. It filled the Rose with joy. He sensed it. "Enjoying the company?" he said, softness in his voice. She squealed in his cabin, drawing a smile from his cheeks.

I will admit, she said, ***yes I am***. There was a pause in the cabin's creaks, as if the Rose was readying herself to share something new. He gave her time, listening to his crew's voices outside his cabin.

"When we find the island, will you help me find Anmar?" It was Mendez's voice, stiff and troubled.

"He's a tough kid," Virginia responded. "He'll likely find us first." There was a shuffling on deck as the crew took turns, helping the Rose with her capstan and sails. "Does the captain do that often?" It was Virginia again.

"Yes, get used to that," Charles replied, almost too quickly.

A rumble reverberated above James' head. ***Giacobbo***, she began. ***There is something you should know***.

"Yes, *mia cara*?" he murmured with still-closed eyes, but kept his ear attuned to his crew's voices.

Charles spoke again. "I trust you should get some sleep for the night. We've got an impossible island to find."

James could only just make out Virginia's voice, likely trying to obscure her words from the captain's cabin. "Does—does the Rose sleep?"

Charles.

Then he heard Charles' response, and he opened his eyes. "No." James heard Charles' voice, distant but clear. "She doesn't need sleep."

His brows furrowed over quizzical eyes. The door to his cabin creaked as it closed, leaving the Wolf and the Rose alone in the cabin. *He can understand me.*

James sat upright in his chair and interlaced his fingers. "How?"

I do not know. But there is something curious about him.

"Then we will use that to our advantage," he muttered.

21

Alexandra

We're not out to get you, captain

The shipwreck around the islands began to materialize as the Silver Rose neared the Devil's Trap. Blown bows bobbed between waves, battered figureheads peaked above waters, wood and sheets floating between the wreck as if they were performers on a dancefloor.

"Captain, we do need some kind of livestock," Thomas said from behind James. "Any chance any of these islands smuggle some?"

The distinctive fog of the Devil's Trap enveloped the Silver Rose as she neared the shipwreck. James groaned and turned to Thomas. "Do we have to?"

"Our crew is growing," Thomas responded. "How about sheep?"

"No!" James blurted, heading for the quarterdeck. "We're not getting sheep."

"How about chickens?" Thomas offered, turning to face their captain at the helm.

"Fine," James said, wrapping his hands around the Rose's helm. "Chicken it is. As long as they don't make a mess." He helped the Rose as she entered the shipwreck. A sunken stern leaned starboard as the Rose entered port. Two cross bowsprits parted languidly, welcoming the Rose deeper into the islands. The Silver Rose rumbled as she sailed through the shipwreck, as though giving thanks to the misty waters.

"Virginia, do you happen to know where your piece of the map is?" James asked.

"Thieves' Den," she called back from starboard.

"Wonderful. It's close. And they've got the best chickens. Or so I've heard," he smiled to Thomas, who clapped and rubbed their hands together.

James turned the helm to port, deeper into the fog. As they neared, Thieves' Den unveiled itself behind the wispy shroud. They docked the Rose safely. James gave her helm a gentle rub and made to dismount.

Thieves' Den was southeast of Pirates' Island. It was one of the smaller islands, and one of the busiest. A shipwreck, half the size of the tavern on Pirates' Isle, had been turned into a smuggling post. Smaller huts of wood and stone sprinkled the island, and some looked like they were homes to pirate residents.

Alexandra and Virginia took the lead, and the crew followed the two to the right of the smuggling post. People carried crates full of rum, fruit and spices. Muffled music came and went as they walked by the weathered buildings. The music died down as they reached a bridge that connected the main island to two islets. They moved through a thicket on the smaller islet until Alexandra and Virginia stopped at a hut, a staircase flanking its left.

"What's this all about?" James started, his alert eyes shifting between the two.

Virginia merely adjusted her gloves and gestured for him to be patient. "Relax, captain. We tucked our half of the map safely here. Wouldn't want those filthy pirates' hands on it, eh?"

Mendez raised his eyebrows at her words *our half*.

Alexandra nudged the door, and it opened with a creak. A hut like this was no place to hide a valuable map, especially with the door that opened so easily.

Virginia must have noticed James' apprehension and she sauntered to the hut, opening a palm to the dark and dusty interior. "After you," she grinned.

Alexandra entered and Charles followed. Mendez stepped cautiously inside, squinting at Virginia. Thomas followed, and James stepped in last. He stood at the door for a moment and examined his surroundings before moving any further.

"Oh, relax," Virginia said, her voice startling him. "It's not an ambush."

He glanced to her and continued forward before she closed the door behind him.

The hut was dusty, its old and dry wood creaking even as the smallest breeze of wind tossed against it this way and that. Virginia joined Alexandra at the center, where the floorboards creaked under them. Alexandra did a little hop and walked one more step then hopped again. The floorboards sounded a hollowness underneath.

Virginia knelt down, brandishing her dagger in one motion as Alexandra lifted a hefty lock to her. Virginia lockpicked it with her dagger, a small *click* coming out of the lock and drawing a smirk from Alexandra. She undid the lock and pried open the boards. "There." She reached in and pulled out a scroll, unfurling it before the crew.

"Well, it's empty," Mendez said, irritation streaking his voice as he and the crew eyed the blank piece of paper.

"Oh, is it?" Virginia turned to face the map in Alexandra's grip. "It'll clear up once we join it with the other half. Poor thing's been locked below these dusty old floorboards for months. Be easy on it."

"May I just say," Thomas interjected, holding up their index finger, "that was really *fantastique*." They joined their index and thumb together and gave it a kiss. "Just amazing."

"Why thank you," Alexandra smiled.

"Shall we?" Virginia opened a palm to the door.

"To the smuggling post?" Thomas asked, their voice charged with excitement.

"To the smuggling post," Charles agreed with a laugh and opened the door.

The crew began to funnel outside, but James waited for Alexandra and Virginia to exit before he left the empty hut. He breathed deeply of the air outside, the smell of rum, bakeries and livestock filling his chest. He flinched at the sting before he met with the two. "Thanks," he said with a nod.

"Any time, captain," Virginia smiled.

"That was—really good. Very clever." He squeezed his hands together. "Wouldn't want anyone—any pirates, really— finding out." James unclenched his hands and scratched the back of his neck, self-conscious of his every move.

"Of course not," Virginia shook her head and gave an agreeing frown.

A thick silence befell them, interspersed with the creaks of the hut and the waves on the shore.

"We're not out to get you, captain," Alexandra finally said.

"You could be lying. You could be working for—" James started.

"Not with the Ordinance, never," Virginia said.

"The Ordinance did nothing good for us," Alexandra asserted. "If you're really James Wolf…"

James threw his arms out and nodded in self-affirmation.

"Then Alexandra and Ginny are on your side," Alexandra told him.

James pressed his lips together. Silence overcame them again. "I'll go—" he began, rolling his index and thumb together, "—help Thomas. With the chickens. And all."

"You do that," Virginia winked. "And here." She presented him with the map. "Keep this with you. You can trust us. We want to screw over the Ordinance too."

The captain held the map slowly with both hands, his coarse fingers wrapping around it protectively. He swallowed and tucked his necklace inside his shirt before he nodded to them and took his leave.

Alexandra watched as James Wolf entered the smuggling post with his crew. She and her wife were now part of said crew—for better or for worse. "Are you sure about this?" she said.

"This is as close as we can get, Alex." Virginia moved over the bridge to the main island. "And besides," she turned her head to the Silver Rose's crew and the docks. The Rose bobbed in the waters, awaiting her crew. "I've always wanted to see the Silver Rose."

"If he wasn't the Ordinance's enemy…" Alexandra started.

"But he is. So, he is our friend."

A small smile made its way onto Alexandra's lips.

"Finally," Virginia smirked. "She smiles."

Alexandra turned and gazed into her eyes. Virginia's lips already had a natural red to them, a red that went well with her hair. The translucent fog scattered the sun's light and gave her lips a tantalizing gleam, as though she housed a fire within them. Virginia held a hand out to her. Alexandra took off her wife's glove and held her hand. She rubbed the scar that crossed Virginia's palm. Memories of stories and love and stolen moments by the *Lucas* courtyard fountain flitted through her mind.

She remembered the forest behind *Chateau Lucas*, where she and Virginia scrambled to get to Dr. Marie after the fight with Elian and his guards. The next day, Virginia, bandaged and slightly drunk, sat by Alexandra and Dr. Marie as she outlined her and Alexandra's escape out of Vienna, away from the Ordinance's grip. It had been seven years since they made that vow to live.

"We're doing it." Virginia's voice brought Alexandra back from Dr. Marie's hearth to Virginia's palm and the salty shores of Thieves' Den. Alexandra faced Virginia and they shared a long kiss before they turned in the direction of the smuggling post.

They rejoined with the crew, a stream of three chickens gobbling and running in front of them just as they arrived.

"How are the chickens?" Alexandra asked.

"They're going to be great," Thomas said, a gleam in their eyes.

"How much?" James asked the woman behind the post.

"Four coins."

James blinked. "How about three coins, one silver, and a pack of exquisite cloth?"

"Depends on the cloth," the woman answered, her arms crossed.

James shifted and reached into his pockets. He pulled out a stack of cloth tied under a neat light blue ribbon. The woman examined them behind the counter. She raised an eyebrow. "Deal. Give 'em the birds!" she called over her shoulder.

"Yes, ma'am!" a man responded behind her and frantically ran to work, bumping his head on a rack of utensils and pots.

"Do you ever run out of cloth?" Mendez asked.

"Never." James handed the coins and the stack of cloth to the woman, and the man handed them the prized birds.

22

James

He's scared, Giacobbo

"What the—?" James' muffled voice came from the stern of the Rose. "Get out of my cabin!" He came out of his door kicking his boot, feathers and chicken gobbles blasting out of his cabin.

"And for the record, Mendez." Thomas scrambled to catch the chicken that ran over the deck. "This is a *señora*, not *señor. Señora Victoria.*"

"Then we'll keep her for the eggs." Mendez walked out of James' cabin, chicken feathers stuck in his hair and bandana.

"Fine! Just come and help me," Thomas said as they and Mendez headed below deck.

The Silver Rose emerged from the fog and wreckage of the Devil's Trap, keeping a close distance between her and the shipwreck. Should she spot any intruder, the shipwreck in the Trap knew her very well.

"Please don't tell me he named the chicken," Charles said as he finished tying a starboard knot. He walked middeck, watching Mendez head below with Thomas, the chicken in arms.

Alexandra nodded. "He named that one."

Virginia shook her head. "He's going to get attached."

James strolled to his crew, rubbing the back of his neck, irritation scattered across his face.

"Say, captain," Virginia said. "Mind if we get a head start on the map?"

"Mon Dieu!" Thomas' shriek rang from below, muffled but very piercing. The crew heard the clanging of pots and metal and the shuffles of chickens, and they rushed downstairs to the panicked cook.

James shuffled down the stairs, his sword already in hand.

"Please don't hurt me!" a young voice cried from behind the shadows of the galley.

"A stowaway," Mendez grumbled, approaching the young intruder.

"No, no, please! Don't throw me overboard! I won't cause any trouble."

Mendez stopped in his tracks. "Anmar?" he said with a frown, recognizing the voice.

The figure in the shadows appeared to have his hands in front of him, quivering.

"Come out, we won't hurt you," Charles said gently.

The person moved forward, the sounds of pans clinging around his feet. He stepped out, his brows furrowing over his brown, sleepless eyes, his hands trembling in front of his face. "I was only hungry…"

"Why didn't you say so?" Thomas lowered their pan, but James still retained his sword.

The boy said nothing, but slowly lowered his arms. Thomas turned to the shelf behind them and handed Anmar a biscuit, a genial smile on their face. The boy wouldn't take it. The mighty ship creaked beneath his feet.

"Diego, please, let me explain." The boy stepped back and almost tripped on a pot.

"I'm sure you can explain why you double-crossed me," Mendez said.

"I'm sorry. But please, just listen."

"Enough," the captain snapped. He held the boy by the shoulder. Anmar struggled in his grips as James lead him up the stairs.

Charles darted behind his captain. "But he saved us back there."

"He could be leading Max to us," James snarled. "I'm closer than I've ever been, and I don't want any more distractions."

The Rose rumbled in his direction. **Giacobbo, he means well. He's just a lad.**

"I was just a lad, too, when the Commodore chased us. I can't let this lad risk anything." He continued pulling Anmar up the stairs as the boy held on to the railing and wrestled against the captain's movements.

Anger and impatience shot through James' body, and he switched to Italian as he spoke to the Rose, hoping his crew wouldn't understand. "I'm already risking the crew's lives by involving them with the Commodore and the Shadows. I can't have another burden on my shoulders."

"You do know I understand Italian, right?" Alexandra said from the foot of the stairs, crossing her arms.

"We're closer than we've ever been, *mia Rosa*. I don't want any more attachments—" James began, anger eating at his words.

He reminded me of you on the day of the Calypso's Wrath, the Rose cut him off with a loud growling creak, the sound coming down the stairs and stopping James in his tracks.

The captain froze, his expression turning pained.

He's scared, Giacobbo.

James gazed at Anmar in the eyes, but spoke to the Rose. "Why didn't you tell me he stowed away?"

The Rose responded in a low, wistful rumble. *I couldn't let you make a rash decision like this.* She rumbled toward her crew. *They're watching.*

Anmar glanced to the captain, then to the crew. He whispered, his lips quivering. "What is he doing?"

Charles appeared to listen as well. He gestured for the boy to wait.

The boy was far from home, or whatever might have sufficed for it. Tears twinkled in his eyes. From what James has seen, Anmar was a strong lad, but in that moment, strength and weakness merged into something James could vaguely recognize as broken bravery. He broke his gaze away from the lad.

A sudden pain racked James' chest and his grip loosened on Anmar. "Let's take this outside the galley," he finally rasped.

"Don't mind the chickens," Thomas called out as they meandered around the squawking birds, the Rose creaking along their path outside the galley, and into the sleeping quarters.

Anmar sat down cautiously at a bench. His eyes spoke of his sleepless nights, and he rubbed his knees with quivering hands, his biscuit still untouched.

Mendez sat facing him on the opposite hammock. "You had enough, didn't you?"

Anmar sighed and nodded.

"How did you get to the Rose?" Mendez asked.

"I don't know. I was scared. I was afraid Max would find out I let you go. I just followed you after that. I don't know… I just broke through a window." He stole a guilty glance to the captain. "Sorry."

"Why did you tell Max about our plan with the map?"

"I didn't tell her. She found out! I was scared." Anmar's voice nearly broke. "You know how she is."

Mendez let out a sigh, and the Rose creaked above and below them. Waves splashed against her hull with a low, bass sound.

"I'm sorry, Diego," Anmar said. "I just— I hope I can… stay here." He rubbed his knees again, his gaze hopping from the captain to his crew. His attention landed on Alexandra and Virginia. "I didn't know you were and Ginysis were part of the crew."

"We weren't," Alexandra responded. "Just had a change in plans."

Anmar stood and walked closer to the two. "Weren't you part of Edenton's contract?"

"Ehhh, we changed our minds. And the name's Virginia. Hello, lad." She winked.

The boy leaned closer. "You're a woman?"

She nodded.

"You're amazing," the boy said. Virginia chuckled. "But not as amazing as this." He lifted a hand, a dagger with a lapis hilt in his palm. Virginia frowned and reached for her belt.

"How did you—" a wide grin replaced her frown. "Crafty. I like the lad," she said to her captain.

James surveyed his crew and massaged his forehead. The lad's skills were impressive.

"What say you, captain?" Virginia prompted.

James glanced to Mendez. He appeared betrayed, but his features did not hide his concern for the lad. James released a breath he did not know he was holding. "Welcome aboard," he said tersely, heading above deck.

Thomas clapped their hands. "And so the crew grows." They gently patted the boy. "You're so skinny. *Mon dieu*, let's make you something to eat." Thomas headed back to the galley.

"I'm fine, thank you—" Anmar began.

"Ah!" Charles lifted a finger in the air. "You're part of the Silver Rose's crew now. You're not allowed to refuse the cook's food."

23

Anmar

I know, chico. *I'm proud of you*

Anmar ate his small but hearty snack. It was grand compared to what food Max was able to feed him. He carried a bowl in hand, filled with a few fruits that Thomas so meticulously cut as they shared some of their culinary insights. They mixed the fruits with grains, softened with a warm liquid, which Anmar secretly hoped it was rum.

"Mind if I join, *amigo*?"

Anmar made room for Mendez, avoiding Mendez's gaze. *Amigo.* Mendez still called him that. He wondered if he really meant it.

"How did you escape?" Mendez sat next to him.

"I snuck away after I let you go."

"I know that." Mendez rested his hands in his lap. "But how did you escape Max?"

Anmar put his spoon down. There were points in Anmar's life when he wished Max would protect him. Not this time. This time, his lingering fear finally dissolved and left behind but a shell of regret. Regret that he hasn't done this earlier.

"I'm almost sixteen." Anmar turned to face Mendez. "I can make my own decisions now. If I want to escape, then I escape."

"Your birthday's not in six months."

"Like you would know." The boy filled his spoon again. "Remember the rotten cake you got me two whole months before my birthday?"

Mendez chuckled.

"Then Ed got angry because it smelled," Anmar said before taking another bite.

"Well, you know what, *amigo*? There's no more Ed now," Mendez said.

Chickens squawked again in the galley. A little burst of laughter bubbled in Anmar's chest. His bowl was empty, but something felt whole inside him. Maybe he was feeling better after this small meal, or maybe it was because he felt relief and openness fill him. Whichever it was, Anmar let that feeling sit in his chest and swim with the bubbles of laughter. He giggled a little.

"I'm sorry I betrayed you, Diego." He set his bowl aside. "I was just scared. You know how she is when she's angry."

"I know, *chico*. I'm proud of you."

The words lingered in Anmar's head like a stubborn but lovely song would worm into his ear. He turned to Mendez with a knot in his throat. He was about to cry again. But this was a different kind of cry. Anmar sniffed and smiled a *thank you*. Mendez pulled him in, and the boy wrapped his arms around his friend. Silent tears slid down his cheeks.

James came down the stairs with Alexandra and Virginia, and the two turned to them. Anmar's heart quivered when he saw them come down the stairs, light illuminating their features in stripes from the Silver Rose's floorboards. They reminded him of his family. He considered himself lucky to find the Rose, and even luckier that the captain of the Silver Rose allowed him on board. He pulled away from Mendez and wiped his tears with his sleeve. He hoped his new family didn't see.

"How's Thomas' cooking young man?" Alexandra asked.

"It's great," Anmar giggled. "Better than the shit Max can provide, right Mendez?"

"You said it, *amigo*."

"Say, lad," Virginia said. "Do you know where Max's next heading was? Maybe we can get a bit of a head start."

"Oh." Anmar pulled the map out of his pocket and held it out to his captain. "I think this might help."

James held the map in his hands, an incredulous smile spreading across his face. "We've got a heading to find."

24

James

Maybe we can go there one day

James placed the map and the key to his table. Mendez joined Anmar's piece of the map with the crew's own, and Alexandra handed him the final piece. The three parchments burned together at the seams, and sealed.

"What now?" Mendez asked.

"The maps are clever," Virginia said. "They won't give the same hint twice."

The Rose creaked. ***Join the key and map. I sense a connection.***

The crew faced James for translation. He looked to each of them. Inquisitive, intent faces. Except Charles. James pulled out the key, his eyes lingering Charles' before he placed the key over the map. The key made two of three corners of a triangle. A lens formed from the corners of the unfinished key.

Anmar moved the lens over the map's surface.

"Clever," Alexandra said.

A little glowing light appeared under the lens, so small and delicate, as though it were a firefly glowing inside the map's fabric. Anmar followed the little light's path over the lens until it slowed down at the bottom right. The little firefly of light pulsed and the map shone bright, strings of light streaming down its wrinkled sheet. The light dimmed, their next destination materializing over the map.

"That's it." Virginia pointed. "That's the place. The last part of the key should be there."

"How do you know?" James asked.

"Because we put it there," Alexandra said. "No one expects to find it in the place exactly where it should be."

"And the doorway?" James pressed on.

The Rose rumbled in his cabin. ***I recognize its source. The doorway will be there.***

James faced his crew, expecting them to beckon him for translation, but kept his eyes on Charles, who was surveying the map. Finally, he said, "Time to set a course."

The crew funneled outside their captain's cabin. James eyed Charles' steps until he could no longer see him.

"Lovely ship." The boy's voice pulled James out of his focus. He turned to see the lad roaming around his cabin. The Rose creaked gently at the cabin's aft to Anmar's boots. The lad followed the ship's sounds and smiled. Waves sloshed against the Rose's hull, and the sun that came through the windows gave the cabin a warm hue.

James sat back in his chair. "Do you believe in ghost stories, Anmar?" James traced the curved edge of his chair with his thumb.

"In all my years of thieving, I've seen some interesting things," Anmar said, as if he had been in the profession for over thirty years.

"Well, you do set a high standard." James leaned forward gently. "The Rose's reputation in the Trap precedes her. What stories have you heard?"

The Rose picked up speed, the waves clashing on her wood. She rocked smoothly and gave a small rumble from the center of the cabin and creaked above the two's heads.

Anmar listened to The Rose's creaks. "So the stories are true," he said, his eyes following the Rose's voice. "No wonder I could barely get through the window. She chased me into the brig after I broke in."

A wild pang stabbed through James' chest and keeled over, his hand flying to his heart. He stood wearily and moved to his closet, looking to hide the incoming symptoms from the boy. "I'm glad you left those two. Max and Eddy, or whatever his name is," James said as he moved to his wardrobe. "They're real idiots." The closet gave small thuds as James looked into it, his voice muffled through garments and wood.

"Tell me about it." Anmar turned to his captain. "Though, they're not as much of idiots as I am."

James turned and rested his hand on the edge of his closet door. "Don't talk to yourself like that on the Silver Rose." He waved a handkerchief and turned back. "Only I can talk to myself like that on the Silver Rose."

The Rose rumbled at the edge of James' bed toward where he stood. ***No one's allowed to talk like that to themselves on the Silver Rose, Giacobbo.*** James laughed and continued looking through his closet.

"What did she say?"

"She said—" James peered into a drawer and looked through another. He had it here somewhere, he just needed to find it. "—that she doesn't allow anyone to speak badly about themselves aboard her deck."

Anmar sat back in his chair and put his palms together. He looked to the ground then to his palms. "Yeah, well, I ran away from my family and home in search of a treasure that doesn't exist. So stupid and naive."

James threw a few garments on his arm and turned to face Anmar. The boy was eyeing the oversized seashell on the windowsill over James' bed. The boy's gaze wandered, and

James followed his gaze to the basket of empty sheaths and swords beside his bed. The boy looked to the ground then to his palms.

James closed the closet door with his free arm. "Well, if you so insist, I'm an idiot too."

Anmar chuckled despite himself. The boy glimpsed back to the swords. "Are those Damascene swords?" he asked.

James glanced at his sword basket as he sat in front of the boy. "Why, yes," he said. "Have you been there? Damascus?"

"It was my home. My father was a blacksmith."

James looked to the ground. "My father was Damascene. He used to take me there. It was lovely."

"Maybe we can go there one day," Anmar said.

James smiled and turned his gaze to the boy. "Maybe."

The Rose gave a quiet creak behind Anmar and followed it with a rumble above James. Anmar smiled and traced the sound. ***Told you he was a good lad to keep around.***

A one-sided smile curved James' mouth. He hadn't spoken about Damascus or travel, or family for that matter, in a good long while. It kept his attention away from the Bite and revenge for once. "So, you fell overboard you say?" James attempted to keep his attention away from the yawning emptiness that ravaged his chest, searching for the barest hint of a foothold that it could latch onto like a leech.

"Yes," Anmar said. The boy's clothes were thin and the fabric's color had long faded. The only color that the cloth retained was a few stains and spots.

"Those clothes don't look very comfortable. Here—" James presented Anmar with the garments in his arm. "Try these instead."

The boy unfurled the garments. He smiled as he thumbed the shirt's cuff. It was made with a smooth, cotton cloth, laced with a simple and beautiful embroidery. Not too different from the embroidery he eyed on his captain's sleeves and collars. And although Anmar had tried to take care of his present trousers, the ones James offered were in a much better condition.

"My mother once made these for me. I grew out of them," James said. "How old are you? Twelve? Thirteen?"

"I'm fifteen!" Anmar half-frowned, half-smiled.

"Oh, sorry," James said. "Well, you look like you're twelve. I used to wear these when I was that age."

"Yes, I get that a lot."

"Which isn't necessarily a bad thing," James said. "Can't do anything about those boots though. Sorry."

"No this is great," Anmar beamed. "Thank you." He paused, the clothes bundled in his fists. "So—can I call you Captain Wolf now?"

"You can call me James," he said. "Now go change." He pointed outside his cabin. "And let's introduce you to the Rose. We wouldn't want to keep her waiting."

25

James

Goodnight sailor boy

Charles led Anmar to the Rose's bow and the young lad began his proper sailing lessons.

"Love for teaching, *non mon amie*?" Thomas called across the deck to Charles, who smiled to them as he knelt beside Anmar.

"Always," Charles called back to Thomas. He introduced Anmar to his first knot: the bowline. The Rose showed Anmar how to untie it, and the boy watched as the rope unfastened itself. Charles tied it back, and the Rose undid it again.

Charles smiled encouragingly. "You give it a try."

The boy tied it and waited for the Rose to undo it for him before he tried again, his beam reflecting the sun's glare as he worked.

"Not bad, *amigo*!" Mendez said behind him. "Nice new clothes you got there." Mendez patted Anmar on the shoulder. "Hey, captain." Mendez turned to James. "How come we don't get clothes like Anmar?"

"I don't have enough clothes for everyone," James said as he made his way to the helm. He stopped midway and called out. "I can make some, if you don't mind mismatched cloth."

"Hull and Wheel Bay. They've got the best garments." Alexandra was pulling the jib line.

James reached the helm. "No. Fool's Stronghold's got the best," he muttered to himself.

The Rose untied her foresails as James aimed for their course. Alexandra climbed the ratlines, and Anmar followed Alexandra's path until the sun obscured his vision. He turned to the stern of the Rose and saw her untie her sails. He turned back to Charles.

"Two questions," he said. Anmar pointed to the stern. "What's that mast called?"

"The mizzen mast," Charles said.

"How can she do all this?"

Charles shrugged and walked mid-deck. Anmar followed. "She's a mystery. The captain said they found her like this."

"They?"

"His parents."

"And what is that particular mystery?"

Charles chuckled. "Maybe another time, Anmar."

The wind blew and the Rose picked up speed. Anmar turned his face to the wind and closed his eyes. He breathed it in: salt, humidity and the breath of the sun.

Thomas walked to Virginia, two bananas in hand. They handed one to her, who peeled it and looked up to Alexandra. "Come down here already," she shouted to her.

"No!" Alexandra shouted back.

Virginia laughed. "Then I'm coming up."

Anmar turned to his captain and made his way up the stairs to the quarterdeck. He stood next to James, eyeing the helm. "May I steer the ship?"

The Rose creaked beneath James' and Anmar's boots. James' hands tightened around her helm, unwilling to give the boy an answer. The Rose gave a small rumble within her helm in response to his grasp.

"Fine," he said and made way for Anmar, attempting to hide his hesitance. "She'll guide you."

The Rose rumbled as he held her helm. *I like his grip*.

"She says you have a good grip," James said, his gaze to the horizon. From the corner of his eye, he saw Anmar smile.

"How does she do all this?"

James clasped his hands together, still keeping his gaze out to the open ocean. He swallowed. "She's always been like this. She's not from around here."

"She's magical?"

"Sure," James said. "Magic."

Virginia and Alexandra were now at the crow's nest, and Anmar saw them share a kiss. The Rose glided through the water, her helm making a low grinding sound as Anmar steadied it. Her sails clapped and became full with wind, her ratlines rattling with increased speed. She clicked and squeaked at her aft, and gave a rumble that traveled mid-deck and stopped beneath James' boots.

Charles' voice reached them as he hopped up the stairs. "It's not magic." He looked to James, who shrugged and grinned.

"Guess you know my story by now." James followed Charles' gait with his eyes.

"I'm all about stories," Charles smiled. "Perhaps it's time I share, Anmar. The captain's parents found the Rose in a…"

Charles' voice disappeared beneath the skittering whispers in James' head, and the stiff grasp around his heart. He frowned and turned his gaze to the Rose's floorboards, his hand moving absently to his chest. The skittering swelled, but as he merely glanced to his crewmates, the creeping whispers in his ears dimmed, and the tightness in his chest loosened. He smiled. It was good to breathe.

Giacobbo, they will slow down the Bite. But you'll need your soul back, eventually.

His smile flattened, his gaze traveling to The Rose's main deck. He blinked once. Twice. He hasn't given his life after vengeance any thought, if such a life was even in his future.

Speak with him. The Rose creaked in Charles' direction, and the captain regarded his crewmate with curious intent.

"... of course, you can't believe every story you hear, Anmar," Charles concluded.

"Anmar," James said, "how about you follow Mendez. I'm sure he's got quite the stories to share."

Anmar's gaze bounced between his captain and Charles. He hesitated but nodded, heading to the stairs. "Thanks. Promise to teach me some more?" he asked in Charles' general direction.

"I have to," Charles replied. "You're part of the crew now."

Anmar waved and headed below. The crew of the Silver Rose funneled together on deck. Alexandra was the first to head below, Thomas and Virginia following her in conversation. Mendez and Anmar followed after them.

James steered the Rose in silence as Charles stayed behind. The sun dipped, dragging the warm hues with it in the west, cool darkness creeping from the east. The Rose lit her lamps in succession, the light casting hazy shadows over her deck. The glow of her lamps bled across her wood and reached the quarterdeck, dousing James and Charles in flickering warm light.

As the Rose sailed through the open waters, the clean sheet of the sea mirrored the blossoming night sky. The warm air carried the scent of a storm with it. Charles headed to tighten the starboard lines at the railing, humming a sea shanty.

"Where did you learn that one?" James asked, laughter entwined in his voice. He released the helm and headed to harness the starboard mizzen sheets. Charles turned to him. The warm lamps cast his right face in a murky light, his left outlined in growing shadows.

"It was a shanty that my sister and I only knew in books." Charles took slow steps to his captain. "I didn't know how the melody went until I started my ventures at sea." He stepped down the stairs. "A good sailor on one of the ships I sailed on taught me the melody."

James finished tying lines and walked to Charles. "It's a good shanty." He took two steps down the stairs, his fingers gliding over the Rose's railing.

"You look at her like you're looking at someone," Charles said. "She means a lot to you, doesn't she?"

"Aye." James descended one more step and sat down next to Charles. The wind blew, and Charles cupped his hands together.

James drew in a breath. "She's all I have. Well, apart from a crew now." He turned to face Charles, giving an awkward laugh. The Rose sent a small creak where they sat. Charles averted his eyes to the floorboards. James narrowed his own, studying him. Something somber was in those eyes, and James wanted to know why.

"Trade ship, you say?" Charles said, massaging his fingers.

James looked ahead. "Aye. They loved her so much." James did not miss the way Charles pressed his lips together. James' eyes traced the tremendous horizon. "I can't let him, or the Shadows, have her."

The Rose's wood groaned starboard to port across the aft. Her mast squealed, and her sails gave a hushed but intent luff. Charles appeared to listen to the creaks then looked to the sea, sky and followed James' stare into the same horizon.

James took his icy gaze off the skies and seas and glared across the Rose. "One of the talismans. It's here. On the Rose. *In* the Rose. I need to stop him. Before he—before he tears her. Board by board to find it." His eyes carried a fearful look over the Rose, from deck to hull, mast to sails. A low rumble traveled from her mighty belly and into her hull.

The figurehead. He wants the figurehead. He'll stop at nothing to get to it, and Giacobbo will stop at nothing to kill him. They are both afflicted with the Bite. It's race against death. I need you to slow it down for him. And once we find him, once I kill him, I need to get Giacobbo his soul back, or it will consume him. He's all I have.

Charles followed her sound, a troubled frown forming across his face. The Rose's wood darkened as the clouds curtained the stretch of sky above. Charles' hair stood slightly on his arms and the back of his neck. He hugged his arms and arched forward, lifting his eyes and to meet his captain's. Silence and a gaze that held the weight of a thousand mountains.

"What did she say?" he asked.

"I think you know quite well what she said, Charles."

He gulped, sucking in a breath to speak. "How long have you known—"

"Oh, she told me the moment you understood her," James said.

"How?"

James shrugged. "I don't know. But you can understand her now. For better or for worse." He faced Charles. "You heard her. The Rose believes there's a life for me after Mitchell. I hope we can prove her right." James clenched his fists, even a passing thought of vengeance reawakening the Bite. Tightness built again in his throat, and he swallowed down the hungry Bite. Leaning closer to Charles, he spoke again. "Help me find Mitchell. Help me kill him before he kills us." His voice carried a plea that he did not intend.

"Of course." Charles looked away. "What is it that you want?"

"To kill him. Before he gets to—"

"I know that." Charles turned to him. "But what about afterwards. She wants a life for you." He gestured to the Rose. "What do you want after you kill the Commodore?"

James huffed and rubbed the back of his neck. "Well. I haven't really given that much thought. I should give that some thought, actually. If the Bite doesn't consume me before that happens."

It won't! A grinding creak sounded beneath James and Charles. *I will find a way to get your soul back.*

The Rose gave another rugged creak under Charles' boots. *You will help me with that, right Charles?*

Another gulp. "Yes, absolutely." He turned to James. "He's my captain, after all."

James continued, pensive. "I suppose I'm going to need my soul back. Somehow. That's the only fitting goal I see after vengeance."

"What about the Rose?" Charles asked again. "What do you want after vengeance?"

She creaked under her captain's feet and the lamps near Charles flickered a warmer hue.

Sailing free and clear without the constant hounding of Mitchell would be lovely. And I forgot how much a crew made me happy, whole.

Charles tried to his wince. He breathed in deeply and clasped his hands tight. Tighter. "So, what do you think of Anmar?"

"He's a good lad," James said. "The Rose likes his presence here. He deserves to stay on the Rose. Better for him here than with the two other idiots, Miranda and Eddy."

"Max and Edward," Charles corrected.

"Whatever." James waved his hand. "I'm closer to one of the talismans than I thought. Should have gotten a crew a long time ago," he said with a laugh and the Rose creaked toward him from his cabin.

The play in the sky began with rain droplets. They fell, small and intermittent, then increased slowly. Charles and James opened their palms simultaneously and looked above. The long drops of rain lifted dark streaks and dots on the Rose's sails and wood. Charles blinked slowly while James drew in a breath.

"Well then, better take shelter below," James said. He rested a hand on Charles' shoulder. Lightening flickered on the horizon. Charles lifted his gaze from the ground to face James. Thunder resounded as Charles' eyes met his captain's.

"*Grazie,* Charles."

"Mhmm." Charles swallowed and nodded. He stood and hurried to take steps down the stairs. "Oh and by the way." He turned to his still-sitting captain. "That knot you tied." He pointed. "You could do a little better."

"Well excuse me, sailor boy." James stood and raised his hands.

"Oh, no, don't call me that." Charles shook his head and grimaced, though he failed at hiding a chagrined smile.

"Goodnight, sailor boy," James said.

"Goodnight, Captain Wolf."

26

Charles

Do you remember the Grimoire?

Dear Gabrielle,

I do hope my last letter reached you and Uncle Wilson. Let me know if the second and third payments reached you. Send your letters to Mrs. Mizza, and she will know how to send them to the Devil's Trap. Do not send them to the Trap yourself.

This assignment is proving difficult. Even more difficult than it was a year ago. I would have taken this job even if I knew the Wolf as I do now, but I wouldn't have expected to feel so torn. You would think me mad, Gabrielle, but the Silver Rose spoke to me. And I understood her! Do you remember the grimoire we found years ago? It had such strange contents, ones that I can only now recognize after spending time with the Wolf. I know Uncle Wilson had warned us against it as children, but I wonder, perhaps, if it would shed any light to my sudden ability to understand the Rose.

I thought only the captain could understand his ship. Which adds more weight to my assignment. She said she wants a life, Gabrielle. A life for herself, a life for her captain. The Commodore promised us a good sum once the assignment is finished. It will promise us a good life. A life that you and I have dreamed of, for us, for uncle. But what of the Rose's life? And James'? And the outcome of this assignment for James and the Rose seems terrible. And I hate to wonder what that could mean for the crew. I assure you, the Rose is unlike any of the stories we've heard. And James, deeper and beyond any story we will ever hear.

He has his life poured into these worthless trinkets, those "talismans," to save her from the Commodore. And the Commodore himself appears to want those talismans too. And a merman promised James those talismans (I cannot wait to share this story with you). It's a race of four and I'm stuck in the middle. During my time on the seas, I had learned to trust whatever story to get me closer to my goal. I am at the last stretch of my goal, and I have to continue to believe that James and his Rose are worth the terrible fate that seems to await them.

Two years of tireless searching and toiling to find him and his Rose and bring them back to the Commodore. I finally found them. But what if I'm working for a murderer, a liar? It will be at my hands that he loses his Rose and his life. And perhaps, the whole crew. There's a child here, Gabrielle. A young lad of fifteen, perhaps. I cannot fathom what the Commodore might do to him.

I want you to understand that I would prefer to fail everyone else in the world before I would even think of failing you and Uncle. You were and still are the one whom I've trusted ever since I gained awareness. When I finish this job, know that I do so with sadness and remorse. But, I also feel relief knowing that we will not lose our bookshop, the place that has been Uncle Wilson's haven, and our home since we lost our parents. The Wolf is soulless. I'm sure he deserves this fate.

Eagerly awaiting your letter, and even more fervently aching to see you,

Charles.

INTERLUDE

Aereon

I will not fail, Nahida

He moved through the waters, flecks of light paving the path to the Ministers. As he reached the pillars that held the gate, the small lights encircled him.

He spoke the entrance phrase with a mechanical tone. "*Tara-mai,* Aereon." A number of flecks of light gyrated down the pillar and swam around his tail up to the markings on his face. Though he has done this many times before, this part always tickled. The flecks of light settled and recognized his signature markings, the gates clicked and unlocked, the sound resounding in the water in a muffled echo.

He straightened his back and cleared his throat as the gates opened, and swam inside, his tail beating through the water anxiously as he approached the Ministers of his aquatic community, Anahiya.

"*Mai,* Aereon," Milithe, the council member, said from high above. She sat on the hollowed rocks, her long tail wrapping around the aged corrals. Small fish and sea critters swam lazily around the Ministers' seats.

Aeron bowed his head. "Milady."

"They are on their way to the island, I see," she mused, rolling a scepter in her hand. The center of it held a small, glowing coral.

"You know what to do," Enos sounded, next to Milithe, their voice coarsely whipping through the waters.

"Place the key on the doorway," Aereon started, "remove the Eye, stab the sacrifice in the heart and use its blood to activate the doorway's release mechanism. Leave before the island becomes unstable." He finished, a sudden weight threatening to tear the commitment in his voice. "I've done it numerous times before."

"You have a sacrifice?" Enos inquired.

"The Wolf," Aereon said. "He is soulless."

"Unworthy," Tethys, the third Minister, spat. "His sacrifice will be his redemption."

Aereon flinched internally. He moved toward a smaller series of rocks and took a seat, fiddling with kelp. He flicked it side to side, watching it sway with the movements of the water. Aereon faced all three council members.

"And are you prepared for the Sentinel to taste his blood, Aereon?" Tethys prompted, flicking his scepter for emphasis.

"That is why I am here." His voice hitched a little. The image of James lying dead on the island's canopy shot sharp in his head. Aereon blinked and breathed, willing the water to rush through his gills and banish those thoughts. He fiddled again with the kelp.

Milithe hammered the ground once, sand erupting beneath the scepter's base and dissipating in ripples. The coral in the scepter's center shimmered a different pattern than her fellow council members. It released a small rock—a gem—and Milithe presented it to Aereon. He swam and took it carefully.

"What of his crew?" Aereon dared to ask.

"It matters not if the Sentinel reduces them to dust." Milithe's commanding voice boomed through the waters. "It is your responsibility to ensure the wolf arrives to the doorway intact for the sacrifice to be complete. Other casualties are immaterial."

He bowed his head slightly. "Does this work like usual?" he asked.

"Yes, it goes to the armor in her left cuff. She will taste the sacrifice's blood before she lets you through. The blood must match." She sat back down and swayed the scepter lightly. "But, Aereon." He looked to face her. She continued when he met her eyes. "I can sense you have a soft spot for that soulless wolf."

Enos spoke next, their voice echoing in the water ominously. "You are one of our greatest generals. I do not want to see you struggling with this decision. All of Nahida's community Ministers have agreed to send the doorway elsewhere, away from the growing Shadow Influence."

Aereon was quick to respond. "I will use my siren song and have it done by his own hands if I have to. I will not fail Nahida."

"Very well." Milithe waved her hand. "You are excused."

Part II

27

The Commodore

I promise you

"Look lively, men!"

Navy men, dressed in the recognizable red and white coats, dotted about the *Hunter*, the Ordinance's flagship, getting the vessel ready to sail in the direction of the island.

Had it not been for Commodore Henry Gregory Mitchell, Edward and Max wouldn't have had their swords sharpened, their bellies filled and their voices heard on the highly esteemed Ordinance ship.

The Commodore walked out of his cabin, his hat under his arm, and peered silently toward Edward and Max. Edward would be simple enough to bring onto the Ordinance's side. He was deeply eager to impress. The Commodore's gaze turned to Max. She was tougher to connect with. Hardened, cold. But despite her distance, she listened intently when the Commodore spoke, and almost always raised an eyebrow and looked away after he was done. It could only mean one thing. Jealousy—a simple emotion to toy with.

He turned his attention back to Edward, who took a seat at the barrels near the bow. The Commodore nodded to his quartermaster and some of his men as to not disturb his new guests.

"Sir," the Quartermaster saluted and walked to his position near the helmsman.

The Commodore nodded amiably and walked to Edward. He appeared to be a young man, perhaps early in his twenties. A difficult age. An age when the passions of youth still bubbled underneath the responsibilities and hardships of life.

"Enjoying the view, Master Edward?"

Edward turned to face him. "Yeah, it's alright."

The Commodore stood and looked out to the sea with him.

Edward snickered. "Max is jealous of you."

"I did notice." The Commodore hummed. "Apologies. I did not intend that."

"She's jealous of anyone with their own ship," Edward responded. He blinked and stole a glance to Max's direction, as if to see if she heard him. The Commodore took a glance as well: She hadn't noticed. She was simply sharpening her sword.

"I see," the Commodore said. "She is an ambitious woman."

Edward scoffed, a sound deep in his chest, and another sly smile formed on his face. "Yeah, she's always wanted her own ship," he said. "Money can buy anything, is what she says. She thought she could buy me and the young lad's loyalty and companionship. Nah." He shook his head. "Not me."

The Commodore gave Edward silence, gracing him with the illusion that his words were very important to the Commodore. A breeze whistled and the sea rushed as they neared the open ocean. The Commodore turned his head slightly to his accomplice.

"Master Edward, mind if I have a word with you and Miss Max in my cabin?" he asked.

Edward shrugged. "Not at all." He turned to Max. "Hey, Max!" he shouted, and she turned to him.

Her eyebrow lifted again. "What?" she said.

Edward stood from the barrel as the Commodore turned to his cabin.

"The Commodore requests us in his cabin," Edward said and followed the Commodore's footsteps. "Don't keep him waiting."

The Commodore glanced to Max. She rolled her eyes, but then followed. He entered his cabin and took a seat behind his captain's table in the back of the ship. The giant aft window framed his outline again, his features still very sharp and clear. He set his hat on the table, uncuffed his sleeves, and crossed his fingers together. He smiled.

"I have a very important task," he began. "Assigned by the Crown."

He opened a drawer to his left and placed a rolled scroll on the table in one motion. The seal was very easy to forge.

"You do know of the Shadow Ordinance, don't you?" he asked.

Edward nodded slowly while Max shook her head. "Why should we care?" she grumbled.

The Commodore sat back in his seat and smiled kindly as he picked up his black-feathered quill on his left, rimmed with a golden color at the edges. He twisted the quill slightly, the letter *L* shimmering under the lanterns and candle lights in a matching gold on the aged, black calamus. Mitchell blinked and began to draw on paper as he spoke.

"You see, there are dangerous creatures among us," he began. "The most dangerous are the ones we think we know." He stole a look to his guests. Edward leaned in his seat, his eyes in close focus and attention. The Commodore continued drawing. "I joined the Shadow Ordinance thirty years ago to protect my home from the horrid influence of the Shadows." He gave his voice a flare of hurt heroism.

"The Shadows?" Edward repeated.

"Yes," The Commodore said. He lifted his quill for suspense, allowing subtle dramatics to seep into the moment, to make it memorable. "Those are no ordinary shadows. These creatures' whispers have more than often brought men to ruin."

Edward shook his head in question. Max was crossing her arms, but her eyes began to show focus. The Commodore continued. "You see, those Shadows often ask people for the most prized possession a human body has, in return for promises of course. Some want money, others…" he glanced to the letter on his quill again as he drew. "Love." He dipped the quill into ink. "Of course nothing is more cherished, more holy than one's soul."

A small gasp escaped Edward as the Commodore finished his statement, and he nodded in emphasis.

"So what?" Max said, uninterested.

"Don't ever think you can live without a soul Miss Max," the Commodore countered gently. "They even asked for mine. I refused of course," he said and brought his quill back with a simple but necessary flourish. "The experience was… grisly to say the least. Which is why the Ordinance seeks to protect people from the Shadows' heinous influence."

"And what about the Crown?" Max asked. "How is it involved?"

"The Crown saw the importance of the Ordinance's work and asked me to expand its influence beyond my home in London. And so the Ordinance was given a fleet, and I traveled to London's most critical alliances and places of interest. Dell'

Armonia was one of them, if you've heard of it. Alas, it has been claimed by the Shadows despite my efforts."

"And are you seeking to prevent what happened to Dell' Armonia elsewhere?" Edward asked.

"Yes, Master Edward," The Commodore responded. "Dell' Armonia is now in a very regrettable shape. I doubt anyone lives there anymore. Aside from the quarantined Shadows of course. And that's why I seek your help."

"Our help?" Edward asked. He was on the edge of his seat now. Max unfolded her arms a little. Only a little. Perfect.

"I must monitor and control the Shadows, and who they influence," he said. "And you," he pointed with his quill to his guests, "have valuable information about very person in question."

"Mendez?" Max said.

"No," the Commodore said. "I don't know who that is."

"Consider yourself lucky," Edward muttered.

The Commodore smiled. "*Captain*," he stressed the word, the side of his mouth twitching. "*Captain* James Wolf."

The two guests blinked. They knew him. He leaned forward, giving them his full attention. "This captain… Dell' Armonia was his home. Of course, I need not explain what the Shadows have done to the mind of this captain." He paused, letting his words hang in the air between his guests for a moment before he continued. "I need to get to him and those talismans." He put his quill down and turned the paper to them. The curved teardrop necklace and the key, circled.

"This *captain* murdered one of my accomplices, a very valuable member of the Ordinance. Admiral Hastie Fleming," he said. "I need to get to those talismans. God knows what more harm this *captain* is planning to do with them."

"Unleash another Dell' Armonia perhaps," Edward suggested, picking up the paper and examining it.

"Heavens forbid," the Commodore said, inflecting an extra flare in his tone.

"What's in it for us?" Max argued.

"I am very glad you asked," the Commodore sat back in his seat. "I must repay you. If there's anything you want. Name it."

"I want my own ship. And enough gold to be my own person," Max said.

"Truthful and direct," the Commodore acknowledged. "A crucial desire." He turned to Edward with a kind smile. "What about you, Master Edward?"

Edward went silent, his gaze finding the floorboards. He glanced to Max with the side of his eye, a muscle working in his jaw.

"Go on, spit it out, Ed. We don't have all day," she said.

"Leave first," Edward muttered.

"What?" Max stood, unfolding her arms fully.

"I said," Edward began, turned his head to her, "leave the Commodore's cabin first. Then I'll speak."

"What are you hiding?"

The Commodore glanced between the two, a smile of utter delight twitching at his mouth. He forced his smile back into kindness, and feigned concern in his eyes.

"Nothing," Edward said. "I have never shared my desires and life with anyone. And I'm certainly not going to do it with you in the same room."

"You know what—" she reached for her sword but stopped when royal men outside shuffled to the cabin door. He door knocked.

"All is well, gentlemen," the Commodore called out. "As you were."

Max clenched her jaw. "I want none of this anyway." She stood and looked to the Commodore. "I will see my ship and my gold."

"You have my word," the Commodore said.

Max shot Edward a hot glare before she stormed out the cabin door, closing it hard behind her.

Edward took a deep breath and turned to the Commodore. "Apologies," he said behind closed eyes.

The Commodore shook his head and lightly raised a hand. "Not at all. I understand the fervor of a strong desire." He sat comfortably, but not too comfortably. He rested his hands on his armchair and Edward invitingly.

"I just want to be with Alicia," Edward said.

"Might I ask who this Alicia is?" the Commodore asked delicately.

"She err—" Edward hesitated, "I love her."

"Ahh. My Alicia would be Lisa," Mitchell responded. The letter *L* shimmered when he glanced. Edward had been eyeing him. Mitchell returned his focus to his guest with a smile.

"Some gold will help me get to her," Edward continued, almost sounding like a little boy asking for a favor. "Will the key help you get to Lisa?"

"No," Mitchell said. He averted his gaze. "She is dead." He swallowed down a growing emptiness before he faced Edward.

"I'm so sorry. I didn't mean to—" Edward began.

"Not at all, Edward," Mitchell assured.

"Might *I* ask what happened?"

Mitchell uttered the terrible word. "Pirates."

Edward swallowed, clearly uneasy. He seemed to wait, considering what to say next. He finally spoke, quietly. "Will the key help at all?"

Mitchell smiled, making eye contact with Edward. "Of course it will." Mitchell sat back in his seat and looked down to his table, his eyes pensive and lost in memory. Edward seemed intent, listening, his hands clenched together over his knees.

"When I was just starting with the Ordinance," Mitchell began, "I had been assigned an important task. Hunt pirates. By any means necessary. They were the most influenced by Shadows." He blinked slowly. "And I did, confidently. Victoriously. I returned home after a six-month journey at sea, bringing those pirates to justice, or to the gallows." Mitchell lifted his gaze to Edward for a second. Edward was engaged. Mitchell did not need to give any flourishes, any simple but necessary gestures and silences. This part of the story was real.

"I had enough money to buy her a ring. I went to the shop first, got the ring and returned to her. She was…" A smile slipped Mitchell's face and crumbled as soon as it formed. "Surprised and happy. She was playing the piano when I entered, playing our favorite piece."

"What was the piece called?"

"She called it *Midnight Moonrise*," Mitchell said. He tapped a few notes on his armchair, almost reflexively. Edward smiled. "I proposed to her that night, and our wedding was to be held three months later. I was stationed in Nassau. I asked a few friends if we could host the wedding at the church near our headquarters. It was near the ocean. I should have waited. I should have held the wedding inland, away from the sea. Like, London or something."

"What happened?"

"Pirates stormed the beach. We were about to exchange our vows when—" Mitchell rolled the ring around his finger. He swallowed and brushed his hands over his mouth briefly before he continued. "She took a hit. Bad. In her back. I held her and we exchanged our vows. She was my wife and I her husband for perhaps thirty seconds. She was killed. I saw the ship. It was teaming with Shadows." His eyes welled with tears. It wasn't part of the act, all of it was real. He wondered if he should remove the tears, exaggerate them, or keep them natural. He simply blinked them away.

There was silence, as if Edward was mourning Lisa along with Mitchell. He let that silence stand.

"I'm— very sorry, Commodore," Edward said, his voice hushed in the rumbling cabin.

Mitchell cleared his throat and returned his gaze and focus to Edward. The Commodore smiled again. "That's why I am very grateful for your help, Edward. Tell me," he said, and steepled his fingers together as he leaned over the table. "What do you know about this captain called James Wolf?"

Edward squinted his eyes. "The one with the brown hair, medium height, terrible sense of footwear and very annoying presence?"

"Precisely," Mitchell affirmed. "He still wears that necklace, right?"

Edward thought for a minute. "Black and looks like a curved teardrop?"

The Commodore nodded.

"Yes. He and his crew were after the same piece we were, the key."

"He has a crew now?" Mitchell asked and raised an eyebrow. "Hmm. Interesting." He looked away, ideas and thoughts arranging in his mind. He took a breath and returned his attention to Edward.

"The Shadows have a strong influence on captain Wolf. Pirates and Shadows. The two together are infinitely more dangerous. My mission is to stop any pirate, especially ones like Wolf, from losing themselves with the Shadows and claiming more Lisas. "

"I understand."

"Thank you for that, Edward," Mitchell said.

"No, thank you," Edward smiled.

Knock knock knock.

Edward jumped.

"Commodore? May I come in?" a calm voice said behind the door.

"Ah, it's the Lieutenant. One moment, Alistair. I will be right with you." Mitchell stood and Edward stood with him. The Commodore extended his left gloved hand, and Edward took it.

"I will reward you handsomely, Edward, as a gift for you unwavering support. As long as you send my regards to Alicia." He flashed a charming grin.

"Thank you, sir," Edward said, a long, hearty smile spreading of his face. He turned and walked to the cabin door. He nodded to the Commodore before he opened and left, nodding to the Lieutenant as he left.

Mitchell sat down as the Lieutenant entered.

"Any news, Alistair? How are the men doing?" Mitchell asked.

"We have a heading, Henry," Alistair sat down before Mitchell. "The trinket led us to it again." He set the necklace on his Commodore's table. Mitchell held the complement necklace and twiddled the upside-down white teardrop shape in his fingers.

"And yet we have still failed to capture *Captain* Wolf," Mitchell said. "You know the lad told me Wolf has a crew now."

Alistair raised his eyebrows. "Well, it shouldn't make a difference."

"It makes all the difference, Alistair. He's got more hands on deck now. We'll never find him in this state."

"Henry," Alistair said.

Mitchell shook his head. "What kind of captain is he anyway? His crew won't last a month."

"Henry," he repeated.

The Commodore turned his eyes to him.

"We'll find him," the Lieutenant assured. He glanced to the quill, blinking slowly. Alistair was one of the few who Mitchell chance to trust. They had been together since their early royal guard days. Through training under the Crown, to joining the Ordinance. From traveling with Lisa, to settling in Nassau, to the pirate attack and Lisa's funeral, Alistair had seen everything with Mitchell.

The one thing Alistair was not privy to was the Shadows' influence on Mitchell. He can't know. Mitchell balled his hands into fists, attempting to rub some heat into the growing cold in his fingers, though he knew it wouldn't help. It had stopped working years ago. He lost track of how long the symptoms began to progress. It didn't matter.

"If all pirates were hanged and I drained all their blood to fill an ocean, my thirst for vengeance would not be quenched." Mitchell clenched his jaw. "The Wolf's blood is worth a thousand of those oceans."

Alistair knew how important it was for Mitchell to find James and make him pay for what he had done to The Admiral, even if it was Mitchell who had done this to the Admiral himself. Another detail that Alistair didn't need to know. The boy was merely a diversion, a scapegoat to fuel the Ordinance's action against him. The Wolf had two of three talismans. Mitchell had only one, and he needed all six to get Lisa back. The Wolf and the Rose have for so long denied Mitchell the talismans, prolonging his hunger and ache. Mitchell was eager for this hunt to end. And it would end with blood.

The Lieutenant gently put his hand to the table, reeling Mitchell back from his thoughts. "Take your time. I will meet you below when you're ready. We've got lots of work to do when we arrive to the island."

Alistair walked out and closed the door gently behind him. Mitchell drew in a breath and reached for the necklace. He thumbed it briefly before putting it around his neck. Lisa had always thought it was an oddly shaped necklace, and she had always wondered where its other half was. She was convinced there was another half, and she was right. When the Shadows deliver their promise and he gets her back, he will finally show her the other half right from the Wolf's neck. He just needed to get to the Wolf and the Rose.

"And then we will be whole again," he murmured. He reached to the drawer to his left and pulled out a small mirror. He tilted it to his face, his arm barely lifting off the armrest.

The circles around his eyes were still faint, but visible. No one must know. Especially not Alistair. The Commodore, the High Ambassador of the Shadow Ordinance must not show a single lick of the Shadow Bite.

With a labored sigh, he rummaged through his drawer again and pulled out the powder. He removed a glove. His fingers were fully doused in the acrid gray of the Bite, numb and cold. The darkness nearly reached his wrists. He wiped a small dab of the powder on his finger, and placed two small streaks under his eyes, masking the growing darkness. He leaned forward into his chair and brought the mirror closer. His eyes, empty as ever. His eye twitched briefly.

Skittering shook his insides, and he failed to bury down a cough, sputtering into his handkerchief. He heaved a dry breath, examining the cloth. It came away stained with the inky darkness of the Bite.

A shaky rasp traveled across his cabin as he set the mirror down. An echo of whispers flitted from the aft of his cabin and dissipated portside in a hiss.

Hhhhhhhenryyyy.

Another whisper threaded in his head and lifted like wisps of smoke. He placed the mirror in the drawer, his gloves back on, and put his hand to his quill again.

"We're getting close, Lisa," he cooed. "I promise you."

28

Max

I propose we wait. Give them a surprise.

The Hunter neared her destination, a mass of land appearing on the horizon. As they neared, the mass focused into disjointed islands peppering the ocean. Tall peaks and thick trees materialized on the flecks of scattered islands that appeared to stretch forever.

The Commodore stood at the bow, looking ahead. A smile perked the corner of his mouth.

A peak took the shape of a mountain on what appeared to be the middle island between the freckle of land. As the Hunter drew closer, the mountain took the shape of a figure. The Commodore peered into his spyglass.

The figure's shape sharpened into that of a stone guardian. She was kneeling on one knee, her head bent down, overlooking the island, her hands over the hilt of her long, mossy sword. She was fully armored, her guard studded with vines, wood and moss.

He lowered his spyglass. "Steady, men, head for the monument."

Sailors and officers of the Hunter scurried over the deck, shouting orders and getting The Ordinance ship ready to moor near the island. While the men moved, Max was below, sharpening her sword, uninterested in the movement around her.

"Aren't you coming?" Edward asked.

"I'll follow when I want to follow." She lifted her eyes off of her blade momentarily. Edward shrugged and began to walk up the stairs to the hatch.

"You look ridiculous in those clothes," Max added in his direction.

Edward looked at his quasi-Royal Navy attire. A double-breasted red waistcoat, a clean white cravat and a polished sword. "Better than what I've been wearing all these years with you."

Max grunted and took her eyes off of Edward as he continued up the stairs. He hurried on deck and began helping the sailors, as though he had been part of the Hunter's crew for many years. His work was not perfect, but it was honest. The Commodore appreciated honest work. He approached Edward with a smile.

"Good work, Master Edward."

"Thank you, sir," Edward replied as he reefed the Hunter's sheets.

"Those raiments quite suit you." The Commodore put his spyglass down. A few spare clothes with a royal air to them were a small necessity. It gave his guests a sense of belonging, and bound them to loyalty. Well. At least one of them.

Edward smiled. "I won't disappoint."

"I have no doubt," the Commodore said, closing his spyglass. "Geoffrey." He turned to his Quartermaster. "Please prepare our bags. The trip will be arduous."

"Yes, sir." The Quartermaster nodded and headed below.

The Hunter's speed slowed as her sails were raised halfway. She neared the island with the monument, a few pillars of stone served as mooring spots. The men threw the ropes, weighed anchor and tied the lines. With the Commodore's orders, three men accompanied him: the eager Edward and the reluctant Max.

"Keep an eye out for the Rose," the Commodore said. "If you see her, get to her by any means. The Wolf and the Rose are nothing to gamble with."

He walked toward the longboat but turned slowly to the Lieutenant. "Take care of the men and the Hunter while I'm away, Alistair. I will be back soon."

"I will, Henry. Safe travels." Alistair did a small salute. Mitchell nodded and entered the longboat, his three men, Edward and Max following suit.

"Are they necessary?" Max glared at the three men.

"We need as many people as we can, miss Max," the Commodore said. "The venture may indeed prove perilous."

The men began to row to the island. Waters turned murky and green as they neared, seaweed and kelp licking the surface of the waters as their longboat moved between castaway logs and broken branches. The shore received the longboat's wood like a cushion. The sand was a nightly blue, speckles of white sand freckling it like stars. It twinkled in unison, something otherworldly. The Commodore held the necklace in his hands and looked out to the vast island.

"It should be this way." He stepped onto the wet sands. Edward followed him first, and Max made sure the three men trailed second before she followed. She felt the soft sands. Too soft. They walked inland toward the lush greens and the noisy and harmonious forest sounds.

"So, Master Edward," the Commodore said over his shoulder, "have you ever crossed paths with mystical items before?"

"No, not that I know of."

"What about you Miss Max?" the Commodore asked.

She squared her jaw. Nothing more mystical than the Devil's Trap and Edenton's map. But this was the Shadow Ordinance, commissioned officers of the crown. She dared not share information like that with people like them. "No. I haven't."

"Prepare yourself, then. I will have…" the Commodore began. But she tuned out his irritating voice. Her mind meandered around possibilities as they entered the thick of the forest.

The island was magnificent. But it didn't cloud the chatter in her head. In fact, the birds complemented the storm of thoughts in her mind. Soon, birds would fly over her own ship. She will have her own crew, three or more men following her lead. She would finally travel freely in the Mediterranean, the Spanish Main, the Indian Ocean. Plundering wasn't the only fun thing on the seas. And the seas were boundless.

The songbirds directed her attention to the vines that curtained tree branches and cloaked the bark. The leaves were dense, large, the green so vibrant, almost glowing. It was darker under the foliage. Darker. Darker…

There was no more Anmar. No more Mendez. And Edward was likely going to leave her when he got his cut of the reward. He was likely going to stay with the Ordinance. She could sense it. Ed would follow anyone with higher influence. He was undoubtedly going to go back to Alicia, which would be regretful for Max, she was sure.

Was she sure?

Their shadows disappeared under the foliage, only appearing intermittently when the trees graciously allowed sunlight through. Soon their shadows became small, inconvenient and transient dark spots, cutting between small streams of sunlight that escaped gaps in the leaves.

How easy would it be to find another crew? She could try Thieves' Den, but she didn't like the pirates there. She could try Tortuga. Nassau?

Ed laughed. "You're very right," he said to the Commodore.

"We're getting closer," The Commodore responded.

Remorse captured her chest, and it angered her. She gnashed her teeth and breathed hard. When she exhaled, she remembered the times she threatened to leave Anmar behind. Countless times. Pirates' Isle, the cathedral, south France, in the prison cell before they escaped. The trees swayed. Then she remembered when she first found him. East of London. Barefoot. Hungry. Now that he wasn't with her, likely for good, a pang grazed her chest again.

Max looked to her boots as she crossed the capricious ground. For a moment, she wished she could just keep walking. Keep walking and never stop. The texture of the ground changed, and she only noticed when her boots hit stone and rocks, instead of dirt and grass. She looked up. Broken walls of stone, covered with moss and canopy stood with the trees. They were almost like the trees themselves, covered as they were in their vines. Obelisks stood guard in the middle of forestry, their surface giving off a peripheral glow.

"Is this it?" Edward asked, intent in his voice.

"Yes." The Commodore stopped and kept his distance. "But which monolith?"

Edward shrugged, and the three men exchanged glances. The Commodore stepped forward, moving his left hand in slow, semi-circles around him, as if sensing the structures. He narrowed his eyes and examined the monolith to his right, slightly longer than his height. It was chipped and broken away, forming a slant along its length. The Commodore brushed some moss off, his head inclining slightly to the left.

He was examining the monolith, it seemed. Max noticed what took the Commodore's attention. Strange letters. Strings, dots and wispy arrows. Triangles with dots, circles with triangles, triangles and squares.

He turned left, brushed the moss on the stone and read the riddles.

"It's close," he said.

"How can you tell?" Edward inquired.

The Commodore continued his unbothered examination. "The Shadows have a peculiar language," he said. "Those lexigrams are not Shadows, but they have some semblance. Two steps forward, if you all please."

They all walked forward with the Commodore, falling a few feet behind him. His left hand hovered and he walked forward once more. He stopped and brushed more monoliths, scanning and reading. The monoliths got thicker, longer, and more densely packed, like the trees around them. They reached the twelfth monolith.

"It's here," the Commodore said.

Edward stepped forward. He cleared the thick canopy in the center of the structure.

"Slimy," he said. Edward wiped his hand on his trousers, gazing at the monolith. It had three small sides of a triangle. One indentation was filled with a piece of the key, nuzzled in, mossy, undisturbed. The Commodore's face slipped a smile so delicate, so sinister, so charismatic.

"Perhaps if we split up." The Commodore eyed the piece. "We can find them quicker once they get here. I will be back at the Hunter. You stay here." The Commodore addressed Edward. "Capture him by any means necessary. And bring him back. Alive."

"Of course," Edward affirmed.

The Commodore turned his head to him, his eyes sparkling in interest.

"Best cover this back over," Edward continued and put back the vines and canopy and made it as though it had been untouched. "The Wolf and his crew may be here any moment."

"An excellent idea," the Commodore said to Edward. "Men, this way." He turned towards the beach and his men followed.

Edward smiled and turned back to the piece and took it carefully.

"What do we do?" Max asked him.

"I propose we wait. Give them a surprise."

29

James

Trust Her

James put the journals back in his drawer and shuffled to his boots. He drank the half cup of water by his bed, dabbed some water on his face, and headed to his cabin door. He tidied his hair and peeked out.

There was no one on deck.

James stepped out, closing the cabin door behind him. Silence had descended upon him, and the squeaking of the Silver Rose's wood was the only sound left on deck. A small breeze spoke to his ears and ruffled his hair as he descended the quarterdeck stairs. He closed his eyes at the breeze's peak. Not long ago, silence on the Silver Rose meant isolation. But today, silence on the Silver Rose meant his crew was below deck.

The Rose pulled down a line and pointed to her hatch.

"*Buongiorno, mia Rosa,*" he said as he headed to the hatch. The Rose creaked back to him as he headed below.

The crew was huddled around Thomas. "*Bon jour,* captain," Thomas said.

"Morning."

Virginia was laughing with Charles over something, her cheeks red with laughter, while Alexandra finished an apple. Mendez walked behind Thomas into the galley to join Anmar, grabbing a handful of walnuts on his way.

"Here," Thomas said. "You're late." They reached below a shelf to their right and handed James a plate. Apples, hard tack, boiled oatmeal and toasted almonds.

"I know." James held his rations. "But those journals won't decipher themselves."

"Won't you let me help with them?" Alexandra asked.

"All in good time," James replied.

"You always say that." Charles reached behind James to the pistachio stash, and James only chuckled.

The crew finished their rations and boasted about the instruments they played. And when they crowned Charles the Champion of Many Instruments, they funneled back on deck.

The sea felt welcoming. Vast, and the sky open. Jade, blue and the white caps of waves waxed and waned in slow succession. Birds flew eastward.

The Rose rumbled beneath the crew's feet. ***"Land, Giacobbo."***

James flicked his spyglass open on the quarterdeck and looked out. He grinned.

The crew turned eastward and gazed. A fuzzy outline of land emerged, then focused into individual islands. Scores of them, clearer moment by moment.

"See that statue over there?" Virginia pointed. A small spire appeared at one of the islands. The spire cleared into a giant structure of an armored woman, kneeling. "Let's go find some trouble," Virginia smirked as they neared.

But her smirk dissolved as soon as it formed. She narrowed her eyes, then whirled on her captain. James was already at the helm, and the Rose was suddenly trimming her sheets. Charles scurried to his captain and James handed him the spyglass.

Royal embroidery outlined the flag. A staff with a light at the end impaling a wispy figure, the words *Lex Umbra* embroidered above it.

"Ordinance," Alexandra swore.

"Ready the Rose," James responded, breathless. The Rose's helm turned port under his guiding hands. "And follow her lead."

The crew of the Silver Rose ran to the masts and trimmed sheets, the ship's sails cupping with the weight of the wind. The Rose picked up speed, her wood groaning with haste. James steered the helm as the Rose entered a cluster of islands, maneuvering near the tall trees and rocks, dangerously close. But he trusted her.

Mendez rushed starboard and pointed to the crowded shoreline boulders, pockmarked with girthy woods. "Over there. They shouldn't be able to see her behind cover."

James turned the helm and the Rose swiveled starboard.

"Ehh—I said behind the rocks captain, not in them." Mendez's voice wavered as he stole a glance at his captain.

But the Rose continued toward the jagged rocks.

"What is she *doing*?" Charles hollered toward James.

"Trust her!" James' eyes didn't leave the Rose's path, and he aimed to the rocks.

"Then we best head a bit low." Virginia lowered herself close to deck. Charles tightened his grip around a starboard rope and looked ahead.

The Hunter was barely visible behind the cluster of islands, peaks and forestry masking the Ordinance ship's mast and sails.

Two fates. He could choose only one.

One signal is all he needed to alert the Hunter. His gaze shot to James. Then the crew. Then the rocks.

The Rose creaked, suddenly reefing her sails as they came close. Her speed rapidly diminished, her bowsprit nearing the boulders. She slithered ropes on her deck to her crew.

"Ready," James called out. "At my mark throw the lines portside."

"Captain?" Thomas called.

James turned the helm port. The tip of the Rose's bowsprit began to turn. The crew's hands flew to the lines. Charles' hands quivered as a line slithered to his feet.

He held it.

"Now!"

The crew threw the lines overboard. The Rose's ropes reached the rocks, vines and tree tightly. Her ropes became taut, and the bowsprit traced a sharp arc as the Rose turned hard.

James turned the helm hard starboard, his muscles pumping against the sea's resistance. The same pumping he felt when he held the Rose's helm in the pirate attack. Images and sounds came rushing back to him, threatening his grip on the helm.

He shook his head and focused. There was no fire on the Rose this time, no Calypso's Wrath. He focused his eyes back from the smoke and fire of his memories to the rocks and green.

"Hang on tight!" James held on to her helm dearly and continued turning until he couldn't turn the helm anymore. Her wood squealed, her ropes and lines rattled, her sails clapped and thundered with the sudden change in inertia.

As she cut through the waters, the rocks turned into boulders, boulders into an alcove, an alcove into a hollowed cave. The Rose lowered her anchor, her capstan whirring rapidly until it finally locked, and the mighty ship came to a jarring halt inside the cave. She rumbled as she fully nestled inside.

Silence descended, thick as honey. The wind blew through the silence, the leaves whistles and the island hummed a distant vitality.

"Hope they didn't hear that." James came trotting down the stairs in a haste. He snagged the spyglass from Charles and looked ahead through the other opening in the cave. "No sign of them." He held his necklace and put it inside a pocket he had sewn on the inside of his tunic.

"How did she…?" Alexandra hissed, pulling herself up and glancing portside.

"That was," Virginia said, almost tumbling on her steps. "Incredible."

"Fantastic!" Thomas adjusted their hat.

"Rather scary, but damn amazing!" Anmar threw a fist in the air. "Can we do that again sometime?"

"I don't think so, *amigo*."

"We should be clear of them, right?" Charles ran behind his captain.

"We should, but I won't risk it," James replied, turning to his cabin. "We'll disembark at the west."

"How do we find her when we're back?" Virginia asked.

"I'll find her," James said and entered his cabin. He hastily ran to his desk and rummaged through a drawer until he found what he was looking for. He pulled out the piece of cloth and gave it a quick sniff, closing his eyes and breathing it in. Still smelled like home. He exhaled a quivering breath, his hand trembling with the cloth.

Aereon. He's here. I sense his energy.

James opened his eyes. "Do you trust him?"

The Rose rumbled softly under his feet. ***I trust him as far as he can aid us. He's of my kind, after all.***

He put his hand on the table and hung his head. "If you trust him, then I will too."

After another long breath, he raised his head, his shoulder tense as stone. She gave a ginger creak and rumble. His shoulders relaxed and he arched his head.

"Be safe, *mia cara*," he whispered gingerly. The Rose squealed above his head, and his shoulders relaxed.

Come back safe, Giacobbo.

He brushed the pieces of cloth against his lips, giving it a small kiss before he rolled it into his pocket and headed outside.

"Let's head to the longboat," James announced. His crew funneled into the starboard boat.

They rowed ashore. The sand embraced the longboat and the crew disembarked. Once James left, last in line for his crew, the longboat rowed itself along the same path back to the Silver Rose.

"She'll find us, don't worry," James said when he saw the concern on Charles' face. Unrolling the map, he looked ahead. "Any idea where we're going, Alexandra?"

She joined James near the map. The map had changed again, a small dot pulsing with faint light now on its surface and ahead of the glowing dot were bold dashes scattered in a funneling pattern.

Alexandra pointed. "Follow the dashes."

The warrior monument's peak appeared behind the thick of trees. The gray and brown stone blended with the green moss. The crew continued through the mushy, salty sands and into the lush grass and trees.

An aura of warmth and humidity roamed the barks and trees. A cool mist calmed this heaviness and encircled the lower branches in slow, cyclical patterns like a thing alive. Mossy branches spread overhead, and canopy curtained those green and patchy branches. Birds sang as though they were within the trees. Some trees appeared to sing without birds. There was an audible but unidentifiable hum among the foliage.

"So," Anmar said. "How is the Rose going to find us? Assuming we make it out of here alive, that is."

"She will." James gave the cloth a tight squeeze in his pocket. This piece of cloth has been with him since the early days of the Rose's in Dell' Armonia. It was one of the few things he had left of home. "She knows."

Alexandra walked through a near-perfect circle of mushrooms. "So, what happens after we get the final piece to this key?"

"Well," James said, stepping over large fingers of roots. "We find the next talisman after that."

"That being what?" Virginia asked.

"I don't know. Mitchell's journals should lead me to the next one." He stroked his necklace and the key in hand.

It was Charles who spoke next. "And what after that?"

"I figure out how to destroy the talismans important to the Commodore and then kill him."

Virginia nodded. "Easy, easy."

Their tread slowed. The forest's sounds grew louder, more harmonious. The wind brushed through the leaves and gave a background sound, while birds gave staccatos and branches gave alto and tenor beats.

"Alexandra," James said, noticing how she was a few steps ahead of him, Virginia right behind her. "How do you know where to go without the map?"

"We've been here before," Alexandra said. She and Virginia examined a tree with vines that hung over the branches. "But of course, to no avail."

"Why?" James inquired.

"Because of these." Virginia stopped, and James saw what she was pointing to.

Obelisks with etched runes were interspersed between the grass and canopy. The runes were graceful, the letters elegant and flowed smoothly from one lexigram to the next. Unlike the hasty lexicon of the Shadows.

"The dashes, I'm assuming," James said as he looked up from the map. They continued and found more obelisks covered in vines and runes, increasing in height and frequency. Trees stood as guards between one monolith to the next.

"Now to get past the barrier," Virginia said.

"Barrier?" James asked.

Alexandra slowed down. "Right here."

Before them stood a formidable monolith flanked by trees left and right, its top obscured with vines, branches and leaves. The rune in its core glowed in a rhythm and encircled a triangle-shaped keyhole. In the center, there were indentations where the three parts of the key would fit neatly. James approached.

"Stop." Alexandra put her arm out to stop him. She narrowed her eyes. "Someone's here."

Click.

The sound of a pistol cocking clicked behind them. James and his crew turned to find Max and Edward, holding the weapons in their hands. Max frowned, while Edward wore an uncharacteristic malevolent grin.

"Nice to see you again, Anmar." Edward raised his eyebrow and flicked the pistol in Anmar's direction.

"Go to hell," Anmar snapped.

"You think you're so clever, don't you?" Edward scoffed.

"You'll regret this, *pendejo*," Mendez growled behind gnashed teeth.

The branches that guarded the walls creaked. The wind blew and encircled them with leaves and debris momentarily, as though the island was reacting to what unfolded.

"Where's the damn key?" James snarled.

"Oh, this?" Edward waved the third part of the key in front of James, his pistol now aimed at him. Edward put the piece in his pocket when he saw the crew freeze. "Finders keepers."

James was seething with rage when Alexandra spoke. "How did you two even get here?"

"Let's just say we had a little help from a friend," Edward said. He turned to face Virginia, rolling the pistol idly in his hand at her. "I didn't know you were a woman, *Ginysis*."

"And I didn't know you were quite exquisite at securing deals. I'm sure Edenton will be most pleased," she said, unperturbed.

Edward eyed the monolith then his eyes fell on James' neck. He smiled and clicked his tongue. "Nice necklace."

James' hand flew to his neck.

"Bet a certain Commodore would be very happy to see it."

Wrath erupted in James' chest like fire, surging through his limbs as he lunged at Edward, only for Charles to hold his captain back.

Edward only cackled. "Look, I'm not the one standing at the wrong end of the pistol here."

"Just give him the talismans and we'll be through," Max said, her grip on her own firearm lazy and jittery.

James struggled in Charles' grip. "Or what?"

Edward grinned, stepping forward. "Either you give us the talismans." He glared into the captain's eyes. "Or, I will kill him." He moved the barrel of his pistol to Anmar's head.

The wind hollered between the crew and the monoliths, and trees shook their branches. Birds spoke urgent songs. The island hummed a lower and deeper note, anticipation in its sounds.

Anmar stood bravely at the end of the pistol and shook his head. "You won't do it."

Mendez hated the words that left his mouth. "Anmar, don't challenge him." He stood paralyzed.

The flaming feeling extinguished into ice in James' chest like fire doused in water. The abrupt change sent a pang of pain in his throat, like frigid fingers gripping his heart, freezing his limbs. He stopped struggling against Charles' grip. His legs locked. Sweat gathered at his temples, and a heavy weight sat on his chest and shoulders. It was hard to breathe.

"I'm not saying this twice," Edward said. "The key. Oh, and do hand over the pretty necklace as well, Wolf."

The branches swayed aggressively. The crew exchanged glances.

"Right," Edward said, and pulled the trigger on Anmar with a swift and cruel motion.

The boy screamed and fell to his hands and elbows. The bullet ripped the air and echoed throughout the forest, the sound ricocheted against the peering obelisks. Anmar clutched the dirt with his fingers, groaning at his stinging leg, and Alexandra and Mendez rushed to him.

Edward swiftly turned his aim to them. "You stay right where you are, or the next one goes to his head."

The Rose's words echoed in James' head. ***He's just a little boy, Giacobbo.***

"Don't give it to him!" Anmar cried, his voice racked with pain.

If the boy dies, they will leave you. The Bite will ravage you. Alone.

"The talismans, Wolf. Now."

But I'm so close.

He reminded me of you on the day of the Calypso's Wrath.

"All right, all right!" James rasped, raising his arms in protest. He reached into his pocket and pulled out the two pieces of the key. Edward held Anmar by the hair and pulled him to his knees, drawing a wild scream from the boy.

Virginia shifted to face her captain.

"Don't even think of it, *Ginny*," Edward warned.

"Well, let us at least see what's behind this barrier. Satisfy both this friend of yours and Edenton, eh?"

James was shaking his head when he spotted Alexandra. She held a small piece of cloth, the wispy and hasty Shadow symbols transcribed on it.

t r u s t

h e r

Edward narrowed his eyes. "Sure," he said. "Why not? But only on the condition that I get the bigger half of the deal."

"All yours," Virginia said. "I'm not the one standing on the safe side of the pistol here."

"Max." Edward jerked his head to James. Max pulled the last piece of the key out of her pocket and threw it to James.

James pulled his necklace and it unhooked from his neck. "You'll pay for this," He hissed, his teeth baring in fury. He threw the necklace to Edward, who caught it with a flick of his hand.

"Yeah, yeah, we get it." Edward rolled the necklace in his hand.

The island was dear. The talisman was dearer. If Anmar lost his life, James would lose his crew's trust. And he then he would be utterly alone, with nothing but the Bite.

In that very moment, James decided that Anmar's life was dearest. He turned and faced the obelisks.

"Clock's ticking." Edward pressed the pistol to Anmar's head.

James put the two pieces of the key into their indentations.

Click. Ba donk.

30

James

Just call me Zammouri

The island's ambiance fell quiet and the light breeze died, leaving the stage open for the obelisks. The pieces of the key blazed against the monoliths, and as the light dimmed, the ground shook. The clattering of boots on grass and the clamoring of muskets drew near.

"Ah." Edward turned to the incoming guards. "His men have arrived. Captain Wolf, I'd like you to say hello to the crew of the Hunter, the Commodore's very own."

The monoliths descended into the round, dust rising through the shaking dirt they fully nestled, save for the one carrying the key. Edward stepped to it and plucked the pieces of the key out of the protruding obelisk. He pointed his pistol back at James, nodding his head toward the open path. "Off you go," he said, swinging the necklace in his hand.

The guards arranged themselves in a semicircle around the crew, the island's mouth behind them. Behind gritted teeth, James turned to the path paved by birches and pines that swayed as the ground settled. Muskets clicked behind him.

"Don't forget, Wolf: I'm going to need you. *Alive*." Edward stressed the final word, cocking the pistol in Anmar's direction, who still clutched at his wound.

James took a step toward the open trees, and Virginia followed. In the corner of his eyes, he saw her wink and grin. Unsure of just what she was alluding to, he readied himself.

Mendez cautiously knelt by Anmar's side, shooting a fiery scowl at Edward as Mendez scooped the boy up to carry him. Edward shook the pistol carelessly, gesturing for him to hurry.

"Careful with that," Mendez huffed, stepping past Edward with Anmar in his arms.

Charles' eyes darted to the crew and the officers, and he took one cautious step toward his captain.

"Follow along, men," Edward called out. "Best find what's in here for the Commodore."

The trees rustled as the crew stepped deeper into the path. As the officers followed, their muskets at the ready, the rustling continued, louder, more intent. The more steps they took, the more agitated the rustling became, deliberately rattling above the intruders of their grounds.

Virginia grinned. She turned to face Edward, arms open to her sides. "Gotcha." She bolted, shouting to the crew, "Run!"

Edward frowned. The crew ran after Virginia just in time. Dirt erupted in bursts as the trees' roots stirred beneath the surface and cut through the ground, planning a speedy path toward the trespassers. Charles elbowed Edward, narrowly jumping out of the way of an incoming birch tree. The pistol flung out of Edward's hand. James snatched it and made haste behind Virginia. A tree cut the ground after he leapt out of its way, roots spindled out of the dirt like fingers.

"How did you know?" Thomas puffed as they ran along Virginia.

"I've heard many stories," Virginia said, out of breath. "I completely took this on a whim."

"What if the stories weren't true? You could have had us killed!" Charles yelled over the lumbering of branches and grunts of men as they thumped into them.

"Just shut up and follow!" Alexandra screamed.

The path sloped downward into a steep descent, and the crew lost their footing in a mad scramble, screaming in unison as the ground rushed to them. Anmar tumbled off of Mendez as he went sprawling.

Trees sliced the earth, roots erupting in their wake. Mendez stumbled to Anmar and carried him over one shoulder. The boy's eyes widened as he spotted an array of spruces and firs hurtling toward them. "Faster!" he called to Mendez. The crew picked up in a sprint, drawing closer to a clearing.

A shot fired in the air, the bullet hitting a stray tree branch, chipping off wood and leaves in a blast. The irked birch tree seemed to slow down, dirt bursting beneath its pronged branches as it turned and faced the sound, facing the unfortunate Ordinance officer.

Two pines and a spruce halted in their haste and turned to the Ordinance soldiers who came out of the forest, stumbling over the unearthed roots. A shiver passed between the group of trees, aiming for the crew, as if they were considering their options. They came to a jarring stop, a low and agitated rumble shaking between their woody branches, before they turned and headed back to the mouth of the island in a cloud of leaves, dirt and grass. The crew watched as the huddle of trees moved with purpose and haste; Edward, Max, and the officers were no longer visible behind the onslaught of arbors.

Thomas let out a low whistle and hunched over, their palms to their knees. They hung their head, a breathless laugh escaping them.

"Now that that's cleared," Virginia said. "Let's go find shelter."

"Ahead of you." Mendez pointed to a lagoon, the water crisp and shimmering under the direct sun, canopy covering half of it in shade.

Alexandra approached and threw a rock to the other side of the small lagoon where more trees huddled. They did not move. "Safe enough," she said, and they proceeded to the lagoon.

Charles' breath felt heavy in his chest, his inhales quick, his exhales heavy.

"Filthy traitor."

He heard the sound of a musket click behind him. He turned and found an Ordinance officer aiming the weapon at him.

A shot fired.

Charles blinked, expecting the inevitable. But the officer collapsed to the ground, James standing behind him, the smoking pistol in his grip. Charles gulped, an unfocused gaze settling on his captain. "Thank you." He exhaled. James brought his fingers to his forehead in a salute and threw the empty pistol away. Charles thought he saw a sliver of a smile on his captain's face before James continued to his crew.

"Easy there," Mendez said as he settled Anmar near the lagoon. He knelt beside him. "I'm sorry, I'm so sorry, *amigo*. Virginia, your dagger, please." He held out his hand and she gave him the blade. Mendez cut a tear in Anmar's left pant leg. "Good thing Edward's a bad shot." He exhaled heavily. The wound was only superficial, but the boy still looked to be in pain.

They're your crew. Do something! His thoughts blared in his mind, tension gripping his limbs. An idea, silly as it was, made itself known among the storm of thoughts. James turned to the lagoon, and whispered, "Aereon." He walked closer to the lagoon and spoke his name, louder this time. "Aereon!"

A twig snapped to his left. James twisted around, unsheathing his sword. A figure stood shrouded in the shadows of canopy. The figure must have noticed the blade in James' hand. The person raised their hands in surrender.

"I mean no harm," the figure said, voice low and raspy, stepping ahead into the sunlight. The light doused his features in a golden glow. He wore long dreads that hung to his shoulders, a beige and navy striped tunic, dark mahogany trousers and carried a satchel around his waist. Though his features were sullen and sun-beaten, his deep–set eyes spoke good intentions. His arms still raised, he took a cautious step toward the captain.

"Who are you? Who are you working for?" James demanded, his warning aimed at the figure.

He huffed and gestured for James to lower his weapon. "Zammouri," he said. "Just call me Zammouri."

"How did you get here?" James asked.

"I'm a ship doctor. I think I'm the only survivor. The ship—"

James didn't let him finish. "Ship doctor?" His eyes flashed with relief, brows furrowed in hope. "Come on, I need your help." The captain led Zammouri to his crew.

"Zammouri. He's a ship doctor." James stood by Mendez and Anmar, afraid to stand any closer and hurt his by his mere presence.

Mendez's shoulders relaxed. He's been shot. It's superficial, but can you help him?"

Zammouri inspected the boy's leg. "Yes, yes, of course. What's your name young man?"

"Anmar, he responded, his hand tightly clutching Mendez's shoulder.

"Anmar," Zammouri repeated. "What a lovely name. You're from Al–Sham, no?"

Anmar's eyes glanced between his injured leg, Zammouri's deft hands, and Mendez. He swallowed thickly. "Yes. I was."

"Lovely place, Al–Sham. I studied medicine there before my passage to Istanbul. I'm from Morocco. Have you been there?" He retrieved a bandage and a cloth to clean the wound. Anmar flinched and shook his head.

"How did you get past the barrier?" Alexandra asked Zammouri, sheathing her sword and looking around her.

"As I was saying," Zammouri said, his attention still focused on his young patient. "I was aboard a ship. It ran afoul and crashed. I've been here for days. Couldn't find a way out. But some mild earthquake happened, and those bizarre stone walls cleared. After that, I was able to find a way deeper into the island."

"Ah, that earthquake would be us," Virginia offered.

"I doubt the ship crashed on its own. Must have been the islands protecting what's inside," Alexandra muttered.

Virginia shrugged. "Whatever it is," she said and retrieved her dagger from Mendez, "I'm grateful you found us. So, are you a traveling doctor?"

"Something like that."

James put away his sword when he heard the familiar humming. He turned and hurried to the lagoon as Aereon's sweet voice swept over the waters. "Hello, Wolf."

"Aereon." James shuffled to him, solace finding its way into his voice.

Aereon smiled. "I see you've made it."

"Your trees almost tried to kill us," Virginia called out to him and her captain. She uncrossed her arms and put a hand to her chest, giving a small bow. "I'm Virginia, by the way."

Aereon gave a small laugh that carried over the trees, the branches shivering along with it. "I'm Aereon. Charmed to meet you all." His gaze traveled from one crew member to the next until his eyes settled on James. "I see you've grown your crew, Wolf."

"I made a promise." *To you, to us.* But he kept that to himself.

"Oh!" Aereon glanced to Anmar and bobbed in the water. "One moment." He plunged back into the lagoon and reappeared a few seconds later with a chalice in hand. "For the young lad," he said, directing his voice over to the crew. He turned to Thomas, who visibly blushed, unsure of what to do with their hands. They finally settled on cupping them and making some semblance of a reverent bow.

"Thomas! Thomas is my name." They struggled not to fumble their words, not to speak too quickly, face-to-face with a merman. "My pronouns are they/them *en anglais.*"

"*Enchanté* Mx. Thomas," Aereon winked. He pointed behind Thomas to a bush of olive-green leaves, punctuated with pastel purple. "See that bush over there? You can make a brew out of its leaves and it will accelerate young Anmar's healing."

The crew got to work but stopped when Anmar called to them. "Wait, before you go," he said to his captain. "I thought you might want this." Wincing, he reached into his pocket and pulled out James' necklace and the key.

James gazed at the piece for a moment before slowly reaching to the talismans with quivering hands. "How did you–"

"I'm a pickpocket, remember?"

James put the necklace around his neck and pocketed the key. He glanced between Anmar, Aereon, and his crew before he finally looked back to the young lad. "Thank you, Anmar."

The crew exchanged knowing smirks and glances. Charles searched for some kindling and Thomas gathered the bush's leaves. Alexandra and Virginia headed to gather wood, while Mendez remained by Anmar's side with Zammouri. James stayed with Aereon.

"Oh well, then." Aereon flicked a hand in the water. "You'll need the final gem for this talisman to be complete." When Aereon saw James frown, he continued. "You didn't think we'd make it that easy, did you? You'll need my help to get past her first, though."

"Her?" James asked.

"The Sentinel," Aereon whispered.

At the mention of her name, the ambience in the island changed. The wind swept, birds chirping through the trees, branches rattling, and leaves shivering.

"The big warrior statue on this island?" James asked.

"Oh, she's not a statue, darling," Aereon corrected behind a smile. "She's one of the most formidable warriors of Nahida, my world. She guards the doorway beneath." He leaned in towards James, his voice hushed, a pensive expression passing over his face, however fleeting. "You need to release the doorway, and I will give you one of the talismans."

James breathed in and closed his eyes. "Thank you." The words left his lips in a whisper. He was leaning closer, nearly toppling over the water bank. Coolness spread near his face, and he realized how close he was to the merman. Aereon, as always, smirked seemingly at James' every action.

31

The Commodore

I don't work with filthy pirates like yourselves

"What is the matter with you?" Edward screamed across the beach. Birds chirped noisily and flew deeper into the island, irritated by the loud intruders.

"You shot him!" Max retorted. "He's just a kid."

"Like you ever cared," Edward said, his voice coming deep within his throat. "Since when were you ever this soft? The Commodore promised you a ship, didn't he?" Max's lip twitched, but she remained silent. Edward continued, taking strides toward her. "You'll get what you want. Why risk it when you're so close?"

"He is just a *child*," she repeated.

"Whom you've slandered and beat and threatened ever since he joined our group," Edward shot back. "Why should you care now?" He wrung his hands, as if ready to strangle her. She stood still, undeterred. He walked away from her and continued. "I'm joining the Commodore's Ordinance."

The words hung in the air like acrid smoke.

"So, you're leaving…" Max muttered. "None of this ever meant anything to you, did it?"

Edward kept his back to her. "My path is far better off with the Ordinance than it will *ever* be with you or your hypothetical ship."

"You'll do anything just to prove yourself to her, won't you?" she jabbed. When Edward didn't respond, she continued. "Alicia. She's all you want. Never mind that you'll end a boy's life to get to her. Never mind that you'll join the Shadow Ordinance just to get to her."

"They do good work."

"Oh, I'm sure you're trying your best to believe that," she said.

"You'd do the same for your ship," he countered. "I'm not different than you."

She sneered. "You're wrong. Our methods differ. I won't sell myself out to a goody-two-shoes Commodore just to get what I want. I earn it."

He arched his neck to the sky and closed his eyes. Then he whirled on her. "Then I suppose you've earned this." He turned to the direction of the Hunter and picked up a musket that had fallen on the beach after the wild tree attack. Though he didn't aim the musket at her. He turned to face the moored Hunter, reloading it with purpose.

"What are you doing?" Max unhooked her crossed arms.

"You were under the flag of the Hunter. This is clearly treason." Edward shot her a scathing look. "Once the Hunter arrives, your actions will be handled accordingly."

"You sound just like Hans," Max said.

Not paying her any attention, he continued. "And once you're dealt with, the Commodore and I will resume our hunt for the Wolf. And you can forget about your ship."

"You bloody bastard."

A grin split across his face and he looked out into the horizon, admiring his newfound autonomy. He aimed the musket into the air and came to fire a shot.

But his grin dropped, his face twisted in shock and pain, the musket falling from his hands and firing a blank shot into the ocean. Blood erupted from his lips with a wet cough and he looked down to his abdomen to find a blade sticking out of it. He managed to cough, blood splattering on the sands.

"I can't let you do this," she croaked, her voice tight as she held the blade against his back. She pulled it out, fear, shock and anguish strewn across her face. Edward fell to the beach, sand drinking the blood that pooled around his body, his eyes frozen in eternal pain.

"Miss Max." The Commodore's voice resounded behind her. "That won't do." She dropped her sword and turned to him. He clicked his tongue. "You've both failed the Ordinance. Worse yet, you've failed me," he said. "Not that it mattered. I don't work with filthy pirates like yourselves."

She frowned, but registered the pistol too late. He fired. Her body jerked back against the bullet and she fell to the sands, her blood mixing with Edward's.

Critters and birds chirped across the lip of the island, music that framed the scene that it had just witnessed. The beach crunched under the Commodore's boots as he knelt before the two and took off his gloves. His fingers were charred with the gray of the Bite fingers. He dipped his index and middle finger into the blood and began to write.

32

The Silver Rose

He deserves another chance

The Silver Rose loaded her cannons, her sails unfurled and her anchor ready to raise at any moment she felt danger. She bobbed in the waters, listening to the echoes of droplets in the cavernous space. The alcove rang in a low, sinuous hum, and the waters around her felt a familiar presence. She creaked in the direction where she was expecting him.

"Hello, Rose," the merman said, finding her exactly where she sensed he would be: squarely facing her rose figurehead, his tail carried by a whirlpool of water.

She squealed as her vines grew longer to meet Aereon, turning her main rose figurehead directly to the merman. He blinked, the markings on his neck and temple glowing a dim light on every inhale. When he spoke next, his siren voice boomed through her wood, rippling through her sails and sheets. "The Hunter is here. You have to follow me. It is not safe for you."

Has the Hunter found—

"No," Aereon hastened to speak. "Wolf and his crew are beyond the first threshold of the island. You'll have to follow me." The gyrate of water that carried him began to descend. When the Rose didn't move or creak, he stopped halfway and turned to her. "Quickly! The Hunter may be looking for you." The whirlpool continued its journey downward and merged with the still waters. He disappeared under the water, leaving a trail of faint but noticeable aura of light and color. It moved southward. She turned her helm and followed.

The light in the waters dissipated as she reached the south end of the island. He had led her into small bay, surrounded by tall trees that swayed in the ocean breeze, facing the mossy and dark armored back of the Sentinel. She was completely hidden from the Hunter. But anxiety tore through her wood, and she called out to him, her rumbles echoing in the waters she floated in. *Aereon!*

Silence and the brush of wind through foliage.

Then she heard the whir of the waterspout.

"We've made it. The Hunter lagged behind." His voice swirled between her masts and finally settled near her figurehead.

Aereon, she creaked in his direction, extending her vines and figurehead to meet him. *What happens now? Where is he?*

"Rest assured, Rose," Aereon muttered. "He is nearing the doorway. I am leading him to the talisman." Odd. He wasn't facing her figurehead any longer. He turned back to the waters, but the Rose's vines snapped and reached for him, twining around his tail and dragging him back.

I am not finished with you. She turned him to face her figurehead. *Is he in danger?*

"No," he said.

More vines entwined around the merman. *I don't believe you. I don't remember much from my time at home in Nahida, but I do know this. Releasing a Nahidan doorway is perilous. Is he in danger?*

The light pulsing from the markings on his neck quickened, and a frown belied his usual calm. She was right about him. He was hiding something.

He finally sighed, strength and serenity leaving his features, replaced by an expression that was utterly new to him. Defeat. Aereon hesitated. When he spoke, his voice came in but a whisper. "It requires a blood sacrifice."

A taut groan resounded in her wood. Her vines furiously wrapped around Aereon, growing and lengthening to wind around his throat. *I can crush you. Right here, right now.*

He fought in her grip, his voice strangled. "I know, I understand you're furious. But just let me finish—"

Why? Thorns grew sharper, threatening to pierce his scales.

"Because I intend to sacrifice myself instead."

The vines squealed as they slowed down around his throat, allowing him some space to continue. The light around his gills and markings swelled, and he breathed heavily, preparing himself for her next move.

She retreated some but not all of her wooden tendrils. *How can I trust you?*

Aereon fully trusted her to do as she pleased with him. To strangle or release him, he seemed not to care. He breathed deep, surrendering in her hold, his voice broken when he spoke. "They have always taught us that those who chose to sell their souls for cheap were unworthy of the life they were blessed with. Unworthy of a second chance." A woeful siren hum escaped him. "But in all of my time, I have never met anyone like him. I love him, Rose. He deserves another chance. Please. Let me get him out of here, alive."

Silence overcame them, save for the sway of branches in the salty breeze and the crash of waves.

"I will give him the island's talisman, unharmed. You need them intact. He must traverse into Simraash, the Shadow world."

How? the Rose creaked.

"That is beyond my knowledge. But his soul resides there. Find a way to get him his soul back. So that I may have a chance at seeing him again. Perhaps not in this life," he added. His voice was somber, but he appeared revitalized. The Silver Rose released him, tenderly, her vines slowly retreating back and squealing as they returned to the figurehead. He then disappeared below the waters, leaving the Rose suspended in the bay, alone.

33

James

I want this

"What is this thing?" Anmar asked as he swirled the brew in Aereon's chalice. Anmar's leg had healed rapidly as he finished the drink.

"It's a bush that grows in my world. It must have found its way here through the doorway, locally." Aereon leaned over the lagoon's bank and rested his elbows on the rich dirt. "Communities in Nahida use it for medicinal purposes and sacred rites."

"It's a miracle," Zammouri marveled. He turned to the merman. "May I have some of that? I'd love to study it."

Aereon smiled and nodded. "You won't find anything like it beyond this island."

"So, you're a doctor?" Thomas asked as they sat, cross-legged near the bonfire the crew had made. Dusk had turned into night, and nocturnal creatures buzzed in the background. Some sounds were familiar—the rhythmic hoot of an owl, the ticks of crickets. Others were foreign, but harmonious, standing out like the sound of a piano in a violin quartet.

Zammouri rested his palm to the earth. "Something like that."

"Something like that?" Mendez repeated, amused.

"I studied in Marrakech. When I found an opportunity to study in Istanbul, I took it. But…" He stared into the fire, as if looking it in the eyes. "I did not finish my education."

"What happened?" It was Anmar who spoke, and Zammouri turned to him. In the rippling glare of the fire, Zammouri's eyes swam with unshed tears.

He swallowed thickly. "My brother. He—he fell ill. I returned to him as soon as I could. But I was too late."

His words settled silence among the crew and ambience until Anmar spoke again, his voice soft and tender. "I'm sorry to hear that."

Zammouri shook his head and smiled, though it betrayed the heavy sadness in his features. "So, you're from Damascus, you say?"

"Yes. The captain's father is from Damascus, too," Anmar said. The glee of an excited young man returned some positivity to the air.

Zammouri smiled and turned to James, bringing a hand to his brow then heart. "Good to meet you, captain."

"Likewise," James said. He reached for a fruit. "Zammouri. Where were you heading before landing here?"

"Nowhere. I needed to get away from Morocco as soon as I could."

Virginia raised an eyebrow. "A ship doctor might not be a bad idea," she said, munching on a crunchy fruit. "Especially with Mendez aboard. You'd fit right in, doctor."

"Hey!" Mendez threw a mango-shaped fruit in her direction. She caught it and laughed.

"She's right, though," Charles said.

"Hang on hang on!" Thomas said. "We haven't even asked Zammouri. Pronouns?"

"He, him."

James' jaw settled squarely. A ship doctor might be a good idea. Anmar seemed to like Zammouri, and his skillset was missing from the growing crew of the Silver Rose. But he was not ready to have yet another crew member, another life, at the mercy of his doomed quest for revenge. The crew of the Silver Rose conversed over fruit and water, the fire setting a cozy ambience and the night giving a sweeping hum as they conversed. And as the fire cracked and the wind rustled through the leaves, the Bite in James' chest tightened, sending spears of frigid pain throughout his heart.

"Excuse me for a moment," James blurted out thinly, knowing that none of his crew registered his haste. He stumbled to the lagoon, compelled by something beyond his control to be next to Aereon. But the merman was not there. Disappointment captured him, settling a cold, heavy weight in his body. James pressed a hand to his chest and he turned to go back to his crew.

"Not so fast, impatient one," Aereon's voice rang around him. "You didn't think I'd make this easy, did you?"

James turned and narrowed his eyes at the source of the merman's voice. It came from the other bank of the small lagoon, hidden behind a canopy of trees.

"Follow my voice, Wolf." His hum came in a near-siren tone, impossible to ignore. James entered through the long and swaying leaves of overhead trees and re-emerged into a most captivating space.

It was, somehow, a little more brightly lit than the other bank, the glow of an unidentifiable light seemed to come from the leaves and water of a murmuring stream. He followed the waters that continued to grow brighter, not believing what he saw next. The stream defied gravity. It arched upright as though a waterfall was moving upward toward its source.

"There you are." Aereon was suspended in the backward-flowing water, his tail moving in opposite directions at a slow, rhythmic pace.

"How…" James followed the water's movements above Aereon's head, where it flowed into a small hill that perhaps led to another water source, or perhaps to some structure unknown to this world. James did not know. He turned his gaze back to Aereon.

"Like I said," Aereon said with a teasing smile. "Mystery island."

James could only grin. He moved closer to the rising water, his nose so close to its rippling surface. Aereon put a hand to its surface as though touching a mirror. James placed his hand on Aereon's. The cool water would have been refreshing and welcoming if he still had the vessel of sensation and life. The soul. He closed his eyes, defeat washing over him. Whether Aereon was about to manipulate the Bite in him again or not, James did not care. The touch between them reconnected him with something he had long forgotten. He let out a brief sigh.

"How does it feel?" James said, his voice carrying the tremor of tears.

"Feel what?" Aereon said.

"Everything." James opened his eyes to prevent tears from welling up. Aereon had been gazing at him, a pensive expression painted across his face. "The water. This." He looked to their joined hands. His fingers shivered against Aereon's webbed palm. The merman studied James' features, a smile slipping through his face.

"When the soul is torn out of its body, it leaves fragments of itself behind. The Shadows don't come back for those fragments. Not worth their time." Aereon hovered closer to the water surface, his nose an inch away from the air. The merman's smile beckoned James closer. "Perhaps it's those fragments that I felt last time we met," James remembered the tightening Bite in his chest that night. "Those fragments might be what you're attempting to connect to," Aereon offered.

"How do I get it back?" James sighed. "All of it."

Aereon's smile faded, a weighty look replacing it. He averted his eyes from James', as if hurt by it.

James grinned, a chuckle escaping him. "So," he said. "How do we get to the doorway then, and where can I find this gem you promised?"

Aereon turned his attention back to James, returning to his usual peaceful countenance. "Tomorrow, move south. You will find the Sentinel. I will meet you there and deliver her the message to let you through. Once you're through, the gem will be attached to the doorway." Aereon opened his mouth to speak more, but halted, a calculating, pensive look gracing his features. He held out his hand through the water-rise. James looked to the merman's hand as geometric shapes materialized over his scaled skin. His frown did not go unnoticed.

"Those, dear Wolf," Aereon said, acknowledging James' gaze that studied the geometries of his skin, "allow me to breathe the air under and above water," Aereon said. "Take it."

Without hesitation, James took Aereon's hand. A buzzing, warm sensation bolted through his hand, his arm and into his chest. He reeled, but held on. The sensation traveled like a current, running from Aereon's hand, into James' heart. He relished it.

"You will have your peace again, Wolf," Aereon said.

"I will get my revenge. Even if it kills me."

"I wasn't talking about revenge," Aereon murmured.

James held his gaze to their hands. Aereon drew his other hand to James' neck. The water dripped through his collar, sensation making him close his eyes. "Then what are you talking about?" Desire laced through James' whisper.

"Your soul." Aereon's voice caressed James' ear as the two drew closer together. "You need all the talismans for that. Do not destroy them before you regain your soul." He hesitated again, but drew a breath and continued, his gills shivering for a moment. "Promise to get your soul back before you destroy the talismans. Afterwards, you may exact your revenge as much as you like on this wretched Commodore."

James could read reluctance on Aereon's features. He leaned closer to the water. "What do you want to say to me?"

The merman shifted his gaze away from James. "The merfolk council has instructed me not to task any member of our community with finding the doorway. It's dangerous."

James snickered. "So, you let us do your dirty work?"

"That was not my intention—"

James laughed. "I'm only teasing. I'll do any dirty work to get to the talismans."

"Finally gained your confidence, I see," Aereon said with a melodic laugh. Then his easy smile dropped, grim. "I won't let anything happen to you. I promise."

James shook his head. "Not enough. You have to promise me that nothing happens to you." Aereon blinked, a reply close to his lips but James continued. "Aye. Promise me that we'll still meet after I release the doorway. That I'll still see you again."

Aereon didn't respond.

"Promise."

Aereon steeled himself and returned his gaze to James'. "I promise. We will see each other again."

James relaxed. Aereon hummed thoughtfully, the sound sending a chill throughout James' body.

"You never let anything go unanswered, do you, Wolf? I love that about you." The merman ran a hand over James' cheek, then trailed to his neck and chest. James' eyes closed, and he tried to connect with whatever fragments of his soul were left.

Aereon opened his mouth to speak, then reconsidered. He brushed a hand through James' hair. "Kiss me." The merman pulled James in, slowly, as though handling a delicate flower.

His nose touched the water. Then his eyes, cheeks, forehead, until his head was submerged, his lips touching Aereon's. In a moment, their kiss harmonized, giving and receiving. James forgot that he needed to breathe. Aereon's laughter echoed through the water. He put a thumb between their lips, giving their kiss a cadence.

"Breathe," Aereon told him. He cupped James' chin and led him back into air. James took a breath and opened his eyes, the air traveling shakily into his throat. Desire flooded the dry well of his chest. It ached, churned. He stifled a cough and drew another breath. "Don't stop." The words left James' mouth before he could think of them. "I need you. I need this."

A pained smile came across the merman's face. "I can't substitute your soul, Wolf. Neither can your crew. Believe me. If I could, I would have done it in a heartbeat." He paused, gazing into James' eyes as if looking for something precious. "You're going to need it back. All of it."

"I've forgotten what a soul felt like." James pressed his forehead to Aereon's, his hair swaying in the water idly, the bridge of his nose half-submerged in water.

Aereon pressed a thumb against James' lower lip. "Would you like me to remind you some more?"

"How?"

Aereon's hand moved to James' shirt and slowly undid it. "Just ask."

James savored every movement, every scratch of Aereon's scales against his skin. He leaned closer to the merman. "Remind me?"

Aereon pulled James in again, and James pressed languid kisses to Aereon's lips. He only emerged for air when he could hold out no longer, dripping wet. The merman draped an arm around James' shoulder, the other sliding down his arm, pulling himself out of the water.

Then, his tail split, peeling in half. Gracefully, he stepped from the water, and onto the wet grass, James watching with wonder in his eyes.

"You can walk on land this whole time?" James asked teasingly. Water moved down Aereon's bare body in rivulets, collecting in small patches where he still retained his scales. It gave his skin an ethereal glow.

"There are lots of things that I can do, Wolf." Aereon pressed himself against James' hips, the pressure of their bodies together sending a wild tug in James' heart. It chased away the tightness of the Bite, replacing it with deep desire and yearning.

James wrapped his arms around Aereon's waist. "Show me," he whispered, allowing Aereon to undress him. The tunic fell to the ground, half-soaked in the water.

But he forgot what was beneath his clothes. A little too late. Aereon had noticed the black tendrils of the Bite marring the surface beneath James' skin, originating from his heart and digging in many directions. Breath caught in his throat and he held Aereon's hand before it reached his chest. His lips quivered with an explanation he desperately wanted to make.

When he forced himself to look Aereon in the eyes, he was met with nothing but reverence.

"You're beautiful, Wolf," Aereon said, kindness so sweet in his eyes.

Tears burned behind James' eyes. "And you're gorgeous," he whispered, moving his hand up Aereon's scaled back.

Aereon's hands played against James' body the way waves lap against a shore. Rhythmic and wanton. James craned his neck as Aereon's touch drew a groan from James' throat. He breathed heavily as Aereon planted a kiss to James' open neck. His tender touch awakened the fragments of James' soul, and his chest erupted in a fiery burst that traveled through his body, massaging his every nerve. The searing hot fingers of desire, or perhaps his soul, played against his heart and muscles and his very breath as if he harbored a star in his body.

As Aereon caressed James' neck, he closed his jaw to Aereon's hand as it moved to his shoulder, then collarbone, every touch rewarding James with a sigh of pleasure. "Don't stop." The words came in a rushed, troubled, vulnerable breath.

Aereon smirked and pressed his body against James'. The merman's hands found the sword belt and he undid it. The sword landed in the grass with a muffled sound, dewed with the water's foam and droplets. His hand then traveled up James' waist, abdomen and finally arrived to his chest, never for a moment deterred by the Bite that ate James underneath the skin. His hand found James' necklace and stilled on it for a moment.

James held Aereon's wrist and whispered. "This stays."

Aereon leaned to James' ear. "I expected nothing less." He led James down to the grass, their lower halves still submerged in the water as the two joined. It drew a small gasp charged with delight from James.

As Aereon settled his hips against James' and moved eagerly with anticipation, the Bite on his skin receded rapidly, shriveling against his flesh. James growled at the sudden movement of the Bite, pressing his head into the grass against the throbbing beneath his chest.

That did not go unnoticed to Aereon. He stopped moving. "Wolf, does the Bite hurt?"

A tormented breath of yearning escaped James' lips, clutching Aereon at the waist. "I want this."

Aereon's hands went to James' wrists, and pinned them against the dirt. He rested his webbed fingers on James' and smiled. "Then we'll take it slow."

The merman continued moving his body on top of the captain's. James savored every breath and sound, connecting with sweet pain and pleasure that made his body shiver. The Bite responded with meager retaliation, attempting to send icy spikes within James' chest. But the heat between his skin and the merman's dispelled the cold tendrils that fought against the blissful fragments of his soul. His cheeks and shoulders reddened with elation as Aereon's scales and the beautifully cryptic markings on his neck and throat shimmered with oscillating light. James gritted his teeth, a groan rasping deep within his throat.

"What's happening?" James begged, his voice breathy, his eyes shut. The piercing pain in his chest intensified as the twinge of pleasure heightened between his hips. He enjoyed it.

"The Bite," Aereon began, his breath quickening as he pushed himself against James, his knees digging into the soft dirt, and his scaled toes sliding within the water. "It feasts on emptiness. It's fighting against the fragments of your soul."

A snicker braided with ecstasy left James' mouth. The Bite attempted again. He moaned as he felt it crawl into his throat, sharp and cold in his gullet.

"Tell me how you feel," Aereon whispered between passionate pants.

"Aereon," he huffed. "Burn the Bite away."

He peeled his hand from the captain's, longing in his movement, and ran his fingers over the withering spindles of the Bite on James' throat. Slow. Even slower.

James whimpered. "Please," he moaned, his free hand flying to grasp Aereon at the hips. He pushed himself closer into the merman, working to fuel the rising fire within him, and purge the remnants of the Bite in his throat.

Aereon chuckled softly, the sound arousing them both, and the two met each other's hungry gazes. James braced himself for Aereon's next move, squeezing the merman's hand and trembling with anticipation. Aereon took that as an indication of consent. He grinned and moved faster, closer until James shuddered with pleasure, an endearing sound of satisfaction leaving his lips. Aereon released a breath of gratification and slumped next to James. Tenderly, Aereon brushed his arm over James' chest, placing his warm and webbed palm over the shrunken Bite. The two lay together, entangled in each other's arms, half immersed in the water, half breathing the radiant air.

Night had fallen. James lay on the grass, his sword next to him, his shirt and clothes lazily covering his skin that glistened with sweat under the moonlight. His arm was wrapped around Aereon's torso, his tail joyfully moving back and forth in the water.

Aereon leaned onto his belly against James' side. He spoke as though sharing a terrible secret. "I'm not supposed to be here."

"Why?"

"The Ministers of my world would punish me if they found out I'm with someone who is without a soul."

James turned his head to him, their eyes meeting, their noses touching. "Why?"

Aereon held his gaze on James. "I don't know."

James did not miss the discomfort in Aereon's voice. The merman shifted away from James, hesitantly wrapping his arms around himself as he lay on his back.

"You're hiding something." James twisted around, one hand to Aereon's cheek, the other to the ground, pinning the merman to the grass and water.

A nervous laugh escaped Aereon's lips. He cupped his hands to James' jaw. "Promise me you'll get your soul back."

"Only if you promise me nothing will get between us."

Aereon drew in a shaky breath. "I promise."

"I—I can try." He brushed Aereon's hair, his eyes studying the merman's every feature before holding his gaze to Aereon's eyes. "I promise you I will try my best to get my soul back."

Aereon sighed a breath of relief. They lay shoulder to shoulder, the water-rise and night creatures adding a background symphony to their joyful breathing.

An hour passed, or two, and Aereon withdrew to the water. "You should, perhaps, return to your crew."

James had dried and began dressing slowly. His trousers were on first, then his sword and belt. He checked his necklace was still on him and nodded. He swallowed down the lump in his throat as the distance between him and the merman grew. Aereon held James' hand like one would hold a fragile bloom. "I will see you very soon, dear Wolf." He gave it a kiss. "If you need me, just sing," Aereon said and disappeared into the shimmering waters.

James frowned, and the knot in his chest returned ruthlessly. He turned his back to the water-rise and reached for his shirt. With each layer that he put on, the warm blaze of his leftover soul dimmed, the Bite replacing it with contemptuous, acrid cold. He was sure the Bite was regrowing beneath his skin. He felt it, crawling and conquering what it thought was its domain. The sensation left his throat dry.

James adjusted his necklace and sword and brushed his fingers through still-damp hair. He stood on the grass, submerged in the night's ambience as he became reacquainted with the James he knew for a long ten years. Soulless. Empty. Vengeful.

"James?"

He heard Charles as he stepped through the canopy.

"Are you all right. We've been looking for you for…"

James blinked and turned to face Charles. "Yes, I'm fine," he said abruptly.

"The—the map," Charles finished. He paused, his eyes searching and studying his captain. "Alexandra said its surface changed again," he quietly said.

James nodded. "I'll be right there." He followed Charles back to their camp and sat by the fire. Charles sat across him, a careful look in his eyes.

"What happened to you?" Virginia asked.

Thomas and Mendez turned to their captain, and Thomas lifted an eyebrow, their mouth parting for a moment. James' hand flew to his hair, his fingers coming wet, embarrassment blooming across his features.

Mendez scooched close to him, a smug grin on his face. "I'm not assuming it rains in patches on this island."

"Santiago, what are you suggesting?" Alexandra smirked.

"Oh, give him a break," Virginia said. "He might have just really loved the pond and shoved his face into it, right, captain?"

James whirled on her. "Why would I do that?"

"I don't know. To drink? Unless, perhaps, it wasn't water that you were drinking." She grinned when he crossed his arms.

"Drinking something else?" Mendez chirped.

Anmar brought the chalice to his lips, hiding a snicker.

"He is quite handsome you know, that Aereon," Thomas added.

"Thomas is right," Alexandra joined in. "Quite the looker."

James turned visibly red. "Let's just have a look at the map, shall we?" His eyes caught Charles'. His weren't carrying joy or mirth like his crew mates. They carried scrutiny, and something that resembled remorse. Charles averted his gaze.

James turned to Alexandra. "The map."

"Right," she said, a laugh slipping from her. "I'm assuming this is the lagoon." She pointed to a rippling blue spot on the map. A faint arrow pointed south of the lagoon.

"And that's the Sentinel," James said.

"Sentinel?" Thomas echoed.

"The statue," James said. "We need to get past her. She guards the doorway."

"And how do we do that?" Alexandra said.

"With the help of Aereon, of course." Virginia threw a smirk to James, who looked away before he spoke again.

"He said he'll disengage her."

"So, you did see him back there!" Virginia said, victorious.

"I did!" James admitted. "Yes, I did. And he kissed me, too. Happy?"

"Very." Virginia threw one leg over the other.

The crew planned their course as the map revealed more of what lie in wait for them. They settled in to sleep before the long trek to the heart of the island.

When James heard most of his crew's sleeping breaths, he stood and shambled back to the lagoon. His hand went to the necklace. If it wasn't for Anmar, he would have lost two talismans to the Commodore. If it wasn't for Mendez, he wouldn't have even found the map. And if it wasn't for Alexandra, he would never finish deciphering the journals.

His heart ached and his hand flew to it. He knocked his chest, and the Bite knocked back, ravenous. He sighed and closed his eyes, remembering the path of Aereon's lips on his own, and the chill that traveled through his body as Aereon's hands traced James' neck.

"Evening, captain," Virginia said.

He opened his eyes and turned to her. "I thought you were asleep."

"Shouldn't you be?"

He shrugged.

"It must be difficult," she said as she stepped to the lagoon's bank. When James frowned, she continued, "Being in love without a soul. The Bite must be wracking your body, hungering for sensation, isn't it?"

His gaze dropped to the ground. Her words struck something inside him, though he did not know if the tight grip around his heart was the Bite, or his own despair. "What do you know?"

"Oh, I know," she assured him.

He faced her. "Did you sell your soul?" Maybe he wasn't alone.

"No," she shook her head. "But I was close. Alexandra's ward, Lucas, was involved with the Viennese Shadow Ordinance," she said. "Not that I cared." She walked to the lagoon and sat, putting her fingers into the cool waters. Ripples traveled across the surface, distorting the reflected night sky. "I was the ward's court boy. But when he found out I wasn't actually a boy, I was thrown out of his estate. Alexandra was to be married to the Viennese Ordinance ambassador, Elian. I was desperate. The Shadows knew. If it wasn't for the risk Alexandra and I took…"

"You would have ended up like me," James concluded and sat down next to her.

"Well, if you put it that way, it does sound a little incriminating," Virginia said, and James managed a smile.

"So, what happened next?" he asked.

"Lucas and Elian were infuriated. They came after us." She lifted her sleeve and revealed a scar across her wrist. "This was the last of the damage. Alexandra saved my life once here," she said, pointing to the scar on her wrist. "And a second time here." She rolled her shirt's collar over, revealing a charred swatch of skin on her shoulder.

James frowned at the familiar markings of the Shadows, and he could not deny the sense of relief and safety in the space between them. He was in fact not alone. "They nearly had your soul," he grated.

Virginia covered her shoulder and turned to face the lagoon. "Nearly. But we escaped, went on the run." She gave a dreamy grin as she stared into the sky. She took a deep breath and continued. "Sure, the Viennese Ordinance is after us. We've hopped ships and escaped gallows. But none of that bothers me. It thrills me. When I'm with her, I feel alive, whole." She then turned to James, her face suddenly taking on a severity that wasn't there before. "If she was too late, if I had sold my soul, I wouldn't be able to feel a sliver of what I do with her now."

James averted his gaze, suddenly feeling ashamed that he could not save anything so dear in his life, including his soul. "I did what I had to do. Ever lost someone, Virginia?"

"No."

His shoulders slumped, and his fingers dug into the ground, scraping dirt from grass. "I don't have any more souls to bargain with," he muttered. His voice caught in his throat, and his hand flew to his chest. "This *thing*. It's eating me up—has been eating me up for years." It took everything in him to face Virginia again. But when his eyes met hers, he wasn't faced with the repulsion he was expecting. He was received with attention and care. His eyes watered. "I don't know how much time I have. For so long, all I wanted was to find the talismans, destroy the talismans in front of his eyes, to destroy his hopes with them. And *kill* him. But…"

Virginia gave him time to finish, motioning him onward with a small gesture.

He gulped, emotion moving in a maelstrom into the Bite's jaws in his every fiber. He let out a sharp breath and continued. "But now I'm starting to wonder if there's something else for me, something beyond revenge."

"Has Aereon given you any inkling of how to survive the Bite?" she asked, quietly.

"He said I'd need all the talismans for that."

"All the more reason for us to kill the Commodore, then," Virginia

James laughed, despite himself. "If I still have enough time after we kill him, that is."

"Well, I suppose that's something for the Silver Rose's crew to arrange," she grinned again, that sly smirk of a fox, as she stood.

James' eyebrows lifted in surprise. Empathy and help were the last things he expected. His lips parted and he turned to her. "So, you'll help me?"

She nodded. "As long as we rid ourselves of Elian and Commodore Michael—err Mitchell. Whatever." She waved a dismissive hand at the name. "If getting your soul back is along our path, then we will damn give it our best." She offered him a hand. He accepted and she helped him up. "I wouldn't wish a soulless life upon anyone," Virginia added, her voice solemn.

He swallowed, thick and heavy. "Thank you."

"Of course," she said. "I suppose we should get some sleep. Long trek tomorrow. Goodnight, captain." Virginia turned back to their small camp.

"Goodnight."

34

James

Yes. Alone.

Alexandra narrowed her eyes at the map, following the dotting line, she pointed through dense forestry. "Through there."

"Couldn't it have led us through a clearing instead?" Charles sighed, trudging alongside his crewmates.

"You sure you can walk this terrain, *amigo*?" Mendez asked, studying Anmar's limp with open concern.

Though Zammouri recommended that the boy's leg remain bandaged and his mobility limited, Anmar was headstrong. "I'll be fine, I promise," he said as he marched through bundled trees and shrubbery determined purpose.

The forest was heavy, wired with foliage and branches. It felt as though it stretched forever, and the crew's every step became heavier as weariness weighed down their breath and pace. The woods dominated the setting. Dirt and earth beneath the crew contorted to the thick roots' liking, the sky choked out by the arbor's wild branches and leaves.

Eventually, as the crew's throats became dry with labored breathing, they reached a clearing, vast and open, beautiful and tranquil. The trees spread a gentle shade over the rich forest bed, and a small stream gurgled its way to the east, landing in a pond that led back to the ocean somewhere behind the forest.

But that was not what drew the crew's awe.

"Is that the Sentinel the merman was talking about?" Virginia murmured, craning her neck to fully take in the stone warrior's scale and splendor, wonder streaking her face.

The Sentinel was at least three times the length of the Silver Rose. Moss covered her stone armor, and vines creeped out of small cracks between her structure. She was kneeling, both hands to the hilt of her sword, firmly planted into the ground like Excalibur to its stone. Her pupilless eyes gazed far beyond the crew at her feet, watching over the island with rapt attention.

James took a step forward, joining Alexandra at the map. He pointed to the sword. "There," he said. "The doorway's beneath the sword."

"So, what now?" Charles breathed, joining his captain's side.

As much as James wanted to keep marching through the day and night to reach the talisman, he had to remind himself to slow down. He was the captain of a living, breathing crew now. He glanced at the boy, whose forehead glistened with sweat, his face hiding a grimace.

"We'll rest here before—"

He was interrupted by the sound of grinding stone, and the crew turned to face the source of the sound in unison. The stone warrior craned her head down, her eyes landing a steely gaze on the crew, the crack of stone against stone splitting through the air. She stood, rocks and debris and the sound of a thousand cracks booming over the island like thunder as she rose to her feet. The ground shivered beneath the crew with her colossal movements.

The Sentinel raised her sword, dirt and grass and roots blasting out of the ground as the stone blade's tip left the earth, exposing the cave beneath it.

"I suppose we don't need the merfolks's help for once, do we?" Charles mused.

Then she raised the sword above her head, not unlike a stone guillotine.

"Not good," Mendez muttered under his breath.

Her sword plunged down, and the crew scattered in directions like marbles. Though the Sentinel's movements were slow, heavy with stone and size, her blows were calculated, deliberate. Her next blow landed near Zammouri and Anmar, the ground erupting and hurtling them back.

The Sentinel drew her sword back behind her, plowing it through the dirt in the crew's direction, the colossal weapon uprooting and snapping ancient trees in its way like mere saplings rather than the living history that they were. The crew split in a sprint, the erupting earth rumbling behind them. Anmar was determined not to let his limp drag him down into his death. But the boy's leg betrayed him, and he toppled over with a pained cry. Mendez yanked Anmar back by the arms as a tree snapped and tumbled over, nearly crushing them both.

"Over here!" Zammouri called out to Mendez, running to a rocky cave formation by the pond. Mendez did not hesitate. He carried Anmar over his shoulder, making for opening to the cave.

The crew was scattered about the field. To her, they were mere ants. None drew their swords. They all knew they won't stand a chance against her. Hers came down through the middle of the open field, and the ground rumbled as stone met earth. The sheer force thrust Charles off of his feet, and he rolled onto the ground. A wet pop came from his shoulder and his hand flew to it, biting down a gasp. He stumbled back against the dirt, barely escaping yet another incoming blow.

Amidst the chaos, James' attention narrowed to the slit the Sentinel had exposed. He bolted to it. But the Sentinel noticed, and she swung her sword in James' direction. The sheer force knocked him off balance, and knocked the air out of his lungs. He rolled onto his side and scrambled off in a mad dash, the sour taste of blood in his mouth.

The Sentinel dragged her sword along the ground, dirt, dust and leaves pluming in the air. She raised it, and swung her sword back down, the crew narrowly missing her attack. The impact sent rocks and roots bursting in directions as Virginia, Alexandra, and Thomas ran to take cover in the cave. A flying branch hit Thomas' head with a dull *thunk*, and they tumbled over, unconscious.

"Thomas!" Alexandra yelled. She and Virginia grabbed them by the arms and pulled them into safety just in time before the Sentinel landed another blow near the cave's opening.

Now it was just James and Charles on the field against the massive warrior. James rushed to help Charles up as he stumbled in the direction of the pond. "Head to the cave. Take cover."

"What are you doing?" Charles shouted, breathless, as his captain sprinted into the heart of danger.

"Just go!" James side-stepped a hurtling rock, and it smashed into an uprooted tree, showering him in splinters. With a strangled sound in the back of his throat, Charles shambled to join the crew.

There was one thing on James' mind: Aereon. He was the only one who could help them get past the Sentinel. He made it to the pond and sank to his knees. "Aereon. Aereon!"

The Sentinel lumbered in his direction, trembles giving way to thundering and shaking through the ground. Her form eclipsed the glinting sun, and she raised her sword, casting James' path in shadow.

"Aereon!" James cried, uselessly shielding himself with his arms.

The swiftness of the merman's response took James by surprise. A siren song hovered over the stream and pond, and the Sentinel stopped, her sword mid-way through the air, dust settling like snowflakes around her blade. James peered at the giant, awaiting her next move.

A splash of water behind James made him turn on his elbow, and he faced Aereon. The merman drew James' sword and cut his own palm in one motion, then joined his bloodied hand in James', placing something shimmering in his hold.

"To her left cuff. Go!" Aereon commanded.

James opened his hand briefly, the emerald gem soaked in the merman's blood. The sound of grinding, moving stone filled the stifled air again. The Sentinel was moving away from James, her hardy steps aimed towards the cave where the crew was taking cover. James wasted no more time and sprang to his feet. He raced to the Sentinel, aiming for where her sword was coming to crash against the ground.

"James!" he heard Charles cry out. "What are you doing?"

He did not attention to his crewmate's warnings. All he could hear was the blood pumping in his ears as he aimed his path to the sword that would crush him. The earth beneath him shook when the immense sword struck, the shock reverberating in his bones. Stone crackled as the Sentinel began to raise her sword back up. He jumped, and scrabbled for the blade. James gained purchase and made his ascent.

"James!" someone shouted from behind the cover of rocks. But he continued climbing, the ground shrinking away from him as the Sentinel raised her sword, bringing him up with her. James secured one step after another, moss and stone adding more peril to his journey to the Sentinel's weapon. He made it to the hilt. The sword cut through the air far too quickly for a titanic statue. It smashed against the boulder, chipping away at the crew's only refuge. James lurched forward, nearly mis-stepping over the edge. He clung to the hilt's guard, securing himself, breath leaving his chest in shivering pants.

Her left hand was moving to the hilt, aiming to grip her sword with both hands.

Now was his chance.

He leapt, the air refusing to leave his lungs as he did. Wind hissed in his ears as he launched through the closing space between her two wrists. James met stone, the force knocking the air out of him. He wheezed and grunted, grasping at vines and her protruding armor pieces. He forced two stiff breaths and he hefted himself over her wrist, twisting to land on both feet and one hand. The Sentinel secured her hands on the hilt in time for her wrist to turn just the right way for James to see where the gem would go. In the center of her armored wrist sat a small imprint in the shape of the gem that he held.

Without warning, wind rushed around him again, and he fell against the stone, bruising his side as he grabbed on for safety. She was swinging her sword back down to the ground, and when he dared to look below, the sword's path was aimed at the heart of the cave. The crew would be pulverized. His heart knocked in his chest, his feet moved with singular speed and, with a grunt, he threw himself onto the cuff, shoving the gem in place.

The wind roaring in his ears abruptly ceased as the Sentinel's movement slowed. Then, with the grinding sound of stone, the Sentinel finally stopped, frozen as a statue should be.

James stood with a muffled groan, his chest rising and falling in sharp breaths, his bruised legs shaking. Her sword was mere inches away from crashing against the cave and crumbling it in on his crew's heads as a tomb.

The wind howled through the Sentinel's form and the remaining trees.

A booming sound rumbled beneath the Sentinel's cuff, and James warily turned to face it. The gem vibrated in place, blood pouring from it. The crimson flowed in the path of veins under the Sentinel's stone skin. The rivers of blood snaked under James' feet with direction and purpose, winding up the statue's arm, shoulder, neck until they reached her face, pooling in her eyes to form blood-red pupils. She turned her head to James, the sound of her neck craning sending tremors beneath his feet. With those scarlet eyes, she fixed him in a glare. Awe and fear bubbled deep in his abdomen, everything in him screaming at him to move, but it was as though his legs turned into the same stone as the Sentinel's. Her glare seemed to last forever. Then, with a motion so certain and gentle, she moved her arm down to the ground, and James scrambled off of her wrist, running to join his crew in the cave.

Charles shuffled to his captain, cradling his shoulder. James took Charles' arm and cracked his shoulder back into place without warning as they passed each other. "Oh, I hate you!" Charles yelled, a gasp logged in his chest.

"I know," James said and took a step inside, counting his crew mates. They were all present, alive but not unharmed.

"Lay low. I will finish this," he said.

Charles stepped forward, his features twisted in concern. "Alone?"

James' gaze flitted between his crew. Thomas lay unconscious, Alexandra setting them down gently while Virginia cradled their head. Anmar's face was contorted in pain as grasped his leg, Zammouri and Mendez by his side. Guilt twisted in James' heart.

"Yes," he said, facing Charles. "Alone."

He cautiously stepped out of the cave and found the Sentinel lumbering back to her post. She faced south, and knelt back down, rumbling as she lifted her sword, exposing the slit. James approached the trench. He whistled. There was a beat, and then it echoed back to him. Scant daylight filtered down into the crevice, and it smelled of damp rocks and shrubs. He breathed deep and took a step inside the lush labyrinth. The moment his last step crossed the threshold into the narrow path, the Sentinel's stone sword thundered into place, using the earth itself as a sheath, casting the James into darkness.

35

James

I promise you, Aereon

James emerged on the other side. The underground safe haven retained a certain shimmer and light, as if it was lit by an unknown sun. A plum bird drifted before him. It landed on a branch that arched over a stream, its water blue as a midday sky, streaked with the hues of a sunrise. Vines and canopy sprawled above his head, clinging to whatever stalagmites the cave offered. A humming symphony of birds, insects, and the stream of water echoed in the dome of the cave.

But one sound stood out: a sinuous buzz that reminded James of locusts. It came from a girthy tree. In its midst sat a circular door, or what appeared to be a door. At its heart lay a gem that looked like an iris, its pupil piercing, the luminescent light that bled from the gem pulsing like a heartbeat.

"You finally made it."

James whirled to the source of that irenic voice.

Aereon was suspended in a small pond. When James reached him, Aereon lifted a wet hand out of the water, and James held it, helping Aereon out of the pond. Water seamlessly morphed into a robe of blue and gold as he stepped onto the lush underground dirt, the cloth's surface retaining an aquatic shimmer. James couldn't help the reverent smile as he eagerly took Aereon's hand and brought it to his lips.

Aereon hummed, a siren tune entwining both of them. "Walk with me," he cooed.

James fell into step next to Aereon, the two's hands intwined. Tranquility permeated through his body starting in his chest and spreading out. James' head began to ring, a sonorous buzzing building between his ears. He cherished it, allowing himself to dream of a life beyond revenge, a life where he followed Aereon's music across the open waters, free from the Ordinance. It seemed silly to dream of such a life, but he the sensation of his hand in Aereon's made every dream feel like a promise. He intended to follow through with it. "Finally," he breathed.

"'Finally,' what?" Aereon asked.

"Finally, the key. The necklace, the Rose," James said. "I'm three talismans ahead of him."

"Wolf," Aereon said. The closer the two drew to the tree, the more intentional the siren song became. "Promise me something."

They drew nearer, the heartbeat synchronizing with James' own, thrumming in his chest. "Anything." James turned to face Aereon.

The merman swallowed, and James could see the glint of tears in his eyes. "Forgive me," he whispered.

A response hovered at the tip of James' tongue, but when Aereon's siren song changed pitch, James' vision blurred. His consciousness slipped away, as if under the grasp of some intoxicant.

He was entranced with the siren song, his senses and wits fully under the merman's control. Aereon cupped James' hands in his own and sung, his music churning in the air and bringing an agitated wind with it. "Place the key over the Eye."

James' hands left Aereon's and he pulled out the key from his pocket, his eyes glazed and his expression blank. The pulsing of the iris in the tree increased, as though it hungered for the taste of the key. The gem—the Eye—responded, blinking rapidly like no gem should. Then, out from its very center came a blade, a shimmer gleaming on its sharp surface.

"Take it." Aereon's voice commanded. And James held it, readiness in his movement. Aereon put his hands to James' cheeks, admiration in his motion as he pulled himself closer to the captain. "Kiss me," he murmured. His siren song turned into an anguished tone.

The wind kicked, the trees rustling with building intention as James leaned in and pressed a kiss to Aereon's lips, the merman relentlessly stretching their kiss and distancing the time to the next shift in his siren song. A gust tore through the air, as if scolding the merman for his delay. His hands slid to James' shoulder and he tore himself away, sharply inhaling for his next note.

"Stab me in the heart," he choked out through tears, a biting tone in his poignant chant.

With his mind captured by the strings of Aereon's song, James pierced Aereon through the chest, red blood splattering and his song morphing into a pained gasp. He wheezed and his siren song died, breaking its spell on James. And the captain came to, Aereon's red blood painted across his skin, the lethal blade still in his hand.

"No," James gasped, choking on the word. Aereon pulled out the blade with a cry.

James watched, the siren song's hold loosening and horror making its way into his eyes, as Aereon's blood drained into the dagger. The blade retreated into the Eye, and Aereon, leaning onto James, placed the Eye back onto the tree, in the center of the key. The blood pooled from the Eye and traveled through the tree trunk, tracing its path throughout the bark and spindling around the doorway. Light erupted behind the door, blinding and fierce, and as the flashbang faded, the key fell from the trunk, the Eye closing as it hit the rocks and dirt. Aereon dropped to the wet earth, cradled in James' arms.

Slowly, awareness returned with the metallic odor of blood, invading his mouth and nose. "Wh—what did you make me *do*?" James cried.

Aereon held the key with a quivering hand, the Eye closed and asleep. "Take it," he sputtered.

James' hand quivered over Aereon's robe, exposing his lethal wounds, his fingers spotted in the merman's blood. "No."

Aereon put the key in James' hand. "Take it. It's yours." He swallowed thickly. "Don't let him get his hands on those talismans."

James stared at the key and gem, its light snuffed, the iris appeared as though it was in a deep sleep. "Aereon…what did you make me do!"

"I'm so sorry, Wolf. Please forgive me," the merman heaved. He put a hand to James' cheek, streaking it in blood. "I couldn't let you be the sacrifice."

"Sacrifice? What are you talking about?" James cupped Aereon's neck. "Just wait. Let me—let me get help. Hang on, please."

He attempted to settle Aereon down, but the merman held on to him, grasping at James' shoulder with whatever strength he had left. "No." The word struggled to leave him. "No use. I'm dying." When James shook his head in denial, Aereon continued, his voice grating within his throat. "The doorway needed a sacrifice. I couldn't let it be you."

"But you promised. You promised…" James pleaded. "You promised nothing would get between us, remember?"

"I know… I'm sorry, Wolf. I'm so sorry," Aereon whispered. "Listen—" he began, a cough interrupting him. "Listen." He clutched James' sleeve. "You have to leave now. Head south. You'll find the Rose. The Sentinel will destroy the island."

James shook his head. "I'm not leaving you."

"You have to—"

"No!" James cried, a torrent of tears streamed from his reddened eyes down his cheeks. "We couldn't bury my father. I couldn't bury my mother." He pressed his forehead to Aereon's, and his came voice laden with sorrow. "This won't happen to me again. Not with you."

Aereon smiled and his eyes began to close. "You're so beautiful, Wolf."

"And you—you're gorgeous." James' throat could barely support his words.

Aereon's golden eyes glistened with tears and they streamed down his face. James wiped them with his thumb as tears welled in his own eyes.

"Wolf." Aereon's hand quivered up to James' lips. "Sing with me."

Aereon began to hum, his voice no longer strong enough to summon a true siren song. James held him close to his chest, Aereon's quiet humming reverberating deep within James' being. He held him and rocked back and forth. Sniffing, James managed to hum with the merman.

"Good," Aereon murmured. "They should be here in no time."

"Who?" James asked, his voice choked with soft tears.

"My brethren."

They kept humming and singing, as though everything was well with the world, as though death wasn't racing toward Aereon. A fragile tune threaded in the air, starting with two, then five and tens of melodies, filling the cavern with melancholy.

A weak smile tugged at Aereon's lips. "They're here."

James peered over Aereon's shoulder. Through tears, he saw the merfolk in the stream, fog swirling around them like a maelstrom. He barely registered their own siren song. It stood in the back of his mind like muffled rain, lashing against a window. All that remained on his mind was honoring Aereon with a burial that was fit for his first real love in many isolated years.

Aereon weakly grasped a hand on James' shoulder, nodding to James in the merfolks's direction. Gingerly, James lifted the dying merman, the robes swaying with James' careful motions, leaving a trail of blood as they approached the pond.

"Wolf," the leader in the waters uttered, her voice scolding, her glare piercing. "You've lost us a great commander. Aereon," the mermaid addressed him, her tone concealing her sorrow with staunchness. "The ministers would punish him doubly so if they knew what he has done."

"It was my choice," Aereon blurted out, the effort causing him to shiver. James held him tight as he heaved in another breath to speak. He coughed, blood coloring his skin and James' hands. "Talori, please. He has nothing to do with the Crisis. Spare him." The leader's gaze, Talori, did not waver. But Aereon continued, his next words addressing Talori with an unspoken tradition. "Please. As my soul's parting gift."

Hushed whispers flitted between the merfolk at Aereon's words. That broke Talori's stoic regard, ever so slightly. Her gaze bounced between Aereon's wounds and James' reddened eyes. She drew a slow, purposeful breath before continuing.

"Very well." She gestured for James to kneel, and James did so readily.

"Talori," Aereon's voice began to fade. "Don't tell the ministers about me and the Wolf." He turned to face James, closing his eyes and smiling despite his pain. "Wolf. Get your soul back," he whispered. "So that I may see you in the next life."

His lips quivered with his pending response. It was a promise he never thought he'd be willing to make. Nothing in life had mattered more than revenge, not in a good long time. But in this moment, nothing mattered more than his soul. "I will. I promise you Aereon," he whispered behind a rattling breath.

Aereon's smile widened and his hand met James' cheek, beckoning him close to his lips. James leaned down to him and they shared a final kiss. Aereon's hand went to James' cheek, streaking his skin with blood, and he breathed his last breath on James' lips. James lifted Aereon to his chest, burying the merman's head into his shoulder. He put his face into Aereon's neck, his shoulders shuddering, his throat carrying a stifled sob. He breath in a choked breath and emptied an anguished cry into the merman's hair.

"You were not meant to survive this, Wolf," Talori said, respect and expectation kneading her tone. "Consider this Aereon's gift. We must honor the soul's final wish."

James nodded, tears streaking his face. His eyes took in Aereon's features, covered in blood and serenity. "Worthless and soulless," he said, suffocated with grief. "But he still loved me. Honored me, despite the Bite." He mustered whatever strength he had to address the merfolk. "Help me return the favor."

The merfolk exchanged gazes, their eyes glittering in the mist like candles. One mermaid drew forward. She raised her hands above the stream and beckoned the waters to her fingers. The water followed, streaming against gravity to her fingers and collected in her palms. She sang a tune that stood out among her fellow sirens and spun a waterbed like a spider spins a web. She led the waterbed to the streambank. "Rest him here."

James lay Aereon down in the waterbed, gently putting the merman's hands across his chest. He caressed his cheek and sniffed. Aereon's robes melted into the waters, his legs becoming the tail that James had tried to commit to memory.

The wind kicked as the bed began to rise, and as it did, water slithered across Aereon's skin, blanketing him. The water washed away his blood, and he appeared as though he was merely sleeping. Light flickered through the waters, casting him in mosaics of blue and orange.

"We send our dead into the afterlife with the colors they've lived with," the mermaid said, "so that their soul may find its passage in peace."

James' gaze shot to her. His lips shook. The mermaid's words echoed in his mind, and deep regret clawed into his chest like a dagger.

"Without you, we wouldn't have lost our commander," she said. James swallowed. He wanted to say something, perhaps to redeem himself, but she interrupted. "But without you and your crew finding this map, we wouldn't have released the doorway. Nahida is safe. Because of you."

The waters of Aereon's bed merged with the waters of the stream. The merfolk sent him below, and they followed, their siren song dissipating as they disappeared below the waters. Silence enveloped the underground cave. The mist fizzled out. Birdsongs quieted. The wind died in the air. Leaves did not rustle.

James dropped to his hands and knees, the wet dirt sinking under his weight, and bellowed a tormented holler.

36

The Crew

Would you come with us?

A thunderous sound boomed outside the cave formation the crew sheltered in. Shockwaves followed, shaking the ground of the island.

"That doesn't sound good," Alexandra huffed.

"Doesn't look good, either," Charles said from the opening of the cave, anxiety tangling his features. The Sentinel slammed her sword across the land, pulling ancient trees out at their roots. The crack of wood snapping filled the air, and Charles shielded himself reflexively. "Oh no," he muttered under his breath.

"What? 'Oh no' what?" Virginia hastened to stand.

He peered out again to find the Sentinel wielding her sword, swinging it at the ground, felling tree line after tree line in her blast's wake. "She's destroying the island." He whirled to face the others. "We have to get out of here. *Now.*" Charles hesitated to step outside the cave. Doubt, indecision and sliver of guilt sliced across his determined face. But he turned to the crew, a fresh idea blooming in his head. An idea too dangerous, but the alternative left was no option. "Head to shore. Find the Rose. I'll go find James." He turned to the direction of the Sentinel.

"You're mad!" Mendez snatched Charles by the arm, stopping his exit from the cave.

"Just find the Rose." Charles released himself from Mendez's grip. "Go!"

And he bolted into pandemonium, the rest of the crew left to save their own skins. They hesitated, but another crash rattled the cave, reviving their motivation. Alexandra helped Thomas up, while Mendez supported Anmar as he stood.

"Can you walk, *amigo*?" Mendez asked.

"Yes," Anmar replied and followed Mendez and Zammouri out the cave.

The crew rushed in the direction of the shore, their steps disrupted by the distant chaos that The Sentinel wrought. She was zealously tearing the island apart. A bitter crack resounded in the air, and the earth beneath them shook violently, knocking Anmar off his feet. A crack came from behind him, and he turned on his elbows to find a tree tilting rapidly in his direction.

"Anmar!" Mendez screamed.

Zammouri bolted and reached the boy in time, hoisting him above his shoulder. One second too late, and both the boy and doctor would have been crushed.

"*Gracias, gracias*," Mendez heaved as he ran alongside Zammouri.

"Shore!" Thomas pointed, breaking through the tree line. The ground's texture turned from grassy to sandy. As the rumbling and crashing of rocks, trees and stone became more distant, the crew could hear the welcoming slosh of waves against the beach.

"Now to find the Rose," Alexandra breathed.

Zammouri was tall, and his height gave Anmar the perfect angle to view the tranquil shore. Its tranquil blue color that budded over the horizon brought a relieved smile to his face. But that smile turned sour when the boy saw what lay on the sands, covered in red. "No." The shock in Anmar's voice built into outright horror. "Zammouri." He thrashed against the doctor's grip. "Let me down. Now. Please!"

"*Dios mio,*" Mendez said, visibly perturbed as he hurried to the beach.

No sooner Zammouri let the boy down did Anmar run and reach Mendez, who sank to the shore, his knees digging deep into the red sand and waves. Anmar threw himself next to Mendez, his hands shaking over the bodies of Max and Edward. Zammouri knelt by the two bodies and put a hand to each of their necks.

"Is she—" Anmar started.

"She's dead," Zammouri announced, testing her pulse. "They both are. Officers?" he asked, drawing away from them.

"No," Mendez choked. "They are—were… idiots."

"Our idiots," Anmar finished.

"Hey, mates," Alexandra called out. Disturbed, she stood looking down at a rock, its surface smeared with red. Recognition and concern weaved across her face. "Come take a look at this."

Virginia stood next to her, and her blood ran cold, the air catching her throat. On the rock, smeared in blood, were the patterns of the ciphers she had seen Alexandra study over the years. Whoever wrote them did so meticulously, gleefully, going over dried arcs and dots again with red to clearly define the glyphs.

"The Commodore's doing." The words left Alexandra's lips thick and heavy. She turned to Mendez and Anmar.

"I don't know what to do." Mendez stood, his gaze still fixed upon the still forms he once knew.

"I can't believe she's—" Tears came down and swallowed Anmar's words. He looked away and Mendez wrapped him in his arms. "We have to bury them." His voice came muffled under Mendez's embrace.

Zammouri stepped up to the pair, clearly unsure what to do with his hands. He resorted to resting a hand on Anmar's shoulder, reassuring and kind. The two remained in each other's embrace for a moment before Mendez pulled away. Austerity was new to his features. Anmar approached the bodies, but hesitated. The boy's hands trembled.

The doctor stepped forward, quick and certain, as though he knew the scenario by rote. "The burial is more for the living than the dead," he said as he picked between rocks. He glanced over his shoulder, addressing his words to Anmar and Mendez. "I've known the pain of loss too many times. Let me help."

Shakily, Mendez closed Max's eyelids, Anmar doing the same for Edward. Though he had seen and dealt death too many times for a lad of fifteen, he appeared visibly shaken this time, his hands quivering and his face ashen. Zammouri stepped closer and carried Max's body while Mendez carried Edward. The Sentinel laid waste to more of the island; a distant, low crash rumbled the sands beneath them. Silently, Anmar lead Zammouri and Mendez to where the sands of the beach met the earthy grass of the island's inner lip. There, the Silver Rose's crew buried Max and Edward, wondering who else they had to bury, and who else they lost in the chaos.

Anmar stood up after leaving decorative rocks and shells on the simple graves, and Mendez placed his bandana over the wet dirt. He turned to the blood-soaked beach and looked out to the sea. Silence fell between the crew, suffocating and tyrannical. The crew exchanged glances, unspoken tension wavering between them. Distant rumbling and crashing echoed in the distance. For all the crew knew, James and Charles could be crushed and broken.

Mendez breathed deep and exhaled, his legs carrying him to the beach. He sat down, absently gazing over the quiet horizon. Anmar shuffled and sat next to him. His words coming coarse when he next spoke. The crew straggled slowly, one by one sitting on the beach as though death and destruction did not consume the island a few leagues behind them.

Thomas pointed out to the waters. "The Rose," they said flatly. The Rose dug through the south waters, anxiously cutting her way to the crew. "What do we tell her?" Thomas asked, their voice soft with defeat.

Zammouri turned to Thomas, thoughtfully. "Who?"

"The ship. She's sentient," Mendez said, as though that was something any sailor should know about the Wolf and the Rose.

Zammouri blinked rapidly, his mouth opening and closing a few times.

"They have a strong bond, the captain and his ship," Alexandra added, her voice resigned and quiet.

Stone and wood cracked in the background. The crew flinched, but could muster little else at that point.

"Would you come with us?" Anmar asked suddenly, addressing Zammouri.

Zammouri hesitated, unsure of how to answer. He settled for joining his hands together, averting his gaze from the sea and his fellows. He swallowed before he spoke. "I've seen many strange things. I expect nothing anymore." He turned to face the crew, who all sat to his left. He saw defeat and overwhelm, and perhaps a promise. He breathed deep and came to answer—

"We've got company!" Alexandra blurted, pointing west.

Virginia stood, alert, and gazed out. Out in the open waters was the Hunter, its flag luffing with the promise of reckoning.

37

Charles

Damn it!

The rumbling and cracking above the trench were constant. Every blow that the Sentinel sent above made the cave Charles trod shake, dust clouding the air. Rocks threatened to collapse over his head with every rumble that reverberated through the tunnel. But he had to find James.

The cavernous space where James had carelessly headed was dim and echoed loudly with the chaos that the Sentinel brought above. He breathed in, the air thick with tangible agitation, and called out to his captain.

"James!" He yelled. The turmoil swallowed his voice. He tried again, his throat coarse from all the shouting. "James. Come on! Answer me."

The only answer was another blow, shaking the ground around him. He clutched at the cold stone, catching his step, a desperate sound caught in his throat. Charles sank down with his back to the shaking rock wall. A sense of failure captured him, heavy and thick. He had failed. He failed Uncle Wilson. He failed Gabrielle. He failed James. Everyone.

In the corner of his eye, he saw a shadow approaching, hazy on the edges. Standing abruptly, he squinted at the shadow. The figure was getting closer. The dust and haze made it nearly impossible for Charles to discern the moving shadow, but who else would it be?

James.

He walked quickly, quicker, picking up the pace until he recognized the outline of a sword. Charles settled into a run. "James!" He called out.

No answer. The figure stumbled onwards, and the closer Charles got, the clearer he could see the figure's steps. Through the dark and clouded air, he recognized James, no doubt. But his steps were broken, hollowed, more wraith than captain.

"James?" He was unsure if that was truly his captain. Charles ran to him, the ground shaking after another blow above the cave. Dust clouded the air again, obscuring his vision. But James was getting closer, and as he did, he saw color. Something… red.

Blood.

Charles hurried to James, who kept taking slow, sluggish steps. Rocks tumbled and fell, narrowly missing his captain's head. Charles could see it clearly now. James' chest, neck and arms were drenched in blood. Fresh and wet.

Just as he reached him, James fell to his knees, and Charles caught him by the shoulders. He shifted his captain to where he cradled his exhausted frame. "James," he breathed. "Whose blood is this? What happened?"

He noticed the whole key in James' grip before he realized James' eyes, reddened with the weight of tears. "Aereon," he whimpered. James hung his head, shuddering with a sob.

"Oh, James," Charles whispered. His hands moved before his mind could protest, and he held James' head against his shoulder. His captain wept. The cave rumbled.

James muttered something, faint and beaten.

"What?" Charles said, unable to make it out. Charles waited for him, as though the cave was not collapsing, as though the Sentinel did not wreak havoc above their heads.

"He made me do it." James meagerly raised the hand that carried the key, stained in Aereon's blood. His eyes were soft, anguished and defenseless.

Tears burned behind Charles' own. *You will be his doom, the crew's demise and the Rose's damnation.* He hated himself for the thought.

The cave rattled savagely and rocks toppled with a crash around them, loosening more of the cave's already precarious structure. A cave-in was imminent. Charles held James by the shoulders, pulling him away. "James, look at me." He put a hand to James' cheek, pure sorrow in those keen, brown eyes. "The Sentinel's destroying the island. We have to get out of here. The crew might have found the Rose."

Beneath James' bloody neck, Charles could see a slithering darkness, slowly, eagerly making its way beneath James' skin, mapping out his veins in a dark web. A building pinch of pain creased his captain's forehead. *The Bite.*

"Oh no," Charles breathed, and hauled James to his feet. "Come on. We have to get out of here." He pulled James up to his feet and led the way.

Their egress was quiet, punctuated by the blows above and the threatening rumbles below. James was dragging his feet, but kept close to Charles, shuffling empty steps beneath an emptier gaze. Charles was used to his captain's quiet and reclusive nature. But this silence was different, laden with sorrow that left Charles uneasy. He tried to convince himself that he didn't care, and only hated himself more for the attempt. Charles opened his mouth to say something, anything, to make James communicate.

But the cave spoke first, echoing in a roar that swelled above their heads, shaking their bones. Rocks loosened and rolled, clouding their vision with dust. Charles pushed James out of the way of a hurtling boulder, shielding himself from another. It smacked against the cave wall with a crack that echoed in the dust, the ground shaking beneath their feet. Dirt and grime filled the air and a coughing fit seized them both. Charles held James by the shoulder, compelling him back up to his feet. He hooked his arm into James', and his captain fell into a hurried step alongside him.

Through the thick cloud of dust and dirt, Charles could see fingers of light flickering from the opening of the cave. A smile made its way onto his face. "Come on, we're almost out!"

"Argh!" James reeled, a pained cry escaping him, muffled by the onslaught of tumbling rocks. He collapsed to his knees, grasping and clawing at his chest. Charles rushed to his side, stunned by what he saw. James pulled on his collar, fighting for air.

Panicked, he ripped away James' shirt to reveal his neck. The Bite slithered out from his chest, like hungry snakes, radiating out into his arms, reaching to cloud his eyes and mouth, choking his breath. Charles dry heaved as dread built in his chest, but in a moment, he threw James' arm over his shoulder and pulled him up, his captain struggling to stay on his feet. In the corner of his eye, he saw dark threads dig beneath the skin of James' hand. Taking a deep breath, Charles fell into step, his feet trying to reach for their rescue, his mind trying to keep up with James' faltering pace.

They were merely inching to the cave opening. As if in response to Charles' alarm, the cave shook again, violently, threatening to collapse on itself and over the pair's heads. More rocks tumbled over, curtaining their exit. There was only room for one of them to make it through. But Charles didn't slow his pace.

"We're almost there!" he cried.

"Go," his captain finally choked out, that one word coming out of him battered and raw. He ripped his arm off of Charles' shoulder and, with a pained grunt, pushed himself against Charles' back.

Charles fell and tumbled over dirt and grass, unable to grasp what just happened. He twisted on his elbow, taking it in. One moment Charles was inside the cave, the other moment he out, blinded by the sunshine and clean air.

"No." He scrambled to his feet just as the cave's opening erupted, rocks cascading against his captain's only outlet. He slammed his hands against the rock. "No! James. James!"

His captain surely couldn't hear him. But Charles searched for a weak point, a hole in the lattice of the stubborn stone. Grunting, he tried pulling the rocks, fully knowing they won't budge. "Open up!" Charles banged against the wall, loosening a cut on his finger. He gasped and drew back. There was nothing he could do.

"Damn it!" He clutched his hair and crouched, letting out an exasperated scream.

James

Sing

James knew nothing but pain. What was he thinking? Pushing Charles out of the cave and leaving himself stranded? He didn't know. All he knew was that pushing Charles out into safety was the only clear thought that stood out among the pain that would not abate.

He hissed behind gnashed teeth, pressing his back to the blocked exit.

The scene of Aereon's death dominated his thoughts. Aereon's blood still clung to James' clothes, the blood that was on his hands. Grief gurgled in his chest, vaporizing into his throat and bringing tears with it that James zealously waited for—for catharsis, in any form he might reach. But the Bite snatched it like a snake plucking unsuspecting prey out of the grass, and dragged it with such speed that James keeled over with the sudden, cutting pain.

Something cold seeped into his boots. In the small light that came from the cracks within the rock, he found water twinkling on the ground. It came slithering in streams at first, then rapidly began to gush.

Despite the crippling pain piercing through his body, James scrambled to his feet, as if the water burned him. The terrible memory came, sharp and unrelenting. Cold caging his muscles, making him forget how to breathe. His legs will fail, then his arms. Then he would be submerged.

He shook his head and his hands flew to his hair, panic gripped his heart. The memory persisted.

It was after the captain of the Calypso's Wrath killed his father. He had run to him, but a crewmate held him back. Before he knew it, the Rose had been pushing him onto a longboat. A board had hit his head and knocked him overboard. The last thing he remembered was panic, before darkness enveloped his vision.

Now, time slowed in that moment of raw dread. The water engulfed him, frigid and biting his limbs. He knew how to swim, but in that moment, terror, grief and rage warred through his limbs, and he sputtered and splashed helplessly.

I'm going to drown down here!

Fear built into terror, and the Bite feasted hungrily, gnawing, cutting and biting every fiber of his being.

He didn't want to drown. Not here. Not how. The memory—the nightmare—of the pirate attack captured him. He forgot where he was. The cave, or the ruthless sea, by the blown hull of the Silver Rose.

"No," he choked. The water had risen to his chest as he was lapsed into memory. He turned to the rocks and hammered them. Air escaped his chest rapidly, not giving him enough time to draw in precious, limited breath.

Sing.

The water reached his neck. He floated, buoyancy carrying his limbs as he thrashed around. His heart raced, pumping with building panic as the Bite ate through him and drained away his strength.

Sing!

The thought stood out among the battling anxieties, and he drew in one last breath and muttered some semblance of a sea shanty just as the water level reached his chin. He tilted his head up and drew one last panicked breath before he was fully submerged.

Then light diffused into the water, and there was nothing. Nothing but a solid room of rocks and water. A vacuum where no one would hear him. A tomb.

James went below and aimlessly tugged on the rocks. Air escaped his lungs, trickled around him in big and small pockets of exhaled air. He gave the rocks one last tug. His muscles were exhausted. And of his breath? Little remained.

He knew how it would go. He'd involuntarily gasp for air only to swallow water. Then he would lose consciousness. Slowly. Too slowly. And then he would drown. He waited for that to happen. He let himself relax, tension melting from his body, and surrendered to the waters. He felt weightless.

Maybe this is it. This is how I will die. Pathetic. Alone.

Maybe my soul will find Aereon's. Maybe I'll even see mother and father again—

The realization came back to him. He had no soul. It's with the Shadows. Despair ate at him. He waited to die.

And waited.

And waited…

Something tickled the sides of his neck. His hand flew to it, the waters resisting his reflex. The tickling traveled to his chest before a pang, too quick for James to register, shot through his neck and chest.

James opened his eyes. Shouldn't he be dead by now?

But he wasn't out of breath. If anything, the water beckoned him.

Breathe.

He became aware of the strange urge to breathe in the water. It surrounded him, the abundance raising a chilling desire in his lungs to breathe. The only sensation he could feel was the cold water encompassing his being, its deep and low sound filling the emptiness and quiet. He dared to move his arms and legs around. His breath didn't feel exhausted by these motions.

Just breathe.

His lungs screamed for air. He breathed.

His neck and chest tingled as water flowed through them, the sensation filling his lungs with the stuff of life. He breathed again. His muscles rejuvenated, his mind waking up, his attention sharpening. James turned to the rocks. A whistle traveled in the water, so clear. So familiar. The light was of contrasting warm and cool hues. It twirled around him, the sound following the light as if it were its source.

Orange and blue. Aereon's colors. Grief blossomed in his heart, and he expected the Bite the react. It crept through his body, drawing strength out of him. He arched inward, his hands flying to his abdomen that was barbed with the Bite's hunger.

But with this grief came something else. Something different, something that he welcomed. Connection. It was warm and shockingly serene. It chased the Bite away, the pain easing and making room for his body to respond in the moment. He breathed in deeply, replenishing his stamina.

The speckles of light came together and moved in the opposite direction from the cave. Back toward the alcove. He breathed again and swam to it, his movement almost unnaturally natural. The light turned to its right and gathered at the bottom of the cave floor. It pulsed, the siren song that beckoned. He frowned, but followed it. It might be his only way out of here. The light began to pulse against the rock. James pushed against it. A muffled crack resounded in the water. The light pulsed again as if pushing against the rock. James pushed again and the rock cracked.

Pressure gathered around him and sucked him out the cave in a rush. He came out the other side, floating and tumbling in the water. When he settled, he opened his eyes.

More water. It was saltier, his eyes stinging slightly. The siren song returned, the light preceding it. It moved around James once before it moved deeper into the water. He followed.

James waved through the waters, the siren song and light accompanying him like leaves on the strong wind. He followed it, not knowing where it would lead him. He breathed again, still unsure how this was even possible, before his breath caught in his chest.

"*Mia Rosa!*" he said, the water muffling his voice. He recognized the Rose's hull underneath the water. He swam to it with haste, as if reaching for salvation.

He saw a rope, and he held on to it. The feeling of the Rose's ropes in his hand filled his heart with safety and vitality. He held on tight and climbed. He gave the waters and siren song one last glance before he resurfaced. He didn't need to gasp for air, but he still did, taking in panicked, petrified breaths as he hauled himself up against the Rose's hull. He climbed until he reached the Rose's railing and pulled himself over, his muscles pumping, his arms shaking.

James rolled onto the deck of the Silver Rose, an agitated creak and rumbled traveling through her floorboards and masts as she greeted him. She wrapped ropes around his arms and helped him up.

Mio caro. The Hunter.

38

Charles

Run, Little Wolf, Run

He finally lifted his gaze up to the horizon and saw the two ships. The Hunter and the Silver Rose. Charles blinked slowly. He knew what he needed to do. But he would be lying to himself if he said he wanted to do it. A longboat appeared on the waters, rowing directly to the crew, and they scrambled onto it. He breathed deeply, hating himself for what he had to do next.

"Charles!" Mendez's voice echoed across the beach. Thomas turned, a smile wide on their face, and Mendez and Thomas flew to Charles, gathering around him as he stepped on the wet sands.

"Where's James?" Mendez asked.

Charles met Mendez's gaze. "He's gone."

Mendez's expression soured, his lips parting slightly.

"What do you mean… gone?" Thomas stepped forward, their brows creased in disbelief.

Charles stepped past the crew and into the longboat. "I mean gone. Crushed. The cave collapsed."

"How come you made it out of the cave unharmed?" Alexandra's voice cut through the air, and even deeper into Charles' heart.

"He pushed me out before it tumbled over him," he answered. Part of him was relieved he did not have to turn James in. But he still had to deliver the Rose. The crew turned to face him as he sat in the boat, and he shrugged. "It was his choice." He tore his gaze away from the crew. That many eyes upon him were crushing. "Come on," he said. "We've got the Hunter to outrun or burn."

Silence overcame everyone, and they exchanged looks heavy with grief. The crew followed, absently. Their longboat cut through the waters toward the Silver Rose as the mighty ship hurtled to the island.

The boat reached the ship, and the Rose hauled it onto her hull. Charles was the first to embark, and he was met with a sword's tip to his neck. At the other end of the sword, his captain stood holding the blade.

"Must we always meet like this?" James mused. Charles only swallowed, surprise bordering on terror wrung through his face.

"Captain!" Anmar said.

Charles spoke, his voice quivering. "I thought you were–_"

"Dead?" James said as he ran up the stairs to the helm. "Not yet."

Charles followed his captain up the starboard stairs. "We've got company."

James held the helm. "The Hunter. I know."

"Your plan?" Alexandra called out to him.

"Open fire," James said, savoring the words as the Rose unfurled her sails and cut through the waters. "They spotted us," he continued as he steered the Rose hard to starboard. A cannon whistled past them, missing the Rose's main mast by a hair. The Rose responded with a series of cannon fire, completely unmanned. Two hit their mark on the Hunter's hull with a crash.

"You going to just stand there?" James called out to his crew, glee in his command. "Open fire!"

The crew clamored around the cannons, filling the muzzles with all manner of cannonballs. But Charles stood frozen, the chaos around him little more than background noise against the stage of his mind. *Turn him in. Both of them. Now.*

I'm not ready.

Turn him in. Get it over with.

"Charles."

Now's your chance.

"Charles!"

Turn the Wolf and the Rose in. Return home.

What happens to the crew?

"Charles!" Virginia slammed into him, knocking him out of the way of an incoming cannonball. "Battle fright, sailor?"

I'm not ready. I need more time.

He didn't answer. He merely eyed the Hunter's mast from where he stood. The Rose rumbled beneath his feet as she tore through the sea. That was all he needed. With his heart quivering in his chest, his throat dry, he hauled himself up and ran below to the gunport. A cannon smashed into the Rose's hull, drawing rumbles and squeaks out of her. On another ship, Charles would have ignored the sounds. But on the Silver Rose, he couldn't help but feel an overwhelming vicarious pain. He kept looking. His legs and arms moved without his mind's awareness as he rummaged through the barrel until he found what he wanted. A chain ball cannon. He headed up on deck, his heart hammering in his chest, his hands shaking with the oath of treachery.

James must have noticed what was in Charles' hands, and he turned the helm just right for the Rose to get within range of the Hunter. Charles loaded the cannon, aimed at the Hunter's mast and—

His breath quickened, his heart raced. He was about to commit treason.

But the Commodore didn't need to know.

Time. I need more time.

The Rose flicked the cannon line, and it brought Charles' attention back to the moment that he could no longer take back.

The cannon fired.

Time seemed to stretch beyond discomfort as the chain ball cut through the air. Charles braced for impact, as if he were on the Hunter himself. He flicked when it hit its mark. The mast cracked, and careened portside.

The crew erupted in celebration. Virginia threw her hands in the air, shouting and yelling names at the Ordinance flagship. Thomas tossed their hat into the air, while Mendez carried Anmar like a barrel, the young lad laughing as Mendez twirled around. Zammouri watched, a laugh escaping him.

But Charles had his eyes on his captain. And he saw something new and terrifying. James raced down the quarterdeck stairs, his sword drawn and his face painted in an expression Charles had never yet seen. He most certainly saw his captain kill before, and that fierce and unbending look in his eyes was not new to Charles. But this one was new. James was a man on the brink of exacting revenge, his eyes crimson with malice, a grin so wicked on his face that he appeared a completely different man.

Alexandra sauntered over. "So, what now, captain?"

James headed to a longboat. Charles jumped ahead of him, putting a hand to his arm and pulling his hand back, leaning away from the blade. "James, wait. No!"

His captain seethed, shoving Charles off with a grunt. But Charles persisted, reaching for James' shoulders now. "Now's not an opportune time for revenge—"

"Now may be the *only* time," James snapped back.

The Silver Rose responded this time, creaking beneath her captain's determined feet. ***You're in no shape to kill him yet, Giacobbo.***

Charles wasted no time to use James' trust. "She's right. We have to stand down and put as many leagues between us and the Hunter as possible."

"Since when can you understand the Rose?" Mendez grumbled, jealousy sharpening his tone as he set Anmar down gently on his feet.

Charles ignored Mendez, leaning closer to James. "The crew's in no shape either."

That seemed to slow James down, even when nothing else had. He swallowed, his face returning to the captain that Charles was familiar with. He turned to face his crew. Anmar still had a limp, and Zammouri was new to the crew. Thomas' smile was wide with victory. Alexandra's eyes were shining with the promise of triumph, and Virginia smirked at her enemy's defeat over the horizon. It was a perfect picture of pure joy. One that could easily be torn to pieces right before James' eyes if he made a single mistake.

Releasing a surrendered breath, James resheathed his sword and addressed his next words to Charles. "He hasn't seen the last of us yet. I'll make sure of that." The Rose turned her helm and braced her foreyard, gathering more wind and more speed and propelling herself away from the Hunter.

Mendez crept behind Charles and whispered, "You think we should tell him about the markings on his neck, *amigo*?"

Charles narrowed his eyes, then huddled around his captain, as if examining a sculpture. Mendez was right. Geometric markings fazed in and out as water was still drying off of James' neck, waxing and waning as water streamed from his hair.

"This looks just like…" Charles began.

"Aereon's," Mendez said.

Silence fell aboard the Rose, as though she were mourning the merman's name.

"What?" James turned to Charles, frowning.

Charles locked his gaze onto James'. "It didn't seem right to tell you while we were holding back the Hunter." He wrung his hands together. "But I think… you're growing the markings just like Aereon. The kiss," Charles finally said, his voice heavy.

"Say, captain," Virginia asked. "What happened to that lovely merman?"

James stopped dead in his tracks.

Charles could see his captain's hand clench the Rose's railings a little too hard. Charles turned to Virginia, shaking his head.

Her expression turned confused, then understanding dawned. "Oh. I see," she whispered somberly.

Silence settled. The wash of the waves over the Rose's hull turned in the direction of the sun, casting her crew in its warmth. Charles could feel her ache through her floorboards, her lines and sheets. She had to get out of here. Away from this island of heartbreak. Fast.

"Zammouri will be joining us," Anmar said in an innocent attempt to uplift the mood. "He's a fantastic doctor."

"Welcome aboard," James said hoarsely.

More silence. James turned to his cabin. A muffled shock reverberated through the waters as the Sentinel made her final blow on the island. She began to tear herself apart, her once–formidable structure falling apart like an avalanche, until she collapsed, a plume of dust enveloping her crumbling form and cascading over what's left of the island's canopy. Dark clouds burgeoned across the sky and devoured the sun, casting the open waters with a dreary glow as the Silver Rose sailed away.

Thomas turned to Zammouri. "Come on," they said. "I'll show you around."

Zammouri followed his new crew member as Mendez and Anmar headed below. Charles, Alexandra and Virginia remained on deck. Virginia's eyes locked onto Alexandra before she nodded to their captain.

Alexandra cleared her throat.

"What is it now?" James said, irritation laced in his voice.

She approached him. "We err—Max and Edward were killed," Alexandra started, "Possibly the Commodore's work. And…"

Charles' heart throbbed in his chest, waiting for her next word.

"He left a message," Virginia finished.

James' hand stilled on the cabin's door. He faced them, his grave silence beckoning his crew to speak.

"It was written in blood. We don't know what it says. Well. At least, I don't," Virginia said, looking to her wife.

James turned to Alexandra. "What does it say?"

She swallowed. "Run, little wolf, run."

Acknowledgements

I would be remiss to start the acknowledgments section of this book without first acknowledging my mother. You have sacrificed so much for us. I could spend an eternity appreciating your limitless dedication and love, and it would not be enough.

To my sister. My other half and first and only best friend.

My writing community friends. Thank you for your valuable feedback and uplifting energy.

Thank you, reader, for joining my crew. I'm a storyteller, and what's a storyteller without listeners?

To all who doubted me and my stories: I win.